LIES

Bare Lies

A gripping gangland thriller with a deadly twist

Nick Rippington

Cabrilon Books

Published by Cabrilon Books

ISBN 978-0-9933323-5-7

Typesetting services by BOOKOW.COM

To Jemma and Sam... keep doing what you do

ACKNOWLEDGMENTS

THANKS to my editor ***Emma Mitchell*** for fighting through long covid and my many email requests to get the job done, and my fab cover designer ***Jane Dixon-Smith***. Simply the best in the business.

Much research was required in order to tell this story and I would like to make particular mention to ***Wensley Clarkson*** for his books *The Curse of Brink'sMat: 25 years of Murder and Mayhem (Quercus Press)*, an incredible insight into a crime that still resonates today, and *Gang Wars on the Costas (John Blake*). I was also enthralled by the book *Snow on the Atlantic: How Cocaine Came to Europe* by Spanish investigative journalist ***Nacho Carretero*** (Zedbooks) which told the fascinating story of the smugglers of Galicia and their close links with the Columbian cartels, which has been turned into a highly entertaining Netflix series. There were plenty more besides but that will do for now.

Finally, huge thanks to my readers for encouraging me to bring about the fourth Boxer Boys novel when at one stage I planned to finish the series at three. Hope you all enjoy...

Epigraph

Special request: An honest review is an absolute godsend to an independent author so please, if you like this book, leave your views and a mark on Amazon, Goodreads or any reputable Book reviewing site. Thanks!

PROLOGUE

Saturday November 26, 1983

HE could have been a snoop from the tax office if it wasn't for the black balaclava pulled tightly over his head. The man's tone was measured and his words mundane, but their underlying message struck terror into the security guard's heart.

'Your name is Peter Flynn and you live at 44 Riddington Road, Hayes, in a two-bedroom flat above a laundrette which you share with your wife and 7-year-old child. We've been watching you for some time. Do you understand?'

He nodded. His mouth was so dry he feared that if he tried to speak his words might be misinterpreted. The syrupy, pungent liquid ran down his face and across his chest, flowing on to violate every pore and crevice of his body. The stench was enough to make him gag, and he flinched every time a thick droplet hit the concrete, the noise assaulting his skull like a jackhammer.

Plink…

Plink…

Plink…

'Please, sir,' he muttered, the foul lubricant spilling from his lips.

'Hear that, Commander? "Pleeeese, sir".' A sing-song voice mocked him. 'Like that TV series about those school kids. Ironic, eh? There was a Peter in that too, but he was a right cool fucker, not like this geezer. I remember the spin-off. What was it called?'

The prisoner almost blurted out *Fenn Street Gang* as he would have done when watching a TV quiz show at home, only for a familiar rattle to remind him of his precarious predicament. The question went unanswered.

Shakashak, shakashak, shaka…

The macabre percussion drilled into his head.

'Let me be clear.' The man they called Commander never allowed his voice to alter in cadence or volume. 'Unless you give me exactly what I require, I will light one of these matches and apply it to the petrol coating your body. It will be such an efficient cremation your family need only brush you into the urn. Say "Yes" if you understand.'

This time the guard croaked a reply, hoping his terrifying quizmaster wouldn't interpret his lack of lucidity as an act of petulance.

'Good. We are on the same page. As an added incentive, I should inform you there is a car idling outside your flat at this moment, just waiting for a signal. If everything goes to plan, that car will move on. But if you fail to comply with our reasonable request, the men inside it will make a house call. You won't want them to do that, Mr Flynn. One of those men has a particular, umm, weakness when it comes to young children. We call him the *babysitter*.'

The captive's fear levels rocketed. He could tell his interrogator didn't make empty threats. If the succinct and measured words alone weren't enough to convince him, then one look into the dark, soulless eyes would do the trick.

'It's been three minutes, Commander. We have to stick to the schedule.'

The new voice was abrupt and impatient, its owner sounding slightly unhinged. Each of the intruders wore a different shade of headwear, and this man's balaclava was mustard yellow. The survivors would later refer to him as The Bully and recall that it was he who transformed a routine Saturday morning shift into an event from which many would suffer the fallout for decades. Had it been just three minutes ago when he had entered their lives?

Today had started like most Saturdays, the men relaxing and sharing some light-hearted banter about that day's football while Errol stood in the kitchen area brewing up for his statutory cup of pre-shift tea. His colleagues called him Errol simply because he shared the surname Flynn with a famous swashbuckling actor. He found it pretty ironic because until now his life had been devoid of heroic acts apart from the day he rescued a neighbour's cat from up a tree, and he didn't think that counted. Certainly, his five years in his job at the warehouse had passed without drama.

When The Bully burst in and ordered them to 'Hit the floor!' he had casually glimpsed at the clock on the wall and noted it was 6.45a.m. Bozza certainly picked his moments. It was only when he realised the practical joker in the group, John 'Bozza' Borowski, was lying beneath a table, his hands laced together on top of his wire-wool hair, that he knew he was in trouble.

'Got a clever clogs, have we?'

Errol felt the full weight of a 9mm Browning automatic smash against his skull and fell, his head catching the sharp corner of a table on the way down. He was so shocked he didn't think much about the injury until later, when they drenched him in fuel and his temple stung like holy hell.

After the assault with the gun, more footsteps had entered the room, urgent and purposeful. Errol's arms and legs had been bound, and a heavy cloth sack yanked over his head and fastened by straps at the neck. His keys were removed from his belt and sent skittering across the floor together with his watch, an eighth wedding anniversary present from his wife. This wanton disregard for his personal property ignited a flicker of anger within.

Before he could dwell on it, rough hands jostled him into the corridor and stripped him down to his Y-fronts. That was when he smelt it for the first time, the instantly recognisable stench of petrol. His plea for mercy caught in his throat as he heard the glug, glug, glug of a container emptying and felt the thick liquid pour down over him. It was only then that the bag was ripped from his head, and he found himself up close and personal with The Commander.

All that had taken place in three bloody minutes? It felt like a lifetime.

As Errol tried to gather his scrambled thoughts, his soaked, quivering frame was manhandled along the corridor, his feet stumbling for purchase. It reminded him of the three-legged race at his kid's sports day when each parent was attached to their child by a rubber band and had to hobble 100 yards across a rutted field to the finish line. Somehow, he and his kid had won first prize, and it was one of his most treasured memories since becoming a father.

Tears swam into his eyes as he pictured heavyset men climbing from a car and making their way to his front door.

He tried to recall seeing a suspicious vehicle in the vicinity of the flat that morning but came up blank. He had no doubts about its existence, though, and knew whatever these people wanted from him he had to deliver.

When they reached the vault, Errol saw his shift manager standing there and felt the deep wound of betrayal. They'd been sold out by one of their own. How else could the gang have known which two men to target?

'It's your turn, you pitiful cunt,' said The Bully. 'Your pal here has kept his part of the bargain. Now bash in your numbers like a good boy and we'll take it from there.'

Errol felt a shove in the back and stumbled forward to the keypad. He moved his hand towards it, then hesitated. His mind had gone blank. The company had changed the codes just days ago, and he knew he should remember the new one. At home, he liked doing puzzles, a pastime which helped his brain retain certain information, though he'd never completed one while doused in petrol with a man standing inches away holding a box of matches. He needed to buy some time.

'The codes are new,' he said.

The words were greeted with a casual slap across the face, the sharp crack echoing around the cavernous vault. He heard the matches rattle again and images flashed instantly through his mind: his beautiful child, so smart and joyful; his devoted wife, fun-loving and quirky. If only he had called in sick that day and stayed at home strumming Ralph McTell, Don McLean and John Denver tunes on his guitar. He had taken up the instrument to find a peaceful place inside himself, far removed from the world's chaos. He wished he could go there now.

'Errol, come on, man… Think!'

The desperate plea from his boss pierced his paralysed mind. The man was risking his own neck to shout encouragement and Errol knew if he didn't act quickly, it would be too late. There was a pattern, wasn't there? He tended to recall the codes by attributing each number to a letter. Why hadn't he come up with an acronym on this occasion? The numbers had to be so blindingly obvious that they would spring into his head instantly.

'Time to blow it, Commander?' asked The Bully.

'He's got 15 seconds,' the gang boss replied. 'Then he's human *Creme Brule*.'

'Tasty.'

Errol's stomach turned to mush, and his bowels threatened to explode, causing him the ultimate indignity in death. Blocking out the cramping sensation, he moved his hand towards the pad.

'I think… yes, I've got it!' he stuttered.

The numbers bore such special significance for him that he couldn't understand why he hadn't remembered them sooner. The area around the vault fell silent as Errol tapped on the pad…

1.2.0.5.

'Fuckin' hero,' said The Bully. 'What was the point in holding out that long, you cunt!' He marched forward and put his hand on the heavy steel gate as Errol held his breath, his heart pounding so rapidly in his chest he thought it might explode.

It didn't.

The gate opened.

The robbers flooded past him, and Errol sank to the floor, utterly spent.

'IT'S A soddin' shoebox,' said The Bully. 'Don't say we've gone through all that grief for a consignment of Clarkes' fuckin' Commandos.'

'Please tell me we bought a hacksaw,' said The Commander.

'Here.' A man in a tweed hat stepped forward, waving the required tool in his hand. They watched him go to work. Within seconds, the metal strap binding the box fell away, and he removed the lid. 'Fuuuuuckin' 'ell!' he exclaimed.

'Let's see,' said The Commander.

The bloke with the effeminate voice chimed in. 'Looks like we've raided Willie fuckin' Wonka's!'

'Who?' asked the Bully.

'You know, from *Charlie and the Chocolate Factory*. It's a kid's film. He hides golden tickets in chocolate bars—'

'All right, all right!' shouted The Commander like an adult stepping in to calm two squabbling toddlers. He moved forward and knelt beside the box, dipping his hand in and lifting out an object the size and shape of a Mars Bar. 'Now,' he said, looking up to see five pairs of eyes staring back at him. 'I can tell you these ain't chocolate bars, boys. If I'm not mistaken, these are gold bars… and looking around this vault there appears to be at least 50 more boxes where this came from. Gentlemen, I believe we have struck the jackpot.'

For a moment there was stunned silence. Then a huge cheer erupted, the robbers jumping around and hugging each other as if they'd just discovered eight score draws on the pools. The vault was alive, the atmosphere charged with electricity. When they had ripped open all the boxes, the final count came to 6,800 gold bars, weighing roughly two-and-a-half tons, with a value of £26.4m, traveller's cheques worth £200,000, £113,000 of polished and uncut diamonds and several hundred pounds in bank notes.

The Commander and his men had pulled off the Crime of the Century.

ONE

May 1999

THE drunk bounced off the corridor walls as the bulky man guarding the door watched with mounting despair. Surely this job entailed something a bit more exciting than having to direct space cadets back to the dance floor. Many of them were away with the fairies, but this hophead was on another planet altogether. To prove he was 'out there' he was wearing some sort of rubber embellishment to his face.

'Jus' a word, bredren,' said the security guard, moving forward to intercept the interloper. 'You cyan cum yah. It's private, see. Gwan wid you.'

'What you on about, mate?' slurred the drunk. On closer inspection, the doorman realised his uninvited guest was wearing a mask of Miss Piggy, a character from TV's *The Muppet Show*. This clubbing business attracted all sorts. 'Out the way, man, I need the bog or I'm gonna...'

The security man's eyes widened as the wasted figure in the mask lurched forward, performing jerking motions, his body going into spasm as he reached for the bottom of his mask, lifting it to expose the mouth. 'Nuh romp wid mi, blood!' the man on duty shouted, as a stream of purple-coloured bile shot out onto his perfectly pressed black trousers. 'Naah, deerty!'

The drunk took advantage of his shock to stagger forward and push on the door handle. Turning to intercept him, the bouncer gasped as his arm was forced up behind his back and a blade pressed to his throat. He had been so busy concentrating on the drunk he hadn't seen the knife man creep up on him.

'Slowly back away from the door,' a gritty voice whispered threateningly in his ear as handcuffs were slapped around his wrists. Was this a police sting operation? It was something he had feared ever since his arrival in Britain six months previously. It wouldn't take long for the authorities to establish that he had entered the country illegally and was wanted back in Kingston, Jamaica, for two gang murders and a rape.

The drunk, having made a rapid recovery, was wrapping some kind of thick duty tape around the doorman's legs. A third voice chimed in, this one well-spoken and businesslike. 'Good... quickly! Piggy, get that door open. Now!'

'Won't budge,' said the man in the Miss Piggy mask, sounding sober and alert.

The doorman felt the knife break the skin at his throat and a trickle of blood run down onto his pristine white shirt. Damn, this wasn't good… even if he survived the ordeal he had failed in his duties and the boss man would consider him surplus to requirements. In this game, that meant something far less amenable than being pensioned off with a nice retirement package. He considered how he might turn things around and gain the advantage but felt powerless. Even from this brief altercation, he could tell the man with the knife was a serious professional.

LESS than an hour earlier, that same knife man had been queuing outside the East London nightspot with his three mates. Chuck Dolan prided himself on his appearance. He wore a neatly pressed black Ralph Lauren polo shirt, stonewashed jeans and retro black loafers over a pair of white socks, all topped off with an olive-green Stone Island shell jacket which flapped open as he moved.

He walked with his left hand in his pocket, nervously caressing an object the size and shape of a cricket ball but weighing twice as much. Running his fingers across the dimples, he embraced the sense of awe and excitement building within him. The M67 hand grenade had been purchased from some of his father's associates working for the Quality Street Gang in Manchester. It contained 180 grams of Composite B explosive and had been used by US troops in Iraq during the Gulf War at the start of the decade. How the Manchester outfit had acquired such a destructive piece of ordnance he had no idea. Part of him wanted to see what damage the thing could do, but he knew to unleash such a weapon in a room full of young people would have horrendous, long-lasting consequences.

Chuck walked quickly, still bristling from the row he'd had with his younger brother, Arnold, on the way to the venue. 'He's barely 16 for fuck's sake!' he moaned, leaning in the direction of his other brother, Sly. 'I'm nearly 10 years older than him, and he should show me a bit of fuckin' respect. What right has he got, telling me what to do?'

'None,' said Sly in his casual, laid-back manner as he thumped his leg in time to Fat Boy Slim's anthem *Right*

Here, Right Now, which was pounding out through the nightclub doors. 'You know he loves winding you up.'

'It works every time, doesn't it? He knows I'll rise to the bait because confrontation is in my nature.'

'Come on, you could eat him alive in a scrap,' said Sly. 'You have to give him credit, though. He came up with this scheme and so far, we ain't done badly from it, none of us. I mean, look at those two in front. They're just school kids. Not many their age can get their hands on that sort of cash.'

Chuck studied the boys walking ahead of them. The one they called Fancy Man lived up to his nickname, decked out in expensive retro Mod gear. In sharp contrast, the other, known simply as Vickers, looked totally out of place among the fashionable young things of Hackney. He was dressed in a pinstripe suit which could have belonged to his dad. In his black tie and sensible shoes, he would have looked more at home behind the counter of the local bank, which, coincidentally, was the work placement he had lined up for the school holidays.

'OK,' said Chuck, relenting. 'Arnie's done well so far, granted, but he couldn't pull this off without us. It's our money in that van. If we hadn't turned over that Post Office none of this would be happening.'

'True,' said Sly, whose close resemblance to his older brother would render a DNA test surplus to requirements. They had the same tidy brown hair falling to just above their eyebrows, the same dark brown eyes, and the same swagger. The only difference was that while Chuck's fringe was dead straight, Sly's separated like a pair of curtains. 'Let's focus on the job, eh? You can't blame him for getting a little antsy after seeing that "thing" you brought along.'

'I ain't gonna use it though, am I?' said Chuck, running his fingers over his new "toy". 'It's a scare tactic. Our old man said you need to put the frighteners on if you want people to toe the line.' He chuckled as they joined the line behind their two mates. In front of their party, a gaggle of barely dressed teenage girls laughed and joked. They would have looked more at home on the sun-drenched isle of Ibiza rather than in the chilly heart of the UK.

The Ottoman Club was down a cobbled side street just off the main thoroughfare running through Hackney, a cosmopolitan London borough with a reputation for grungy chic only surpassed by its notoriety as the homicide hotspot of the capital. Nicknamed the Murder Mile by the red-top tabloids, the area had become synonymous with narcotics-related crime since Jamaican gangsters came to the fore in the late eighties. Though the murky world of drugs seemed far removed from the fun-loving youngsters around them, Chuck knew the two things were inextricably linked.

The first mass police raid on a crack den took place in nearby Dalston, where Errol 'Rankin' Dread, once dubbed the most dangerous man in Britain and the number one Yardie Godfather, made his home. Since then, the official number of gun-related incidents had exploded. Armed Response Vehicles, or ARVs, were seen on the streets of Hackney more than anywhere else in the capital. That evening the boys had passed one idling on a street corner in response to an incident the previous week when a Turkish man had been shot six times in broad daylight.

Most right-thinking young people would steer clear of a business attracting such mindless bloodshed, but at that moment Chuck and Sly Dolan, Fancy Man and Peter

Vickers were walking straight towards its epicentre. They were members of a fledgling gang known as the Boxer Boys, so called because they hailed from the Boxers' Estate, a tower block-saturated area of Barking, six miles away. Though the town didn't have Hackney's well-publicised reputation, the young men intended to put it on the map. They'd had a taste of the riches drugs could provide and were keen to sample more.

The two bouncers on the door were now chatting up the girls, trying to look rugged and act charming at the same time. The biggest perk of their job was that female customers openly flirted with them in order to get through the door.

Chuck took his time assessing the men. He wasn't impressed. They were smug and overconfident, having spent too long on the weights and not enough time on their general fitness. He doubted they could last three minutes in the ring, which was where the eldest Dolan had honed his own particular skills. To him, fighting was all about speed of thought and deed. You needed to learn how to hit and how to avoid being hit as well as working on accuracy, endurance and discipline. They were all attributes Chuck possessed in abundance. The contrary part of him hoped things didn't go quite to plan so that he could demonstrate those skills and unleash some pent-up anger and frustration.

The heavier set of the two bouncers was now unhooking the rope and standing aside for the girls, ogling their backsides as they shimmied past in their colourful summer skirts. Once they'd been swallowed up by the dark interior of the club, he focussed back on the queue.

'ID?' he asked Vickers.

'Umm… I… hang on…'

Great, thought Chuck. Arnie's little mate was going to fuck things up at the first hurdle. Pete Vickers was a quiet kid by nature and lacked the self-confident arrogance of the others. They had gone through the plan meticulously with him earlier that night. He had a fake driving licence in his wallet and all he needed to do was flash it. He was now fiddling around in his pockets, the nervousness plain for all to see.

'I think you're in the wrong place, pal,' said the bouncer. 'Youth club's back that way. What do you think, Moses?'

The other bouncer, a squat man with a shaved, bullet-shaped head, moved forward, opening his mouth and grinning. He reminded Chuck of one of his boxing heroes, the legendary Iron Mike Tyson, the comparison confirmed by the gold tooth that took pride of place in his mouth.

'You look about as 18 as I do,' Moses said to Vickers. 'Do I look 18 to you?'

'You obviously don't use moisturiser.'

The bouncer's expression froze. He looked as shocked as a charging rhinoceros stopped in its tracks by a tranquiliser dart. His head slowly turned in Sly's direction.

'What did you say?'

'I said you should use something on your skin, like the adverts say. It would take years off you.'

'Oh… comedian, are you?'

'You want tickets?'

As Moses pushed Vickers aside and moved towards Sly, Chuck felt his fingers close around the grenade. It was an instinctive move and as soon as he realised what he had done, he released the object quickly, balling his right fist in his pocket instead. *Bloody hell, Sly!* It was far too early to start trouble, but his younger brother couldn't resist the opportunity to demonstrate his quick wit. They hadn't even got past first base and if they lost their cool now, the entire mission would have to be aborted. What would his little brother Arnie say then? He already believed Chuck was a sandwich short of a picnic and if it all kicked off, it would only reinforce that judgement.

'He didn't mean nothing by it, mate,' he said, moving forward and putting Sly in a headlock. 'I'm sure we can sort this out. It's his birthday, and he's just in a good mood. Sometimes he doesn't realise when the joking should stop. He genuinely thinks he's a funny guy. He's actually done a couple of open mic stand-up shows down the town hall.'

'You see me laughing?' said Moses.

'No, sir.' The deferential term stuck in Chuck's throat. All he really wanted to do was tear down this muscle-bound statue. Later, maybe. 'I think I've got something to make you smile, though.'

'Woaaah!' Tyson's mate moved in, bristling for a bit of the action. 'Watch yourself, Moses, he's got something in his pocket!'

'Hey, let's keep things civil, boys,' said Chuck, lifting both hands up in a surrender gesture. 'I've got a treat for you, that's all.'

'What does he mean, Ryan?' asked Moses.

The bouncer called Ryan shook his head. 'Steady, fella,' he said, the Irish inflection coming through in his voice. 'No sudden moves or you'll be on your way to Homerton A&E.'

Chuck opened his raised hand.

'Excuse me?' Ryan was confused.

'Look, I ain't bought the kid his birthday present yet so figured this might be the time,' said Chuck. 'All he wants is a good night out. Let us in and it's all yours.'

'How much?'

'50 quid,' said Chuck, waving the bunch of notes. '£25 each… providing you let the boy up front in, too. I know he looks a bit young but I'll vouch for him, he's 18. Look, he's found his driving licence now, see?'

The two bouncers looked at each other. Moses took the document from Vickers' hand, gave a slight nod, and his mate returned to the rope and detached it.

'Can't see the harm in it,' said Ryan. 'You boys don't look like troublemakers. If anything happens, though, you'll have to deal with us, and we might not be so kind on the way out.'

TWO

THE noise and psychedelic light show hit Chuck full force. He stood still for a moment, watching hundreds of figures weaving unworldly shapes in the main body of the room, their forms rapidly changing colour before disappearing into the mist pumped out by a dry ice machine. Like an amphetamine-crazed freak playing hopscotch in an amusement arcade, the DJ bounced around behind a bank of record decks, switching from one to the other while occasionally lifting a pair of oversized headphones to his ear.

The music had changed now, a slapping bass funk hammering out from the speakers as a female singer wailed about it being a 'catastrophe' but telling them not to worry or panic. Chuck recognised the song as the latest release from London duo Basement Jaxx, who had rapidly made a name for themselves on the club scene.

Catastrophe.

That's exactly what someone's got coming to them, thought Chuck, peering through the manufactured smoke in the hope of glimpsing the others. Eventually he caught sight of Sly and Fancy Man walking purposefully off to his right and set off at a jog to catch them, pushing a protesting partygoer out of the way as he went. 'Oi!' shouted the irate clubber, but the heavy bass beats drowned him out and Chuck wasn't paying attention, anyway.

'Chucky boy, what are you having?' Sly asked his older brother when he finally caught up with them.

'Having?'

'Yeah, I'm in the chair,' said Sly. 'We could do with a little livener before getting down to business.'

'What the fuck are you talking about?' said Chuck. 'A livener? This ain't a jolly boys' night out. We're here for business, right? We need to keep our heads clear. Just imagine what Arnie would say if he thought we were in here partying.'

'You weren't bothered about what the kid thought five minutes ago. You said fuck him, and I say the same. Let's get a bit of Dutch courage down us. We can sort the other thing when we're good and ready.'

'Don't be a prat all your life, Sly. One sniff of the barmaid's apron and the sight of a bit of skirt and you're off on one. Look, at any time one of these bozos could recognise us and sound the alarm. It's got to be in and out. Quick job, no messing… where the hell's Vickers?'

'Needed the loo,' said Sly. 'Nerves, I guess. Afterwards, he was gonna take a look around, see if the coast's clear then report back. Let's have a drink while we wait. Can't hurt, can it, Fancy?'

The boy with the blond, shoulder-length hair looked embarrassed. He didn't want to be drawn into a family dispute, so said nothing.

'Not going to happen,' said Chuck. 'Come on. That little drug peddler Tigger told us exactly what we needed to do. Vickers will be as handy as a chocolate teapot in this scenario, anyway. I don't even know why he's here. He should be with Arnie doing what he's good at, wielding a calculator.'

'We can't do it without him, bro,' said Sly. 'Whatever you think of him, he's a clever fucker. He and Arnie worked the whole thing out together, you know that. Plus, he's got all the equipment.'

Chuck put his arm around his brother's neck and pulled him close. 'Well, if it's his plan he should know we can't afford to lose the element of surprise, right? It could make the difference between carrying this crazy thing off or crawling back to Arnie with our tail between our legs.'

Chuck felt a hand come from nowhere, long elegant fingers covering his eyes. His initial instinct would be to strike back with his elbow, but something stopped him. A smell; familiar and alluring.

'Guess who?'

Oh fuck! He hadn't bargained on being recognised at this crucial stage of the operation, particularly on 'foreign territory'. He bought his nerves under control.

'I would recognise that perfume anywhere – Anais Anais … and if I'm not mistaken that means the person this hand belongs to is the beautiful Abigail Lee.'

He spun around to look at her. She hadn't changed much since he'd taken her virginity on a school trip when he was in his teens. Abby Lee might have been two years younger than him, but even back then she had been mature for her age. They got on so well that they continued to see each other for more than a year afterwards at neutral venues across central London. Sadly, the relationship ended abruptly when her family emigrated to Spain.

'Still looking gorgeous,' he said, meaning it. Her long blonde hair flowed down her cheeks, gathering in bundles at her uncovered shoulders. Her smoky green eyes reflected his own image back at him and for a moment he was glued to the spot, unsure of what to do. She was wearing a ruched neon lime dress which beautifully showcased her trim figure and shapely legs. His eyes were drawn to a dribble of sweat running down into her cleavage as she blew upwards in the direction of her fringe. He looked away quickly when she caught him gawping.

'It's flippin' hot in here,' she said. 'Come and join me? It's my 23rd birthday celebration and you're the best surprise I've had yet.'

'Sorry, don't dance,' he said, looking around for a way to extricate himself from the conversation, all the while knowing he really just wanted to spend the next few hours in Abby Lee's company. 'When did you get back, anyway?'

'About six months ago,' she said. 'I had the chance of some work over here with a PR company promoting fashion brands. I love it. Mum and Dad are still in Spain though so I'm sharing a flat with a friend…'

'Chuck,' said Sly, nodding towards the entrance to the bar where Vickers stood, beckoning them.

'Look, it's really great to see you, Abby, but I gotta make tracks.'

'Oh, OK.' She looked hurt.

'Seriously, I'm only here to find someone, then I've got to go. Look, give me your number and I'll call you… promise. It's not a brush off. I really want…'

'Now, bro!' hissed Sly. 'We gotta go.'

'Wait!' she said. She moved across to a table, reached into her handbag and pulled out a business card. Returning, she attempted to push it into his pocket. For a moment he panicked and grabbed her hand, worried she might touch the grenade. Then he gave it a squeeze and took it from her, feeling her squeeze back. The contact lasted barely a second, but he could still feel her fingers in his hand long after she had walked away to be swallowed up by the fake smoke and swaying bodies.

'Was that the element of surprise you were on about?' asked Sly, chuckling.

'Fuck off, Sly,' he retorted, still peering into the crowd through which she had disappeared like a ghost. Abby Lee had lost none of the magnetism she possessed as a teenager.

VICKERS led them to the top of a circular staircase then set off down a corridor before stopping at a set of double doors. He looked both ways before pushing down a handle and ushering them into a function room.

Considering the compact nature of the club, it was a large space with tables and chairs dotted around. 'Lock it!' hissed Vickers to Fancy Man, who was the last one through the door. He did as he was told. Vickers walked to the far end of the room and retrieved a large sports bag from under a table. He unzipped it and started passing out blue boiler suits. 'Tigger may be a bit of a prick but, to be fair, he's done the job.' They started pulling on the one-piece suits.

'Here you go, you look a dead ringer for Miss Piggy,' Vickers said, throwing a polythene bag to Fancy Man. The blond boy wasn't happy with the comparison, but was more upset at having to cover up his stylish clothes. With little time to argue, he slipped the item from its covering and pulled it over his head. The famous character from *The Muppet Show* stared back at them.

Happy with the effect, Vickers threw masks to the two Dolan boys, who swiftly transformed into Fozzy Bear and

Animal. 'Always fancied you for this role,' Vickers said as Chuck became the mad character who played the drums on the popular puppet show.

'Yeah, OK, Kermit, you Muppet,' said Chuck as he looked up to see Vickers wearing the face of the show's main character.

Vickers began repacking the bag with their old clothes, making sure nothing would be found later to bring the police or a rival gang to their door. Chuck felt the adrenaline pumping around his body, knowing the next half hour could define the rest of his life. If things went right, then it might lead to untold riches, but the price of failure would be catastrophic. Until now, they'd been playing at gangsters, getting into the odd scrap and distributing small quantities of marijuana and pills throughout their local neighbourhood. Now they were about to pit their wits against the real players in the game, and it was a frightening prospect.

Chuck Dolan lived for these moments, though. He had faced plenty of dangerous encounters in his quarter of a century on the planet, and he had emerged victorious from nearly every one, considering the rare setbacks that came his way as lessons to be learned. He had been brought up by a tough, uncompromising father who had never been averse to handing out 'a slap' when he considered it necessary. At primary school he'd been the target of one particular bully. Luckily, what he learned at the local boxing gym enabled him to fight back and emerge stronger from every challenge.

'You got the stuff, Vickers?' he asked the younger man.

'Right here,' said Vickers, tapping his pocket. 'Remember, if we get split up, we'll rendezvous in the car park at The Hope. Good luck, boys.'

THREE

'NOT more interruptions! Who the fuck can that be now?'

The man behind the desk was olive skinned, his shiny black hair brushed with precision so it sat immaculately across his forehead. He was wearing a beige suit and black shirt with a black and silver diamond-patterned tie. The pièce de résistance was an 18-carat gold tie pin his mistress had bought him for his 28th birthday.

Though he had roots in Cyprus, he was born and raised in North London and had risen up the social scale thanks to his shrewd business sense. In his early 20s he had noticed during a personal journey through London's clublands that thrill seekers were desperate for a new, cheap drug to enhance their 'rave' experience. Having bribed numerous bouncers to turn a blind eye to his activities and weed out any rivals, he had introduced ecstasy to the London club scene and pretty soon amassed a small fortune. Investing in the Ottoman Club seemed a natural progression. He had taken it over as 'a favour' to a client who had fallen into debt because of raging coke and gambling habits.

Moving into murkier waters meant the Cypriot was bound to come into contact with sharks, and pretty soon he was visited by the biggest fish in the ocean, a Turk called Ishmal Calderon Durak. He presented the Cypriot with a fait accompli. He could carry on moving product, but he had to use Durak as his sole supplier. In return the Turk expected a large cut of the profits, explaining that he was the one taking all the risks and footing the bill to bring the drugs into the country.

The door handle rattled again, but it didn't open.

'Oh, for Christ's sake!'

Surely it couldn't be Durak again. The Turk had paid him a visit barely 20 minutes ago just to keep him on his toes. He had scooped up a wodge of cash from the table, dumped the suitcase down and left the club in the company of a small-time drug dealer called Mitchell Tiggs. The Cypriot couldn't imagine what those two might have to say to each other, but knew the drugs business took all sorts.

Bump!

Now this really was taking the piss. Where on earth was that muscle-bound Yardie Winstanley, or Stanley as he preferred to be known? The bloke wasn't his first choice for special protection duties but his usual bodyguard, a tough young Somalian known as Abs, was unavailable tonight and the Jamaican came highly recommended.

Unable to concentrate with the noise going on outside, the Cypriot finally got to his feet and walked around the table. Just as he was reaching for the door it flew off its hinges, the thick-set doorman following on immediately as if he had been used as a battering ram.

'Jeez!' The Cypriot jumped aside to avoid the bodies piling through, a maniacal looking tough guy wearing an Animal Muppet mask lying across the Yardie's back. Two scantily dressed girls peered in through the open doorway having taken a wrong turn for the toilets, only to scream and beat a hasty retreat when they saw the chaos in front of them. Damn! He had a gun in his desk drawer, but his path to it was blocked.

Crack! Without warning a character in a Fozzy Bear mask hurdled the two figures on the floor like an Olympic Steeplechaser before landing a powerful punch on the club owner's jaw. He wobbled, stumbled, then crashed to the floor as his assailant leapt on top of him and held him there. 'You got the stuff, Kermit?' his captor shouted, and the Cypriot began to realise he was under attack from a rival drug gang. If he did what he was told, he could walk away from this and plan his revenge. He would disperse search parties far and wide to ask questions, and when he found out who was responsible, he would take back what was his, with interest.

Kermit the Frog was fiddling with something in his gloved hands while Fozzy Bear held the club owner in place. With alarm the Cypriot saw the needle and watched the smaller guy tap it a couple of times before kneeling down beside him. 'Sorry about this, Alexis,' said the Kermit character. 'If it's any consolation it's supposed to give you a really good buzz.'

Wiggling and bucking ferociously, he tried everything he could to escape. He hated needles at the best of times, even when handled by an NHS professional, so the thought of being poked by some ignorant young gangster filled him with dread. He didn't even know what was in the syringe but had learned of certain things being injected into underworld bosses with fatal consequences. It was vitally important he remained conscious and in control.

'Need some help here!' shouted Kermit and Miss Piggy raced to help Fozzy Bear restrain the club owner. Defeated, the Cypriot felt the pinprick in his neck, sensed the fluid rushing into his arteries, and lay still, scared to death of what the next few seconds would bring. The Muppet intruders were frozen to the spot, watching him as silence descended on the room. They became blurred and fuzzy like a badly tuned TV before he lost his battle for consciousness.

'FOR fuck's sake, Vickers, man. He doesn't look very well!'

'Jeez, shout my name why don't you?' Pete Vickers rounded on Fancy Man.

'No one's gonna hear,' said Fancy Man.

'You don't know… walls have ears.'

'No, they don't.'

'Look,' said Vickers, trying to bottle up the adrenaline coursing through him. 'Let's just get on with it, eh? Grab his other arm, would you?'

'Jeez, he's heavy,' said Fancy Man. 'How are we gonna get him out of here?'

'There's an emergency door just down the corridor, in case of fire. It leads to some steps at the back of the building. If anyone is suspicious, we'll pretend he's drunk. Problem is, he's a dead weight and we might need some help.'

'We'll handle it,' said Chuck. 'What do we do with this geezer, though?' He indicated the dazed bodyguard he was holding face down against the broken door.

'Handcuff him to the desk,' said Vickers. 'We don't need him… we just need enough time to get away.'

'Got any more knockout stuff?' asked Chuck. 'It seems to work pretty bloody well.'

'It should do,' said Vickers. 'Its main purpose is to tranquilise horses. Some ravers have started taking it, the nutters. They call it Special K, but its actual name is ketamine. He's had an extra-large dose. We needed him to go bye byes, not start tripping. I only bought enough for him, though.'

'Well, I hope you got the dose right,' said Chuck, his eyes questioning. 'The plan sounds good but there's a danger someone might see him on the way to the fire escape… he's a well-known figure around here.'

'I doubt they'll recognise him once I've finished,' said Vickers. He dipped his hand in his pocket, pulled out another latex mask, and slipped it over the unconscious figure's head.

'Ha ha, mork mork mork… you're enjoying this casting role aint ya?' said Sly. 'Fozzy Bear and Animal escort the Swedish Chef from the premises. To be fair, kid, you've thought of everything.'

'I hope so,' said Vickers. 'If I haven't, we're dead men. Fancy, you scoop up the gear on the table, put it in the suitcase and bring it with us. I'll bring the duffle bag with the clothes, leaving these two to look after Cyprus Alex here.'

Chuck leant over and grabbed the Yardie, pulling his head back and slamming it against the door for good measure. He needed the Jamaican disorientated because though he looked harmless in his current state, the man wouldn't have been up here guarding the boss if he wasn't useful. These criminals from the Caribbean had established themselves as a force since arriving on the scene. The newspapers were full of stories of drive-by shootings south of the river in places like Brixton and Peckham, motorcyclists gunning down rival gang members in broad daylight before making their getaway.

Dragging the Yardie over to the desk, Chuck turned to Sly. 'Keys?'

Sly threw over a bunch, and Chuck twisted them in his hand. Finding the right one, he then pushed it into the lock and turned, removing one of the bracelets. He was reaching to attach it to the table leg when a clubbing right hand caught him in the side of the head. The eldest Dolan boy fell forwards off balance but managed to avoid the Yardie's wild, flailing fist a second time. He was trying to grab the keys, but Chuck kept them at arm's length. Sly squatted over the prisoner and dealt him a crunching blow. With the big man stunned, Chuck took full advantage, grabbing an arm and twisting it. There was an audible snap, and the victim screamed. Without hesitation, Chuck slipped the other cuff on. The doorman was shaking with rage and pain.

'Oh fuck!' Chuck looked up. The profanity had come from the Kermit the Frog character, who was staring at something on the floor.

'Shit!' said Fozzy Bear, his voice muffled behind the mask. 'Run… now. Get out!'

Chuck twisted to see what had alarmed his two accomplices. The grenade was rolling gently on the floor, and there was a small metal clip lying next to it.

FOUR

'AH, Mr Durak,' said the kid, his light brown hair falling ruler-straight across his eyebrows like a latter-day Beatle. He pulled the man in the dark suit into the back of the beaten-up red transit van. Though the new arrival looked like he spent a lot of time in more upmarket establishments, appearances could be deceptive. Ishmal Durak had done business against every kind of backdrop, from the opulent clubs of Monte Carlo to the rat-infested hovels of London's inner city.

'I know this isn't the poshest gaffe in which to meet and for that I apologise,' said the boy. 'My name's Arnie Dolan and I run a little operation called the Boxer Boys... you may have heard of us.'

His visitor gave no hint of acknowledgement as he folded himself over, taking a seat on a rusty wheel arch.

'Well, that's you,' said Durak. 'I'm surprised you're allowed out on a school night.'

Arnie ignored the jibe, sitting back and keeping his mouth shut. He had learnt that you were more likely to find out what you wanted from a person if you let them talk without interruption. 'Nah, I ain't never heard of you,' said Durak eventually. 'Me, on the other hand, you know, so I am sure you realise my boys ain't far away. If you're trying to turn over me or my business, I'll have your entrails spread like a carpet from here to Dalston.'

If the younger man was worried about the prospect, it didn't show in the electrifying blue eyes locked on his guest. 'Look, let's not fight,' he said. 'I do, indeed, know who you are. That's why we are here. Tigger?'

Mitchell Tiggs climbed in and closed the back doors, then squeezed through and leant into the front seat, returning with a briefcase. Tigger didn't look like a typical clubber. He was decked out in an unfashionable denim jacket and jeans, his peppery hair falling like rats' tails onto scrawny shoulders, his face under attack from a serious dose of acne. His sole purpose for being at a place like the Ottoman Club was to sell drugs.

Placing the case in front of The Turk, he popped the latches. The visitor leant forward and eyed the contents, then sat back and studied Arnie's impassive face. The schoolboy didn't flinch, though his insides were churning. This was a make-or-break moment for the self-appointed leader and founding member of the Boxer Boys. He would either walk away with a deal or his bones would be discovered years later inside the foundations of one of London's many new millennium developments.

Durak nodded slowly. 'Very impressive,' he said. 'That's a lot of money. Perhaps we do have something to talk about. What can I do for you?'

Arnie leant forward and lifted out one of the bundles of £50 notes. 'It's what we can do for you, Mr Durak. Let's just say this is a little gift from us as a token of our respect. We're hoping it paves the way for a long and prosperous relationship. You have the product we want, and we want to be your exclusive business partner, helping to distribute it throughout the East End. This is a downpayment.'

'And what if I said I already had an "exclusive" agreement with someone to do just that?'

Arnie sat back, his whole demeanour radiating confidence. 'Well, I think that deal is about to be terminated,' he said.

TIME froze before Chuck broke the spell, his shout setting off a series of events.

'Run!' he commanded, and Vickers paused for barely a heartbeat to look at the club owner, unconscious by his side. The next instant he turned around, scooped up the bag at his feet and leapt through the unguarded doorway, Fancy Man following with a briefcase in his hand.

'Go on, Sly! What the fuck are you waiting for?'

'You.' The one-word reply struck Chuck to the core.

'Help me, then!' he said, reaching over and grabbing the prone Yardie. Sly quickly sprang into action and between them they dragged their groaning adversary across so that his body was lying on top of the grenade. Both men turned away and crouched, making themselves into small targets and raising their arms to protect their faces…

Nothing happened.

Chuck felt a hand grasp his shirt and pull him towards the door, his feet scrambling for purchase. The next thing he knew he was out in the corridor and running at full pelt away from the danger zone. Gradually, it dawned on him something was missing. His brother! He turned to see Sly cowering behind the damaged door, holding it in place as a defence against the blast.

Boom!

THE van rocked, a loud echoing crunch reverberating around it. Tigger was the first to react, jumping into the front seat to see what had happened.

'Shit!' he said.

'What is this madness?' demanded the Turk.

Although Arnie had little idea what had taken place, he could hazard a good guess.

Fuckin' Chuck!

As soon as he'd seen the grenade earlier that evening, he'd been afraid the operation would go pear-shaped. He also knew that it was impossible to put a leash on his psychotic brother. Chuck Dolan might have been nine years his senior, but his lack of foresight made Arnie seem like a rocket scientist by comparison. He knew, though, that this was not the time to lose focus. The key to rescuing the operation was for Arnie to maintain his cool under pressure.

'To attract the attention of a businessman like yourself, Mr Durak, I think you would agree that sometimes you have to make a big noise,' said Arnie, offering a handshake. 'It looks like our competitors in the market may have hit a slight snag.'

'So, your big idea is to put a club which earns me a great deal of money out of business? I'm not sure you've thought this through.'

'There are many ways to skin a cat, Mr Durak.'

'And no doubt you have tried them out,' said the older man, a note of sarcasm evident in his voice.

'Look, I think perhaps we need to discuss this in a quieter and more civilised environment,' said Arnie as the first wails of emergency sirens penetrated the van.

'I should get back to my men,' said Durak, rising and moving towards the back doors of the van.

'Wait!' said Arnie. 'Do you want to risk unwanted attention from the filth? Please. Let us deliver you safely to your doorstep, Mr Durak. It will only take a few minutes and by that time I hope I will have convinced you that we would make the perfect business partners… especially when it seems a new gap in the market may have arisen.'

'Let me make a call,' said Durak, removing a sleek-looking device from his pocket, one of the newer and more expensive phones on the burgeoning mobile market. He turned away from Arnie, punched in a few numbers and began talking in his own language. Turning in the opposite direction, Arnie then leant into the front seats where his drug-dealing accomplice was staring out of the window, his face reflecting the flames from the building opposite.

'Where's our fuckin' driver, Tig?' he whispered anxiously.

'I… I dunno, Arnie. He must have scarpered.'

'Shit! Can you handle one of these?' The rattails bobbed as the boy's head shook in the negative. 'Great! Then I've no need for you either. Get out.'

'What?'

'I can handle it from here… make your own way home,' said Arnie. 'See if you can find the others while you're on your travels. I want to know what the fuck went wrong.'

Gingerly, the drug dealer pushed down on the handle and slipped out of the front passenger door. It was now just Arnie and a Turkish killer alone in the van. The schoolboy knew his decision-making had to be spot on over the next couple of minutes. Anything else and he was a dead man.

As the sirens increased in volume, he hurdled the front seat and settled behind the wheel. Looking around, he found the keys to the van nestling on the passenger seat.

He felt a mixture of relief and anger flood through him. The driver they'd enlisted for the job had been careless, but the mistake might just have saved his skin. He picked up the bunch of keys, inserted one in the ignition, and twisted. The engine rumbled into life; the van making a teeth-jarring crunch as he thrust it into gear.

'Are you old enough to drive?' asked his passenger after finishing his call.

'Of course,' replied Arnie, though the truth was his only driving experience had been limited to late-night spins around Sainsbury's car park with Sly. There were also the occasional trips to Dagenham to fuck around on the Go Karts, but he wasn't sure that counted. As he touched his right foot to the accelerator and eased the other off the clutch, the van lurched forward, sending the Turkish gang leader flying in back.

'What the hell…?'

'Sorry!' shouted Arnie above the racing engine as it belatedly dawned on him he had to shift gears. The van slewed across the narrow road, mounted the kerb and just avoided a gaggle of dazed-looking clubbers, unable to comprehend what was happening. Cracking the window open, his ears were assailed by anguished screams, smashing glass and running footsteps, all played out against a backbeat provided by the emergency services.

Approaching a junction, Arnie realised he was on the wrong side of the road and swerved to avoid a police car heading in the opposite direction, its lights and siren adding to the cacophony of chaos.

'If you have a death wish, I'm sure I can oblige,' said the Turk, his knuckles bleached white as he clung to a leather strap hanging from the roof of the van.

CHUCK looked back just in time to see his brother's body lift from the ground and fly in his direction. Attempting evasive action, the eldest Dolan boy rolled into a ball before taking the impact full force. For a moment there was only darkness, then he realised he was squeezing his eyes shut. Slowly he opened them to find his vision impaired by rolling clouds of smoke. Making a quick inventory of body parts, he found they were all where they should be.

Looking down, he saw his brother's inert figure. Lifting Sly's mask slowly, Chuck cringed at what he saw. His face was covered in cuts, blood and grime. An unfamiliar sensation pricked at the corners of Chuck's eyes, and he tried to remember the last time he had cried. It had to be almost 20 years ago when his father had walked him into the park across the road and set fire to his football kit in a bin. On many such occasions, he had been able to endure the pain thanks to his close ties with his younger brother. It had always been him and Sly against the world. For one harrowing moment he was confronted with a nightmare vision of life without his amusing, brave and crazy sibling. If blocking that doorway and taking the brunt of the explosion was his last defiant act, it summed up for Chuck how selfless and devoted his younger brother had been.

FIVE

THE cough caused Chuck to jump back sharply, as if he'd been tapped on the shoulder by a ghost. Looking down, he saw Sly open an eye and grin. 'Fuckin' 'ell, I said if we came here we'd have a blast, didn't I?' he said.

Chuck punched him in the shoulder.

'What the fuck?'

'That's for playing dead, you bastard!' stormed Chuck, but behind the mask he was smiling. 'I was just trying to work out what I was going to say to Mum and Anj. Let's get out of here or we'll end up behind bars.'

'Shit, what's this?' Sly reached up and pulled a sticky globule from his hair. When he opened his hand he gagged reflexively, the lump of bloody meat like an off cut on a butcher's chopping board.

'Drop it!' ordered Chuck. 'Don't think about it... What's that?'

The younger Dolan looked down at a shard of wood embedded in his calf.

'Fuck!'

'Wait,' ordered Chuck, ripping the sleeve from his boiler suit and holding it loose in his hand. With the other, he reached down and pulled the sizeable fragment of wood free before his younger brother knew what was happening. Colour drained from Sly's face as blood gushed from the hole that was left, but Chuck acted quickly, tightly wrapping the material around the wound and tying it. Sly gasped. 'Don't be such a baby,' Chuck said, fitting comfortably back into the hard man persona he'd spent years perfecting. 'Now, let's get out of here. Which way did the others go?'

'Dunno,' said Sly.

'Never mind. We'll have to go out the way we came in.'

As the two brothers moved further down the corridor, swirls of smoke parted in front of them and they saw a familiar figure. It was Moses the bouncer, his expression one of confusion. Chuck realised he was still wearing his Animal mask. Acting instinctively, the eldest Dolan boy lashed out, the punch catching the doorman by surprise. Delighted his quick reflexes had been restored to full working order, Chuck followed with the perfect uppercut with his right, watching with satisfaction as his opponent's eyes glazed over and he crashed to the ground.

'Downstairs… now!' Chuck waved his brother through. Sly hobbled forward, pushing dazed clubbers aside as he descended two steps at a time. Chuck followed, casting around him in an attempt to calculate the best escape route. On the ground floor the beats were still going, the club's patrons oblivious to the chaos taking place above their heads as they made shapes to a song about a boy being 'Sweet like Chocolate'.

'Fire!' he heard a female voice shout from above. 'Help! Fire!'

The music stopped, and the lights went out. There was a moment's silence followed by a babble of voices all speaking at the same time, asking questions for which they were unlikely to get an answer. Taking advantage of the confusion, Chuck barged past people on the way to the exit. Then a loud rumbling sound assaulted his eardrums, and he turned, Sly abruptly pulling to a halt in front of him.

'What's that?' Chuck asked.

There was a cracking sound like thunder, and a sea of startled faces turned upward in unison.

'Abby!' Chuck shouted, deserting his brother and charging onto the dance floor as plaster, dust and rubble rained down onto him. His hand shot out, and he tugged at the girl in the green dress. She turned in his direction, eyes wide with shock. 'This way,' he ordered, his voice barely carrying above the cacophony of mayhem.

'Chuck, is that you?'

She looked around for her mates, but Chuck knew there was no time for politeness. Still holding her firmly by the hand, he began bundling his way through the dense barrier of partygoers ahead.

Whump!

Hesitating for a second, he looked over his shoulder to see a huge chunk of ceiling fall away and a grotesque, misshapen figure drop through. A high-pitched burst of feedback assaulted his eardrums, and it took him a second to realise it was one continuous scream. Chuck thought for a minute his ears were playing tricks with him before realising it was the piercing wail of a fire alarm. Feeling a tug at his sleeve, he turned back.

'What have you done?'

Though he could barely see her, he moved in the direction of the voice. 'Why does this have to have anything to do with me?' he shouted.

Reaching up, she grabbed at his face, her hand coming away with the Animal mask. She waved it at him. 'Because you're wearing this?' she said. 'What's the mask for, Chuck?'

Before he could reply, Sly was at his shoulder, shouting in his ear. 'The exit's filling up,' he said. 'If we don't get out of here now, we're dead.'

'Toss it!' he shouted to Abby, but she didn't react. He snatched the mask from her and threw it as far as he could in the direction of the dance floor before ploughing forward, dragging her behind him in the direction of a haven of light.

In front of them one girl stumbled to set off a macabre domino effect, bodies falling into each other and dropping to the floor. Sly swerved to avoid the blockade, and Chuck and Abby followed in his footsteps. Now the only thing standing in their way was the doorman called Ryan, who was trying desperately to bring some order to the mass exodus. Chuck released Abby and charged forward, barging Sly out of the way and wrapping his arms around the bouncer's waist, the momentum carrying them both out onto the street. Taking advantage of the element of surprise, Chuck brought his forehead crashing down on the bridge of his disorientated victim's nose, then stumbled to his feet.

'What now?' said Sly, gazing down at the prone doorman.

'Back to the van,' said Chuck.

'We might have a problem there.'

Sly nodded in the direction of the opposite pavement, and Chuck followed his gaze. Their escape vehicle wasn't there.

A BUS HORN blared as the van swerved out of the side street and into the late-night traffic. Shifting gear, Arnie put his foot on the accelerator then quickly jammed on the brakes, the vehicle bucking then briefly travelling on two wheels before coming to a halt by the side of the road, the engine stalling as it mounted the kerb.

Arnie glanced in the mirror to see his passenger prostrate across a bench in the back. Slowly the Turk pushed himself into a sitting position. 'You're trying my patience, boy!' he growled.

Arnie didn't respond. Instead, he leant across and threw open the door. From a small alley to his left, two figures emerged, running forward and jumping into the passenger seat. The last one in closed the door.

'Do me a favour, Fancy,' said Arnie. 'Take the wheel and get us out of here. I have things to discuss with our guest. Head for Dalston, we're dropping him home.'

Having issued his orders, Arnie rolled over the seat and landed in the back. The engine roared to life again, and the van slipped smoothly back into the flow of traffic, a procession of police cars, ambulances and fire trucks passing by on the other side of the road.

'I hope you and your "friends" here don't intend to try something stupid,' said Durak.

'We don't want trouble,' said Arnie. 'We know the rest of our lives wouldn't be worth living.'

'In all fairness, those lives wouldn't last very long.'

Arnie nodded. 'Understood,' he said. 'Look, I'm sorry things haven't exactly gone to plan, Mr Durak. I'm banking on the contents of the suitcase being adequate compensation for any losses you might incur from the imminent closure of the Ottoman Club. Still, if we have proved anything to you it is that your current arrangement wasn't very … umm… secure. As you pointed out yourself, we're just a gang of kids yet look at the damage we've caused.'

'There's something else.' The two men swivelled to see Pete Vickers leaning over from the front passenger seat. Beads of sweat rolled down his forehead, coming to rest in his thick black eyebrows. He passed a second briefcase over to Arnie, who placed it on the floor and released the catches before flipping the lid open.

'We got your drugs back, Mr Durak,' said Vickers.

'Hmm,' the Turkish gang leader mused. 'To be fair to you, I didn't expect to see them again.'

'We felt it best not to leave them lying around,' said Vickers. 'It could have led to some awkward questions.'

Durak looked thoughtful. When he spoke again it came out as just one word – something none of them had ever heard before.

'Sorry,' said Arnie. 'We don't speak Turkish.'

'*Yüreklilik*,' repeated Durak. 'It is what you British call spunk, I believe, and you boys have plenty of it.'

The two gang members in the front seat began giggling, but Arnie kept a straight face.

'Of course, you find the word spunk funny,' said Durak. 'You are just boys and to you it is something smutty. It also means courage, though. There is something about you, Mr Dolan, that reminds me of myself when I first set foot in this country. I was an outsider, a foreigner, and it wasn't easy to become accepted. There were a lot of people who didn't want us here. It made me toughen up pretty quickly, I can tell you.'

He looked slowly around the van, his stare settling on each boy in turn. 'We young Turks were not unlike you Boxer Boys,' he said. 'We had to confront our enemies head on. By the time I was 14 I was earning lots of money but holding onto that money took bravery. As my "business" grew I attracted the attention of some of your British "Faces". I lost friends along the way, but I never lost sight of my goal and now' –he spread his arms – 'I think you can see how far I have come.'

His piercing stare locked on Arnie, trying to detect signs of weakness in the boy's eyes.

'Some would say what you did at that nightclub tonight was foolhardy and stupid…' Durak's voice rose as he spoke, but he brought it under control instantly. 'It was also brave. Spunky. You made a statement. I can't say I approve totally of your methods, but I can understand.' He picked up the case of drugs and passed it to Arnie. 'I will give you a trial run. I believe I could have cleared £50k with the contents of that case. If you can do better than that over the next month, this could be the start of a brand new alliance. Now, I think this is my stop, boys… you can let me out here.'

SIX

A PROCESSION of police cars pulled up in the middle of the narrow street, doors flying open and officers climbing out. They headed for the nightclub entrance, knowing their first job was to limit casualties as best they could. Standing there, breathing heavily from his earlier exertions, Chuck watched with morbid fascination.

'What's going on?' asked Abby, shouting in his ear so she could be heard above the discordant sirens.

'How should I know?' he said.

'Give me some credit,' she said. 'I'm not your average thick bimbo. I remember you from old, Chuck Dolan. You were always telling me about the scrapes you got into at school.'

'Bloody hell, Abby.' He felt it only right to act like the wounded soldier. 'This is a bit different from stealing the library keys! We haven't seen each other for years. I could have changed, you know? Right now, we need to get moving. Let's discuss this another time.'

Breaking away, he marched in the direction of a police officer who was erecting a barrier across the entrance to the street. He then turned and gripped his brother's arm, indicating to Abby that she should take the other. He was acutely aware that he and Sly were still wearing their boiler suits and that the clothing would be saturated in forensic goodies. He could only hope the officer was too wrapped up in the chaos to notice the significance of what they were wearing.

Spotting them, the policeman stopped what he was doing and headed in their direction. Sly, tuning immediately into Chuck's wavelength, assumed the role of an injured clubber, his battered and bruised face adding authenticity to the scene. They were just three victims of the mayhem, trying to make their way to safety.

'You guys OK?' asked the cop.

'My brother,' said Chuck, nodding in Sly's direction. 'He's in a bad way. He was hit by falling debris when the ceiling caved in. We need to get him to a hospital.'

'Ambulances are on the way,' said the officer.

Sly groaned.

'We can get a taxi.' Abby joined in the charade. 'I've phoned ahead. I'm sure the emergency services will have enough to deal with. I think he's concussed but his injuries aren't life threatening.'

'Well, if you're sure…' Their questioner turned back to another officer, who was putting the finishing touches to the barrier. 'Let 'em through, Josh. This guy needs a hospital.'

Hobbling past the blockade, Chuck kept his head down for fear he might be recognised. He was hardly a stranger to law and order in the area.

'This way,' said Abby, turning right onto Mare Street, the main road through Hackney. 'We'll go to my place. My flatmate's away. No one will ask questions provided we're discrete.'

Sly chuckled, easing up to his full height and brushing off the attention of his two protectors. 'It's not like we'll attract attention looking like this,' he said.

'Don't worry, everyone keeps themselves to themselves around here,' said Abby. 'There are a lot of different nationalities, asylum seekers who have experienced much worse, and illegal immigrants who have no interest in alerting the authorities to their whereabouts.'

Chuck shrugged. 'Sounds lovely,' he said.

TO reach Abby's flat they had to pass under a viaduct located on a cobbled street off the main road. The streetlights had been damaged by vandals some time ago, giving it a dark and eerie aura. Each of them kept their own counsel, frightened to speak lest the horrific images they'd witnessed were replayed in their minds. Heads down, they put one foot in front of the other until a green space appeared to their right, illuminated by a single street lamp.

'Chuck!'

The shout sent a tingle of alarm through the older of the two brothers, but once he was over the initial shock, he realised the voice was annoyingly familiar. 'It's all right,' he told the others, turning to face the new arrival. 'Tiggs?'

'Thank God,' said the figure, his face bathed in shadow.

'How did you find us?' Chuck asked the dealer.

'I was hanging around afterwards and saw you from across the road. Thank God you guys got out. What happened?'

'I could ask you the same bloody thing!' stormed Chuck, his pent-up frustration getting the better of him. He charged forward and pulled the drug dealer into the glow of a streetlight. 'Where did the van go, Tigger?' he demanded. 'You fucked off and left us!'

The boy raised his hands, shielding his face from the inevitable blow. It didn't come. 'A... am I in a van now?' he stuttered. 'It was Arnie. He went without me. Had that bloke Durak with him. I hope...'

'Fuckin' Arnie,' said Chuck. 'I should have guessed.'

'I'm sure he had his reasons,' said Sly, stepping forward into the light. 'Particularly if he was negotiating with the Turk. Maybe he's planning to come back for us later, eh, Tigger?'

'Sorry, boys,' said Tigger, keeping his eyes on Chuck. The older Dolan boy clamped a hand to the back of his collar.

'OK, you snivelling twat, tell us exactly what happened.'

'We heard the explosion,' said Tigger. 'Arnie thought it best not to hang around. The driver had done a runner though, and he told me to get out and find you. Then he drove off. Shit! I thought he was going to collide with a car load of fuckin' filth.'

'Arnie can't drive!' said Sly.

'I ain't telling porkies,' said Tigger. 'I dunno what happened to Moxy. He must have done a runner.'

'I hope our brother knows what he's doing, Sly,' said Chuck. 'If he's got it wrong, he's bought himself a one-way ticket to East London Crem. Kidnapping Ishmal Durak ain't the smartest thing he's ever done. Look, you'd better come with us, Tiggs. We need to piece it all together.'

Chuck felt a hand grab his arm and spin him around. 'Seriously?' said Abby, her green eyes boring into him like lasers through the darkness, the frown lines vivid on her forehead. In a strange way it turned him on. He remembered she could be quite feisty when they were teens, putting up a fight when she wanted her own way. 'The bloke's a fuckin' drug dealer,' she hissed, her eyes flitting in the direction of the new arrival. 'Just look at him! He's on something now. You expect me to let him into my flat? I'm taking a chance with you two, but at least I think I know you. How do I know I won't wake up to find my valuables gone?'

Putting his hands on her shoulders, he looked down at her earnestly and when their eyes met it reminded him of the chemistry they once had. For him, it was still there, and he was banking on her feeling the same. He was slightly ashamed to use it to his advantage so soon after meeting up again, but felt there was no alternative. 'I need him, Abby,' he said. 'I've got more questions, and he's got the answers. I wouldn't be asking if it wasn't important.'

'That's the point,' she said. 'You didn't ask.'

'Well, I'm asking now,' he said. 'Look he won't touch any of your stuff. I guarantee it. He wouldn't dare. He'd rather cut off his own hands than have to deal with me.'

Abby locked in the stare, searching his eyes.

'It's on your head then, Chuck Dolan. You got that?' Turning to Mitchell Tiggs, she said, 'Right, you, I swear if you lay as much as a finger…'

'I… I won't touch a thing,' said Tigger. 'Promise.'

'Yeah? A drug dealer making a promise. Where have I heard that before? Just so as you know, I'm only agreeing to this because Chuck asked me, OK? You're his responsibility.'

Turning on her heels, she led them through a gateway past a sign announcing 'London Fields'. Walking in single file, they passed a bench where a loved-up teenage couple were too preoccupied to notice the four bedraggled figures. As they approached the far side of the park, a new noise assaulted their ears… the low, familiar chatter of a helicopter passing overhead.

ABBY'S flat was located behind a bakery, the main entrance to the block a broken piece of chipboard that had once been a door, the lock rendered useless long ago. She pulled it open, the sound of wood scraping on concrete jarring Chuck's already battered nerves. Following Abby inside, he found himself in a dimly lit corridor lined with greasy, ageing wallpaper. Along its length were a number of doors painted in an assortment of garish colours.

Abby led them up a narrow staircase to a second-floor landing where she stopped in front of a newly painted blue door. Chuck knew all about squalor from his early years growing up on the Boxers Estate but couldn't remember anything this run down. He had assumed Abby was earning good money with the marketing agency, but the surroundings jarred with the impression he had of an upwardly mobile young woman who took enormous pride in her personal appearance.

Fiddling in a handbag branded with the logo of a famous Italian designer, Abby eventually produced a bunch of keys, putting one in the lock and twisting. When the door opened, she stood back to let them enter and when he stepped inside, Chuck realised his first impressions had deceived him. It was surprisingly spacious, bright and cheerful and tastefully decorated. There were a few pictures of fashion models adorning the walls, intermingled with framed posters of music, film and sports icons of the era. A life-sized photograph of the rap star Eminem shared equal billing with Brad Pitt from Fight Club and David Beckham in Manchester United gear.

'Nice place,' said Chuck. 'Who's the United fan?'

'No one,' said Abby, her mood softening. 'We just both think he's fit. Same with Marshall…'

He looked at her, confused. '…You know Marshall Mathers? Eminem? Then, of course, there's the lovely Brad.'

'And here was I thinking you'd been saving yourself for me,' he said with a cheeky smile, reminding her they had been prised apart through no fault of their own. Touching his upper arm gently, she moved swiftly on into the front room.

Despite the windows being shut they could still hear the sirens, while now and then the glass was illuminated by flashing lights as an emergency vehicle passed on its way to the Royal London Hospital in Whitechapel. 'Make yourself at home,' she said. 'One of you can sleep on the couch and I'll make up a temporary bed for the other.'

Sly dived onto the couch while Tigger looked about vacantly before assuming a position cross-legged on the floor.

'So what am I supposed to do?' asked Chuck.

'You can have my flatmate's room. You'll have to take a shower first, though. Where are your clothes? You weren't wearing those dungaree thingies when I saw you earlier.'

Chuck felt the onset of panic.

'Sly,' he said. 'Where's the sports bag with our gear in?'

His brother thought about it. 'Vickers was looking after it… Mind you, in all the panic…' He saw his older brother mime a zip fastening across the mouth and fell silent.

Abby must have sensed something was up, but did well to hide it. 'Right, well I've got some tidying up to do,' she said. 'Put the TV on if you want. I'll see you later when you're all settled.'

'IT might have been destroyed in the explosion,' said Sly.

'You think? We'd better hope so. They're fucking clever bastards these days. You've seen those TV dramas. If there's any evidence left at the scene, they'll find it. Even a stray hair containing a bit of DNA and, pow, you're a goner.'

'True,' said Tigger.

'What can we do?' said Sly.

'I don't know,' said Chuck. 'I need to speak to Arnie and see if he can figure it out, as long as the little sod still has his head attached to his shoulders.'

'He'll be all right,' said Tigger. 'Arnie's clever, and his plan's a good one. Durak wasn't happy initially, but I could tell he was impressed with that briefcase full of money. Your brother can be pretty persuasive, too.'

'Let's hope so for his sake… and ours,' said Chuck. 'Whatever happens, we'll need to keep our heads down for a while.'

'We'll be like *The Outsiders*.'

'Eh?'

'There's this film… Matt Dillon's in it,' said the drug dealer. 'It's about these kids from different parts of town, one lot rich and the other lot poor. Well, one of the rich kids gets stabbed to death and they have to go on the run …'

'Oh fuck off, Tig!' said Sly. 'How is this helping?'

'Yeah,' said Chuck. 'Tell us a true story, y'know, like what happened in the back of that van between Arnie and the Turk… then maybe we'll be able to establish how long we've got left to live.'

SEVEN

HE tapped gently on the door.

'Who is it?' she asked.

'Chuck.'

'Hang on… OK, come in.'

He moved the handle slowly, feeling nervous with anticipation. If there was one good thing to come out of this mess, it was the reunion with a girl he thought he would never see again.

Feeling vulnerable with just a towel wrapped around his waist, he entered the room.

'Hi,' he said.

She was sitting at a small dressing table with a vanity mirror, removing the meagre traces of make-up that had survived the nightclub chaos. A pair of strappy green stiletto shoes stood to one side of her, the designer handbag to the other. Her pose revived a long-forgotten memory in him of a scared little boy in front of a similar mirror, his mother applying foundation to his eye with the intention of disguising an ugly bruise. Chuck had been eight at the time and had been drawn into a confrontation with the playground bully. Not only had he suffered painful injuries, but he'd also got in trouble with the school for fighting. His mother's intention had been to hide his bruises from his father, but the old man walked in on them and punished them both. Big Mo had given her a verbal lashing for painting his eldest son like a 'China Doll' then turned on young Chuck for his 'weakness'. He still remembered his dad's words, clear as if he had said them yesterday. 'My son's a punchbag for the little scrotes around here? That ain't right!' A hard slap to the face followed, and next day Chuck was marched down to a local boxing gym for his first lesson in how to defend himself.

'Ahhhh, that's better,' said Abby, turning to face him. 'You've showered.'

She was dressed in a long, white kimono with Chinese dragons floating across her trim belly. The dragons swayed rhythmically as she rose from the chair and moved towards him. 'The room, OK?'

He suddenly felt envious of those dragons, and as his body started to react, he felt his face redden.

'Yes, all good,' he said, quickly lowering his hand to strategically cover his embarrassment. 'Not sure what we do about clothes tomorrow, though. We only have those boiler suits.'

'Pile the dirty ones on the floor in the hall and I'll put a wash on,' she said. 'Hopefully with an extra spin they'll be dry by the morning.'

'You're an angel,' he said, rubbing the rough knuckle of his left hand against the delicate skin of her cheek. She blushed, turned and gathered a towel from the chair. He watched her, marvelling at the perfectly painted copper-coloured nails decorating her slender fingers.

'OK,' she said. 'I need a shower too. I must be stinking. You settle in and I'll see you later.' Rising on tiptoes, she planted a kiss on his cheek, making his stubble tingle.

She smelt pretty good considering the night they'd endured. There was still a faint aroma of the perfume he'd recognised during their first encounter in the nightclub. With a lingering glance over her shoulder, she left the room.

Standing there for a moment, he studied the compact little bedroom with its baby pink walls and fluffy white carpet. Noticing some pictures in frames on her dresser, he walked across, curious to know if there was a man in her life. In one photo, a bikini-clad Abby stood on a sandy beach with her arms around two girlfriends, while in another a younger Abby blew out candles on a cake emblazoned with 'Happy 18th birthday'. A third showed a slightly older Abby standing in front of a purple Mini Metro, ripping up an L plate.

Pride of place, though, belonged to two older, blinged-up people in summer clothes raising cocktail glasses in the direction of the camera. Her parents, he guessed. He didn't recall ever meeting them during the brief time he and Abby had been an item back in the early 90s. Looking at the burly man in the picture, his neck adorned by a gold chain and jewellery dripping from his wrists, he wasn't sure they would have got on. There were plenty of fathers who had warned their daughters off 'going out with a Dolan', even though the more rebellious girls went through with it anyway to experience the apparent "thrill" of being with a bad boy. Mr Lee certainly didn't look the type to take prisoners. His wife, however, had a quirky, fun-loving smile, the dimple on her cheek firm evidence that the apple didn't fall far from the tree. He guessed she had to be in her mid-40s but her playful disposition made her look younger.

Chuck turned away from the photographs and walked out, padding along the corridor to the room belonging to Abby's flatmate. Before he entered he paused, listening to the gentle splashing of water from behind the bathroom door opposite, imagining the course the stream would take as it flowed over and around his ex-lover. He could hear the low mumble of conversation coming from the front room and guessed Sly and Tigger were ensconced in a late-night movie while discussing the dramas of that evening.

Recalling his recent encounter with Abby, he wondered if he had interpreted the signals right. Did the slight incline of her head as she was leaving the room mean what he thought it did? He really wasn't very good at taking hints from members of the opposite sex, but he knew if he didn't act now, he might not get the chance again. Fighting his innate shyness around girls, he turned back to face the bathroom door then gently pushed down the handle.

AT first he could make out little in the steam-filled room but as his eyes adjusted, he saw the kimono on the floor, resting on a white rug. In front of him was a pastel-blue curtain embellished with red hearts, and beyond it he saw a shadow moving in sultry rhythm to a silent soundtrack. The conflicting inner voices were screaming at Chuck now, one ordering him to walk out, the other demanding he take the plunge and satisfy the urges coursing through him.

He couldn't recall feeling so aroused at any time since he'd discovered girls weren't just annoying, giggly creatures that played with dolls. He was almost ashamed of the wanton need that possessed him when normally he was a paragon of discipline. What if she rejected him? Could he take it? How would he know if she had really meant to send him a signal or whether his brain was simply playing tricks with him? Maybe she was just one of those girls they used to label a prick-tease at school, leading him on only to reject him when he responded to her hints. His mind was full of silent questions and the answer came from an unexpected source, a hand emerging from behind the curtain, grasping his and pulling him towards the mist. He let the towel fall at his feet.

'I'm glad you came,' she whispered, as he joined her under the hot jets. She nibbled on his ear, and he felt a tingle pass along his body, suppressing the strange desire to laugh out loud.

Grabbing his hand, she placed it on a hardened nipple and he gently rolled it between his fingers, gasping in appreciation. It was full and square, protruding proudly from a half-moon of gently curving flesh. Placing his whole hand over her breast, he shivered again as he traced the small goosebumps on her skin, something he hadn't expected with the temperature of the water so comfortably warm. Shuddering, she put her lips to his eagerly then buried her face in his neck, her breath coming in short, sharp bursts.

Moments later, her mouth was on his again, biting his bottom lip gently. A strange sound, half groan, half growl, escaped from deep inside him as long nails tenderly explored the length and breadth of his erection.

'Stop!' he moaned, stepping back before it was too late, gasping as he tried to put his thoughts in some semblance of order.

She pulled back, upset and confused. 'What's wrong? You don't like it?'

'The opposite,' he said.

'Ohh!' she said as all became clear, the smile creeping across her lips. 'Then maybe…'

She turned to face the wall, grabbing his hands and pulling them forward so they enclosed her breasts once more. Looking down, he watched her shift position, pushing her buttocks towards him and spreading her legs. He had to shut his eyes to keep his rampaging libido in check.

'Fuck me, Chuck,' she murmured.

Taking a breath, he summoned every emotion inside him, concentrating his feelings, thoughts and desires together in one place. When anticipation threatened to overwhelm him, he opened his eyes again and looked down at the beautiful girl in front of him, the girl he'd thought about, dreamt about and fantasised over since the day she'd walked out of his life just over eight years ago.

Thrusting forward with his hips, he plunged into her deeply, the faintest squeak from her lips acting as a fanfare to their electrifying union, the sound so excruciatingly erotic he needed to hear it again… and again… and again.

EIGHT

'YOU look shagged out mate,' said Sly, a mischievous grin on his face.

Chuck threw the boiler suit at him… hard. 'Get this on,' he said, ignoring the question hanging in the air. 'We've got things to do today if we want to stay out of the cells.'

'That good, eh?' said Sly. 'I couldn't get in the bloody bog last night. I needed a piss, but I heard you two going at it in there. Uhh, Uhh, aah…' He started improvising the orgasm scene from the film *When Harry Met Sally*. Unable to handle his brother's mickey-taking any more Chuck dived forward and pulled back the quilt. Sly moved quickly to cover his embarrassment.

'Hey!' he shouted. 'I'm naked under here… No need for that.'

'Serves you right… perv! I bet you had a good squint through that keyhole, didn't you?'

'Couldn't see much… it was a bit misty.'

'They got a name for people like you, something French … *voyeur*, that's it.'

'Who's a *voyeur*?'

Both boys turned to see Abby standing in the doorway, dressed in the Chinese kimono. They looked like kids caught with their hands in the biscuit tin. Chuck felt a stirring within as he remembered that same dressing gown discarded on the bathroom rug the night before. 'Oh, ummm, nothing,' he said. 'Sly reckoned he saw one of your neighbours stripping off in the window last night, that's all.'

She flicked her head dismissively. 'Lucky Sly,' she said. 'Boys will be boys, I guess. I'll put the kettle on, and I should be able to rustle up some bacon, sausage, eggs and toast. OK?'

'You're a treasure,' said Chuck. 'Don't put yourself out on our behalf, though.'

'It's OK, I'm off work today,' she said. 'I've got nothing pressing on.'

Abby had nothing pressing on last night either, he thought, and had to keep himself from grinning, the memory causing further stirrings down below.

'Thanks, babe,' he said. She reserved a special smile for him, then turned and left the room.

'You're a treasure,' mimicked Sly in a high-pitched voice.

'Oh, fuck off, Sly,' he said, moving quickly to plant a solid punch on his brother's exposed arm.

'Owww! No need for that. I'm an injured man.' He pointed at the bandage on his leg, which now showed only a few spots of blood after Abby had cleaned the wound and provided him with fresh dressings the night before.

'Serves you right,' said Chuck. 'What's with Sleeping Beauty?'

They both looked to Chuck's left where strange moaning noises were emanating from a bundle of rags in the corner. It wriggled before two arms shot out and stretched for the ceiling. 'W… what's going on?' said Tigger.

'Get up, Tiggs, we got things to do,' said Chuck. 'Put the telly on.'

The drug dealer searched around. 'Remote?' he said.

'Fuckin' 'ell, Tigger, you had it last, you bloody waster,' said Sly.

'OK…OK.' Tossing the blankets aside, he finally found what he was looking for, then pointed it at the TV and pressed a button. The screen came to life, and he surfed through the channels until a buxom brunette sprang onto the screen, lying on a bed talking to a showbiz personality.

'What the fuck's this?' demanded Chuck.

'It's the *Big Breakfast*,' said Tigger. 'Ace show! I watch it every morning wiv me Cornflakes. It's got this lovely bit working there now, Kelly something… she took over from Denise van wazzername. She's a bit thick mind but she and Johnny Vaughan are good together.'

Chuck leapt forward, grabbed the control from Tigger's hand and switched channels.

'Hey!' said the drug dealer in protest, before registering the stony expression on Chuck's face. 'OK, fine,' he said huffily.

'I ain't after watching soft porn in the morning, Tigger, and I didn't ask for your opinion on breakfast TV.' Chuck waved the remote at him like a weapon, the message clear. 'This is serious. We need to know what sort of shit we're in … so sit back and shut the fuck up.'

Tigger did as he was told. There was now a male newsreader on the screen, looking sombre as he read out the headlines.

'*Four people are now believed dead after an explosion ripped through a nightclub in the London Borough of Hackney last night*,' he said, looking earnestly into the camera. '*It is the second major incident of its kind in less than a week, following Saturday's attack in which 48 people were injured in a bomb blast, including a one-year-old boy.'*

'That's a relief,' said Chuck.

'What?' Sly looked incredulous. 'Fuckin' hell, Chuck, people died. How can you say it's a relief?'

'I meant for our sake,' said Chuck. 'That bomb in Brixton completely slipped my mind. People are naturally gonna link the two incidents which means they won't be looking for us, at least, not yet… Not until all them scientists and forensic geezers sift through the debris and find clues. It gives us some time.'

'Time for what?'

'Time to get our heads together. Come up with a plan,' said Chuck.

'What happened in Brixton?' asked Tigger.

'Bloody hell, Tiggs, have you been living under a fuckin' rock?' As he said the words, it dawned on Chuck that it was a fair assessment. The kid reminded him of a book from his childhood, *Stig of the Dump*, in which a caveman somehow came to be living in modern times. 'There was this massive explosion in Brixton market… Nail bomb, or something. They think it was terrorists, or maybe someone with a grudge against blacks. All I'm saying is it can't do us any harm if they're thinking this is an organised attack. Now, shut up and listen.'

The news reader had been joined at the table by a man in a spotless police uniform, silver buttons shining under the studio lights. '*With me now is Assistant Commissioner Max Cooper of the Metropolitan Police*,' said the newsreader. '*Assistant Commissioner, is there anything more you can tell us?*'

The man leant forward, subconsciously brushing back his black hair. He seemed young to have risen to such a high rank in the organisation, but the greying sideburns hinted that he was probably in his early 50s. Whatever his age, AC Cooper looked distinguished and authoritative.

'*Thank you, Simon*,' he said. '*I'm afraid it's far too early to speculate whether this latest incident is linked with the one in Brixton. At this moment Crime Scene Investigators are at the club trying to piece together what happened.*'

'*Can you tell us anything about the victims?*'

'*There are four known fatalities, and we are in the process of trying to notify their next of kin*,' said the officer. '*Until then, we cannot release their identities. Of course, many more victims have been taken to local hospitals to be treated for their wounds. Some are in a serious way, and we are praying they pull through.*'

The interviewer nodded, encouraging the high-ranking officer to continue. '*Personally, I find this a cowardly and despicable act*,' said Assistant Commissioner Cooper. '*It seems young people out for a fun night have been deliberately targeted, never anticipating anything like this would happen. The Ottaman Club is a compact venue so this incident would have taken place in an enclosed space, the youngsters having little or no warning as to what was about to happen. You can just imagine the ensuing panic as they scrambled to escape the scene.*'

'*Of course*,' said the newsreader. '*Assistant Commissioner, there have been increased reports of terrorism acts around the world. Since last year's attacks on the US embassies in Tanzania and Nairobi, an international group called al-Qaeda has come to the fore. Is it possible that some kind of terror cell exists in Britain as some commentators are suggesting? After all, this country's armed forces have been fairly active in the Middle East and our special relationship with America could mark us out as a target, according to some.'*

'*I am not going to speculate on that*,' said Assistant Commissioner Cooper. '*We need to have the evidence in front of us before we draw any conclusions. We still need to ascertain the device that caused the explosion and will also be studying CCTV footage from both inside the club and in the surrounding area, with the hope we can identify who was responsible and bring them to justice.'*

'*Of course, Assistant Commissioner*,' said the newsreader. '*Just before we let you go, another theory which has been mooted is that this could be some kind of gang reprisal attack. This particular area of London has earned the dubious nickname Murder Mile and has seen its fair share of gruesome deaths over recent years. What are your thoughts on that?*'

'*Look, all I will say is we can't rule anything in and we won't rule anything out*,' replied AC Cooper.

'*Assistant Commissioner Cooper, of the Metropolitan Police, we thank you for your time.*'

Chuck turned off the TV and sat back.

'What next?' asked Sly.

'We need to speak to Billy Big Bollocks… wherever the hell he is.'

'I forgot about Arnie,' said Sly. 'Shit, he could need our help.'

'If he's upset Durak and his Turks it's already too late,' said Chuck. 'Do you want to take them on? I know I don't. Listen, Arnie's big enough and stupid enough to look after himself. He knew it might come to this. Before we start making wild assumptions, let's see if we can get hold of him, shall we? We need to get our asses in gear. You heard what that copper said. If someone recognises us on CCTV, we'll be joining the old man behind bars.'

Sly shuddered. 'No thanks,' he said. 'I quite enjoy my life as it is. What should we do?'

'In the words of ET, "Let's phone home".'

'IS ARNIE about, Mum?' said Chuck.

'What the hell have you boys been up to?' asked Beryl Dolan.

'Is he there?'

'Well, he was supposed to be at school today, but when I went to get him up, he wasn't in his bed,' said Beryl. 'Bruce said he hadn't been in all night. With you and Sly both out too it don't take one of them birds with a crystal ball to work out you've been up to somethin'. It was only me, Bruce and our Anj for breakfast, so I'll ask 'til I'm blue in the face… What were you doing last night?'

'For God's sake, Mum. I'm 25 and Sly's 19,' Chuck said, doing his best to sound affronted. 'We don't have school and we can do what we want.'

'Not when you're with my Arnie,' she said. 'I'll have the truant officer around here. He's only 16 for God's sake. He's supposed to be preparing for his exams. You boys lead him astray.'

'Sure, Mum,' said Chuck. 'If it wasn't for us, our Arnie would be the next Albert bloody Einstein.'

'He's a clever boy,' she said. 'Cleverer than you two dopes, anyhow. Weren't you supposed to be on site today? Your boss rang asking if you were sick, cos you hadn't turned up. What was I supposed to tell him? I said I hadn't seen you, but you were probably on your way. You're going to lose another job if you ain't careful, son, and I need that money cos you two eat me out of house and home.'

'Stop with the nagging, Mum.'

'Well, come on then. Tell me what's going on and... hang on, you didn't have anything to do with that business, did you? It was all over the news and the radio, only a few miles from here down in...'

'Shut up!'

There was an instant silence on the other end of the line.

'Well, I...'

'Sorry, Mum, look... do us a favour and go and find a payphone, then ring me back on this number.' Beryl fell silent, allowing him to read out the digits. She wasn't stupid. She'd spent most of her life covering up for her criminal husband of 20 years, Maurice Dolan.

'Leave it with me,' she said. 'But when I call back, I expect answers.'

CHUCK watched the battered black van pull up opposite and saw his mother gingerly climb down from the passenger seat. She strode over to where they were standing in the Tesco's car park off Mare Street.

'Boys, for God's sake, what trouble have you got into now?' she asked. 'And what's wrong with your leg, Sly. You're limping.'

'Just a cut,' he said. 'Nothing to worry about.'

Chuck and Sly stood with their hands behind their backs, ready for a parental bollocking.

'I can't believe you two,' she said. 'People died, you know. What in God's name happened?'

'It wasn't supposed to happen like that. Honest, Mum,' said Chuck. 'It all got out of hand and the less you know the better. It was just bad luck. Someone had some sort of … device and it went off accidentally.'

'What device? Oh, never mind, you ain't gonna tell me the truth, I know. I'm disappointed, though. After all I've been through with your father, I don't deserve this grief. I'll end up in an early grave.'

'Mum, we need your help,' said Sly.

'I've sorted it,' she said.

'What do you mean?' asked Chuck.

'Look, I've been through enough of this malarkey in the past to know what to do in a crisis. Don't forget your dad was on the run for a whole year before the old bill caught up with him…'

'Sure,' said Chuck. It had never dawned on him before how much his mother must have been involved in his father's escapades.

'I've arranged for you to stay with your grandfather for a while,' she said. 'Out in Spain. I spoke to him on the phone after you told me what was going on and he's making arrangements. You're leaving tonight.'

'Tonight?' said Sly, shock registering in his voice. 'But, Mum… clothes? Passports?'

'All in the van, together with some money to tide you over,' she said. 'I had to raid the piggy bank but once you're out there, I suspect Granddad Billy will put you to work so that you can earn your keep. He's got quite a few little businesses on the go and a couple of fit young men are exactly what he needs to help him out. He ain't getting any younger.'

'Jeez, I haven't seen him since…'

'You were 12, Chuck. Sly was 6. We spent a brief time there on hols. In fact, your sister was born out there if you remember… in your granddad's villa.'

'Christ, yes,' said Chuck. 'I remember that holiday. He's got a fab place in Marbella. Thanks, Mum.'

'Come on then, we got no time to waste,' she said, turning and heading for the van. 'You have to be in Southampton by tonight for the boat crossing.'

'Boat? Really?' said Chuck, feeling a strange sensation in his stomach.

'It will be easier than plane. Not so many checks.'

The boys followed her over to the van to be greeted by a man with black curly hair leaning through the window, a big smile on his face. 'Right, boys?' he said.

'What's he doing here?' said Chuck, suspicion clouding his voice.

'I had to bring your clothes and passports,' she said. 'If you thought I was going to carry all that on the Tube on my own, you've got another think coming. No way, Jose. I saw Stan outside the flats this morning and he kindly offered to help. He was on his way to the market anyway, so it's only a slight detour.'

The sight of Stan Marshall made Chuck suspicious. The man had flitted in and out of their lives ever since he was a young kid, and he knew his dad wouldn't approve. Beryl Dolan would never hear a word said against the market trader, though, and regularly visited his stall in Walthamstow when the kids needed footwear. Chuck recalled the first time he clapped eyes on Stan, when he had visited the market to buy his first pair of boxing boots. The man always seemed pleasant enough, but he might as well have had DODGY written across his forehead in permanent marker pen. If they were to remain under the police radar the fewer people who knew what they were doing, the better. It was done now though, and they couldn't turn back the clock.

Chuck watched Stan climb from the cab and walk around to the back of the van. When he pulled open the double doors, Chuck saw two holdalls sitting in front of rows and rows of shoe boxes. Lifting them out, Stan handed one to each boy. Once they had collected their bags, the boys walked into a big hug from their mother. Though she was only petite in comparison to her two eldest sons, she could still reach around them both. Again, Chuck was reminded of his days growing up on the Boxers' Estate. He wondered when he might see it again.

'Passports,' she said, holding the burgundy-coloured documents in front of her like a fan. The boys took one each. 'There's money in the zip up pockets of the holdalls – not a lot but enough – and you pick up your tickets from the ferry point when you get there. OK?'

She took turns looking each of them in the eye until they indicated they were clear about the plan. 'Right,' she said. 'As soon as Arnie shows up, I'll tell him to get in touch. Look after each other.'

'Always do,' said Chuck.

NINE

CHUCK leant over the side of the bottom bunk and retched into a bucket. He didn't think there could be much more of the disgusting yellow bile left, but he still felt awful. His brother lay on the top bunk, trying to suppress a giggle and failing. Chuck would have given him a slap if he'd been able to summon enough energy.

'You get any whiter I'm gonna call the Ghostbusters,' said Sly. 'Gramps should have booked you a coffin, not a cabin.'

Chuck ignored the jibe. He'd never been very good on the water. Even relatively calm boat trips on the Thames had caused his stomach to churn like a spin dryer.

'This must be the famous Bay of Biscay,' said Sly, oblivious to the fact Chuck just wanted him to shut up. 'I read about it. It gets a bit choppy at times. Boats have capsized …'

'Gnmmph.' Chuck tried to speak, but instead reached for the bucket again.

'Sorry, were you trying to say something?'

'F… fuck off, Sly,' Chuck managed. At times he found his younger brother's humorous attitude uplifting. This wasn't one of them. 'Go for a… fuckin'… walk or somethin' and leave me alone.' The words sucked up all his reserves of energy. He hadn't felt this helpless or incapacitated since his time in hospital as a child after his father knocked him unconscious with a baseball bat. It had been an accident, of course… like most of the old man's actions. Even so, the memory was still painful 17 years later.

'Well, thanks for trying to cheer me up, little bro,' said Sly, in a poor impersonation of Chuck. 'Sod it, I'll leave you to your misery.' Clambering down from the top bunk, Sly grabbed his stonewash jacket and pulled open the door. 'You're doing me a favour anyway,' he said as a parting shot. 'Bloody stinks in here. I'll be on deck if you need me.'

As Sly disappeared to explore the ship, Chuck lay back on the bed, putting the wet flannel to his face and reflecting on the previous 30 hours. At about this time last night he was tucked up in bed with Abby having had the most exhilarating sex of his entire life. It had been amazing to get back with her after all these years. The difference now was that they no longer had to settle for the odd, nervous fumble, fearing that at any moment they might be caught in the act. They were both older and wiser, with more time to get to know each other and discover what each other liked.

Abby Lee had made his heart beat that bit faster from the moment he'd first spotted her on the lawn outside that Scottish castle, sitting among friends. She was wearing the standard uniform of her school, but it looked like a fashion statement on her, the white, pleated shirt rolled up to the elbows and her tight navy-blue skirt revealing just a tantalising portion of smooth, tanned thigh. The intoxicating view had him hypnotised, and he was rendered speechless when he realised she was heading in his direction.

'You're Chuck Dolan from Barking, aren't you?' she asked, causing his two mates to snigger. He was so tongue-tied he could barely nod. 'Right,' she said. 'We're from

Wood Green, but we've heard all about you. See that girl over there?' She was pointing to a small dumpy pal with brown curly hair. 'That's Crystal, and she fancies you. Will you go out with her?'

He wasn't sure how to answer. A refusal, and he would probably never get the chance to speak to this vision of beauty again. Accept, and he would not only be forced to meet a girl he had no interest in, but he would also risk having the piss taken out of him by his pals.

'I'll think about it,' he'd said, taking the safest option. 'I'm not sure she's my type, really.'

'Oh,' she said. 'You have a type. What is your type then, Mr "Big Shot" Dolan?'

She was taking the mickey out of him, something people who knew of his reputation would never dare try. Coming from her, though, he could take it. In fact, the sparring was fun, more challenging than any he'd faced at the boxing club. He fixed her with his deep brown eyes and said nothing. It was a small but significant victory when her cheeks began to colour, and she looked away.

'Bluuuurgh!' For fuck's sake, would this torture never stop? He had hoped recalling a pleasant memory might take his mind off his current predicament. Apparently not. He was so glad Abby wasn't a witness to his current shame and wondered what she was doing at that exact moment.

He'd barely had time to get to know her again before they'd parted. At least she'd promised she would visit him in the summer once she knew his location. It wouldn't be hard to organise because she'd be going back to visit her parents on the Costa Del Sol, anyway.

He thought now of their rushed farewell, the brief kiss on the lips that left him wanting more, the little wave and wink she gave him as he disappeared into the taxi and the faint smell of her perfume which stayed with him for the next few miles. He tried to hang on to the scent, only for it to fade on the way to the station. Throughout his life he had brushed away disappointment like a bug, his dad's insistence he 'Man Up' drumming away inside his head every time something didn't go his way. This time, it felt like his heart had been ripped out and discarded, like the takeaway boxes littering the back streets of Hackney.

Despite Sly's best attempts to lift his spirits on the subsequent train journey, Chuck had been unusually quiet, and his mood had turned even darker when they reached the docks. Seeing a large cruise ship in port revived a long-forgotten memory which hit him like a speeding truck, smashing his breath from his lungs. The last time he had been in a similar setting he'd been among thousands watching the *Queen Elizabeth II* set sail for the Falklands, having accompanied his father to say goodbye to his uncle. A soldier with the Scots Guards, Clive Dolan had been in fine spirits that day, lifting young Chuck above his head and calling him his 'favourite' nephew. A few months later on his return, his uncle was sullen, gaunt and distracted, a husk of the man they'd known. It wasn't long afterwards that Clive had died and for reasons Chuck kept buried deep down he still felt partly responsible.

That was just the start of a period of bad luck for the Dolan family, closely followed as it was by his father, Big Mo, getting arrested and subsequently imprisoned for a Post Office robbery in Kent. The only bright spot to emerge from that unhappy time was the birth of Arnie, so called because Arnold had been Uncle Clive's middle name.

During Big Mo's long periods of incarceration, Chuck had acted as a father figure to his siblings and a crutch for his mother to lean on. He'd had enough practice, having shielded Sly from parental meltdowns and rows from a very young age. Even so, he'd found it almost impossible to form the same bond with Arnold. Even as a toddler the kid had a rebellious streak and was inclined to do things his own way, no matter the guidance he received from his older and wiser siblings. By the time he reached his teens, Arnie was a tough loner with an instinct for an opportunity and a drive to follow through, whatever the dangers presented. The force of his personality made him impossible to ignore, which was why his two older brothers were now sailing far away from family, friends and the old flame Chuck had just managed to rekindle.

'Bloody Arnie,' he muttered, rolling over for another close encounter with the bucket at his side.

SLY never got as far as the deck. He was distracted by a sign reading 'Captain's Bar' which stood between him and the blustery outdoors. Stepping inside, he wasn't surprised to find just a smattering of customers. They were dotted around various tables in the large room. Wandering over to the counter, he waited patiently as the portly, balding barman dealt with someone further along the bar. 'P… pint, please… l… lager,' the young man was saying.

Sly watched the barman fill a pint mug and place it in front of the customer, who handed over a £10 note. Despite the stammer, Sly could detect a trace of a Cockney accent. Walking in the direction of the till, the man looked over and nodded at Sly. Then he stopped short and turned back to the other customer. 'Excuse me, sir, I can't accept this,' he said. 'This note is not legal tender.'

'W… w… what do you m… mean?' said the young man. 'I… I got it out of the cashpoint at the f… ferry terminal.'

'That's as maybe, mate, but it's a fake. Look.' He held it up to the light in front of the kid. 'There should be a watermark here, see? But there isn't. Means it's a forgery. Have you anything else?'

'N… no, sorry. It's all I've got.'

'In that case…' The barman picked up the pint and started walking away with it.

'Hold on, fella,' said Sly. 'Let's not be hasty. I'm sure it's a genuine mistake. Here, let me get that for him.'

'Well, if you're sure, sir?' said the barman. He walked back and placed the pint in front of the other customer. Sly held his own tenner to the light to check for the required watermark. It would be highly embarrassing should he be caught out the same way. Satisfied, he walked across and handed the note to the barman.

'And what would you like, sir?'

'The same please,' said Sly. He began walking back to his spot in the bar when the voice made him stop and turn.

'Would… it be ok if I… I joined you?' said the customer. 'I've been all on my tod 'til now. If you don't mind me s… saying, you sound like you're from my neck of the woods.'

Having been shut up with his ailing brother for hours, Sly grasped the opportunity for a two-way conversation with both hands. He was a much more gregarious creature than Chuck and sought out company wherever he could find it. He didn't like everyone, but you had to do something pretty despicable to get on the wrong side of him.

'You're from London?'

His new acquaintance made an instant decision, climbing from the bar stool and stumbling in Sly's direction. Sly shot out a hand to prevent him ending face down on the floor. 'Ch… cheers,' said the lad. 'My name's Lucky.'

'Sylvester… but people call me Sly.'

'Cool,' said Lucky. 'Like Stallone?'

The barman delivered Sly's beer and walked away.

'That's pretty much it,' said Sly. 'If you don't mind me saying, you don't seem very lucky. It's a nickname, right?'

'Of course. It's stuck with me ever since… well, forever. Real name's Luke Chalmers, see?' Sly gave him a blank look.

'My second name… Chalmers, hence Lucky Charm.'

'Ahhh.' Sly took a sip of his lager and let the welcome refreshment slide down his throat.

'Y…You on your own?'

'No,' said Sly. He wondered if his new friend was gay. It sounded like a pick-up line. Putting aside his misgivings, he explained about Chuck.

'He's sick? Poor bloke. People tell me it's a pretty b… bad crossing,' said Sly's new companion. 'Luckily, I have decent s… s…sea legs. P… p… probably thanks to my uncle Ron. H… he lives down in H… H… Hastings and used to take me out on his boat to teach me the r… ropes. I thought at one stage I might take up sailing for a liv… liv … living. S… sorry about the st… st… st...'

'Don't worry about it,' said Sly. 'Where are you going?'

'Spain.'

'Aren't we all?'

'S… sorry.' Lucky wobbled onto a stool then steadied himself by grasping the bar.

'You look like you've had a few, Lucky,' said Sly.

'D… drowning my sorrows, y'know?' he said. 'Not a lot has been going for me recently.'

'Snap.'

'R… really? Why, what's gone wrong?'

Sly was about to explain his predicament before a vision of Chuck came to mind. His big brother wouldn't like him telling tales out of school to complete strangers. 'Just a few issues at home,' he said.

'Sure,' said Lucky, taking a big gulp from his drink. 'Well, they're all after me… C… cops, criminals…'

'Public enemy No. 1, eh?' Sly laughed, wondering why the police would be pursuing this harmless-looking kid.

He sensed Lucky was having an internal debate with himself. Taking another drink, the boy seemed to come to a conclusion. It was obvious to Sly that he desperately needed to get something off his chest.

'Have you heard of the H… Hole in the Wall Gang?' he asked. Sly shook his head, but said nothing. 'They've been in the news – a group of f… faces from south London. Hardened criminals, you know… bank robbers and stuff?'

An image of his own father popped into Sly's head. 'Know the type,' he said.

'Well, I met this bloke in clink, like…'

'Prison?' Sly was surprised. Lucky didn't look old enough to have spent time behind bars.

'Afraid so,' he said. 'Not pleasant but I was a bit w… wayward at school and on leaving I f… fell in with a bad crowd. I… I'm pretty good at maths and science and shit. M… my foster mum always said I was too clever for my own g… good.'

'And you're running away to Spain because…'

'It's a long story.'

'We have nothing better to do, have we?' said Sly.

'Well, there was this bloke in p… prison who found out I knew how to clone cards,' Lucky said, lowering his voice.

'You cheat at poker?'

Lucky burst into laughter, rocking on his stool so much he was in danger of losing his balance and toppling over. Sly noticed the barman glaring at them from a distance and thought there was a good chance they could be asked to leave. Lucky was clearly more drunk than he had first suspected.

'Not those t… type of cards, silly!' he said, louder than necessary.

'You need some fresh air,' said Sly. 'You can tell me the rest out on deck.'

TEN

STINGING arrows of rain tore at their faces. Grabbing Lucky by the arm, Sly guided him to a more sheltered area. It was dark, but the roaring sea was lit by an eerie green glow, reflecting light emanating from somewhere below them.

'So what's the big joke?' shouted Sly to make himself heard above the cantankerous winds. 'You were laughing at me in there.'

'S… sorry, Sly,' shouted Lucky. His curly blond hair whipped around his face, and now and then he brushed it aside with a hand. 'It's j… j… just that when I said cards, I meant credit cards not gaming cards. I obtain people's details then produce f…fake cards in their name. Where I went wrong was sharing my secret with one of the blokes inside, though I had little choice. I needed someone to have my back in there. It was pretty sc… scary, and I was y… young and alone.'

Sly had a good idea what Lucky meant. He'd encountered some of the worst dregs of society on his occasional trips to see his dad in Belmarsh, a Category-A prison in south-east London.

'This guy offered me p… protection provided I did him a f… favour when we got out.'

'What favour?'

'A b… bank job, but not one where you break in. We were going to do cashpoint machines.'

'You can do that?'

'In theory.'

'What went wrong?'

'I d… don't really know,' said Lucky. 'Perhaps the geezer let too many people in on the secret. He was a bit of a loud-mouth, full of himself, liked to show off to his buddies as if he was the b… big noise. Trouble is, when too many people get involved there's always a danger someone will sn… snitch on you, for their own personal reasons. Maybe they got caught for something else and the cops offered them a deal. For whatever reason, things went wrong.'

'How far had you got before it went tits up?'

'I… I'd fixed up a machine to collect details from a branch in Borough Market. Just one day collecting people's bank card information c… can prove highly lucrative. Unfortunately, before we could make use of them the old b… bill discovered my equipment and started asking questions. As soon as word got out, I figured it was time to split.'

'I get you,' said Sly. 'Because of the cops.'

'Worse,' said Lucky. 'The people I was dealing with were h…hardcore villains. Most of them knew each other from back in the 70s having worked together before and trusted each other implicitly. When two of their pals were dragged in and questioned, they started the search for a m… mole. Of course, I had no such connections, and I figured pretty soon the f… finger of blame would point at me. Do you know what those sorts of people do to a g… g… grass.'

'I can guess,' said Sly. 'You didn't though?'

'What?'

'Tell the Bill.'

'Of course not!' Lucky looked affronted. 'I w… want to make a killin' as much as the next man. The last thing I imagined was sailing far from home. As soon as I heard about the arrests, though, I knew I couldn't hang around. Fortunately, I had this little escape to the Costa Blanca all planned out just in case things went wrong.'

'You said you didn't have any money, though. How does that work?'

'Oh, I have plenty,' said Lucky. 'Trouble is, it's funny money, see. I got a printing press in the garage at home which produces dosh on demand… or did before I was forced to dump it.'

Lucky took a wallet from his pocket, opened it and pulled out a bundle of £10 and £20 notes. 'That b… barman had every right to be miffed. I'm gonna have to stay out of his way. When it was a bit busier, one of his colleagues wasn't q… quite so careful in checking my money so when they cash up at the end of the night…'

'…There will be forgeries galore,' said Sly, finishing his new friend's sentence. 'Bloody hell, Lucky, You're full of surprises.'

'Thanks,' said the young man, interpreting it as a compliment. 'What about you? W… Where are you heading?'

'Chuck and I are going to stay with our grandfather for a while.'

'Chuck?' Lucky laughed again. 'Sounds pretty appropriate given his current st… state. Where does Granddad live?'

'Just outside Marbella.'

'Nice,' said Lucky. 'Bit more upmarket than Benidorm where I'm going. It's where the low-life British tourists flock to in the summer. Why didn't you fly?'

'Granddad organised it,' said Sly. 'Bit of a spur-of-the-moment thing. He's sent someone to pick us up when we get there. Look, maybe we should find the lounge and get our heads down for a bit. I'm shattered.'

'I thought you had a cabin?' said Lucky.

'Yeah,' said Sly, drawing out the word. 'I'd rather spread out over a couple of uncomfortable chairs than listen to my brother living up to his name.'

'I SUPPOSE you're fuckin' Millwall are ya?' said Chuck when Sly introduced his brother to his new friend. The older Dolan boy was still grumpy from one of the roughest 24 hours of his life.

'Most blokes are around my way but I'm Palace for my sins.'

'Hmmmph,' said Chuck.

'Don't worry about him,' said Sly to his new friend. 'He's always this miserable.'

Once the ship had docked, their passage through immigration was fairly rapid, and they found themselves on the Spanish mainland, keeping an eye out for their transport. Chuck was giving Lucky surreptitious glances, trying to work out what his game was. He loved Sly to pieces, but his brother had got in plenty of scrapes through his trusting and spontaneous nature. Now he seemed to be joined at the hip with this new friend, even though they'd only met each other a few hours earlier.

'There,' said Sly, pointing to a man standing by a large dark grey transporter van. He was holding a sign in his hands, the muscles on his tanned forearms straining to escape his tight-fittingT-shirt. The sign simply read 'Dolan'.

'That's our ride,' said Chuck.

Sly stepped forward, looking his brother in the eye. 'Can we give Lucky a lift? It's a long way to where he's going. He's a good guy and maybe we can make a detour, drop him off…'

'Sorry, Sly,' said Chuck. 'There's a reason granddad has sent someone to pick us up. He's got some "business" for us. I'm sure Lucky can't have come all this way without a plan.' He locked eyes with Sly's friend.

'It's fine S… Sly,' said Lucky, his stammer kicking in hard under the weight of Chuck's stare. 'M… my mate t… told me I c… can get a bus from here to Zaragosa and from there a train to Barcelona. I'm in n… no hurry, I can take in some of the t… tourist sites.'

'Well, if you're sure, mate,' said Sly. He moved forward and wrapped his new friend in a hug. Chuck turned away, unable to handle all the fake camaraderie. Sly had known the lad barely 24 hours and was acting as if they were best buddies, just because they had shared a beer together. One day his trusting nature would backfire badly.

Chuck shook Lucky's hand briefly, picked up his bag and set off over the road. 'Be Lucky,' said Sly to his friend before following in his brother's wake.

'Always am,' said Lucky. 'Hey, once I'm settled, I'll come and find you to give back that money I owe you. We can have a night on the razz.'

'YOU Chuck?'

The eldest Dolan boy nodded. 'Yeah,' he said. 'And the waster following me like a puppy is Sylvester.'

'Nice to meet you,' said their muscle-bound driver. 'I am Rafael, but you can call me Rafa. I am your granddad's *brazodorecho*, how you say uh, his hand on the right?'

'Right-hand man.'

'Si. Your grandfather, he marry my sister-in-law, Alisha, five years ago but I work for him ever since he first come out here in 1985. I introduce them. I guess you could call me, how you say, matchmaker?'

'Right,' said Chuck. 'I forgot he remarried. We didn't get an invitation.'

'It was a quiet ceremony,' said Rafael. 'I guess because it was his third marriage, he wanted to keep it, you know, under the wraps. Not everyone would think the age difference acceptable. Also, your mother was close to Viola, his second wife…'

'Yeah,' said Chuck. 'Our mum doesn't like flying and isn't that big on socialising at the moment anyway, so I don't think she would have come.'

'Sure, well, before we head back to civilisation, I'm afraid we have to take a trip to La Costa da Morte to pick something up for your grandfather,' said Rafael.

'Where?'

'Ah, in English you would call it the Coast of Death.'

11

'SOUNDS dangerous,' said Chuck. 'Should we be worried?'

'It depends on how easily you frighten,' said Rafael. 'It is one of the most beautiful places in Espana. The scenery is fabulosa, but it has a disturbing past. They talk of smugglers, ghosts and pirates… not to mention witchcraft.'

'Like you say, though, that's just history,' said Chuck.

'Yes and no,' said Rafael. 'The smugglers still exist, but nowadays it isn't tobacco, clothes, jewellery and food they are interested in but the white snow, cocaine.'

'Shit,' said Chuck. 'Is that why we're here?'

'Your grandfather tells me you are a clever boy, Chuck. I am sure you don't need me to answer that question. Are you the policia?'

Chuck laughed, but inside he was finding the latest revelation hard to grasp. He remembered the old man so well from his childhood and had always suspected Billy the Kid Dolan of criminal activity, but nothing involving drugs.

In his mind's eye, Chuck pictured him as a gentleman robber, targeting jewellers and high street banks. A successful one at that, simply because he had managed to stay out of jail and retire to the sun, unlike his eldest boy, Chuck's father Big Mo. Drugs was a whole different ball game, though, a business more associated with the young. Granddad Billy had to be nearing 70. It seemed an old dog could be taught new tricks, after all.

'Listen, this should be, umm, straightforward,' said Rafael. 'Please do as I say and let me do the talking. We'll be out of here soon enough.'

'What nice little Spanish hideaway are you taking us to, Rafa?' asked Sly, leaning forward from the back seat.

The driver smiled at the younger boy in the mirror, but the hard glint in his eyes contained no humour. 'It is six hours from here, a mansion on the hilltops behind a quaint fishing village. It's a shame it's so late because it would be nice to show you the beauty of Galicia. Don't be deceived, though. There are many bad people here who survive off the proceeds of *la blanca*.'

Feeling drained from the rough crossing, Chuck settled back and closed his eyes, allowing Rafael to concentrate on the long drive. He awoke some time later to the sound of rain hammering on the roof of the van. Glancing at the dashboard clock he noted it had just gone midnight. Chuck could count on one hand the hours of proper sleep he had enjoyed over the last three nights, and this was going to be another long one. 'Will we stop somewhere?' he asked Rafael. 'After the job, I mean. We could both do with some proper shut eye, couldn't we, Sly?'

Looking into the back seat, he saw his pale-looking brother nodding in agreement.

'The nature of our business means it is better to work at night,' said Rafael. 'Your grandfather has given me permission to stop off at a small hotel where you can rest up and be fresh to meet him tomorrow night at his villa in Torrevieja. Hopefully, barring complications, we should make the stopover by 3ish.'

'Hang on,' said Sly. 'I thought he lived in Marbella.'

'Ahh, he does,' said Rafael. 'He has two homes, but he has business on La Costa Blanca at this moment in time.'

'Balls,' said Sly. 'I was looking forward to spending time among the jet set. Imagine all the totty!'

'Sorry,' said Rafael, expertly swerving around a large, water-filled pothole in the road. 'That is a matter you will need to take up with your grandfather.'

'Jeez, how the hell can you see where you're going?' said Chuck.

'I am used to it,' said Rafael, who had barely reduced his speed despite the shocking driving conditions. The wipers were fighting a losing battle to clear the windscreen, while at the same time a swirling mist was rolling in from the Atlantic, somewhere off to their right. 'I have done this journey many times and always the rain, the mist, the wind furioso. Can you imagine being out on a boat in this weather, unsure where you are heading?'

It was a scenario Chuck didn't dare think about. His stomach was already twisting in knots, a muscle memory from his recent experience of the Bay of Biscay.

'Who are we meeting?' he asked. 'I appreciate the need to be secretive, but we'll be there soon enough and surely it would be better if we're fully prepared.'

'It is down to your grandfather to fill you in on, how you say, "the gen" but I guess it can't hurt to tell you the bones. We have dealings with one of your grandfather's closest associates: La Rana.'

'That's a nickname, surely?' said Chuck, feeling excited. 'What does it mean? Snake? Lion? Ghost, perhaps?'

'It means The Frog.'

Chuck burst out laughing and Sly, leaning over from the back, joined in. 'Bloody hell, they could have picked a scarier name,' said the elder Dolan. 'Hardly sounds like a gangster… reminds me of the character Del Boy and Rodney used to go on about in our favourite TV show *Only Fools and Horses*. Remember Sly?'

'Freddie the Frog.'

'That's the one.'

As the brothers fought to subdue their giggles, Chuck noticed that Rafael's stern expression didn't change.

'If you treat La Rana with such disrespect, you are dead men walking,' he said.

Chuck wrinkled his eyebrows, disbelieving, yet unsure.

'How so?'

'La Rana is a cartel boss from Colombia,' explained Rafael. 'The frog we are talking about is this big…' He raised his fingers, holding them no more than two inches apart. Sly was unable to control himself, rocking backward and forward as the laughter took hold.

'And what's this frog supposed to do,' he asked. 'Lick you to death?'

'Quite possibly,' said the Spaniard.

At that instant the van hit another hole in the road, veering violently to one side before Rafael brought it under control. Chuck glanced in the mirror at his brother. Sly's face had totally drained of colour, the humour being replaced by fear.

'This tiny frog is dangerous?' said Chuck.

'One of the most dangerous animals in the world,' agreed Rafael. 'The Golden poison frog lives in the Chocó rain forest on the Pacific coast of Colombia. I see a documentary on the TV. It lives happily in family groups, a friendly animal, but completely deadly to its enemies.'

'Why?' asked Chuck.

'There is poison stored in its skin which acts as a defence mechanism against predators,' said Rafael. 'Local tribesmen extract this poison by exposing the frogs to heat then soaking their hunting arrows and darts in it. A dart dipped in such poison is effective for up to two years, so you must take care in how you handle it, no?'

'Sure,' said Chuck. 'So why do they call this Colombian La Rana?'

'Ahh, it's an interesting story,' said Rafael. 'I don't know whether it is entirely true, but I have no reason to doubt it. Apparently, there was a battle between the cartels back in Colombia and business was suffering. La Rana invited 10 of the top gangsters in Colombia for dinner to talk things over. Only La Rana lived to eat dessert.'

'What happened?'

'The details are… um, sketchy, as you English say. The most popular theory is their knives and forks were coated in poison, but I can't see you could guarantee they would pick up their cutlery at the same time… it seems, how you say, the big flaw in the tale. Maybe there was a toast, with the poison applied to the stems of wine glasses. It wouldn't need much. One frog contains maybe one milligram of poison…'

'You'd need an awful lot of frogs then,' said Sly.

'Not at all,' said Rafael. 'That is the beauty of the Golden poison frog. The poison is so… um…'

'Toxic,' said Chuck.

'Si. The poison is so toxic that one milligram is, in fact, enough to kill between 10 and 20 people.'

THE clock on the dashboard had just ticked past one when through the mist Chuck saw the mansion come into view.

It looked like one of those haunted houses a bunch of kids would always dare each other to enter in films, only for their bravado to backfire on them. Despite that, visitors had to admire its grandeur.

Built in the style of a French chateau, its turrets and battlements loomed large above them, a warning to any invaders that the castle was heavily defended. Rafael pulled up in front of a pair of 14-foot-high ornate iron gates, which bore a coat of arms and were topped with spikes. The Spaniard stopped the van and pulled on the handbrake, then stepped out. Thankfully, the rain was finally relenting, and his two passengers waited with anticipation, listening to heavy drops of water bounce onto the roof from the extensive vegetation around them.

Rafael approached the gates, pressed a button on a panel and muttered a few words, then turned his face up to look into an expensive camera peering down from a gate post like a curious bird of prey. There was a creaking and the gates began to move, inviting the new arrivals into the belly of the beast.

'Remember, let me do the talking and we'll be on our way in no time,' said Rafael, climbing back behind the wheel and driving into the lair of the Colombian Cartel boss.

'Fuck,' said Sly. 'Are we invading some kind of government military base? Look at it… it's bloody huge and I'm guessing those aren't toy guns.'

The van was passing a line of bulky, dark-clothed soldiers carrying weapons. 'La Rana's men,' said Rafael. 'Pick your nose in a suspicious way and they will cut you in two with those AK47s.'

'You can't hide a fortress like this without the authorities knowing, surely,' said Chuck.

'Who says the authorities don't know… of course they do,' said Rafael. 'La Rana is very clever, though. They are taken care of by, how you say, expenses, and the drug money is so important to the area that no locals would dream of telling tales. They know what "reward" they would receive. In these parts, they have a phrase: La Rana's tongue stretches a long way.'

As they drove up to the front of the mansion, Chuck caught sight of a welcoming committee at the building's entrance. A debonair looking man, his greying temples making him appear wise and authoritative, was dressed in a beige suit and wearing a colourful cravat displaying wild and exotic patterns. He looked every inch the boss, but the question was crying out to be asked.

'Why is he in a wheelchair?' said Chuck.

'Oh, he fell out with a rival a few years ago,' said Rafael. 'It's a long time since anyone saw that rival. La Rana always equals the score.'

'Well, I don't know about Joe 90 there but his bird's a bit tasty,' said Sly. 'I would.'

Chuck realised his brother was drooling over the tall, elegant woman at the man's side. She looked all business in a black trouser suit, her dark hair falling straight to her shoulders. Chuck estimated her age at around 40. 'Bit old for you, Sly,' he said. 'She'd suck you up and blow you out in bubbles.'

'Think of all that experience, though,' said Sly. 'I reckon she'd give you a wild ride. She's got that look on her face. Pure filth…'

'Continue to talk like that my friends and we won't get out alive,' said Rafael.

Sly laughed nervously. 'Sure,' he said. 'I can understand why La Rana would be the jealous type with a bird like that for a wife.'

'Yes,' said Rafael. 'Only that "bird" IS La Rana.'

12

AS RAFAEL wandered off to take care of business, Chuck and Sly were still coming to terms with the fact one of the most powerful figures in the Colombian drug cartels was a woman. They were now sitting on a wooden bench in a room just off the main hallway, having been led there by armed guards. Chuck leant back to study the ornate, carved wooden ceiling with its cherubs and scantily clad figures, pondering how high up the criminal scale you had to climb to live somewhere this opulent.

'Come on, Chuck, admit it, you would,' said Sly.

'For fuck's sake, give it a rest,' hissed Chuck, eyeing the guards at the door nervously. 'You heard what Rafael said, she is strictly out of bounds. Whatever you're thinking, it will only end in tears… and probably worse. Fuckin' hell, do you ever stop thinking about getting your end away?'

'Says the man who spent the night shagging his ex before we left for Spain.'

'That's different.'

'Of course it isn't. That bird in there is the same as any other. She has the same urges, the same body parts and functions… Maybe they call her the Frog cos she likes a good riveting. You thought of that?' He laughed out loud.

'There really is no saving you, is there?' said Chuck, shaking his head. 'One day that thing between your legs will get you into a heap of trouble. Make sure it isn't today, eh?'

The Dolan brothers sat in silence for a while, Chuck continuing his inventory of the room, admiring the intricately laid wooden tiles which converged on a central point in the middle of the floor. In other circumstances, the luxury of their surroundings might have lured him into a false sense of security, but the guns nestling in the guards' holsters made sure he stayed alert and on edge.

Eventually, the door opened and Rafael poked his head around. 'Right, *mis amigos*, come and earn your *dinero*. I have some bags that need carrying to the van. OK?'

'Sure,' said Sly, jumping to his feet. Chuck rose and followed the two of them out of the door, the guards not far behind. The echo of their feet bounced off the walls and high ceiling as they made their way to a room farther down the corridor. Rafael pushed open a door, and they entered. It was empty apart from four hessian sacks and two black suitcases placed in the middle of the floor.

'Grab two bags each and please be careful,' said Rafael. 'What is in them is worth far more than I suspect you boys have seen in your entire lives.'

Once they were loaded up, Rafael led the way out to the van then placed the suitcases on the driveway. Flinging open the back doors, he ordered the boys to remove a stack of cardboard boxes from within. When they had done so he climbed in and ordered Chuck to pass the bags to him. Once he had stored them away, he placed a blanket over the load and jumped out again, ordering them to load up the boxes again so the sacks were hidden from view. 'Time to go,' he said, slamming the doors. 'I expect you are looking forward to your sleep.'

'Where's the lovely senorita?' whispered Sly to Chuck.

'Behind you,' said a husky, deep voice. The younger Dolan turned to find La Rana staring at him through piercing dark brown eyes. She brushed strands of hair from her face, blown there by the stiff breeze sweeping in from the Atlantic. Her long legs were encased in black fishnet stockings, teasingly visible through the peekaboo split sides of her trousers. Her shoulders were encased in a silver-flecked black bolero jacket. Chuck had to admit she was an extremely attractive woman.

'So, these are El Nino's grandchildren,' she said.

Rafael stepped forward quickly.

'Si, Senora,' he said, bowing reverentially.

Waving him aside, she stepped forward and ran her eyes the length of Sly's body. Grasping his chin in her hand, her long, blood-red nails dug painfully into his skin. She turned his head to the left, then right before slowly nodding her approval. Chuck shot Rafael a look. In two minds how to react, his fists bunched in his pockets. He received an imperceptible shake of the head in response. The Spanish night air pulsed with tension.

'A little bird tells me you would like to do things to me,' she said coyly, her face now so close to Sly that Chuck thought she was going to kiss him. She was at least an inch taller than his brother, though the height difference could be accounted for by the length of the stiletto heels on her strappy black sandals. 'I make you hard, no?'

Before Sly could react, her other hand shot out and grabbed him between the legs. He yelped, and Chuck stepped forward.

'No, no, English boy!' she said, a rigid finger shooting out in his direction while her other hand remained buried in Sly's crotch. Chuck felt the nozzle of a gun resting against his spine. Raising his arms slowly, he then opened his hands up to reveal he wasn't carrying a weapon.

'Please, Senora,' said Rafael. 'El Nino is expecting his boys back in one piece. They are family and you, of all people, know what that means. If they have upset you in any way, I can only apologise. They mean no offence. They are new to the country and don't understand the way things work here. No disrespect was intended. This one is just a kid.'

'Hmm,' she said. 'That may be so, but his body gives him away. He is what the English call very swollen. He wants to fuck with me. If I cut him now, I think he would bleed very much, no? Perhaps maybe I should slice it off and spare him further embarrassment.'

'N... no, please,' said Sly. 'I... I didn't mean...'

She closed her fist, making him gasp, then let go, laughing loudly. 'You have big cajones for a little one,' she said, nodding appreciatively. 'I like that. You should be careful about who is listening, though, when you choose to be disrespectful to strangers.' She waved her hands in the direction of one of the guards. 'Hugo there has excellent English, which is why he was specifically assigned to look after you. He told me you had lots to say to your brother about what you might like to do to me. Well... I'm sure it would be fun, but I try not to mix business with pleasure.'

She turned to Rafael. 'You have what you need?'

He nodded.

'Don't forget to tell El Nino of my concerns. There seems to be a lot of attention being paid to our boats these days, too much. I have a strange feeling there is a topo – a mole – in our organisation who is tipping off the policia and the coastguard to our schedule. I hope my friend El Nino isn't playing La Rana for a fool. He will discover soon enough that she is not.'

'Of course, Senora.'

Turning to Sly, she winked. 'It won't be tonight, English boy… The future?' She left the question hanging in the air.

13

'FUCK!' said Sly, turning to clamber back into the van as a large German shepherd bounded towards them, growling and barking. Chuck couldn't wait to stretch his legs after the eight-hour journey through the heart of Spain but was hoping for a warmer welcome. He held his nerve, though, and when the animal was just a few feet away a voice shouted, 'Major! Stop!'

The dog came to an abrupt halt, standing to attention like a soldier, its nose in the air and its eyes alert and attentive. It licked its lips slowly.

'Don't worry about 'im.' The cockney tones, though disguised and slightly smoothed out since the last time Chuck had heard them, were familiar. Then he saw the old man walking across the shingle in slippers and cream-coloured silk dressing gown. 'Here they are then,' he said. 'My boys! Any problems, Rafa? Behave, did they? I hope so. Let's have a look at yer then. Fackin' 'ell, Chucky. Last time I saw you, you was barely a teenager… and Sylvester, are you coming out or you going to hide in there all night, you little chicken?'

Sly poked his head around the door, then stepped out gingerly. The dog licked its lips again but didn't move or make a sound. 'Now come and make friends with Major. Give him a stroke. He's fine. He won't bite.'

The younger Dolan walked tentatively forward and placed his hand on the dog's head. It sank to its haunches, grateful for the attention. 'Sorry,' he said. 'I love dogs but Major took me by surprise, didn't you, boy?' The animal looked up at him through big brown eyes.

'Good, good,' said the old man. 'You two will get on fine, I'm sure. But, my, how you've shot up. You were just a little ankle biter when you last visited with yer mum.'

It was early evening and though they hadn't slept properly for four days, they were keen to take in the surrounds of the colourful and expansive villa spread out before them, knowing this would be their home for the foreseeable future.

'Hi, Granddad,' said Chuck. To him, the old man seemed smaller somehow, shrunken from the days he used to lift Chuck into the air with giant, calloused fingers dripping with sovereign rings, the words *Mum* and *Dad* inked on the digits. He wasn't particularly tall, unlike Chuck's father Mo and Uncle Clive, but he was solid, like an immoveable piece of oak furniture. Mind you, Chuck's main recollections of his grandfather stemmed from his childhood. Now a grown man standing at 6ft, Chuck imagined he could comfortably fit the old man under one arm.

'Welcome to Casa Billy,' said his grandfather, opening his skinny arms wide so that his jewellery jingled in the quiet surroundings. 'I know you were anticipating a trip to Marbella, but there's been a change of plans. I bought this little spot of heaven a few years ago after me and wife No. 3 got hitched. You remember the old hacienda at Sierra Blanca? I thought we needed to expand a bit because Alisha loves her horses and, well, I had the money and felt it would be a good investment to buy a ranch. When I die, who knows, you could own a piece of this if you play your cards right.'

'Bloody hell, Gramps,' said Sly. 'You ain't going yet, are you? We only just got here!'

Billy chuckled. 'Ahh, your mother told me you're the joker of the family. No, boy, I plan to stay around and enjoy the fruits of my labours for years to come. It's my intention to get to know you geezers a bit better... me grandkids. We see your Auntie Cilla's brood now and again, but never you lot. Come on, come on, grab your bags and let's go inside.'

It was still a pleasantly warm evening, and the brothers were clammy and smelly from their long journey. Both felt a bit cheated, too, having heard so much about what Marbella had to offer, but beggars couldn't be choosers. They were there to hide out and being off the beaten track wasn't necessarily a bad thing. As they passed through the imitation Greek stone pillars guarding the entrance, a refreshing coolness swept over them, reviving them instantly. 'Air conditioning,' said Billy, noting their expressions. 'Couldn't live without it, to be honest. It was never this toasty in Chigwell. It's hot enough to boil a monkey's piss out here.'

As they deposited their bags in the hallway, Billy hung back to whisper a few instructions to Rafael. Diverting his attention indoors, Chuck saw a raven-haired woman dressed in a bright pink bikini emerge from beneath a pastel-peach archway. He guessed she was in her 30s and was immediately intrigued. Was she perhaps the daughter of his grandfather's new wife?

'Welcome, welcome,' said the woman, her smile as warm as the weather. 'Come on in, boys, and make yourselves comfortable... this is your home now.'

Granddad Billy materialised from behind them. 'Ah,' he said. 'I see you've met the lady of the house. Alisha, this is Chuck and this is Sylvester...' For a moment they hesitated, and Chuck realised Sly was as shocked as him at the age of their new grandmother. He walked forward and held out his hand, only for the young woman to wrap him in a warm embrace.

'It's lovely to meet you,' she said. 'William has told me so much about you.'

Chuck raised an eyebrow. He had only ever heard his grandfather called 'Billy' or 'The Kid' in the past.

'Back in the day they used to be around my house in England all the time and, I must say, it was a privilege to watch them grow up,' said the old man as Sly walked forward to be greeted in the same manner. 'Unfortunately for... um ... logistical reasons we haven't seen as much of each other over the years as I would have liked. Hopefully, this will give us a chance to get to know each other all over again.'

'They are big, strong boys,' said Alisha, grabbing Sly's arm. 'I am sure you will find plenty on the estate to occupy them.'

Chuck raised his eyebrows and turned to his grandfather. 'Estate? Exactly how big is this "little" bolt hole of yours, Granddad? I remember the Marbella pad. That was big enough.'

'It's hard to keep track,' said Billy. 'Let's see... the house has nine bedrooms, four bathrooms, a gym, an office and a swimming pool. Then there are the stables and the paddock for the horses, plus the garden, of course. But never mind all that malarky, what I really want to show you is me boozer!'

'What?' said Sly.

'Oh yes, boy, I got me own rub-a-dub… sorry, pub,' said the old man, chuckling at his grandson's expression. 'I've got four beers on tap and a variety of spirits, not to mention a full-size snooker table, a pinball machine, a jukebox and a couple of bandits. It's a home from home, but it's rare I get the chance to share it with anyone. Rafael's OK but he ain't up to snuff on the old green baize… more suited to pocket billiards if you ask me!'

He started to laugh uproariously, breaking down into a coughing fit. The dog began to run around him, barking, its eyes shining with obvious affection. Alisha moved forward and rubbed the old man's back while Sly, having conquered his fear, knelt and gently petted the animal, which turned and licked his fingers. The old man's jewellery jangled again as he tried to bring his breathing under control.

'Oh dear, it looks like you boys have got him all excited,' said Alisha. 'Let me get Naomi to show you to your rooms, and when you have settled, I've enough paella to feed all the Costas. It will be ready in about half an hour, so why not freshen up and I'll see you then. Naomi!'

A diminutive figure, her face framed by a bob of black hair, emerged from the archway. She was wearing a black-and-white uniform with white sandals and looked about 10 years younger than her mistress. 'Can you show the boys to the rooms we made up today, please?' Alisha said. 'Hopefully, they will have everything they require for their stay with us but if not, please see if you can help them out in any way.'

Chuck noticed the grin creep across his younger brother's face when he clapped eyes on the maid. Immediately, he stopped fussing the dog and stood. Chuck knew exactly what was on Sly's mind.

Here we go again, he thought.

'KNOW what we need after a nose bag like that?' Granddad Billy walked over to the jukebox in the corner of his 'personal' pub. '…A bit of the Rolling Stones.' He patted the retro music machine before pressing in some numbers on the keypad. 'This little beauty has been reconditioned. It's not much younger than me but plays all my pukka old vinyl records. I spend hours in here listening to the old tunes. It gives me peace from the trouble.'

'You've got troubles, Granddad?' asked Sly.

His granddad smiled. 'Ha ha… I can see I'm gonna have to teach you boys a thing or two. It's the old cockney rhyming slang ain't it? Trouble 'n strife? Wife! I can hide away down here and Alisha, God love her, won't come in… She knows an Englishman's home is his castle, don't she? I can raise the drawbridge and sit here with my music, my favourite tipple and my own thoughts.'

Jingling guitar sounds emerged from the speakers and Chuck recognised the wail of Mick Jagger announcing he wanted to do a paint job on a white door.

'How did you meet her, Granddad?' asked Chuck.

'Boys, boys, call me Billy,' said the old man. 'I can't be doing with this granddad nonsense… makes me feel old.'

'Ain't you supposed to be as old as the woman you feel?' said Sly. 'That must make you about 26, Gramps!'

Billy the Kid gave his grandson a steely look, fists balled at his sides. Chuck wondered if Sly had pushed things too far. It wasn't unusual for his brother to test the boundaries. He didn't seem to possess an off switch. When something popped into his head, he had to blurt it out, no matter whom it might upset, his objective to elicit a cheap laugh from his 'audience'.

'Why…' Billy lurched forward, grabbing Sly's head and thrusting it under his arm. It was a surprising show of strength for a pensioner. Rubbing his knuckles across the boy's skull, he said, 'You little tinker! Ha ha! Bloody hell, Sylvester, son. Your mother was right. You're a real card and no mistake. I reckon you could be the next Jim Davidson… heard of him? Love a bit of Jim, I do. Met him once da'an the West End after this gig. We got well and truly hammered on single malt. Talking of drinks, take a seat, boys. What can I get you?'

'Let me get them, Granddad… um, Billy,' said Chuck. 'I worked in the Hope for a short while, so I know what I'm doing.'

'The Hope and Anchor? Is that old place still going?'

'It's our local,' said Sly.

'Had many a barney in there,' said Billy. 'Good times. Well, until that business with your Uncle Clive that is. Never went back after that. Can you pour me a Guinness, boy? Could do with a good stout… apparently it puts years on your life. Not that I'm doing too bad… right, Sly? Look at Alisha. Cracking piece, ain't she? Bowled that young lady right off her feet, I did. You boys keep your eyes off her, OK? I know what it's like being your age. I used to chase all the skirt back in the day when I had lead in me pencil and didn't need prescription drugs to get it up.'

Too much information, thought Chuck. He wondered if Sly got his "No filter' gene from the old man. He went to the bar and returned carrying three pint glasses, passing the Guinness to his granddad before placing lagers on the table for him and his brother. 'You'll like that Spanish pop,' said Billy. 'It ain't bad. Too gassy for me, though.'

Billy took a sip of the Guinness then drummed his hands on the table along with the music. Eventually the song came to an end and he struck up conversation again, telling them about how he had been devastated when his second wife Viola died from cancer seven years after they moved out to Marbella. For a couple of years, he had suffered from acute depression caused by the loss of his loyal and loving companion, and it had only been after a great deal of persuasion from Rafael that he had accepted a dinner invitation.

At the meal, he'd met Rafael's wife and been introduced to her sister, Alisha. They had got on so well that night he'd mustered the courage to ask her on a date and they'd married within the year.

'I know the age difference seems weird,' said Billy. 'But she is a bit older than she looks and keeps me young. With a bit of help from the pharmacist I'm able to satisfy her needs.' He indicated to where his spindly legs poked out of knee-length khaki shorts. Unbidden, a vision of the old man pawing their ravishing young hostess came to Chuck, which he found difficult to wipe from his mind. Unaware of the impact his confession was having on the older boy, Billy continued.

'I'm pretty lucky, I know,' he said. 'A lot of the old gang have been taken by time or fallen victim to… well, let's just say the past. Many of us came out here at different times. The old bill wouldn't let us rest back in England and with plenty of young, keen villains wanting to push you off your perch… well, I just needed a bit of peace.'

'Doesn't sound like you're slowing down much to me, though, gra… Billy,' said Chuck. 'Our little expedition in the north tells me you're not sitting around enjoying sunsets with your pipe and slippers… unless that was talcum powder in those bags we brought back.'

'You can't look a gift horse in the mouth,' said the old man, taking a sip of his pint. 'I see opportunities, always have done. No point in having all this money if you can't make it work for you. Who knows? Maybe you'll be the beneficiaries if Her Majesty's tax collectors, the cozzas and a few, let's say, jealous types don't catch up with me first.'

'The drugs business is pretty messy,' said Chuck. 'Lots of young idiots out there ready to cut your throat to get an advantage in the market.'

'I let the little tossers get on with it,' said Billy. 'With any luck they will bump each other off. That's why I've come up here for a bit, see. Marbella's been taken over by these young wannabe gangsters, all shooting their mouths off and acting the "big I am". I ain't a fan of that white powder to tell the truth, but if people like sticking it up their noses who am I to argue? If I don't supply it, someone else will. The Russians, Colombians, Irish… there are even lots of new faces out here from the Baltics who fled after the war to avoid their comeuppance. I tend to steer clear of the distribution side of things. For me it's about making the proceeds "disappear".'

'You're a fence?' said Sly.

Billy, defying his age, moved quickly to cuff the younger Dolan around the head again. 'Not a very nice thing to call me, Sylvester,' he said. 'It makes me sound cheap somehow, like Nick the Greek down Soho… Look, let's say I got lots of fingers in lots of pies. I bought myself a share in a golf course, I've a handsome stake in one of them water amusement parks down the road, a couple of clubs, one up the road in Benidorm and another in Marbella, and four or five motels like the one you stayed in last night… and then there's the highly lucrative timeshare business. I put my hard-earned cash to work, and it comes out smelling of roses, know what I mean?'

Sly nodded. Chuck couldn't quite see what the difference was. A fence was a fence, surely.

'Anyway,' said the old man, leaning back and tapping his hand faster against his chair as Elvis belted out 'Hound Dog'. 'Sounds to me like you're hardly beginners when it comes to this type of thing. Yer mother tells me you got yourself in a bit of a fix. Still, I don't blame you for trying to make a bit of coin. Maybe you need to learn from the expert, though. I've been around since dinosaurs roamed the earth and the rozzers ain't laid a finger on me. Your dad? He's spent more time eating The Queen's porridge than your mother's. Shame, but I figure I must have been doing something right… your turn, Sly. I'll have another Guinness before we call it a night.'

Sly collected the glasses and walked off towards the bar, and Chuck felt the old man's eyes settle on him. 'How the hell did you manage to burn down a nightclub?' he muttered.

'Who told you?' Chuck couldn't imagine his mother revealing their secrets over an open phone line.

'My head don't button up the back,' said Billy. 'I read and I watch the news… we get the BBC here too. That

Hackney fire was a pretty big tale, and just minutes after I saw it on the TV your mum rang and told me you needed a holiday, and possibly a long one. I can do simple maths.'

Chuck sighed, still unsure whether he was doing the right thing confiding in the old man. Then again, advice from someone who had managed to steer clear of the law for his entire life couldn't do any harm. 'It was an accident.'

'Shit!' Billy whistled. 'Some accident.'

'Well, all right. There was a grenade, but I never intended for it to go off.'

'A grenade?' Billy raised his voice, incredulous. 'You're fackin' kidding?'

'I know, I know… I should never have taken it. That's what Arnie said.'

'Arnie?' Now Billy looked like he had seen a ghost.

'You know, our younger brother?'

'Sorry, of course,' said Billy. 'It was your Uncle Clive's middle name, y'know?'

Chuck nodded. 'Of course,' he said, leaning closer to the old man. 'Why do you think Mum and Dad named him that? It was a tribute to Uncle Clive. I remember him, even though I was only a nipper when he died. Dad took me to Southampton to say goodbye when he went off to war.'

'Shouldn't have gone,' said Billy. 'Stupid army.'

'Our Arnie's only 16 but he's wise beyond his years,' said Chuck, steering off the touchy subject. 'He had this plan to put the frighteners on a rival gang… show the main man in our area we were serious. The plan was to kidnap this drug-peddling nightclub owner and present him to the big cheese. I told Dad about the plan and he advised me to get in touch with some mates in Manchester. They sold me this grenade.'

'I should have guessed your dad would be involved.'

'He was just trying to help,' said Chuck, springing to the defence of his father. 'It was meant to be a tactic to scare off our rivals, but when the thing went down, the grenade fell out of my pocket and…'

'Kaboom!' said Billy. 'Nice one, son. And where was young Sylvester while all this was going on?'

'Right there with me,' said Chuck. 'He saved my life, risking his own neck to stay with me when I thought I was toast. He might act like a tool sometimes but when the shit hits the fan, he comes through.'

'And so he should,' said Billy. 'That's what family is about, son. In my business, too, it's about trust. The old gang I used to work with, they were the salt of the earth, and you could rely on them to have your back. Unfortunately, it all changed when I moved out here… now you spend every waking hour looking over your shoulder, wondering when they're coming for you.'

'Who's coming for you, Gramps?' Sly asked, putting another pint of Guinness down in front of Billy.

'It could be anyone, anytime, anywhere,' said Billy the Kid Dolan. 'That's why I was glad to get out of Marbella for a bit. When I learnt you were coming, well, all the better. At a time like this it's nice to have true family to rely on. Not just the locals who, let's be honest, can be bought for the price of a cold San Miguel.'

14

'YOU said you were planning to spend a lot of time in the water when we got to Spain, but ain't this taking it a bit too far?' said Sly. He doubled over with laughter as Chuck slammed his club hard against the immaculate turf, anger and frustration distorting his features.

'Never mind, son,' said Billy the Kid. 'You had a bit of a bare lie… it was a tricky shot. Fish out another ball and try again.'

'I've nearly run out of soddin' balls,' said Chuck, wiping sweat from his brow. The climate was on the toasty side of warm. 'They aren't cheap either. I thought six would be enough, but I'm down to my last two and we've only played seven bloody holes. Jesus. The fish have more balls than me. I didn't think this game would be so bloody difficult.'

'Oh yeah, my old mate Charlie made 12 on a hole once,' agreed Billy. 'At the end of his round he smashed up his clubs and never played again.'

'Charlie?' Sly was already becoming obsessed with his grandfather's past and the dodgy acquaintances he had made down the years.

'Charlie Wilson,' said Billy The Kid. 'One of the Great Train Robbers. Dead now. He was a neighbour of mine in Marbella and some bastard executed him on his driveway, then escaped on a push bike, cheeky fucker. Nine years ago we lost Charlie, God rest his soul. That's why I move about a bit. You never know who's got it in for you… your shot, Sly.'

The younger Dolan boy took a lofted club from his bag and surveyed the idyllic view in front of him. The sun sparkled off the lake to his right and the gently undulating expanse of green rolled out like a carpet in front of him, skirted by trees. Just to his left at the bottom of the hill a red flag sat limp against its pole, indicating an absence of breeze.

Once he'd lined up the shot, he took two casual practice swings, then addressed the ball, pulled the club back and smoothly brought it down in an arc. The small, white sphere soared into the clear blue sky and all three men watched admiringly as it landed around 180 yards further on, perfectly dissecting two bunkers before bouncing on a few more metres and coming to rest on the edge of the beautifully manicured green. Sly pumped his fists and did a little dance. It made Chuck even grumpier to see his younger sibling rubbing his nose in it.

'Lovely shot, son,' said Billy the Kid. 'You've played this game before, ain't ya?'

'Just a few times, Gramps,' said Sly. 'There aren't many courses out our way that will let ordinary geezers play on 'em. I've been down Epping with a couple of mates in the past and I also like letting off steam on the driving range.'

'I'd say you're a natural,' said Billy.

'He's a waster is what he is,' said Chuck. 'He messes around on golf courses while the rest of us are out working.'

'Working?' asked Billy. 'What exactly do you do, son? When you're not letting off grenades in nightclubs, I mean.'

Chuck let the dig slide. 'I help a scaffolder put stuff up and pull it down,' he said. 'I also work as a labourer for a local builder and, well, there's the odd bit of security work, too…'

'A lot of physical stuff then,' said Billy. 'No wonder you got them muscles, son. As it happens, I'm in the building trade myself. Got these timeshares along the coast.'

'What's a timeshare?' asked Sly.

'It's a holiday flat that those who like coming to places like Marbella every year can buy a share of, perhaps a two week "portion", so that certain dates are reserved for them when they fancy a bit of sun. There's good money in it, anyway. You can make a fortune if you play your cards right and don't stick rigidly to the rules.' He winked.

'Fore!'

Billy and Sly immediately crouched down, covering their heads with their arms. Chuck, confused by the shout, looked back up the hill and saw an overweight man staring down at him, his hands cupped to his mouth. Feeling something brush his ear, Chuck dived to the ground, believing he was under attack. Behind him he heard a 'plop' and turned to see a white ball rolling down the hill in the direction of the green. Realising what had happened, Chuck finally snapped.

'You fuckin' wanker!' he shrieked, climbing to his feet and racing across to where a golf buggy stood, red seats shaded beneath a white canopy. Clambering aboard, he put the cart into drive and turned it around before pressing his foot to the accelerator. The owner of the stray golf ball wore a confused expression as the buggy made its way up the hill towards him.

'What the fack are you doing, son?' Chuck heard his grandfather's shout but ignored the question. 'Come back, would ya? You're holding up play.'

'Fuck play,' muttered Chuck. 'The only thing I'll be holding up in a minute is this fucker… by the neck. He nearly decapitated me.'

'Chuck, stop! Hell, tell him, Sylvester…' Chuck detected a note of desperation in his grandfather's voice and allowed himself a malicious grin. *Serves him right for making me look a fool out here*, he thought.

Chuck saw double chins wobbling beneath a flabby face as he closed in on his quarry. The golfer was gawping at the buggy hurtling towards him and motioning with his hands to two burly men who had been caddying for him and his partner. 'Ah, that evens things up,' muttered Chuck, taking his foot off the pedal and bringing the buggy to a halt 20 feet away.

'Oi, you fat bastard, you nearly knocked my fucking block off!' he shouted, grabbing a three-wood from his bag and hefting it in his hands before climbing off the buggy and ascending the final slight incline to the top of the hill. As the two bodyguards stepped forward, Chuck's target scurried backwards.

'Is that a knuckleduster?' said Chuck, noticing one of the two heavies adjusting something on his fist. 'How quaint. I hope you know how to use it, my friend, or I'll be ramming it up your fuckin' ass. I'm told the operation to remove them can be pretty painful.'

The man charged forward, egged on by the baiting. Big mistake. It was exactly the response Chuck wanted. He liked fighting on the back foot. Bouncing on his feet, he weaved his head out of the way of the anticipated punch before planting a powerful body shot into the ribs of his attacker. A satisfying crunch suggested he'd broken through bone, and he watched with glee as the muscle-bound loser crumpled to his knees. Following up, Chuck launched his knee into his rival's face and watched as the spark departed from his eyes.

Sensing the other heavy behind him, Chuck grasped the fairway wood in both hands and swung around, striking the charging bodyguard in the side of the head. It was the best shot he'd played all day, stopping the mullet-haired giant in his tracks. The man wobbled on two unsteady feet before Chuck's forehead crashed into his nose and sent him toppling down to join his mate.

Adrenaline flowing, Chuck refocussed his attention, picking out the blundering fat man making for the distant clubhouse.

'Stop, son, stop, for fuck's sake!' shouted Billy the Kid from somewhere behind him.

Chuck set off at a trot, his right fist balled and his left holding the shaft of the club. He could see dark hairs pinned to the head of the three-wood by a red, sticky substance. Blood. Even at this sedate speed, he was gaining on his target, the man's bloated, red face betraying his fear as he cast a nervous look over his shoulder. Having lost concentration, his left foot caught the lip of a bunker and he lost a one-sided battle with gravity, the ankle twisting as he collapsed face first into the sand.

Leaping into the trap after him, Chuck placed his foot on the fat man's head and pushed down. His victim spluttered for mercy, his 22-stone bulk wriggling like an overfed serpent in the sand. 'Please,' he said. 'I'm a business associate of Billy's! You want cash? I can give ye cash.'

'I ain't after your shitty money,' said Chuck. 'I just want to play a round of golf without some twat trying to knock my fuckin' block off. If you know my grandfather, then you should know you don't mess with the Dolans...'

Increasing the pressure with his left foot, he placed the other one to the side of the man's body and wriggled like a professional golfer preparing to play a sand shot. Lining up the club with the man's head, he slowly pulled it back over his shoulder. 'Fore!' he shouted. The fat man shut his eyes.

Before Chuck could finish the job, though, he felt two arms wrap themselves around his knees and send him flying across the prone form of his victim. 'For fuck's sake!' he exclaimed, fighting to free himself from his assailant, who was hanging on for grim life.

'That's it, Sylvester, son,' said Billy the Kid, looking down on them from the edge of the trap. 'I don't think the England rugby captain Martin Johnson could have performed a better tackle.'

'TEL, I must sincerely apologise for my grandson's actions,' said Billy the Kid as he joined the fat man at a table in the 19th hole. 'What can I say? The boy's headstrong. Those bodyguards of yours aren't up to much, though. I suggest you get some better ones.'

The fat man looked through the expansive window into the car park where the two hired helps were leaning against a large black BMW nursing their wounds. 'You could be right there Billy boy,' said the man called Tel in a broad Belfast accent. 'Bloody useless, the pair of them, steroid-slurping nonces. God knows how they got this far without getting themselves blown up or weighed down by bricks in the Irish Sea. One of those two UVF rejects has to drive me home tonight. It should be interesting. The one with the knuckleduster has cracked ribs and the other a nasty case of concussion. As for me' – he lifted his foot and rested it across a seat – 'My ankle's the size of a frigging golf ball!'

'In all honesty, you've only got yourself to blame for that, Tel,' said Billy. 'You know the course etiquette. You should be more careful when taking your shot.'

'I'll be honest with you, Billy boy. I've never hit a shot that clean in me bloody life. I was as surprised as yer man when it just missed his head… and I did shout a warning.'

'Who were you playing, anyway? Can't see anyone I recognise in here.'

'Little Gerry Docherty,' said Tel. 'As soon as he registered the look in yer boy's eyes, I didn't see him for dust. Nice to know who yer friends are, eh?'

'Says the devout Orange man who spends a lot of his time drinking with IRA renegades.'

They both laughed. On the other side of the room, Chuck and Sly sat opposite each other, nursing pints of lager.

'LOOK at 'em,' said Chuck. 'Bosom fuckin' buddies. I thought our granddad's motto was you put family first, not consort with the enemy as soon as their back's turned.'

'He has his reasons,' said Sly.

'Really?' The older Dolan boy leant across the table; his features contorted with anger. 'And what were you doing, anyway, making me look a dick when I was just about to teach the bastard a lesson?'

'I had to, Chuck,' said Sly. 'Granddad pleaded with me.'

'I've been fighting your corner ever since we were kids,' said Chuck. 'Where was our lovely granddad while we were growing up? Out here, basking in the sun and living the life of Riley. Then the first chance you get, you take his side against mine. Some bloody…'

'It wasn't like that,' said Sly. 'I was doing you a favour. Apparently that fat fuck, as you kindly called him to his face earlier, was a big noise in one of them protestant paramilitary gangs back in Northern Ireland. Granddad told me he's not one to mess with, and there are a lot of people on his payroll. One word from him and apparently Torrevieja becomes a no-go area to us for the rest of our bloody stay. I don't know about you but I'm quite looking forward to a night out touring the clubs and chatting up the senoritas. We could be here for months.'

'Figures,' said Chuck. 'You stopped me from doing the biz because you want to get your end away. Selfish twat.'

Sly shrugged. 'You'll thank me one day. Anyway, apparently, he's not the only one we have to look out for. The Irish virtually run the town, ex-paramilitaries on both sides. Far from being sworn enemies, it seems they've buried their differences and carved up the place between them. Talk about dedication to the cause… or not. Granddad was saying that recently they've been challenged by the Russians and other eastern European gangs. Fortunately, Granddad gets left alone because he doesn't do any of his business around here, other than own the golf course and the timeshares, which he runs along with the fat man. He supplies the fat man with high-grade cocaine and doesn't step on the toes of the Irish when it comes to the vice industry. Granddad told me most of the Costa Blanca criminal fraternity are members here because they know he's discrete. He turns a blind eye to their wheeler dealing and they keep his club going with their memberships, green fees and the money they spunk behind the bar. It's a win-win for him but a delicate balance and he daren't rock the boat. Let's face it, Chuck, the last thing he needs is you running amok like Godzilla in Tokyo fucking Harbour.'

Sly was the one person able to talk sense into Chuck. 'Fair play I guess,' said the older Dolan, the cooling lager taking effect and lightening his mood. He watched his grandfather return to the bar where a steward was holding out a phone for him. The old man picked it up and spoke for a few seconds, then returned it and walked directly over to their table.

'All right now, Chuck?' he said. 'Calmed that nasty temper of yours?'

'Sorry, Billy. It was just…'

Billy leant forward until his mouth was a few inches from Chuck's ear. 'I know,' he said. 'The thick Mick is a prick and, quite frankly, deserved a beating. Believe me, though, the two idiots you smashed up aren't the most dangerous of the characters on his payroll… not by a long way. I have to live among these people and I don't want any wars. Now, what's done is done. We have more important things to discuss.'

Billy sat down next to Sly and pointed a gadget over Chuck's shoulder. The eldest Dolan boy twisted to see a large TV screen flicker to life. Pressing a few buttons, Billy skipped through the channels until the BBC World News logo materialised in the corner. Filling the screen was a familiar face. 'Don't tell me we're on bloody *Crimewatch* now?' said Sly, feeling uneasy at the prospect of gaining instant notoriety on the popular real-life crime show.

Billy refused to answer though, his expression one of serious concentration as he played with the controls. The well-known BBC newsreader Jennie Bond appeared on the screen, the other face prominent over her shoulder. 'Shut up and listen,' Billy ordered.

The newsreader looked grim. '*Within the last few minutes police have confirmed that the BBC Television presenter Jill Dando has been stabbed to death outside her west London home. She died in the ambulance on her way to hospital. There are no more details at the moment.*'

For seconds, silence engulfed the golf club bar. Then everyone started talking at once.

'That's the bird who presents that crime show, ain't it?' said Chuck.

'That's what I was saying!' said Sly. 'Fuckin' hell! Who done her? Some big wig criminal, no doubt, upset with what she's been saying.'

'Can you shut up and listen, boys?' said Billy. 'I don't know exactly what happened or who did it, but one of my pals back in the smoke tells me she was shot, not stabbed, and that there is a massive manhunt underway for her killer. You know what that means, don't ya?'

Chuck and Sly stared at him blankly. 'Jeez, it's bleedin' obvious isn't it?' he continued. 'With the police having such a high-profile case to solve it means that a little nightclub incident in Hackney is gonna slip well down their list of priorities, comprende?'

This time the brothers nodded slowly, the realisation dawning.

'Good,' said Billy the Kid, 'because for a moment there I was beginning to think you two were even thicker than you look.'

15

SLY'S only previous experience of horses was sitting in front of the television watching the old man scream obscenities at them as they 'stole his money'. It was one of the rare times he'd been able to spend time in his father's company, a brief interlude between prison sentences. Maybe that was why it remained such a treasured memory, particularly as one of Big Mo's many broken promises was that one day he would take his boys to watch the horses 'in the flesh' at Epsom or Kempton Park. It had sounded like a great adventure at the time, but the closest Sly got to realising the dream was riding a donkey on the beach at Great Yarmouth.

When Alisha asked him to help her care for the animals in exchange for a decent daily rate, it sounded fun. Not only would it be an adventure he could tell his mates about when he eventually returned to London, but it gave him a chance to ingratiate himself with the beautiful woman his grandfather had somehow hoodwinked into marriage. The whole scenario came with the added bonus that he could get extra material for his stand-up routine, knowing the relationship between humans and animals provided an endless source of funny stories.

All well and good, but what he hadn't bargained for was a knock on the door at 6a.m., the lady of the house insisting he wash and dress quickly before accompanying her on an early morning hike across fields to the stables. The prospect would have been punishing at the best of times, but to be forced into doing so while nursing a banging hangover from the previous day's golf 'session' made it feel like a medieval act of torture.

Sly took a quick shower, then donned the overalls Alisha had provided and a pair of riding boots loaned to him by Rafael. Not only were they a size too small and pinched his toes, but a quick glimpse in the mirror confirmed his worst suspicions: he looked an absolute tool. What would the boys in the Hope say if they ever got wind of this? Before leaving his room, he looked around tentatively to make sure his brother wasn't lying in wait with a camera to capture his embarrassment.

He found Alisha in the dining room, drinking from a glass of tomato juice and occasionally picking at cold meat and cheese from a platter in front of her. She invited him to dig in, too, but he shook his head, his stomach protesting at the very idea of topping up after the way he had indulged himself the night before. If drinks in the 19th hole hadn't been enough, on his return to the villa they had been invited for a nightcap in Billy's pub.

'Any coffee?' he mumbled.

Alisha turned to the serving hatch separating the dining room from the kitchen. 'Naomi?' The maid appeared at the hatch. 'Young Sylvester here would like a cup of coffee if you would be so kind.'

When she entered the room shortly afterwards, Sly was able to take a proper look at the maid for the first time, having been too tired and dishevelled to pay her much attention on his arrival at Billy's villa. The girl was attractive in an understated way, her plain uniform highlighting a certain natural beauty. She wore minimal eye shadow and mascara, just enough to perfectly accentuate her deep brown eyes, and her skin was vibrant and tanned thanks to limited exposure to the fierce Spanish sun. She glanced at him as she put the mug down, sending a tingle up his spine. Unable to resist, he gave her a subtle wink and she smiled shyly before picking up Alisha's discarded breakfast things and heading for the kitchen door.

'She's a nice girl,' said Alisha, interrupting his thoughts. 'Billy agreed to take her on for a mate of his back in London because she was struggling to find work over there. She's been with us since just before the wedding. Right, let us make tracks shall we, as your grandfather says?'

SLY wasn't sure what to expect and when he reached the stables and saw the Andalusian, he was overcome by the sheer size of the beast. He always thought he was quite tall but felt dwarfed by the animal, its torso standing level with his shoulders. It had a long main of hair running from its majestic head then down its neck and coming to a halt at its dazzling white, gently curving back.

'Meet Caja de Oro, Sylvester,' said Alisha. 'He is the man, the pride of our stable...*El Semental.*'

Sly shook his head, indicating he didn't understand. 'Ahh,' she said. 'Sorry. It means he is a stallion, a proud gentleman of Andalusia. Many, many years ago these special horses were bred in these parts and Caja is very special ... he was a wedding present from your grandfather. The name means gold box, and it was on our honeymoon that

Billy brought me here to show me the villa, the stable and finally, my lovely Caja. I couldn't believe it when he told me this wonderful creature now belonged to me. To be truthful, I cried. Such a wonderful gift.'

You old devil, thought Sly. Billy had gone up in his estimation. He didn't know about his grandfather's relationship with horses, but the ageing lothario certainly knew how to get a woman eating out of his hand.

'How many horses do you have?' he asked.

'In total, four,' she said. 'I ride Caja only on special occasions. Now, come on, I think he wants to make friends, Sylvester.'

Sly felt rooted to the spot.

'What's wrong?'

'Ummm… look, I've never been this close to a horse before. I know nothing about them. Do they sense that? I'm worried he'll bite. He's got a big set of gnashers on him.'

'Gnashers?'

'Sorry, teeth.'

'Ahhhh,' she shook her head. 'Well, he hasn't bitten anyone yet. In fact, for such a powerful animal he is very gentle, aren't you, Caja?' She patted the stallion's nose, and it tilted its head in Sly's direction, as if assessing the stranger. He could see his own reflection in the warm, dark depths of the animal's eyes.

'I think he wants to make friends,' Alisha said. 'Come here.'

Reassured, Sly moved slowly forward and put his hand out, tentatively patting the stallion's nose. It didn't flinch.

'Why don't you talk to him?' said Alisha. 'He likes that. It keeps him calm.'

'What should I say?'

'Anything… anything that is on your mind. As long as you speak softly he will be happy.'

Sly reflected on how he had a knack of making people feel at ease when he first met them, like on the many occasions he'd chatted up girls. What was his technique? The answer was crazy, but it was worth a try.

'There was this horse that walked into a bar,' he said, looking into Caja's eyes. 'The barman asked him, "What would you like to drink?"'

Caja put his head down and shook it slightly, as if he had heard the joke before and wasn't impressed. Tough crowd. Sly held his nerve and carried on. 'The horse said, "I've never been to a bar before. What sort of drinks do you serve?"'

His equine audience seemed more engaged now, Caja raising his head again and showing interest. 'The barman replied, "Well, we have beer, we have wine and we have spirits."'

Now Sly's audience was hanging on every word. '"Spirits sound good," said the horse. "What are spirits?" The barman replied, "There are lots of spirits… you could try gin, or vodka, or even whisky. Come to think of it, we actually have a whisky named after you." The barman pointed to a bottle of White Horse on the shelf. The horse looked confused. "Named after me?" he said. "What, Eric?"'

Suddenly, Caja tossed his head and bared his teeth before making a whinnying sound. Sly stepped back and studied the animal. He could have sworn the stallion was laughing.

Sly bowed to his audience.

'See, he likes you,' said Alisha. 'You have bonded. Would you like to ride him?'

The question caught Sly unawares. He was about to blurt out 'You must be joking' then, recalling his stand-up act for the horse, he began laughing.

'I've never ridden a horse in my life,' he said.

'True,' said Alisha. 'But I bet before today you had never told one a joke either. There's a first time for everything.'

Then she began laughing too.

When she finally managed to suppress her attack of the giggles, she said, 'Honestly, Caja will take great care of you. I'll get another of my horses, Rocco, and show you how to prepare him. We will take a gentle trot around the paddock. Nothing fancy, but it is a chance you would not get in England. No?'

'No,' he agreed.

It was the horse itself that made up his mind for him. As he removed his hand from the animal's nose, Caja de Oro shook his head, then nuzzled against the boy from Barking and gently nudged him.

'Oh,' said Sly, surprised by the horse's demand for attention. 'You like that, do you?'

He started stroking the horse's nose again before moving around and massaging the back of its neck, letting the soft, silky texture of its mane flow through his hands. A warm sensation flowed through him that had nothing to do with the sun slowly rising into the sky and burning off the early morning dew.

He realised he was besotted.

IN THE following weeks the early morning trip to the stables was transformed from a necessary chore into a labour of love. Sly learnt how to prepare food and water for the horses and was even happy to carry out the dirtier jobs, like mucking out the stables and clearing manure from the paddock. In return, he was given a few basic riding lessons by Alisha and soon got the hang of it in the company of the magnificent Andalusian stallion, though he had a sneaking feeling it would take just one wrong command for the animal to summon all its power and charge off with him helpless in the saddle.

It made an unlikely friendship, the boy from the crumbling inner city estate and the animal born to run free on the sun-blessed Costa Blanca, yet Sly trusted the animal more than any human he had ever met, bar Chuck perhaps.

At night he would lie awake wondering why that might be. Perhaps it was because he knew how small and vulnerable he was in the presence of something so wild and powerful. Yet there was an innocent and peaceful air about Caja, and he felt safe in the stallion's company. More than that, he felt wanted and needed. Being responsible for the well-being of another living creature gave him a purpose in life, transforming him from a selfish brat into a useful member of the human race.

16

'IT'S RAMMED in here, Raf!' said Sly, placing a tray of drinks on the table and looking up at the big screen on the wall.

'Si. Everyone comes to Mulligan's when there's a big match on. It's even busier tonight because many Irish support Man U.'

'Should be one hell of a game,' said Chuck. 'I'm a Hammer and it's traditional for us to hate United, but no Englishman with an ounce of self-respect could want the Germans to win. I'd be well happy if Fergie's mob can see off Bayern Munich. What about you, Raf?'

'I am a supporter of Valencia, but I like United, particularly that Ryan Giggs.'

'Yeah, he's exciting to watch,' said Chuck, grabbing one of the beer glasses and putting it to his lips, letting the cold lager slip down his throat. It was hot and stuffy inside the bar, and the noise level was rising.

'I'm glad you made your peace with the Irishman, Chuck, otherwise we would have had to travel 40 miles in the opposite direction to see the game, no? Or even head to Marbella for the night.'

'Wouldn't be so bad,' said Chuck.

'Probably would have missed the first half,' said Sly.

'Anyway, I wouldn't say I made peace exactly,' said Chuck. 'Call it an uneasy truce. At least I shouldn't have to worry about his muscle men tonight. I expect they're still nursing their wounds.'

'Your grandfather says you, how you say, bashed them good. You must be careful. You will gain a reputation.'

'Billy wasn't happy,' admitted Chuck. 'He's right, though. I need to keep my head down and my nose clean. It's hard to believe we've been out here for just over a month and this is the first chance we've had to get into town for a beer. Cheers!'

He lifted his pint in the direction of the other two men before taking a thirst-quenching mouthful. 'Great… that hit the spot.'

'I hear there were some United fans in town last night,' said Sly.

'They were all over the place,' said the Spaniard. 'I think they came early to Spain so they could stay somewhere cheap and enjoy a few drinks and a bit of sun. Some bought tents and camped on the beach, and many didn't have tickets. They were going to buy them on the black market in Las Ramblas before the game.'

'We've missed a trick there, bro,' said Sly. 'We could have bought some tickets and sold them on… we would have made a fortune!'

'Typical of my brother,' said Chuck, addressing his comment to Rafael. 'He's always looking for an angle to fleece the hard-working public.'

'Why not?' said Sly. 'Most rich fuckers would do the same to us. I don't hear any bankers bleating about the poor people of Barking, and they carry out daylight robbery.'

ENGLISH optimism had been shaken within six minutes when Bayern went ahead. After that, the standard of the game fell well below expectations. With time ticking by in the second half, Sly had wandered off to find other sources of amusement.

'Your brother doesn't seem that keen on football,' said Rafael.

'He has a short attention span,' said Chuck. 'To be fair, this is as dull as ditchwater. So what about you, Rafa? Where do you live when you're not here?'

'Down south near your grandfather's place in Marbella,' said Billy the Kid's right-hand man. 'A place called Estepona. Unfortunately, when we are here, I don't get to see my wife and kids so much, apart from weekends. I have two boys and a girl. Your grandfather does give me long breaks though and I always make sure he is in, how you say, the safe hands. Some of the English homes in the area have been broken into and the elderly owners threatened and robbed. That won't happen at the villa. The guys guarding it are either ex-servicemen or people I brought in who used to work for the Spanish police. Anyway, what about your family? You must be missing them.'

'Not a great deal, to be truthful. I sent them a postcard, "Glad you're not here". And I don't miss Barking one little bit.'

'How many of you are there?'

'There's Mum, Sly, two other brothers – Arnie and Bruce – and a sister, Anjelica. It's a big house but, still, you can feel suffocated at times.'

'You boys sound like stars from action movies: Sly Stalone, Arnie Schwarzeneger, Bruce Willis…?'

'…And Chuck Norris.'

'Sorry?'

'Bloody hell, why was I named after the only one people don't know?' said Chuck. 'Norris was the first real action hero and my dad named me after him. He's an American Martial Arts expert who appeared in the Bruce Lee films. When Sly came along, Dad decided to stick with the theme. Where is Sly, anyway? It's ages since he went for those soddin' beers...'

'He is, as you English say, distracted?'

Chuck focussed on the section of the bar where Rafael was pointing and saw Sly in animated conversation with two women. Their clothing left little to the imagination. The brunette's hair tumbled in waves down her back to just above her bottom, the hem of her white skirt stretching just a bit further until it gave way to two shapely legs balanced on high-heeled white sandals. The other girl, a blonde, was small and thick set, wearing a fake leather mini dress that barely covered her over-large breasts. Even from where Chuck was sitting, he was pretty sure she wasn't wearing a bra. Her suede boots extended up to her thighs.

He watched for a while as the two girls laughed politely at whatever line Sly was spinning them. His stand-up act worked around 50 per cent of the time, and on this occasion he seemed to have won over his audience. Then again, they might be humouring him. There was no chance of Sly quitting now, though. Having sniffed an opening, he would be like a dog with a bone... a hard bone if Chuck knew his brother.

'I'll get the beers,' said Chuck. 'Otherwise we'll be waiting until next year's Champions League final.'

'SO what brings you beautiful ladies to a dive like this?'

asked Sly, touching one of the girls on the arm and looking them both in the eye in turn.

'You ask that of all the girls?' said the one with the large breasts, her eyes twinkling as she teasingly popped the strawberry in her mouth from the cocktail he'd bought them. He detected a slight eastern European accent, maybe Polish or Czech.

'I wouldn't say that, no,' said Sly. 'Then again I don't meet gorgeous ladies like you every day.'

'Oh please, it's too much,' said the blonde, her face blushing scarlet. 'This is nice drink, the ménage a trois. You try?'

She held her glass out towards him, but he waved it away. 'Cocktails aren't my thing really,' he said. 'It ain't good to mix your drinks.'

'Oh, come on, darlink, where's your sense of adventure?' the dark-haired girl said, her long eyelashes flashing in his direction. She had introduced herself as Rula and he was so captivated by her stunning looks he found it hard to concentrate. 'I bet you've never had a ménage a trois.'

Sly was pretty sure she wasn't talking about the drink. 'Hmm, can't say I have,' he replied, deciding to play along. God, these girls were desirable, and he hadn't had sex for more than a month. Were they really offering him a threesome? He heard some of these eastern European girls were pretty game, and where was the harm in pushing things as far as he could? Bloody hell, just thinking about getting these two between the sheets was making him horny. A threesome? That would be something to tell the boys about back at the Hope.

'Another drink, Sylvester,' said the blonde one. 'We get you in the mood for partying, no? We like the English very much. They have lots of stamina, particularly if they have a little sniff first. Think you can satisfy both of us, Mr Sly man?' From her handbag she pulled out a vial and waved it in his face. Well, it was a night out and he was hardly going to look a gift horse in the mouth.

EVERYONE was on their feet, cheering, shouting and urging on the men in red. The match had gone into injury time and one of Manchester United's substitutes, Teddy Sheringham, had just made it 1-1. Chuck and Rafael had joined the group around the TV, adding their voices to the hubbub. Chuck leant into the Spaniard to make himself heard.

'It looks like we're in for a bit more drinking,' he said. 'It will be extra time now. Those Germans look dazed, and I really think United can win it. I hope it doesn't go to spot kicks, though. We English never beat the krauts at penalties.'

'Look, United have won a corner,' said Rafael. They focussed intently on the screen, wishing for something incredible to happen.

'Beckham's going to take it,' said Chuck. 'He's from round our way you know, a place called Leytonstone in east London which isn't far from where I live. I guess that means one of our own could win the Champions League.' He chuckled nervously.

The English commentator built up the tension. '*Is this their moment*?' he said. '*Beckham, into Sheringham…*' There was a groan from the pub crowd as the player who had done so well to score the equaliser appeared to miss-kick with the goal at his mercy, only for the ball to run on to another figure in red, loitering at the far post. '…*AND SOLSKJAER*

HAS WON IT!' screamed the commentator as the Norwegian striker, another United substitute, deflected the ball into the roof of the net. For a moment, people were frozen to the spot, not sure what they had witnessed. Then alcohol was flying everywhere as the pundits of Mulligan's Bar in downtown Torrevieja went crazy.

'*Manchester United have reached the promised land*,' said the commentator as Chuck began looking around, anxious to share the moment with his brother.

'Raf, have you seen Sly lately?' he shouted. The Spaniard looked in the direction of the bar, but it was difficult to see anything with all the crazy celebrations going on. He shook his head. 'Do you mind if we look for him?' said Chuck. 'We both have things to do tomorrow. I want to head back at a decent time.'

They split up and pushed their way through the crowd in different directions, meeting back at the same spot 15 minutes later. 'I've looked everywhere,' said Rafael. 'Your brother must have disappeared with las mujeres.'

'Who?'

'Those women. Prostitutes I suspect.'

'Fuck,' said Chuck. 'What a dipstick! This is so typical of my brother, Rafael. He gets into these scrapes and nine times out of ten they don't work out well for him. We have a saying in Britain – "if he fell into a barrel of tits he would come out sucking his thumb". And that's when he's at home, somewhere familiar. In this case, he doesn't even know the place or the people he's with. He's had a fair bit to drink, too.'

Rafael nodded. 'I think maybe we should look for him outside. I wouldn't trust these people. They aren't always what they seem.'

They began heading for the door when a familiar figure materialised, blocking their path. Chuck sensed there was trouble ahead. 'How are your ribs?' he asked the bodyguard he had last seen on his grandfather's golf course.

'On the mend, no thanks to yous,' the man growled.

'If you want them to heal properly, I suggest you move or you'll be back to square one,' said Chuck.

'And if yous wants to see your kid brother again I suggest you come with me,' said the man with the strong Ulster brogue. Suddenly Chuck didn't feel so sure of himself. Had these Irish bastards got hold of Sly as an act of revenge? He would have been such an easy target in his inebriated state.

'Come on,' said the Ulsterman. 'The boss wants to speak to you.'

'SO, let's get this straight, fella,' said the Irish gang boss as he sat behind his desk in the small office at the back of the pub. 'One minute you want to launch my head onto the ninth green, the next you're asking me to help find yer wee brother. Interesting.'

'Look, it was that useless lump of a bodyguard of yours who said you wanted to see me. If you have Sly I'll… '

Rafael jumped in front of the angry young man in an effort to diffuse the escalating tension. 'Please, Senor Tel, Billy would be extremely grateful if you could help find his grandson,' said the Spaniard. 'Chuck here is obviously very upset. He means no disrespect.'

'Let the fucker speak for hisself,' said the Ulsterman, rotating his swivel chair in Chuck's direction. The eldest Dolan brother felt the strength of the fat man's steely glare boring into him. 'A wee hot head, Mr Dolan, is what ye are,' he said. 'The likes of you are ten-a-penny in these parts. Carry on the way you are doing, and you won't live long. It's a dangerous place.'

Chuck looked at Rafael, interpreting the message in the Spaniard's eyes and opting for a strategic withdrawal. 'Sorry, I was out of order,' he conceded. 'On the golf course, and just now.'

'You were indeed,' said the Ulsterman, extracting obvious pleasure from making Chuck squirm. 'Now, I've had my poker game interrupted when I was on a bit of a roll, and once again it involves you Dolan boys. Well, listen up. If I help you get your brother back, I expect a favour off ye in return. You're a big strong lad with a hell of a punch. Your wrecking ball antics have, in effect, left my staff numbers depleted. I should thank ye really for showing me those boys were next to useless, but by doing what you did you've left a big hole in my operation that needs filling.'

'Sure,' said Chuck. 'But my grandfather…'

'Let me worry about Billy Boy,' said Senor Tel. 'Now, I'm guessing the last time you saw Sylvester was in the bar. One of my men spotted something interesting on our CCTV. Shall we take a look?'

17

SYLVESTER DOLAN was entering the Promised Land. He had a girl tucked under each arm and wasn't quite sure if he was leading the way or they were carrying him. The Spanish beer had given him a buzz, but that had been turned up a notch when the blonde one, Mihaela, had persuaded him to inhale from a small glass vial. After a quick trip to a cashpoint where the girls insisted he request the maximum amount of Euros permitted, they had then led him to the hotel where he'd booked a room in which the three of them could 'party' the night away.

Mihaela was nibbling on his left ear now while Rula whispered such naughty innuendos in the other he feared he might peak before they reached the room. 'We make a nice sandwich for you, Sylvester,' she was saying. 'We will be the bread and you will be filling us.' Her hand drifted down, long red nails gently scraping the length of the bulge in his khaki shorts. 'I love – what do you English call it? – the big banger, no?'

When they entered the corridor at the top of the stairs, the trio could barely squeeze into the cramped space side by side, their coordination badly affected by alcohol consumption. Bouncing off the walls, they finally managed to reach a door marked with the number 6 at which stage the blonde pulled away, fitting a heavy brass key into the lock and turning it. When the door opened, she dragged Sly into the room then flopped on the king-sized bed and tugged him towards her by his belt loops. Behind them, Rula closed the door.

He watched with fascination as Mihaela unzipped his fly. In the garish light of the white-walled room, he was able to fully focus on her for the first time, or at least the hand which was working its way inside his pants. It was large for a woman's hand with knuckles red raw, as if she spent the days working a labour-intensive job. He noted her skin was wrinkled and flaky and realised the impression he had formed against the backdrop of a dimly lit bar was slightly wide of the mark. This was not a blemish-free, youthful girl, but a fully grown woman with a suitcase full of life experiences.

Oh well, beggars couldn't be choosers. Falling backwards against the shabby purple quilt cover, he tried to focus on something mundane, just for a few seconds, to keep his rising libido in check. The crumbling plaster on the ceiling had seen better days, a circular pattern swirling around a ceiling rose from which one exposed light bulb hung limply. He tried to avert his eyes from the glare, finding it difficult to focus and beginning to feel nauseous. Surely he wasn't going to ruin what promised to be the most exhilarating sexual experience of his life by throwing up?

Before he could reflect further on his condition, Rula loomed above him, her long eyelashes so close to his face he could see gloops of black mascara clogged in them. Her face was chalky from too much foundation, the skin pock-marked, as if she had suffered from a complaint as a child and had been left with a permanent reminder. She kissed him so hard on the lips their teeth collided, then pulled away abruptly, the weight of her body dropping down on the bed somewhere out of sight above him. Before he had time to draw breath, two muscular thighs clamped down hard either side of his head, making his nausea levels rise.

This wasn't how he'd envisaged things. In his mind's eye he had seen himself as the leading character in an X-rated porn classic, the dominant male feasting on the delights of two vulnerable and compliant young female victims. In reality, they had immobilised him like professional wrestlers pinning a rival to the canvas. A hand at his groin gripped and pulled hard, forcing him to let out a yelp and exclaim, 'Hey… careful!'

The body on top of him pushed down even harder now, and he found it difficult to breathe. He tried to wriggle into a position where he could suck in more oxygen, but the girl had the lower body strength of a gymnast, the muscles so taut he imagined this was how a car accident victim felt when they were fitted with one of those braces which immobilised the head.

'Mmmmm, mmm…' His protests came out muffled and incoherent. It crossed his mind to fight off the two crazy bitches, but he felt extraordinarily weak in the face of this surprise onslaught, and didn't think his limbs would oblige.

'Right, English bastard, do we have your attention?'

What the fuck?

A man's voice.

Could one of his lovers be a transvestite?

Just as he thought he was going to black out, the pressure on his head eased slightly, the girl on top shifting and rising from the bed. He breathed in greedily and almost gagged.

'Girls, you go now,' said the male voice. 'We talk business with this man.'

On the blurry edges of his vision, Sly saw Rula pick up her handbag and walk around to where her friend was waiting, chewing gum impassively. 'Ciao Sylvester,' the blonde girl said. 'It was good to meet you, but sadly our night of fun is over.'

As the door slammed shut behind the girls, Sly saw two out-of-focus figures in front of him… and one looked suspiciously like they were holding a gun.

'THIS here's Sammy, my top boy,' said Senor Tel as a giant of a man bowed his head to enter the small office. Chuck noted the livid 8-inch scar running from above his right eye to below his square jaw. The eye continually watered, a sign he had suffered damage to the tear duct which had never properly healed. Chuck wondered how this colossus of a man had obtained the disfigurement but decided it wasn't the time to ask. 'These boys need your help, Sammy,' said Senor Tel. 'They've a wee emergency.'

Sammy remained silent as he walked across the room and inserted a tape into a video recorder on the small table resting against the side wall. The mean and moody type, thought Chuck, but he had little doubt the bloke could handle himself. The big man handed the remote control to Senor Tel, who pressed a button. A mono picture appeared on the screen with a clock in the top, right-hand corner. As the video rewound and sped up, the clock ticked backwards. 'There he is!' shouted Rafael. 'He is with the two, um…'

'Tarts,' said Tel. 'Yes, I see.' He pressed pause then allowed the film to roll forward at its normal speed. Sly was to the right of the screen, leaning in to one of the girls, whispering something, when the other one wrapped her arm around his neck and moved her hand towards his nose. Suddenly, Sly's head jerked back and he span around. The girl was laughing, showing him a small glass test tube she was holding in her hand.

'Looks like yer man's been on the poppers,' said Tel. Chuck raised an eyebrow. 'Have yous never come across poppers? How old are ye, son? Have yous not been to a rave or two back home? It's a drug, Amyl Nitrate. Supposed to give you a bit of a lift in the lower regions, if you get my meaning. These girls were keen to put yer boy Sylvester in a frisky mood.'

Wouldn't take much, thought Chuck as he watched the girls gather around his brother, lapping up every word. Now and again he would lean across the bar and order more drinks, his two friends seemingly intent on sampling everything from the cocktail menu. As the three toasted each other, a loud cheer went up in the background.

'That was the equaliser,' said Chuck. 'He couldn't have left that long ago.'

'I don't know, Chuck my friend,' said Rafael. 'The match finished nearly an hour ago.'

'Look!' Tel interrupted their discussion. They turned to see Sly drink the rest of his pint and head for the exit, his arm linked with the dark-haired woman. For a moment, her blonde accomplice was nowhere to be seen.

'Where's the other one?' asked Chuck.

'This is what my man Sammy noticed.' Tel pointed out the blonde standing in the corner of the shot outside the women's toilets. She was in animated conversation with a man in jeans and a yellow football shirt.

'Fecker.'

A hush fell on the room, the others shocked into silence by the big Ulsterman in the corner simply because it was the first word Sammy had uttered since his arrival. 'One of the lads who was at the golf club with me recognised your brother and pointed him out to Sammy,' said Senor Tel. 'They watched him talking to those girls and when Sammy later saw the blonde bint meet with that man things piqued his interest, isn't that right, Sammy?'

'Wee scrote arrived in town a couple of months back,' muttered Sammy in a gruff, low voice. 'Romanian. He and his pal are out to make a name for themselves. Mean bastards. No scruples. They've been running these girls, sending them into town to lure gullible tourists. The punter is offered a good time and the girls persuade him to take out money then lead him to a hotel. Before he gets his kicks, these feckers storm in and rob the sucker. They play hardball: knives, shooters… rumour is that the dead man they pulled out of the drink the other day was one of their victims.'

'Is there a particular hotel they use, Sammy?' asked Chuck, struggling to suppress a feeling of rising panic.

'Aye,' said the big man. 'A rat-hole tailor-made to attract vermin like that. You want to go there?'

'You bet.'

'Wait here.'

The big man left the room without another word.

'Where's he going?' Chuck asked the Irish gang boss.

'Not far,' said Senor Tel. 'The thing you'll learn about Sammy is he never goes anywhere without his "tool kit".'

18

THE MAN in the brown, faded leather jacket stood with his back to the door, a pistol in his hand. He kept it trained on a spot between Sly's eyes while the character in the yellow football top attached plastic ties to his wrists. 'Wh … what do you want?' he stuttered, feeling self-conscious about the fact his trousers and pants had been removed and his private parts were on view for all to see.

'We want all of your money,' said the man with the eastern European accent. 'Cash, credit cards, anything of value. You write down pin numbers, yes? Taking advantage of the ladies comes at a price. What he got, Marius?'

'Hey, I saw you in the bar!' said Sly to Marius. He tried to think of something to say that would get the younger man to look on him as a person rather than a prisoner. 'Who were you supporting?'

He was rewarded for his inquiry with a fist to the face. Blood trickled from his nose and a numbing pain told him it was probably broken.

'No talk,' said the man with the gun. 'We're not your friends. I would happily kill you here and now.'

The man in the football top waved a long-bladed knife in the air.

'N… no, please.'

Smash.

With his hands tied, Sly turned his head but was powerless to stop the second punch colliding with the side of his ear. The ringing sound echoed around his skull and for the first time he realised he was in serious trouble. These guys weren't interested in small talk.

'My wallet is in my shorts,' he said. 'Take it. There are 200 Euros in there. Take it all.'

Smash.

The punch connected with his throat this time and left him struggling for breath. He rolled over and puked on the bed clothes.

'We look stupid?' asked the gunman, who seemed to be in charge. 'We tell by clothes alone you are worth more than 200 Euros, English shit.' He leant forward and picked up the designer shorts, rifling through the pockets and coming out with Sly's wallet. It was a cheap black plastic job he had picked up from the ferry shop on the trip over. Keeping the gun trained on Sly, the man let the object dangle from his hand so that the compartments fell open.

'Right, Mr umm Syl…ves…teer Doolan,' he said. 'You have many credit cards: Mastercard, Barclaycard, Visa… if we took you to the bank I think you could raise much more than 200, yes?'

The man in the football shirt pulled Sly back up into a sitting position. He tasted sick in his mouth and needed a pee desperately, though he was sure his body's reaction was a consequence of his predicament. The gunman threw the shorts in his direction.

'Put them on,' he said. 'We go for walk.'

'Look, those cards, most of them are just for show, there is nothing…'

Smash!

This time he was sent reeling by an open hand to the side of the face.

'Help him,' said the gunman.

'What? You want me to put his trousers on, Luca... Merde! That is disgusting. You do it.'

'I can't,' said the man by the door. 'I have the gun.' He waved it around in front of him.

Bloody hell, thought Sly. It was like being a reluctant witness to a lover's tiff. Perhaps these bastards weren't quite as united and professional as they wanted him to believe.

'I always do dirty work,' moaned Marius before breaking into what Sly could only imagine was a string of expletives in his native language.

Tap... tap... tap.

The men stopped what they were doing and froze. 'You expecting someone?' the man with the gun whispered to their prisoner. Sly shook his head.

'What if it is hotel manager?' said Marius. 'Maybe this bastard...'

'Luca, it's me.' Sly recognised the voice as belonging to the girl called Rula.

'What you want?' demanded the gunman. 'We told you "Go". You should be in clubs, finding more punters.'

'Very sorry,' said Rula. 'I lose my keys. Perhaps they fell out of my bag when it was under the bed? I don't want to leave any, ummm, evidence.'

The gunman flicked his head in Marius' direction. The man in the football top tutted loudly, then dropped to his hands and knees, searching underneath the bed. He emerged moments later, shaking his head. 'I see nothing,' he said. 'It's bloody filthy man.'

Luca tossed his head grumpily. 'Fuck, this is not good, girl,' he said, turning in the direction of the door. 'We're busy. You will have to come and look for yourself but be quick.'

He turned the key in the lock… and all hell broke loose.

The door crashed in, slamming the gunman against the wall. Seeing his opportunity, Sly lifted his bound feet and lashed out, smashing Marius in the nose and sending him flying backwards, blood spurting from the wound. A nose for a nose, he thought with satisfaction. First through the door came a lumbering giant Sly had never seen before. He grabbed Luca's gun hand and squeezed so tightly there was a loud snap before the weapon fell with a dull clunk to the carpet. The gunman screamed.

Chuck was next in, scooping up the jettisoned pistol. 'Don't anyone fuckin' move,' he shouted, holding the gun sideways like a gangster in a movie. Sly knew his older brother had never fired a pistol in his life, but wasn't going to let his captors in on the secret.

'You OK, Sly?' he asked.

The younger Dolan boy nodded. 'Bit tied up at the moment, Chuck,' he said. 'Can you call back later?'

'You'll be the death of me you fuckin' idiot,' said Chuck. 'I promised Billy I'd stay out of trouble and look how that's turned out.'

'Sorry.' Sly realised his brother's mood left no room for banter. He often thought Chuck had undergone a sense-of-humour bypass at birth.

'We've got to get out of here, now!' Chuck moved across the room to where the knife lay, bent down and picked it up. The kidnapper in the football top sat against the wall, nursing his broken nose. Swiftly, Chuck sliced through

Sly's bindings. 'Put your bloody clothes on, you embarrassment. How often have I told you that worm dangling between your legs will get you into trouble?'

Looking towards the open door, Sly saw Rafael holding the dark-haired prostitute by the throat while pinning the blonde to the wall with his other arm. She looked far less cocky now. Suddenly Sly was overcome with rage. 'Go ahead and strangle the bitch,' he told Rafael. 'I won't stop you.' Marching over to the blonde, he took over, raising her up with one hand so that she was hanging like a hunting trophy on the corridor wall. 'Was this the sort of big bang you had in mind?' he asked, pulling back his fist. Vivid purple blotches began appearing on her face, her lungs being starved of oxygen.

'Leave it, Sly!' said Chuck. 'We don't hit women and the way you're acting you'll bloody kill her. The last thing we need is another murder charge hanging over us. We'll run out of places to hide.'

The younger Dolan stared into the girl's frightened eyes and let go. She dropped to the ground like a ship's anchor, but the heavy fall didn't knock any of the bravado out of her.

'English bastard!' she muttered. 'I bloody kill you next time; Bite your little cock off.'

He thought about launching into her again, but at the last moment dropped his fist to his side, turned around, and marched swiftly down the corridor towards the stairs and the exit.

'SHALL we follow him?' Rafael let go of Rula so that she could tend to her injured friend.

'I guess so,' said Chuck. 'Job done I think.'

'Wrong,' said Sammy, marching the Romanian called Luca to the doorway. The man's arm was being held up behind his back at an unnatural angle and looked like it might be broken. His grey pallor told a story of fear and unfathomable pain. 'Don't you dispose of your rubbish in England?' said the giant Ulsterman.

Chuck still had the gun trained on Marius. Without his knife, the boy in the Romanian football shirt looked like just a normal frightened teenager, one that presented no danger to four grown men. 'Let's tie them up and leave them,' he said. 'We can call the police anonymously and leave them to deal with it.'

'No.' The Ulsterman held up Sly's wallet and threw it onto the bed. 'Yer man Sylvester's wallet,' he said. 'They know who he is and, because he called you by your name, they will soon know who you are, too. If we leave them, they will just return to seek revenge on you. I know this type. They need a lesson they can't forget.'

'What do you suggest?' asked Chuck.

Ignoring the question, Sammy handed Luca to Rafael. 'Take them outside and wait for me,' he said.

19

'WHAT is this place?' Chuck asked Rafael as they sat in the back of the Land Cruiser. Behind the wheel, Sammy had returned to his natural state, silent and brooding. The roads were empty apart from the occasional delivery lorry on its way to restock the supermarket shelves of Torrevieja. In the distance, Chuck saw a large expanse of water spreading out in front of them. 'Is that the sea?'

'It is the pink lake,' said Rafael, who was sitting directly behind the driver.

'Eh?'

'Very famous,' said the Spaniard. 'We have many salt lakes in these parts. For two centuries the city has profited from this natural resource but this one is different.'

'Because of its colour?'

'Exactly,' said Rafael. 'It is the big attraction for the tourists. You can't bathe in the lake but you can take a tour around it and there is much wildlife, so it is popular with children. You know flamingos? There are maybe 2,000 here.'

The Land Cruiser stopped and Sammy got out. Removing a set of keys from his pocket, he unlocked a gate.

'Why is the lake pink?' asked Chuck.

'It's no big secret,' said Rafael. 'In the lake is a unique plant that is coloured like this. Many shrimp feed on this and the flamingos feed on the shrimp, which is why they are such a beautiful colour. The lake is said to have healing qualities, which is why many of your old people settle here … they believe living close to the salt lakes is good for their health.'

Sammy climbed back behind the wheel, put the land cruiser in gear and drove through the gates.

'So why are we here?' whispered Chuck. 'It's a bit dark for sightseeing.'

Rafael shrugged. 'The natural parks extend for maybe 25 kilometres. There are not just lakes but reed banks, marshes and the famous salt mountains. A good place to conduct business if you want to keep it a secret or hide…'

He left the sentence unfinished. Looking through the windscreen in front, Chuck saw a pair of large white pyramid-shaped hills rise up on either side of them, dwarfing the vehicle.

'How's he doing?' asked Chuck, leaning forward and addressing the driver.

Sammy looked down at Sly, who was draped across the passenger seat, his head to one side, a low rumble emitting from him every time he breathed. 'Sleeping it off,' said the Ulsterman.

Chuck settled back in his seat, letting his eyes close and his mind drift. It had been a fraught night, and the adrenaline was slowly ebbing from his body. He was about to follow his brother's example and doze off when the car pulled up abruptly.

Rafael nudged him. 'We are here.'

Sammy slid back the side door and Chuck climbed out, Rafael exiting from the other side and coming around to meet them. Without saying a word, Sammy went to the back of the vehicle and opened the boot. Chuck peered into the cramped space. Two sets of eyes blinked out at him, fear radiating from them in waves.

'IS he gonna dump them in the lake?' whispered Chuck.

Rafael shrugged.

In front of them, the two prisoners, hands tied behind their backs, stumbled along the rutted pathway. 'If he was that worried about things coming back on us, why did he let the girls go?' asked Chuck.

'He gave them, how you say, the ultimatum,' Rafael replied. 'They now must work for Senor Tel. They have been sworn to secrecy over what happened, and I don't expect them to go against Sammy's wishes, do you? The Irish have the local policia in their pocket in these parts. Everyone knows this. Cops don't get paid a lot out here, so the extra money is welcome. Anyway, what would these women tell them? "We are prostitutas who were robbing an English tourist when his friends turned up and kidnapped our pimps?" I think this unlikely. I doubt the girls even know the names of the people they were working for… These Romanians came to this country illegally. Reporting things like this is not the way it works in this part of the world. You English have a phrase. "You are living by the sword…"?'

Chuck corrected him. 'You live by the sword, you die by the sword. You don't think…?' He shuddered, even though it was a relatively warm night.

Sammy looked over his shoulder, his eyes steely and unreadable. Even though it was dark, the scar on his face was clearly visible. A large shovel dangled from his right hand. Chuck could only imagine it being used for one thing in the circumstances: Digging a grave. The two young men in front must have been petrified. Chuck felt pretty uneasy himself.

Sammy led them around the lake on a pathway constructed from wooden planks. They had to proceed in single file, so Chuck took responsibility for the kid in the football top while the one named Luca followed behind with Rafael bringing up the rear. Looking at the prisoner under his command, Chuck wondered what sort of upbringing Marius had endured, remembering his own early years in Barking. To be fair, Chuck had never felt deprived of anything and imagined that for this kid to travel so far from home things must have been a lot worse. Despite the way the boy had treated Sly, he felt a twinge of sympathy. Obviously, Marius had been abandoned to fight for his own survival.

'Here,' ordered Sammy, stopping in the shadow of one of the salt pyramids. Chuck gave the kid a reassuring look as he left him in the place the Ulsterman indicated. Rafael placed Luca beside him. With their backs to the lake and the salt mountain looming in front of them, the prisoners appeared trapped. Sammy slowly reached inside his pocket.

Suddenly, for their older captive, the tension proved too much. Luca turned quickly and ran into the lake. It was an ill-conceived escape plan with zero chance of success, chiefly because the deeper he went into the water, the slower he moved. A loud crack ruptured the air and the

Romanian gangster lurched forward, his hand gripping the back of his knee.

'Eejit!' said Sammy, lowering the pistol. 'Bring him back.'

Chuck didn't particularly feel like a late-night dip and was relieved when Rafael put his arm on his wrist and whispered, 'I'll go.' Kicking off his shoes, he waded out into the water to where the injured young man was thrashing about, a dark slick forming on the lake's surface. Rafael grabbed hold of his jacket collar and hauled him to his feet.

'Aaaargh!' The scream pierced the night air, and in the distance Chuck saw a cluster of dark shapes rise into the sky. Birds or bats?

Unfazed, Rafael emerged from the lake and dropped the prisoner on the bank. His knee was a bloody mess, and small squeaks of pain had replaced the screams of agony.

'Stand yer man up next to his pal there,' said Sammy.

'But he can't...' One look at the Ulsterman persuaded Rafael to bite down his protest. He turned to Chuck for assistance and between them they raised Luca and put him where Sammy had indicated. He wobbled in place on his one good leg, the other hanging uselessly in the air. Sammy walked forward until he towered over his victim, then lifted the man's chin so that their foreheads were almost touching. The scene reminded Chuck of an adult preparing to lecture a small child. A new smell filled the air: Human excrement.

'Do ye know what we do with prisoners who make a run for it in Belfast?' asked Sammy. The Romanian's confused expression indicated he didn't understand the question. His lips shook violently, and he tried to respond but no words came out. Sammy put the pistol to the side of the man's head and pulled the trigger. Chuck and Rafael put their hands to their mouths in unison as the body slumped to the ground, blood and brain tissue forming a random pattern across the foot of the salt mountain.

'Fuck!' The phrase escaped Chuck's lips involuntarily. He was unable to look away from the dead body. The lips weren't moving but the piercing scream still echoed in his ears. Then he realised the noise wasn't coming from the dead man but the teenager in the football shirt.

'Don't fret yourself, I haven't forgotten you, boy,' said Sammy.

Chuck began to move, feeling obliged to intervene on behalf of the kid, but a hand shot out and held him in place. 'It is Sammy's show,' hissed Rafael. 'We cannot interfere.'

'How do ye fancy a six pack?' Sammy asked the remaining prisoner. The boy blubbered incoherently and shook his head, clearly not understanding what was being asked. Some of the dead man's blood and brain tissue was stuck to his face. 'Oh, I think ye would. Most young fellas would kill for one.' The boy's eyes fell automatically to his dead friend and his sobs gathered pace. 'I'll make it quick,' said Sammy and, without warning, smashed the gun into the side of the teenager's skull. The boy dropped to his knees and Sammy followed him down, turning him onto his back and straddling his torso. Then he grabbed his prisoner's left arm and fired a bullet straight into his elbow from point-blank range.

Bang.

The shot reverberated across the barren land, the body twitching and writhing in pain, the boy's mouth open in a hoarse scream ear-shattering in its intensity.

Bang.

This time a bullet tore through the right elbow, the boy's shrieks dying as his larynx failed to sustain its agonising protests and he began to lose consciousness. Chuck had seen some brutal things in his time having grown up as the son of Big Mo Dolan, but he couldn't remember meeting anyone as callous, unfeeling and inhumane as this ex-paramilitary killing machine.

There was a moment of respite as Sammy pulled out a box of bullets from his pocket and loaded the pistol again, enough time for Chuck to look away and pray to a God with whom he had never engaged in his life. The appeal went unanswered. Instead, Sammy said, 'Make ye'self useful, you two. Grab that spade and dig the wee dead bastard over there a grave in the salt, would yous?'

It was an order delivered as casually as if they were being asked to drive to the store and buy him a packet of cigarettes. Chuck was trapped within a tangle of emotions. On the one hand, he wanted to run, to hide, to leave this hateful place behind and never return. On the other, he felt an impulse to charge forward, rip the gun from Sammy's hand and put a bullet through the sadist's brain. When Rafael moved though, he did too, and between them they grabbed Luca's body and hauled it to the bottom of the salt pyramid.

As Rafael set about work with the shovel, Chuck kept his eyes on the Spaniard, flinching as the shots continued to ring out at intervals behind them.

Bang.

Bang.

Bang.

Bang.

20

FOR A moment he couldn't see her. Then Chuck caught a glimpse of the distinctive blonde locks swaying into view from behind an excessively overweight tourist who was loaded up with luggage and cajoling his skinny wife and entourage of kids towards the exit.

When the holidaymakers moved away and his eyes locked on hers, his heart sped up and it was as if some unseen force had turned up the temperature, his cheeks suddenly hot and clammy. He tried to move forward but his feet felt melted to the floor and all he could manage was an inane wave. His insides were a mess of emotions – happiness, comfort, love, desire – and he felt more nervous than he ever did before a fight.

She was wearing a baby pink vest top, gentle blue hot pants and a pair of flowery flip-flops and was tugging a bulky case behind her. There was another heavy-looking bag flung over one delicate shoulder. Despite having only just arrived at Alicante Airport, her legs were tanned, while her face seemed fresh and natural despite the fact she had been on the go for hours. If Chuck knew Abby as well as he thought he did, she would have topped up her make-up before landing.

'Hey, you,' she shouted cheerily from 100 metres away. 'Are you going to help me with these bags or just stand there with your tongue hanging out?'

Rumbled, he didn't know how to respond. 'Oh, uh, sure, I wasn't…'

'I'm teasing, silly,' she said. 'I've managed this far. I always over pack and this time I had to bring the winter stuff, too, just in case. Sometimes it barely reaches 70 degrees over the Christmas period.'

She laughed, the dimples forming on either side of her mouth as the smile consumed her face. Then he was out of the blocks and sprinting across the short gap between them, wrapping himself around her like a faithful dog who'd been parted from its owner for too long.

The flowery scent of her hair was as familiar to him as a favourite pair of jeans. He kissed her neck and squeezed her until she gasped. She responded willingly, her long painted nails digging into his tense shoulders to send shock waves of tingling anticipation racing down his back. Their lips crashed together and the sweetness of her kiss was intravenous, the drug intoxicating, making him light-headed. Just as quickly, she pulled away.

'Damn!' she said.

'What is it?' For a moment he thought her actions a form of rejection.

'I had my sunglasses in my pocket.' She pulled out a pair of crumpled spectacles, one dark lens falling out of the frame and into her hand. 'They're Gucci, cost me a fortune! Now look at them.'

'Fuck 'em,' he groaned, still on a high from the adrenaline. 'I'll buy you another pair. Two! I'm earning good money now.'

'In that case…' She walked over to a rubbish bin and discarded them before loping back in his direction, her long, shapely legs a magnet for his eyes. This time the kiss went on uninterrupted for a good 20 seconds before they emerged from the clinch, breathless and beaming.

'Come on,' she said. 'I don't think the police in these parts are too keen on outward displays of affection. If we go any further, we'll end up in a cell. Where's the car?'

'GRANDDAD'S always been a bit mad when it comes to Christmas,' explained Chuck as he drove the red Ferrari 360 through the gates of the villa.

'Yes, I can see that,' said Abby.

On each side of the driveway there were life-sized model reindeer, inflatable Santas, snowmen and other paraphernalia associated with the festive season. The decorations were rigged up with fairy lights in every shade imaginable, the characters illuminating when the sun went down.

'I think it was his second wife Viola, my grandmother, who started it,' said Chuck. 'She thought it would be nice for us kids. I always loved going around their house in Chigwell at this time of year. You could see it from miles away. God knows how much it cost them in electricity… I'm surprised they didn't short circuit the entire East End.'

'Who are those guys?' She pointed to a couple of heavy-set men in suits patrolling the grounds. 'They don't look like elves.'

'Security,' he said. 'A lot of ex-pats get targeted by foreign criminals around here, so Granddad decided to beef up his protection.'

'Hmm, I wouldn't fancy being a burglar bumping into them. Is that what I think it is?' She was pointing at one particular figure with a Mac-10 machine gun slung across his back.

'Uh, yeah,' he said, embarrassed his girlfriend had caught sight of Billy's personal militia. 'It's just a deterrent.'

'Scary.'

'You get used to it.' He changed the subject. 'Look, I can't wait to introduce you to the family and give you the grand tour.'

He spun the sports car around the giant Christmas tree at the centre of the turning circle and brought it to a halt. The Ferrari belonged to Alisha and as soon as she learned Chuck's girlfriend was flying out she insisted he borrow it to pick her up from the airport. It was a smooth drive, and he hoped that one day he could own a similar top-of-the-range motor. That ambition was a step closer now he was working for Senor Tel and earning decent money, even though it meant he had to spend far too long in the company of Sammy McMahon, the man he now knew as The Shankill Whisperer.

Chuck had wanted to know all about the man after the incident at the pink lake and had badgered Billy for information. His grandfather had described Sammy as a 'total psycho' who had been a top figure in a paramilitary gang called the Shankill Butchers. There was one particular punishment for which he was renowned. He would shoot his victims through the elbows, the kneecaps and the ankles. 'Six shots, six pack, you see?' his grandfather had explained. 'Poor sods could end up crippled for life or worse if a shot missed its intended target.'

Remembering the punishment dealt out to the young Romanian kid, Marius, Chuck had no wish to spend any more time in the company of the Ulster madman and begged to work for his grandfather instead, but the old man insisted he fulfil his obligation. 'In a way, you will be working for me,' Billy said. 'Ever heard the phrase, "Keep your friends close and your enemies closer"? Senor Tel and I have a couple of combined projects: Building work, hotels, timeshares, all that palaver – but I don't trust him an inch. My constant fear is he'll screw me over. Think of yourself as my inside man, the Barking equivalent of James Bond.'

'What are you smiling at?' said Abby. 'You're like the cat that's got the cream.'

He put his hand on her knee and let it linger there, feeling the warmth radiating from her skin. 'I am,' he said. 'You're here, aren't you?'

'Ooooh corny!' She slapped his arm playfully. 'Remove that hand now you soppy apoth or someone might see. I wouldn't want to shock your grandfather.'

'Speak of the devil.' Chuck looked past Abby, and she turned to see an old man peering through the passenger window. The proximity of his wrinkled, tanned face to the glass, his unblinking eyes staring at her, made her feel slightly uncomfortable.

'Shit! Has he been there long?' she whispered.

'Don't worry, he doesn't bite.'

The door sprang open and a wrinkled, sweaty hand grabbed hers firmly, pulling her out of the car. Chuck watched as the love of his life was drawn into an awkward embrace. He wasn't surprised at her reaction. The forceful nature of everything his grandfather did could be unsettling for those who didn't know him.

'Let's look at ya, treacle,' he said, releasing her and holding her at arm's length. His eyes travelled her body, adding to her obvious discomfort.

'Billy, she's tired,' said Chuck, aware it was time to intervene. 'She's been on the go all day. Do you think we could get into the house first?'

'Of course, where are my manners?' said the old man. 'Come, my dear, come… Alisha's dying to meet ya. Now, where are ya cases? I'll get the maid to sort 'em and take 'em up to your room.' He winked at Chuck as if to say 'and your room too'. It was the kind of inappropriate gesture associated exclusively with elderly relatives.

Fortunately, Alisha materialised to dispel the awkward atmosphere. 'Hello, darling,' she said, moving forward to plant two showbiz air kisses on either side of Abby's cheeks. 'I hope your journey was good. It's so nice to have you visit. Now come, come… we have a spread fit for a queen. You must be hungry after your flight.'

She led their guest into the villa, Chuck and Billy following on behind. 'Bloody hell, boy, you're punching above your weight and no mistake,' whispered the old man, his hand on the small of his grandson's back.

CHUCK was consumed with nervous anticipation as he led Abby down the hallway towards the bedroom. They'd enjoyed a fabulous night, Alisha providing them with a selection of succulent home-prepared tapas dishes which they washed down with the delicious local red wine. Abby had been subjected to 20 questions from Billy and his wife but handled them effortlessly. He supposed it helped that she worked as a media professional in the fashion industry and spent most of her days fending off queries from different sources.

She'd told them how she and her mother had moved with her stepfather to the Costa del Sol shortly after her

15th birthday. Her parents hired a private tutor, and she quickly mastered the language before enrolling on a fashion, business and media course at the local college.

Once the meal was over Billy invited Chuck to his pub, insisting, 'Let's have a game of snooker and leave the ladies to their gossip.'

Chuck declined, though, keen to get his girlfriend to himself after all their months apart. Unlike Sly, who still seemed intent on working his way through the female population of the Costa Blanca, Chuck had resisted all temptation. In fact, he couldn't imagine being with another girl despite his reunion with Abby having been so brief.

'Alisha likes you,' said Abby. 'She is such a bright, charismatic and talented young woman I must admit I was a bit surprised.'

'What you really mean is: What the hell is she doing with my lecherous old git of a grandfather? Don't worry, I've been asking myself that same question since we got here. Apparently, she likes his sense of humour and, well, maybe it's at the back of her mind that he isn't getting any younger and at some stage all this will be hers.' He waved his arm around.

She slapped him playfully on the arm. 'That's a terrible thing to say! I'm sure they're very much in love. To suggest she is a gold digger just isn't on, Chuck Dolan.'

'Takes all sorts,' he said with a shrug of his shoulders. 'It's not like he went to charm school.'

She laughed. 'They do say opposites attract.'

'Like me and you?' he asked mischievously. 'Here am I living the jet-set lifestyle in Spain while you slum it back in Hackney.'

She slapped his arm again, just as the maid walked out of a room to their left, stopping for a moment to stare in their direction before hurrying off down the corridor without a word.

'What was that about?' asked Abby.

'Oh, that's the maid. Billy brought her out from England a few years ago. Didn't trust foreigners poking around in his business, I guess.'

'Maid? Bit old fashioned, isn't it?'

'You've met him,' said Chuck. 'Everything he does is based on the past.'

'Yeah, I guess so,' said Abby. 'Did you see the look she gave me?'

'I don't think it was aimed at you,' said Chuck. 'She probably feels guilty. That's Sly's room she just left.'

'Oh, really? Bit of a boy, is he? I hope you haven't been up to anything similar, Chuck Dolan.'

He feigned a stare of wide-eyed innocence. 'Me?' he said. 'Now what would be out here for me?'

'How about a never-ending supply of bikini-clad nymphos?'

'Nah,' he said. 'You know I'm the shy type. Not like my brother. He thinks he's chocolate when it comes to the ladies.'

'As long as he doesn't lead you astray,' she said. 'Now come on, Mr Faithful, it's bedtime.'

He felt a familiar tingle spread up from his toes as he pushed open the door to his room.

21

CHUCK lay spread-eagled across the bed, utterly spent. It had been everything he had anticipated and more, from the moment Abby had removed a garment from her suitcase and teasingly promised she was going to, 'Slip into something more comfortable', before disappearing into the en suite bathroom.

She had re-emerged in a white baby doll nightie that left just enough to the imagination, her toned skin glistening in the light from the bedside lamp. Unable to control his excitement he had leapt off the bed and moved towards her only for her to slip away, insisting she would dictate the course and pace of their lovemaking. Rather than being frustrated by this, it merely poured fuel on his inflamed ardour.

Moving as rhythmically as a dancer, she had soon relegated him to the role of mere spectator, hypnotising him with her beauty. He had wanted to touch and taste every inch of her, but whenever he tried to make a move, she'd pushed him firmly back down, those long, perfectly manicured nails pressing assertively against his chest.

This was a new experience for him. The few girls he had been with in the past had expected him to make all the running. The Abby he remembered from their teens was sexually naïve whereas this more mature version was so poised and confident he found it impossible to believe it was the same girl whose virginity he had stolen years ago during a fumbled few seconds in a garbage-strewn back alley.

Rising and falling above him, her long hair had weaved patterns inches from his face and as she neared climax the small squeaks emanating from deep inside her throat became more frequent, in sync with the movement of her hips. She was like a long-distance runner building towards a sprint finish and in those final moments he was totally wrapped up in her. By the time they fell breathless and weak across the bed, neither of them could express in words their feelings of unbridled joy and contentment. No matter what happened in later life they both knew they were unlikely to feel as connected to another human being as they did at that moment.

Abby reached across and lifted the ludicrously expensive chocolates from the bedside table. They had been Alisha's night-time surprise for the couple; the box sitting delicately wrapped in tissue paper on the pillow. Opening the lid, she studied them for a moment before lifting out a chocolate and biting into it. She released an 'mmmmm' of satisfaction, and Chuck felt aroused again when he spotted a slither of the gooey soft centre hanging from her bottom lip.

He had a more pressing need than sweet confectionary. Planting a kiss on the tattoo of the three coloured butterflies – red, green and blue – on her shoulder, he then rolled from the bed and pulled on a pair of shorts before picking up his pack of cigarettes and slipping through the hessian curtains onto the veranda.

The first inhalation of nicotine in the Spanish night air sent his head spinning, and he grasped the wooden rail for balance. Despite the time of year, the temperature wasn't too cold, and he welcomed the cooling breeze to calm his libido. For a moment he thought he saw a figure disappearing into the trees in the distance. Then, remembering his grandfather's beefed-up security, he relaxed, leaning back and blowing smoke rings into the air.

'Chucky?' Abby's term of affection was the prelude to a question.

'Yes, babe?'

'You never mention your dad. I've met your grandfather and Alisha, and heard all about Viola and your mum, but not your dad. Why? He isn't dead, is he?'

He wondered if he should lie, to tell her that Big Mo had run off with a fancy woman or was away working on the oil rigs, but if this relationship was going to stand a chance, he knew he had to be honest. He stubbed out the cigarette in the ashtray on a small ornamental table and stepped back inside. Was he ashamed of his father Maurice Dolan? Almost certainly, but despite all Big Mo's faults he loved him, nevertheless.

'Prison,' he said, flopping back onto the bed and brushing a smear of chocolate from the side of her mouth before kissing her. He could taste the sweetness of the confectionary on her lips.

'What did he do?'

Chuck pushed himself onto his elbow and looked down at her. 'You name it,' he said. 'Armed robbery, assaulting police, escaping custody… my dad was notorious back in the day. I guess he still is now.'

'Wow. How do you feel about that?'

'Listen. We grew up in a tough neighbourhood and when I was a kid, there were no jobs,' said Chuck. 'My dad did his best to help his family survive. Much of it was illegal, yes, but he did it all with the best of intentions. When he first went inside, he had two kids, me and Sly, with a third, Arnie, on the way… he wanted a better life for us and that's what we got. Now he's paying the price.'

'How did he make things better?'

'My mum used some of the loot from his jobs to get us out of the tower blocks and into a decent house. Yes, she took advantage of his crimes and if she was wrong to do that, then shoot me. Some people never have to lift a bloody finger in life but live in the lap of luxury. Is my dad a worse crook than them? No. They are just better at hiding it, the bankers who rip off ordinary people or those property tycoons who call in favours from their political chums. If you look around you, nearly everyone's got a scam going, particularly out here.'

'I know what you mean.'

'What about your dad, then? Did he never do anything wrong?'

She giggled. 'Strangely enough, he's one of those rich crooks you're talking about. I wouldn't wonder. That's how we could afford to move out here. He loves living it up in the playground for the wealthy. You'll meet him tomorrow when we get to Marbella. He's OK, to be honest.'

'He's your stepdad though, isn't he? I'm talking about your real dad.'

She fell silent, the question removing the smile that had been permanently fixed to her face since their lovemaking. Colour drained from her cheeks and sadness descended on her. 'He's dead.'

'I'm sorry,' he said, kissing her temple. She snuggled up to him and he fell back on the bed, stroking her hair. He felt a tear drop land on his chest and wondered if he had gone too far. 'I shouldn't have asked. It doesn't matter.'

'No, no, it's fine,' she said, brushing away another tear. 'I never get a chance to talk about him so I'm glad you asked. He died a long time ago, when I was just a nipper. I can't remember much about him really, so there's very little to say. One minute he was in my life and the next he was gone. When I was eight, he was taken into a home. Mum said he had mental health issues. It's all a bit of a mystery, and I guess she thought I was too young to understand. By the time I was old enough to question her, things had moved on and Geoff was on the scene. It didn't seem right.'

'That sounds similar to what happened to my dad's brother Clive… my uncle,' said Chuck. 'He fought in the Falklands War and never recovered. They have a name for it these days – post traumatic stress disorder, or PTSD.'

'Mum says the day I was born was the biggest thrill of Dad's life.' The tears were flowing freely now, and he moved a finger to gently wipe them from her cheek. She rewarded him with a sad smile. 'For someone who acts like a hard nut, you're a soft touch. Do you know that, Chuck Dolan?'

'Shush, don't tell anyone,' he said, grasping her fingers and brushing them against his lips. 'You'll destroy my reputation.' She moved her hand and laid it against his cheek. 'So, how old were you?' he said. 'When he died, I mean.'

'Nine,' she said. 'I'd got up for school and mum sat me at the dining table and told me he'd passed away in the night. I'm not sure how, but I overheard my Aunt Vera whisper something about suicide which, she said, was a sin in God's eyes. She was very religious, but I am pretty sure her words hurt my mum because we never saw her after that. I remember Mum shouting at her and asking how on earth she could know what was going on inside his head.'

'Did you visit him in the home?'

'Just the once,' she said. 'Mum dressed me up smart, and it was nice, as I recall, a big old stone building with flowers lining the driveway and a large garden out the back where residents would sometimes sit. When I saw him, he looked like a shrivelled old man, yet he was only 48 when he passed away. He never said anything, just sat in this chair and stared out of the window while Mum told him what we'd been doing.'

'He sounds a very troubled soul.'

'He was,' she said. 'I remember there was some sort of incident. I think it's why Mum never took me again. A care assistant tripped and spilt a jug of water. It was an accident but it really upset Dad. He leapt from the chair and started running around, screaming. It took two large orderlies to grapple him to the ground. He was shouting, "Come and hurt, Come and hurt". He looked petrified. A nurse told us we should leave after that, and I never saw him again. Mum said it was just one of his bad days.'

'Poor bloke,' said Chuck, 'Poor you, too.'

'Oh, it's a long time ago now,' she said. 'I haven't thought of it in ages. My stepdad Geoff has been really good to us … he's a proper father to me though I'm a bit nervous about you meeting him. He isn't everyone's cup of tea. He's a bit, umm, brash. Even so, it's down to him I now have a job which I love in an industry I love. If I hadn't moved here, none of that would have happened.'

'I'll be on my best behaviour,' said Chuck, lifting her head, their lips engaging in a long, slow kiss. 'I promise.'

'Oh, I know you can be good,' she said, her hands slipping under the sheets. 'Care to show me how good again?'

22

'HERE, geez, 'ave some of this… you'll love it. Freshly caught today. It's supposed to put lead in yer pencil, not that a strapping young lad like you should be worrying about that.' The man with the heavy gold chain around his neck passed across the bowl of calamari, a big grin plastered across his fleshy face. Chuck wasn't a fan of seafood but took a couple of the battered squid rings to be polite.

'Dad!' shouted Abby, her cheeks colouring.

'Oh, Geoff, there's no taking you anywhere,' said Abby's mum, tapping Chuck's hand. 'Ignore him, love. Any chance to embarrass us and he takes it, isn't that right, Abby?'

'Yeah, and he bloody succeeds most of the time,' Chuck's girlfriend replied in mock anger.

'Come on, lovely, you know I only tease cos I fink the world of ya? I've got to put them through the father test, ain't I? Don't want my little girl picking up with any old Jack the lad.'

'You mean someone like you,' said Abby's mum, and they all laughed.

Chuck had been told that if you wanted to get an idea of how your girl might turn out in later life, you just had to look at her mother. He had no complaints on that score.

Philippa Lee had the same twinkle in her green eyes, while the dimples in her cheeks were complimented by the laughter lines around her mouth. If he looked more closely, he could see how her skin had aged through constant exposure to the Spanish sun, but it took nothing away from her sex appeal. Thank God he hadn't bought Sly with him. By the end of the night, his younger brother would have almost certainly made a move. He smiled to himself.

'Care to share the joke?' asked Geoff.

'Sorry… I was thinking about my brother.'

'Older or younger?'

'Younger. I'm the oldest of the lot. There are four boys and one girl.'

'Big family,' said Geoff. 'It's good to have siblings. You can rely on them to have your back… well, some of them.' He glanced at his wife.

'Oh, don't go off on one about your Arthur again,' said Philippa. 'We're having a nice time. There's no need to spoil it. Chuck doesn't want to see our dirty laundry aired in public… not while he's eating.'

'Let's just say there's a bad apple in most families. Other than that… good as gold. I've got five in my family too, two brothers and two sisters. Whereabouts are you from in the smoke then, Chuck?'

'Barking,' said Chuck. 'It's in east London.'

'Oh, I know Barking,' said Geoff, skewering a lump of chorizo with a cocktail stick and popping it into his mouth. He chewed with enthusiasm, unaware some of the red paprika sauce was running down his chin. There were splashes of it on his dazzling white shirt. 'When I lived in Wood Green, I got about a bit and went out east a lot on business back in the day. It was convenient because it was just off the North Circ. What did you say your name was? Your surname?'

'Dolan.'

'Wait,' he said. 'You're not one of "the" Barking Dolans?' He put his hands in the air, making imaginary quote marks.

'I… um… didn't know there was such a thing.'

'Oh yeah… they're notorious, kid.'

'Oh, here we go,' said Philippa, trying to lighten the mood. 'Prepare for a history lesson. You'll get used to it, Chuck. He loves spouting his old London war stories.'

'I remember one guy,' said Geoff, continuing as if his wife hadn't interrupted. 'Absolute nutter. Everyone knew him as Big Mo. He anything to do with you?'

Chuck was thrown by the question and thought once again of disowning his jailbird father but suspected the lie might catch up with him. What did he have to lose, anyway? His girlfriend already knew the truth.

'My dad,' he said.

'Really? Bloody hell, boy! He was a bit tasty, back in the day. He…'

'… has been in prison most of my life, to be honest,' said Chuck.

Philippa picked up a bowl of patatas bravas and shoved them in her husband's direction. 'Come on, Geoff, you're making the boy feel awkward. Now, be a good soldier and get some of these down your neck. You know how you hate food going to waste.'

He shrugged, the gold chain glinting in the sun as it bounced on his breast, a mass of greying hairs rising from his stomach to cushion the blow, the shirt fighting a losing battle to cover his large frame. 'Don't mind if I do,' he said.

'Nothing to be ashamed of, anyway. The fact is your old man ain't even the most famous face in your family.'

'Dad!' said Abby.

'OK, OK, sorry, hon,' he said. 'You gotta be proud of your heritage though, Chuck. It makes you who you are.'

Chuck nodded, relieved that the interrogation seemed to be coming to an end. He lifted a piece of cured meat to his mouth and popped it in, looking over Geoff's shoulder to the marina and the luxurious yachts sitting grandly on the millpond stillness of the ultramarine carpet of the harbour. When Abby had described where her parents lived, he thought she'd been exaggerating, but he realised now that, if anything, she had been underplaying the sheer magnitude of wealth that cocooned Puerto Banus.

He had never in his life eaten lunch in such opulent surroundings and felt a fraud, believing people like him were more suited to the grubby plastic tables, chessboard tiles and chippy attitudes of the staff at his local greasy spoon café. That wasn't to say he couldn't get used to this life. The longer he sat there sipping on an invigoratingly cold lager and savouring the multifarious culinary delights on offer, the more he wished he could stay longer around Marbella. Unfortunately, the Ulsterman expected him back at work in the New Year. Suddenly his thoughts were distracted by Philippa leaping to her feet and pointing.

'Hey, you!' she screamed. 'Stop him! Bloody Nora, that bloke's just nicked my soddin' bag.'

SLY sipped from a glass of Coke at a corner table, looking out of the window and wondering what his brother was doing. He was disappointed. Rather than sexy senoritas, most of the customers at the Spanish megastore were middle-aged men and women, dragging small children in their wake. He bet at that exact same moment his brother was ogling talent on the seafront.

Sly had been looking forward to the move to Marbella. That was why it was all the more disappointing that he was spending his first day in the café of this giant supermarket in a shit-hole called Fuengirola. It sat just off the N340, which Rafael had described as the 'Road of Death' because of the number of fatal traffic accidents that occurred along the route. Sly could relate to the term. At that moment, he was seriously losing the will to live.

When Chuck had announced he was meeting Abby's parents in Puerto Banos, Billy had offered to drop them off. Sly had psyched himself up, convinced the outing would be a glorious distraction from the mundane routine he had got used to back at the villa in Torrevieja. It wasn't that he didn't enjoy helping Alisha with the horses; he had surprised himself at how quickly he had become attached to them, particularly the wonderful white Andalusian stallion Caja. He felt they had established a real connection, the kind he had never experienced before.

Sly's only previous experience of animals had been an uneasy relationship with Arnie's bull terrier Stevo while at times he had amused himself throwing stones at the feral dogs living on the Boxers' estate. Now, spending time up close and personal with such a clean, well-groomed and alert thoroughbred had allowed him to embrace nature in a way that he never would have thought possible. Still, he could treat this as a holiday – a break from the norm – and believed he deserved it for proving himself so adaptable and helpful to his grandfather's young wife.

On the way south he had peered through the windows of the Volkswagen Transporter Multivan at the perfect blue of the Mediterranean, imaging white-crested waves crashing around him. He couldn't wait to stroll along the beach, taking in the sights and sounds of the popular British tourist destination. That had made it all the more disappointing when Rafael had turned the van around after dropping Chuck and Abby off and headed straight out of town again. Sly had begged his grandfather to let him out, too, but Billy had just sneered, telling him he would only be a 'spare prick at a wedding'. Now, as he nursed his drink and looked around him, he was left to dream about what might have been.

Borrrring.

Billy and Rafael were deep in conversation with a couple of 'business associates' at the other end of the expansive café. In fact, all around him tough-looking men hid behind an array of gangster's camouflage – jewellery, tattoos, sunglasses, hats and scars – while whispering to each other across grubby tables. It reminded Sly of a new trend that had just started up in London called speed dating, where you were rotated around a room and given a short space of time in which to convince a member of the opposite sex that you were worth a punt. Perhaps this was speed dating for gangsters. Outside the window, a police officer on a motorbike sat scribbling notes in a small, black book, although no one seemed remotely concerned about his presence.

Sly noted that the thug opposite his grandfather was becoming animated, poking a finger in the old man's direction. Billy seemed unfazed, though, reaching across and placating his companion with a gentle tap of the hand. With his free hand, Sly's grandfather slid a folded slip of paper across the table and the man picked it up, glimpsed its contents, then refolded it and stored it in an inside pocket of his leather jacket. Sly wondered what was written on the note, but before he could give the matter further thought his grandfather had risen and moved across to another table to join a dark-skinned man in a white flannel suit sucking on a fat cigar. Rafael remained talking with the other man for a few moments before joining Billy the Kid. The same process then began all over again.

Draining his can, Sly then stood and walked out of the café. His grandfather could be tied up for ages and he thought looking around the store would help pass the time. It contained mainly foodstuffs, aisle upon aisle of fresh fruit and veg eventually giving way to giant chest freezers crammed with fish and meat. When he came to the ice cream cabinets, he tried to translate the labels, wondering what brands might be the equivalent of those sold at home.

'Sly? Sly Dolan?'

Stunned to hear his name in a supermarket thousands of miles from home, Sly stood instantly, banging his head on the lid of the freezer.

'Oww!' He rubbed at the area then span around. 'Lucky?'

'Well, what a turn up for the bleedin' book,' said the young man he'd first met in the middle of the Bay of Biscay. Lucky moved forward and gave Sly an awkward hug, then stepped back quickly in case he had broken some sort of male protocol. 'S… sorry,' he said. 'It's just… well, it's good to see a friendly face. We… we got on so well on the b… boat, didn't we?'

'Sure,' said Sly. 'I thought you were in Benidorm, though.'

'D… didn't w… work out.'

'Sorry to hear that, mate,' said Sly. 'Hey, why don't we get some ice creams and take them outside for a catch-up, eh?'

Luke Chalmers grinned. Sly couldn't help thinking the south Londoner's over-the-top reaction to seeing someone he had met only once in his life meant a darker tale lurked beneath. Hearing all about it might help relieve the sheer, unrelenting tedium he had been subjected to up until now.

Paying for the treats, Sly then allowed Lucky to lead him to a sheltered area of the car park where they could escape the unrelenting scrutiny of the midday sun. They sat on the kerb, sucking their lollies and enjoying the refreshing coolness on their tongues.

'So, how did you end up here mate?' asked Sly.

'It's a long s… s… story,' said Lucky.

It will be if you're going to stutter your way through it, thought Sly, before internally chastising himself for his unkind thoughts.

'I hooked up with my m… mate Rob and everything was fine for a while. We were repping for one of those h… h … holiday companies that offer breaks for 18/30s, y'know, the ones you hear about which are more like orgies. It was even wilder than I thought and g… g… great fun. On the side, Rob was also making a tidy piece selling drugs to the tourists. He knew a courier who made regular trips up from Gibraltar and could s… supply us with weed and stuff. I thought he had it all figured out. What he didn't tell me was how dangerous it was.'

Sounds familiar, thought Sly, but he nodded attentively, encouraging Lucky to continue.

'One night we were in a bar, sorting out a stag party with E's. Everything was going great until these blokes appeared and grabbed Rob. Fortunately, they didn't realise we were together. I followed them to the waterfront. They searched his pockets, made him s… s… strip then took him on board this b…. boat. I waited for ages, but he never came back. It was a n… n… nightmare.'

'Fuckin' hell,' said Sly. 'They killed him? Who were they?'

'R… R… Russians probably. They're trying to take over and they ain't like us Brits… no sense of decency and fair play. I thought about going to the police but they are so c … corrupt it might cause me more trouble in the long run. My only option was to get away. A bloke I knew suggested I could get work further south. I won't lie, I… I was kind of hoping I might bump into you, remembering you said you were coming down here. I didn't think I'd find you in Fuengirola, though. I was told to meet a guy here to discuss some c… courier work, hoping I might earn enough money to get home. The heat must have died down over there by now.'

'Sure. Look, I could ask my grandfather if he has anything for you,' said Sly. 'In fact, speak of the devil. Here he comes now. Over here!' He waved in their direction.

'W… wait!'

'What?'

Lucky's eyes were focussed on a couple walking towards his grandfather, pushing a trolley. 'I remember you told me about him. Doesn't he go by the name Billy the Kid?'

'That's right.'

'Shit! I think he's in big danger.'

23

CHUCK snapped out of his daydream and looked along the street to where a young man dressed in a Hawaiian shirt and scruffy, cut-off trousers was running towards the more heavily populated area of the waterfront, a designer Gucci bag dangling from his hand. Without thinking, Chuck shoved his chair back, allowing it to crash to the floor as he set off in pursuit.

'Chuck, don't! It could be dangerous. We'll call the—'

Abby's words faded away amid the clinking of cutlery on plates, the hubbub of polite conversation and the rumble of nearby traffic. People swivelled and watched out of curiosity as the determined young Englishman made progress through the canopied outdoor area of the restaurant before running into the street. His adrenaline soared as the thrill of the chase fed his inner desire for confrontation, something that was rarely satisfied. He had always kept himself fit through jogging, skipping and gym work, never forgetting the routines he'd become used to as a young boxer.

Pedestrians swerved out of the way, registering their protests in a variety of colourful languages. He lifted his knees higher, closing the gap on his target with every step as the thief lost valuable momentum by slowing and looking over his shoulder. Despite his scruffy attire, he had a pair of designer trainers on his feet, so white they could have been purchased – or stolen – that very day. By contrast, his skin was the colour of walnut, his black hair gathered in tight curls on top of his head.

Distracted by his pursuer, the thief crashed into a street vendor's table of souvenirs and lost his momentum, stumbling and falling to the floor. Chuck was just a few feet away when the youth clambered to his feet and turned to face him, the bag lying on the floor between them. He muttered something in a language Chuck didn't understand then thrust his hand forward, making a swift movement with his thumb. A blade materialised as if from nowhere. As he lashed out with surprising speed, the sharpened implement grazing Chuck's arm as he leapt back out of reach.

'Leave the bag there and go and we'll say no more about it,' said Chuck, realising the weapon had turned the odds against him. His knife-waving assailant showed no sign that he understood English.

'Leave him, Chuck!' said Abby from somewhere behind him. 'The police are on their way. Let them deal with it… You'll get yourself killed!'

Chuck didn't know how to back down, though. From the moment he stood up to the school bully at his primary school 17 years earlier he'd vowed never to take a backward step again. Fortune favours the brave his uncle Clive had told him before heading for the Falklands. It was a mantra Chuck had followed to that day.

Grabbing the street vendor's table, he whipped around in one motion and threw it at the thief. The flimsy piece of furniture slammed into him and sent him stumbling backwards. Whipping off his shirt, Chuck bunched it around his fists and pulled it taut, holding it out in front of him. He could feel the heat of the late December sun on his back, burning into his flesh, but it only stiffened his resolve. The quicker this was over the better.

His opponent let out a high-pitched squeal, pushing the table aside and lunging forward, his movements lightning quick and perfectly coordinated. In response, Chuck weaved on the balls of his feet, as he'd been taught to do, moving his head out of harm's way as the knife flashed past his face. Sensing his rival off balance, he quickly wrapped the boy's wrist in the cotton clothing and pulled the ends tightly so that his assailant had no leverage to thrust again. Summoning all his strength, Chuck used the boy's momentum against him, unleashing a blow with his free hand against the side of the thief's face. Rocked by the power of the punch, the handbag snatcher's head whiplashed back, and Chuck released the shirt so that he fell to the floor. Following him down, Chuck straddled the figure, raining blows on the back and side of his head until all the fight drained from his wiry adversary. Grabbing the knife hand, Chuck arched it backwards and, drained of strength, the thief had no choice but to release the weapon.

'Pull a knife on me, would you, you little fucker? I should break both your arms,' said Chuck, whispering menacingly in the thief's ear. He might not have understood the words, but the sheer venom with which Chuck delivered them made their meaning abundantly clear. From beside him, a policeman appeared and picked up the abandoned weapon. 'We take him now, yes?' the officer said. Reluctant to release his grip, it was only when a hand dropped on his shoulder and he heard a familiar voice that Chuck emerged from fight mode and returned to reality.

'Come on, son, you've done your bit,' said Geoff. 'Apple didn't fall far from the tree, I see. You're a bit tasty, too. I suspect you've overwhelmed the ladies here with your gallantry. I can certainly see why our Abby thinks you're a keeper.'

As another policeman helped lift the dazed and bloodied thief to his feet, Chuck stood and walked into a tight embrace from Abby. 'You're a bloody idiot,' she said, long nails digging into his exposed back, her physical reaction betraying her true feelings.

When she eventually let go, Philippa, the Gucci bag tightly clasped in both hands, stepped forward. 'My hero,' she said, releasing one hand from the expensive accessory just long enough to stroke his cheek. 'Thanks so much, Chuck. I don't know what's going on around here these days… you need eyes in the back of your head. If it's not these blessed north Africans coming here illegally by boat, with their thieving, raping and drug dealing, then it's the Russians, the Albanians and all those other lawless bastards. To be honest, for such a wonderful place it really is starting to live up to its reputation as the Costa Del Crime. Now let's get back to the table… I hope all the excitement hasn't put you off your pudding.'

'Shit!' said Chuck, remembering something. 'My phone … I left it in my jacket.'

'Oh, that old brick,' said Philippa, laughing. 'Don't worry, Abby's got it. She was moaning about how heavy it was. With all these new-fangled mobiles on the market, she wondered why you haven't bothered with an upgrade. I think you can expect a new one for Christmas.'

'Sly, my brother, keeps telling me the same thing but I've kind of got used to it.'

'Here you go,' said Abby, handing it over. 'Which reminds me… It's got a bloody awful ringtone. It was going off just now. Maybe you have a message or something?'

WITHOUT warning, Lucky broke into a run, heading for the van. At the same time, Sly saw the man lean into the trolley and come out with an automatic weapon. There was a staccato burst of gunfire, the windows of the van imploding as bullets tore into it. Where was the motorcycle cop when you needed him? The gunman turned and Sly froze with fear when he realised the weapon was now trained on him. Feeling vulnerable and petrified, he looked around frantically for cover. A single shot rang out.

It had come from behind the van, pinging off the shopping trolley and distracting the man with the machine gun. He span back towards the van and unleashed another volley of gunfire. At the same time, Sly heard a rumble and saw a motorcycle racing at speed across the car park. It pulled up beside the trolley, the rider making exaggerated hand signals. Sly realised it was the woman who had earlier been helping to push the trolley. Dropping the gun, the shooter jumped on the back of the bike and it screeched out of the car park, leaving smoke trails in its wake where rubber met gravel.

24

'THEY shot him right in front of me.'

Chuck was met by his brother at the entrance to the waiting area. Sly was as white as chalk, his hands shaking, that confident swagger nowhere to be seen as he blurted out the words. As soon as Chuck had heard the garbled phone message, he had raced into the road and tried to flag down a taxi, only for Geoff Lee to catch up with him and offer the services of his driver. Now 30 minutes later he was at the accident and emergency department of La Hospital Costa del Sol just a short distance down the road from where the shooting took place. After making inquiries at the desk, Chuck had spotted Sly's slumped body on a bench. Realising how serious the situation must be, he had broken into a jog, his heart pounding from fear.

'Billy?' asked Chuck nervously.

'He's OK. A few cuts and bruises…'

'Thank God. Then…'

'Rafael didn't make it. He was hit six times, a couple of bullets to the head, one piercing an artery. There was nothing they could do. It sounds like a professional job. Bastards. Who the hell…?'

'I don't know, Sly, but I'm starting to realise how dangerous this place is,' Chuck said. 'I'm not sure our grandfather's as in control of things as he likes to think he is. Poor Raf.'

'Gramps was talking business with some dodgy looking geezers before it all kicked off. One bloke didn't seem to appreciate what he was hearing.'

'It doesn't make sense,' said Chuck. 'Why the hell doesn't he retire? He's made enough money. All that wealth ain't going to stop a bullet, is it? Billy might have been a proper player in the old days, but there are younger, more ruthless criminals around now. I've been hearing all sorts of horror stories.'

'What's wrong with your arm?' Sly indicated a bandage that Philippa Lee had hastily applied to Chuck's knife wound at the harbour.

'I had a disagreement with some thieving toe rag with a knife,' said Chuck. 'He hasn't got one now.'

'Oh.'

'He's in a cell. Where's the old man?'

'On the ward.' Sly flicked his head towards a door on the right. 'They're checking him over. Like I say, a few bumps and bruises but he got off pretty lightly compared with…'

'We have to get him out of here. The cops will be asking questions and I don't think he'll welcome the attention.'

'What about wheels? The van's pretty shot up.'

'I'm on it.' A familiar face appeared at Sly's shoulder. Luke Chalmers was just replacing a phone in his pocket. 'There's a b… back entrance. You can leave that way. A taxi's waiting. The police are two minutes away, so we have to move quickly.'

'You were on the ferry,' said Chuck, thinking out loud as he clapped eyes on the new arrival. 'Lucky, isn't it?' He turned, raising his eyebrows at Sly.

'He lived up to his nickname,' said Sly. 'If he hadn't turned up, Granddad would be dead, too. He spotted what was about to happen and risked his life running out and dragging Billy to the floor, protecting him with his body. Bravest thing I ever saw.'

'Sounds like it,' said Chuck, unable to keep the note of suspicion from his voice. He was wary of everyone and everything, and didn't believe in coincidences. 'Stroke of luck you were on hand. Aren't you supposed to be in Benidorm?'

Sly stepped forward, shielding his friend from the questions. 'He was. It didn't work out, so he came down here looking for work. We just bumped into each other…'

'Well, best of luck with the job search,' said Chuck. 'And thanks for organising the taxi. You should get off. We wouldn't want to hold you up.'

'No!' The three young men wheeled around at the sound of the gruff voice. Billy the Kid Dolan was walking out through the double doors, a crutch tucked under his right arm and his left knee bandaged. 'This young man saved my life. Luke, isn't it? From what Sylvester tells me, you're a bit down on your luck, son. How would you like to work for me?'

'You sure, Billy?' Chuck walked over in his grandfather's direction. 'You know nothing about…'

'Ah, Chuck, you're here,' said Billy. 'What's the problem, son? Think I've lost me marbles? I landed on my arse, not my head. Of course, I'm sure. This kid reacted like lightning. If he hadn't assessed the danger so quickly, I'd be dog meat now. Heaven knows I need someone with his wits about him after… shit! How do I tell Alisha about poor Raf?'

'We'll think about that on the way back,' said Chuck. 'Right now, we need to get moving.'

'SO you're from south of the river, son?' said Billy. 'I knew a few boys over there when I was younger… did a couple of highly lucrative jobs wiv 'em. Don't recall the name Chalmers, though. What's your background?'

'I'm from Bexley,' explained Lucky, leaning forward from the back of the cab. 'My family lived in Bermondsey originally. Dad wasn't a crim, though. He was legit, from what I've been told, worked security, among other things.'

'Oh,' said Billy, leaning across the back seat to address his new employee. 'He still with us?'

'No,' said Lucky. 'He died very young, in a fire, I believe. Then a short while later Mum was killed in a car accident on the A3.'

'Sorry to hear that, son. Who brought you up then?'

'I was taken into care at the age of eight,' said Lucky. 'My aunt looked after me for a while. I'd been staying with her when the accident happened, but she fell ill with cancer and died a year later. Social Services put me in a home. There were a few foster parents during my childhood, but nothing lasted. I went off the rails a bit.'

'I feel sorry for kids who grow up not knowing the real meaning of family,' said Billy. 'Still, you're one of us now.'

'I should probably t… tell you I've b… been to jail.'

Billy chuckled. 'So has half the East End.'

'Got done for forging bank notes – had my own press and everything. It took a special task force to track me down. They didn't get all my equipment, though.'

'Well, in my mind that makes you a bit of a celebrity,' said Billy. 'Christ knows, I could do with someone making me money – it would be easier than my current line of work. Tell me, though, that thing back at the supermarket? It was as if you knew what was going to happen.'

'Before I bumped into Sly, I was having a cigarette outside and waiting to meet someone about a job. That was when I overheard these people talking. One used the word 'ejecutar'. I speak a bit of Spanish and knew it meant execute. Of course it aroused my suspicions when your name came up… though they referred to you as El Nino Billy. As they were talking, a woman joined them and one of the guys disappeared into the building. Later when I was with Sly, I saw the couple pushing a trolley and thought they looked suspicious. Remembering the previous conversation I had overheard, I asked Sly if you were known as Billy the Kid. When he confirmed you were, I put two and two together and knew I had to act fast.'

'Very sharp witted, son, luckily for me,' said Billy. 'Terrible about Rafael, though. He was a good guy and a reliable worker. You have to be able to trust people out here and we were very close. Still, anyone prepared to risk a bullet for me deserves a chance. Come and work for me and I'll make it worth your while. Oh, and don't worry about what my eldest grandson says, he thinks you're pinching his job. I'd tell you the work comes with a health warning, but you know that already. Some might say you've got the T-shirt.'

25

CHUCK felt the nausea rising from the pit of his stomach as he watched the Shankill Whisperer go to work. The oldest Dolan boy would never have described himself as squeamish, but the former paramilitary's capacity for sadism was off the scale. His victim on this occasion was a teenage drug dealer, but any crime the kid had committed could never justify the punishment.

Chuck had spent the last week trying to persuade his grandfather to let him stay in Marbella and help run the business. Things had been subdued after Rafael's shooting, but being down south had enabled him to spend time with Abby before her return to England. He'd enjoyed the uplifting Millennium Eve Party her parents had thrown at one of the elegant hotels in the old town. Abby's dad Geoff had even offered him a security job, thinking him ideally suited to dissuading criminals from targeting the top-of-the-range motors in his showroom.

However, his pleas to Billy fell on deaf ears, the old man's monosyllabic responses a sure sign his mind was wrapped up in his crumbling relationship with Alisha. On one particular evening Chuck and Sly had heard raised voices from the couple's bedroom, Alisha giving full vent to her feelings over Rafael's death in a string of Spanish expletives that needed no translating. Later, they heard the door crash shut and the sound of the woman's sports car revving outside.

Both boys felt a huge amount of sympathy for her. Not only had she lost her brother-in-law, but Alisha also had to bear the brunt of her sister's wrath for having 'taken up with that *delincuente ingles*'. Maria had been left without a husband, and her three kids were fatherless.

Seeking out a sympathetic ear yet strangely reticent to confide in his own grandchildren, Billy had spent more and more time seeking the counsel of his new employee Luke 'Lucky' Chalmers. He obviously considered the young Londoner a kindred spirit because they shared similar backgrounds, having both been forced to rely on their own wits to crawl free from the poverty trap. At times Chuck even suspected the two men of plotting to keep him out of the loop, which he considered a massive personal snub. Billy always talked about loyalty and family, yet the old man had distrusted him ever since that golf course incident, even though he had bent over backwards to make amends.

Chuck acknowledged that saving Billy's life was bound to afford Lucky a degree of special treatment, but what did anyone really know about him? Sly swore blind he was a 'really decent bloke' but the man himself admitted starting out as a conman, forging money and organising elaborate bank scams, actions which suggested he'd spent a great deal of his young life pulling the wool over people's eyes. His spiel might work on his brother and grandfather, but Chuck took nothing at face value.

CHUCK and Sammy had left the battered body of the young drug dealer hanging from the kitchen door of his apartment like a macabre re-enactment of the Crucifixion. Sammy had hammered rusty nails through his hands and feet then gone to work with his favourite device of torture, a baseball bat encrusted with metal spikes. On leaving the apartment, Chuck had glanced back, thinking the young victim couldn't have possibly survived, only for a feeble cough to rob him of that single crumb of comfort.

The haunting image stayed with Chuck for the rest of the day. When his "shift" was over, instead of heading straight back to the Torrevieja villa to drown his sorrows, he got in the rusty runaround his grandfather had given him as a Christmas 'gift' and drove to one of the poorer neighbourhoods of the Spanish city. Here, blocks of half-finished flats stood close together and broken street lamps added a surreal, eerie affect.

During his time in Spain, Chuck had learnt that many expat criminals entered the property market in order to make big profits from minimal outlay. To exploit a loophole in Spanish tax regulations, building works were left incomplete, a scam to which local politicians turned a blind eye in exchange for backhanders. He was beginning to realise corruption was rife in this part of the world.

Pulling in at the kerb, Chuck reached into his glove compartment for the tool he would need, then stepped out, taking care to avoid a steaming pile of dog faeces on the pavement. Crossing the road he walked passed a dilapidated recreation area where shoeless kids wandered aimlessly, a couple of them running over when they saw him, bony fingers reaching in his direction for a handout. When they realised they were getting nowhere, they headed back towards the crumbling playground equipment where a platoon of feral dogs had set up camp.

This is even worse than the Boxers, thought Chuck as he turned the corner, walking into a human blockade of three emaciated girls. One of them, realising he was a foreigner, attempted sign language to communicate her various skills, though Chuck's attention was fixed on the track marks winding up her arms. When he focussed on her face, he saw a knotted tangle of rope-like hair partly obscuring a vacant expression. Despite her well-worn look, he realised she was roughly the age of his kid sister Anjelica and he was suddenly overcome by an acute sadness. Who cared for this girl's welfare, and what future did she have?

He dug in his pocket for a fistful of loose pesetas and thrust them into her hand then shook his head when she grabbed for him and tried to lead him away. He wanted nothing in return, consoling himself with the knowledge that for a brief time the girl would be able to cloak her miserable life in opioid-fuelled oblivion.

Entering the block of flats, he climbed the stairs to where the wreckage of the front door stood. Pushing it aside, he expected to walk in on a corpse, his intention to give the kid a decent burial before the rats and maggots got to work. Instead, Chuck detected the feint flicker of an eyelid and realised his prayers had gone unanswered. Taking a set of pliers from his jacket pocket, he worked painstakingly for more than five minutes to remove the mangled and deeply embedded nails. When he was done, the body flopped forward, and he nearly crumpled to the ground under the dead weight. Taking a moment to regain his composure and summon his strength, he then hoisted the boy in a fireman's lift and carried him downstairs to the car.

Fifteen minutes later a young man with horrendous injuries was deposited at the reception of the local hospital by a Good Samaritan whose identity was hidden beneath a hooded top. The doctor who saw the patient was a veteran of many road traffic accidents but had rarely encountered anyone in such a grave condition. Nearly every bone in the young man's body was broken. He had a collapsed lung and limbs so badly damaged he would be crippled for the rest of his life. The face would require years of reconstructive surgery while the reproductive organs would never perform their primary function. It was as if the very Devil had gone to work on him with every tool at his disposal.

Had the victim arrived any later at the hospital, death would have been assured. The doctor couldn't help questioning whether the Good Samaritan had done his patient any favours at all.

'WHAT'S happening?'

'All good. In fact, more than good.'

'The Turk on board?'

'Loves us, mate.'

Arnie was in a chirpy mood. He'd sent a text message instructing Chuck to call him from a payphone at a certain time. While it all seemed cloak and dagger, the younger man had made it clear they needed to be ultra-careful in their communications with each other. All it would take was one alert copper with a listening device, and a whole heap of trouble would rain down on their heads.

'I don't reckon he thought we could handle it,' said Arnie. 'It ain't a small job, believe me, but things have gone better than we could have hoped.'

'Don't tell me that waster Tigger is organising this,' said Chuck. 'It's a bit out of his league.'

'I ain't stupid, Chuck,' said Arnie. 'Yes, Tigger has his street teams dealing with the everyday stuff, but that produces just a small fraction of our profits. It's Vickers who's come through big time.'

'Oh?' Chuck was surprised. Arnie's mate spent most of his time with his nose deep in one book or another.

'He got some work experience at one of them big banks down Canary Wharf,' said Arnie. 'His work mates invited him on a night out and, hey ho, turns out they're a bunch of cokeheads. Chances, eh? "Work hard, play hard", they told him. When they realised he wasn't some wet-behind-the-ears kid but had "connections" they were all over him like a rash. He could do them a more favourable deal than their regular supplier and when they sampled the product, they realised it was far better. Apparently, even the big cheese likes to powder his nose and the geez only turns around and offers Vickers a bleedin' job as a reward "for all his hard work". Since then, we've been moving the Turk's stuff like it's going out of fashion, all through the offices of the big city companies. We've even had to go back to him for more. He thinks all his Christmases have come at once.'

'I'm pleased for you, Arnie,' said the older Dolan, though his tone implied the opposite. There was something about his brother living the life of Riley while he and Sly were marooned in a foreign land that stuck in Chuck's throat. Arnold might be family, but the two of them had never hit it off. Deep down, Chuck had to admit he felt jealous of the younger man's confidence and apparent success. The kid was nearly 10 years his junior but somehow had adopted the role of head of family with Big Mo locked up.

'Don't forget about us as you stroll about like Barking's version of Scarface,' said Chuck. 'If we hadn't done that post office, you'd still be picking pockets on street corners.'

'Fuck off, Chucky,' said Arnie. 'You'll do all right from this when the heat dies down. There's a tidy little stash waiting here with your names on. I'll keep it safe.'

'When do you think we'll be able to collect?'

'That's the million-dollar question,' said Arnie. 'Jill Dando's murder kept the old bill busy for a time, but now they've arrested some geezer…'

'Oh?'

'Bloke called Barry George.'

Chuck was shocked. 'What, the darts player?'

'That's Bobby George, you dimwit.'

'Hey!'

'Keep yer hair on, just pulling yer leg,' said Arnie, though his older brother found the lack of respect infuriating. 'The truth is the old bill put out some CCTV footage from the night club on *Crimewatch* last week. It was a bit fuzzy, but anyone who knows you boys would be able to identify you. It doesn't prove much, mind, it just shows you knocking over a bouncer and bursting outside. The problem will come if those forensics experts find fingerprints linking you to the scene, off grenade fragments or something.'

'Shit, that reminds me,' said Chuck. 'The bag… the one with our clothes in…'

'Don't worry, Fancy Man rescued it. Still, you need to stay put for the time being, for your own sake and the business. The Turk won't be happy if the filth start sniffing around.'

The events earlier in the day were still fresh in Chuck's memory, watching the Whisperer go to work and then delivering a savagely beaten youth to hospital. 'So you're telling me I have to stay at the beck and call of these fuckin'

Irish psychos Granddad has me working for, while you live it up back home?'

'Don't be a wanker all your life!' said Arnie, his temper rising. 'If anyone's to blame, it's you. I told you that fuckin' grenade was a mistake, but would you listen? That's the trouble with you, Chuck, you don't...'

Chuck slammed the phone down, interrupting his brother in mid-rant. When it rang again, he ignored it, stepping out of the booth and walking back to the car. He was seething and needed a drink. Looking across the road, he saw a cosy bar with dim lighting. He probably shouldn't drink and drive, but he just needed one to take the edge off.

Bloody Arnie.

Lashing out, his fist struck a brick wall. Feeling nothing at first, he was about to repeat the action when the pain finally registered, and he studied his knuckles distractedly. They were grazed and red, flakes of skin hanging off, a mess.

Bloody Arnie.

When he got back to England, he would teach the little oik a lesson in manners rather than take out his anger on stone walls. Cursing under his breath, he moved on, stopping outside the bar, which he now realised was a cosy restaurant catering for locals. The windows were tinted and the interior so dark he wondered if they had shut up early.

The board outside offered the usual array of tapas dishes, but some were unfamiliar to him. Still unable to speak the language properly, he was used to Sly helping him out, but his younger brother had been lucky enough to get permission to stay on in Marbella. Still, *cerveza* was *cerveza* wherever you chose to dine, and all he needed was one cool, calming beer to sluice Arnie from his mind. He was about to enter when something made him retrace his steps. Putting his hand to his brow to cut out the reflective glare of a nearby streetlamp, he screwed up his eyes and peered into the gloomy interior.

Well, well, well, he hadn't been mistaken.

Hunched over at a corner table, oblivious to the outside world and the figure watching her, was the maid, Naomi, sipping from a glass of red and looking much more sophisticated and classy than usual. Her dark hair had been given the full hairdresser treatment, looking luxuriant and beautifully shaped to highlight her pretty face, and she wore a strikingly elegant red dress as opposed to her daytime uniform. No wonder he had needed a double take.

Conscious of the need to be discrete, Chuck pulled his head back from view but kept his eyes on the table as Naomi moved forward, speaking animatedly to her dinner companion. There was nothing remarkable about the man sharing her table, who wore an ordinary grey suit and was leaning forward to hear what she had to say. When he turned to signal to the waiter, though, Chuck's mouth fell open in disbelief. Even if he hadn't seen his face, the blond curls were unmistakable.

They belonged to Luke "Lucky" Chalmers.

26

CHUCK was still mulling over the ramifications of this secret liaison when he stepped through the front door of the villa 40 minutes later. Was it a simple case of Naomi and Lucky having a fling? They were both young adults with the same urges and desires, after all, and shared other common ground too, having moved abroad to find work. Working close to a good-looking member of the opposite sex could understandably nurture a mutual attraction. And yet…

Chuck didn't like secrets. Full stop, and for good reason. At a tender young age, he had worked out that both his mother and father had been embroiled in deceitful affairs during their long and tempestuous marriage. In fact, he suspected his mother still enjoyed the odd liaison with Stan Marshall, the father of Arnie's best mate, Gary. It had been Stan, after all, who had driven his mother to Hackney in order to deliver their passports and bags on the day they left England.

As well as Chuck's natural suspicious nature, there were more concrete considerations that set the alarm bells off in his head. Lucky had only just started working for his grandfather, yet he seemed so comfortable in Naomi's presence it was as if the two of them had known each other for ages. Some people can act like that – Sly for instance – but Luke Chalmers didn't strike him as that sort. For a start, the stutter suggested someone prone to anxiety and nerves who might struggle to strike up new relationships.

Perhaps the biggest stumbling block to any relationship between Naomi and Lucky was Chuck's grandfather. Billy the Kid paid his closest confidantes handsomely and expected them to be focussed and committed. Those attributes were non-negotiable, and it was vitally important for Lucky to stay switched on, given the recent attempt on Billy's life. A distraction of the female kind would not sit well with Billy's expectations for his new employee. Lucky's presence in Torrevieja itself was no surprise. He'd driven Chuck back from Marbella, explaining he needed to familiarise himself with the Torrevieja villa and Billy's security staff in order to do the job to the best of his ability. Should the old man discover an ulterior motive for the journey he would definitely not be impressed.

No sooner had thoughts of his grandfather popped into his head than Chuck noticed the light on in the stairway leading down to the pub. On further investigation, he found a hunched figure perched on a stool, his head resting against the bar counter.

'Billy?' he inquired tentatively.

'What? Who's that? Stay back!'

'It's me, Billy. Chuck. You OK?' He noted with alarm there was a handgun lying on the bar in front of his grandfather.

'Oh, it's you, son. Shit! What time is it?'

'Just gone midnight. What are you doing here? I thought you were still in Marbella. You weren't due back for a couple of weeks. What happened? You haven't been attacked again, have you?'

Chuck climbed onto the bar stool next to his grandfather. The shadows falling across the old man's face made the stress lines more pronounced. Light from the stairwell reflected on the tiny flecks of grey that nestled on his scalp. For the first time it occurred to Chuck that, far from being a criminal mastermind, Billy the Kid was merely an old man with little time left to enjoy his ill-gotten gains.

'The cops came,' said Billy. 'They popped up in Marbella, bold as brass.'

Chuck froze. He was hoping the longer he heard nothing, the more likely the Hackney thing would go away. 'More to the point it was a couple of cops and some insurance geezer,' said Billy. 'They made all sorts of wild allegations, accusing me of being a key figure in a big robbery back in the day. They're putting a case together to have me extradited to the UK.'

'Are they right? About the robbery?'

The old man avoided the question. 'Where's Lucky?'

Chuck thought about what he'd seen that night but decided to keep his powder dry until he could find out more. Spill out his concerns to Billy and the old man might think it was sour grapes. Chuck hadn't been happy with the appointment from Day One.

'I told him to take the night off,' said Chuck. 'We weren't expecting you back. Anyway, never mind him for a minute. Can they do that? Arrest you and send you home?'

'I don't know, son. I guess so. For a long time, there was no extradition treaty between the two countries, which is why all the big-time crims came out here. Unfortunately, that changed some time ago.'

'Even so, where's the evidence?'

'It wouldn't be the first time the police fitted someone up,' said Billy.

'You need a lawyer,' said Chuck. 'You must know a few good ones.'

'Money grabbing bastards,' said Billy. 'Give 'em an excuse and they'll take you to the cleaners.'

'For God's sake!' Chuck was rapidly losing patience with the stubborn old fool. 'What's the point in having all this money if you can't use it to save your skin?'

'Hey,' said Billy, a cold hardness entering his voice. 'Show some respect.'

Chuck considered arguing the point, but Billy's tone made him think twice. The old man was right. He had been brought up to respect his elders, particularly the males in the family. On occasions it had been a hard lesson. Tough love, Big Mo called it.

'Well, what else can you do?' he asked.

'I have options,' said Billy. 'That's why I'm down here, thinking things through. There is one thing I know would make this all go away in a flash, but by putting the wheels in motion it could bring more trouble down on our heads.'

'Right,' said Chuck. 'Well, I guess we have to weigh the options up.'

'That's for me to do, not you,' said Billy. 'I don't want you involved in this…'

'I'm already involved, Billy, like it or not. You told me you wanted us to keep an eye out for you, and that's what I intend doing. If there is anything…'

Billy sat silently for a moment, staring at his empty glass. Then he grabbed the bottle of whisky at his side, looking into it for answers. When he tipped it up, the last few drops landed in his tumbler.

'Lean over and get another bottle, son,' he told Chuck. 'And get yourself a glass, too.'

Chuck did as he was told. Billy wrestled with the lid, then poured them both a large shot.

'Like whisky?' he asked.

'Never really drunk it,' Chuck admitted.

'Don't know what you're missing,' said Billy. 'These single malts are fantastic. Your old man wasn't much for it, I grant you. I tried to get him interested in the finer things in life, but he was having none of it. Me? It helps me think.'

Chuck took a large gulp. He felt a warm sensation at the back of his throat.

'Hey, steady with that,' said Billy. 'That's a Macallan 1926. It's been described as the holy grail of whisky, and you've just treated it like some cheap cooking lager.'

Chuck put the glass down. 'Sorry. It's nice.'

Hearing a noise behind him, he spun around. Sly was entering the pub, a serious expression on his face. 'Did Granddad tell you why we're back?' he asked. Chuck nodded. 'And did he mention this?'

The younger brother took an envelope from his jeans pocket and handed it over. It had a large bulge in the middle, and Chuck emptied the contents into his palm. A brass bullet. He twisted it, then gave it a closer inspection. The word "Puta" had been roughly engraved on the side. 'This is some sort of joke, right?' said Chuck.

'See me laughing, son?' said his grandfather. 'You ain't forgetting that a month ago someone tried to blow my brains out?'

'Sorry, I didn't mean it like that,' said Chuck. 'It's just, well, this is like a scene from a movie, you know, the *Godfather* or something. People don't do this in real life unless, of course, they're playing a trick on someone. It's a bit over the top, don't you think? What does *puta* mean?'

'Whore or prostitute,' said Billy.

'The fact it's written in Spanish suggests someone local,' said Chuck. 'To be honest, Billy, we don't even know it was meant for you. It could be for someone else.' He glanced at Sly knowingly.

'Oh, great!' said Sly. 'Why look at me?'

'Because you can't keep it in your pants,' said Chuck, shrugging. 'It's not that far a stretch to believe some angry husband or boyfriend might call you a "whore".'

'Fuck off.'

'You sure you haven't been upsetting anyone in Marbella? There are some pretty naughty characters down there who wouldn't take kindly to you shagging their wives.'

'No!' Billy raised his voice suddenly. 'Leave your brother alone, I'm pretty sure that ain't it.'

'We have to look at every possibility, Granddad,' said Chuck.

'Look, there are things I ain't told you boys,' said Billy. 'Things that, when you hear them, might make you think differently. I didn't tell you after the supermarket incident because I thought maybe that was a one-off, y'know, some bloody Russian trying to flex his muscles. I've put feelers out in an attempt to get to the bottom of it but, so far, nothing. I even suspected our Irish friends or even the Colombians – they told Rafael they weren't entirely happy with our arrangement – but not a whisper. At times it's hard to know who you can trust.'

'Family, Billy,' said Chuck. 'You should know you can trust us. I get the feeling you've been shutting us out though, especially me. You've been relying on Lucky, but how much do you really know about him?'

'I know he nearly took a bullet for me,' said Billy. 'That merits a degree of trust, don't you think? What you got against the boy?'

'Yeah!' Sly joined in. 'You've never liked him, Chuck. I think he's a great bloke. Ever since I met him on the ferry, he's been nothing but straight with me.' He turned to his grandfather. 'Chuck's always like this…anyone I meet needs his seal of approval. Hell, I think I'm old enough…'

'… To make your own decisions.' Chuck finished his sentence. 'Yeah, like with them two birds in Mulligan's.'

'Fuck off! That's different.'

Yes, thought Chuck, *and do you know where your brilliant "mate" is now? Enjoying an intimate dinner with your current piece of skirt, that's where.* He said nothing, though, fearing it would dissolve into bickering and distract them from the task at hand. If he was honest with himself, he had no proof that anything was going on sexually between the two members of Billy's staff. Unlikely as it seemed, Lucky and Naomi might just be having a spur of the moment 'work outing'.

'I fancy a beer,' said Chuck after finishing his whisky. 'You, Sly?' His brother nodded. 'Go on then, do the honours. I've been working my bollocks off for those bloody Irish bastards all day.'

Sly moved to the other side of the bar and started filling a pint mug from a beer tap. When he finished, he handed it over. 'You're jealous, Chuck. Admit it,' he said, refusing to let the matter rest. 'Of Lucky, I mean. Well, here's something else to wind you up… when we get back to England me and him are going into business together. I'm tired of being pushed around by you, Arnie, everyone. He's a bright bloke… knows lots of technical things about science and physics and stuff. We're gonna do cashpoints and make lots of money.'

'Ohh?' said Billy. 'And what about me? Last time I looked he was employed by me on a fackin' good wedge.'

'This won't be for a while, Granddad,' said Sly, realising he had given away too much. 'You ain't getting any younger, though…'

He fell silent, immediately realising his mistake. *That's the real Sly*, thought Chuck, *opening his mouth before engaging his brain.*

'What?' Billy's face flushed red. 'You're killing me off already, are ya, ya serious waste of baby batter? Fuck me! Your old man should have jizzed in a hanky.'

The crude insult took both boys completely by surprise, and for a moment no one spoke. Then Chuck roared with laughter, and Sly joined in.

'Fuckin' hell, Billy, that's a bit uncalled for,' said Chuck, wiping away tears, his expression failing to back up the outrage suggested by his words. 'That's my brother – your grandson – you're talking about.'

'Yeah well, he said he wanted to kill me off,' said Billy. 'Shit, maybe the bullet's from him! I mean, it turned up in the postbox without a stamp or nothin'. It could be an inside job.'

'Oh, come on!' said Chuck. 'Think Sly's clever enough to come up with such a devious plan? Look at him…'

Sly gave his brother an angry look before Billy banged his whisky glass on the table to attract their attention. 'Enough of this frivolity,' he said. 'We ain't here for a cockney knees-up and a stand-up show. This is fackin' serious.'

Picking up the bullet from the table, he rolled it around in his hand. 'The truth is you're right, Chuck. I've been shutting you out to protect you. I have a duty of care to you, and your mother would never forgive me if you came to any harm getting involved in my business.'

'Oh, come on, Billy!' Chuck almost spat out his drink, having just taken a large gulp. 'That's bullshit. You've got me spying on an ex-Ulster paramilitary while working alongside possibly the most violent psychopath I've ever met. Jeez, on our first day in this country you dispatched us to meet the leader of a Colombian drug cartel who has a reputation for poisoning people who upset her. Then just recently you dragged Sly to a dodgy Spanish supermarket where some of the most violent criminals on the continent do their business. I would hardly call that keeping us out of the frigging firing line. Damn, Fred West has a better reputation for childcare.'

Sly chuckled at the reference to the infamous child murderer, but Billy didn't see the funny side. 'Don't associate me with that fackin' nonce,' he said. 'Look, the trouble is you're as headstrong as your father. If you get wind of what's upsetting me, you're likely to go charging in, fists flying, causing all sorts of grief and that sort of attitude is what will get us all shot.'

'Fuckin' 'ell!' said Chuck, finally losing his temper. 'You're still thinking about that bloody golf incident, aren't you? That was yonks ago, Billy. I haven't embarrassed you since then, have I?'

Billy shrugged his shoulders. 'No,' he conceded, 'but you're like a busted kettle, everything always bubbling under the surface. The water's boiling away and when the explosion comes, it will be monumental. None of us want to be in the vicinity when you go off.'

Silence fell again, Chuck desperately trying to keep a lid on his anger.

'He's right, bro,' said Sly, taking the stool next to Chuck. 'You have got a tendency to fly off the handle.'

He wasn't prepared for the punch which caught him flush on the cheek and sent him flying, his shirt and shorts drenched in Spanish lager by the time he hit the floor.

'There she blows,' said Billy.

27

IT WAS 15 minutes later, and things had finally calmed down. Sly had gone for a change of clothes, while Billy and Chuck had moved to a table and now sat in brooding silence, sipping on their drinks. When the younger man returned, he went to the bar for refills. He was about to take a seat next to the old man when Billy pointed to a shelf above his head.

'Pass that book down, son.'

Sly read the spines of the assorted well-thumbed paperbacks stacked there. 'Bloody hell, which one, Gramps? There's *The Stud*, *The Bitch*, *Hollywood Wives*? I never had you down as a Jackie Collins fan.'

'Not them, you joker,' said Billy. 'They were Vi's. That one there, the big one.' He was straining forward, pointing at a hardback which was approximately the size and shape of the bulky annuals Chuck had received for Christmas as a child. It had a colourful cover, a variety of bright pictures decorating the front. Sly lifted it down and read the title. '*The Guinness Book of Records 1985*,' he said. 'Good one, Gramps. Nice and up to date.'

'All right, funny guy, pass it here, sit down, drink your drink and listen, would ya?'

Sly did as he was told and watched as the old man ruffled through the pages. 'Now where is it… page 385 if the old watch and chain serves me right.' He looked up and registered their dazed expressions. 'Watch and chain means brain in the old Cockney lingo,' he explained. 'Yep, here it is, Chucky boy.' He handed the book over, open at the chosen page.

'What's this?' asked the older Dolan brother.

'Read it and find out,' said Billy.

Chuck took a swig of his fresh pint. 'OK,' he said. 'Greatest Jail Break. In February 1979, US Army Colonel —'

'Not that one,' said Billy. 'Underneath.'

'OK,' said Chuck. 'Robbery.' He looked up to make sure he had the right entry. His grandfather nodded.

'Robbery,' Chuck repeated. 'The greatest amount lost in a robbery was on November 25, 1983, when £25million – it says in brackets here—'

'Don't worry about the bloody brackets!' said Billy. 'They've just converted the figure into American dollars for the benefit of the yanks… If memory serves it translates to $35m.'

'Right… £25m worth of gold in the form of 6,800 bars in 76 boxes were removed by six masked men from a vault of Brinks Mat Ltd at Heathrow, England. Phew…' He whistled. 'Impressive.'

'It was,' said Billy. 'Each one was about the size of one of them Dairy Milk chocolate bars.'

Suddenly Sly twigged. 'Fuckin' hell, Gramps. That was you? Good work! You stole—'

'Shhhhh! Keep your fackin' voice down, Sylvester, would ya? You never know who's listening. I've been able to keep this… thing… quiet for a very long time, even from those closest to me. Alisha doesn't know and even Raf didn't have a Scooby… anyway, I ain't told Lucky or any of the other staff, either. Better that way. A little knowledge can be a dangerous thing.'

'In what way?' asked Chuck.

'Let's just say people have been killed just for jabbering about it. Still, with everything that's been happening lately I felt I had to put you in the picture. I've heard what you said about trust, Chuck, and as my flesh and blood, you have a right to know the truth.'

Billy pointed a bony finger at Chuck. 'I'd heard good things about you through the grapevine, son, but didn't want to tell you too much until I was able to judge you for myself. That's why I was glad your mum sent you out here. I thought it would be good for you both to get to know your granddad and learn about your heritage. I had to suss out your loyalty first though and gauge your ability to keep your mouths shut.'

He stopped for a minute, looking down at the bullet in his hand. 'Chuck, you need to reel in that temper of yours, but you're a good man to have around,' he continued. 'Sylvester, I'm impressed by your dedication. Alisha's delighted with how quickly you got to grips with caring for the horses and finds you an excellent worker. She says that although you were a bit nervous, you conquered your fears and threw yourself into the routine. I can't doubt your bravery, son. You stuck with your brother during that Hackney business when it would have been easier to run and save your own skin. That suggests you have your priorities right … family, family, family.'

He paused to look over his shoulder, but the door to the pub remained shut. 'Alisha has always had more than an inkling my business is, well, not totally legit,' he said, lowering his voice to a whisper, as if someone might be listening. 'Hell, she'd be crazy if she didn't cotton on. She only has to look around her, the house here and the villa in Marbella. They didn't cost peanuts. Of course she ain't happy about the Rafael business and I can understand that. Her sister's gone off on one and she's feeling guilty so is turning her rage on me. Fine, I'm a big boy, I can take it. I'm not sure how she would react, though, if she knew the whole story.'

Chuck and Sly exchanged a glance before the younger man pointed to the book. 'That raid was 17 years ago, granddad,' he said. 'Surely the gold's all gone.'

'You'd think so, right, but gold ain't as easy to get rid of as all that,' said the old man. 'I'm not saying it's out there in its original form. It may have been smelted down, moulded into jewellery, or maybe deposited in an offshore bank or invested in a Texas oil field. It doesn't matter, people still want the money it generates and there are those who believe they've been cheated out of their fair share. That one robbery caused more grief and suspicion than any other. If I snuffed it, I could guarantee there would be a stampede to dig up every acre of land I own in the search for a nugget or two.'

'Some of it is buried here?' Sly looked incredulous.

'Of course not, you dipstick,' said Billy. 'I'm just saying people would suspect it was. You try losing that much gold, it ain't easy. Remember I told you about those cops and that insurance man wanting to extradite me? That's the sort of attention it brings… and it's not just the authorities.

This mystery has taken on a life of its own – gold or no gold. It's reached the point where people have been shot in their own homes as part of this glorified bloody treasure hunt. I'm telling you, there's animosity and suspicion, hatred and vendettas… people have written fackin' books about it. They call it the 'Brinks Mat Curse' because most of those that had something to do with the original robbery have ended up in prison or, worse, dead. Touch wood. Until now I've stayed under the radar, but things happening lately have made me a bit… let's say, twitchy.'

'You mean Rafa's death and this?' Chuck held out the bullet.

'Yeah,' said Billy, his face becoming animated. 'Look, I've never been a worrier. I've always had decent protection… I can afford it. But when one of your closest "associates" is gunned down outside a Costa Del Sol supermarket in broad daylight and you get tipped off that back home another of your old gang got murdered in a busy London street after walking out of a pub with his bird, you begin to suspect things ain't on the level.'

'Could be a coincidence,' said Chuck. 'The narcotics business is dangerous enough as it is, and I don't suppose any of your dead pals were sitting around twiddling their thumbs. They could have upset someone over something entirely different. People are always bumping each other off over drug deals gone wrong.'

'Ahhh,' said Billy. 'What you can't know, son, is that just about everything is linked back to that one heist. Where did the money come from to pay for all that ecstasy flooding the UK? A few years ago, three blokes were shot dead in a Range Rover down Essex way – I bet you heard about it.'

Both men nodded.

'Brink'sMat related, I'm sure, even though none of them was in the original raiding party,' said Billy.

'I think we get the picture,' said Sly.

'Boys, I'm just telling you this because I want you to be wary of what goes on around you… I need you to be my eyes and ears more than ever, to keep me informed of anything out of the ordinary.'

It was the perfect opportunity for Chuck to mention his suspicions about Lucky and Naomi, but he let it pass. He needed to gather proof otherwise the whole discussion would descend into another row.

'I don't get about much these days what with the high blood pressure and other health problems,' Billy continued. 'You boys do, though. What you hear and see is going to be invaluable to me over the coming months.'

'Sweet,' said Sly. 'Tell us though, Gramps. What was it like being on the original raid?'

'Ahh, I figured you might want to know more,' said Billy. 'It's time to break out another bottle of the best single malt.'

'WE didn't have a clue it was gonna be that much,' said Billy, having told them the full story of the raid. 'Not even close. And we hadn't really prepared for it. When we saw them gold bars all sitting pretty in them boxes, it was too much to take in. Do you know how much all that gold weighs?' His rapt audience shook their heads. 'About three-and-a-half tons,' he said. 'Can you believe that?'

'How did you get it into the getaway vehicles?' asked Sly.

'Vehicles?' Billy the Kid laughed. 'We weren't the army, though we planned it like a military operation. We had a limited budget and one of the boys got his hands on a battered old Transit. When it came to loading it up, we formed a line as if we was doing the fackin' conga and passed them boxes hand to hand into the van. When we drove away the bloody axles were bending under the weight, and we thought there was every chance the old bill would find us sitting on our arses amid this heap of metal at the scene of the crime. Fortunately, it was early morning and there weren't many about or someone would have noticed something dodgy. The van was scraping the floor and making a right old racket and we sat shoulder-to-shoulder in the front in complete silence. I kept looking back, expecting that at any moment the gold would disappear in front of my eyes.'

'Like a dream,' said Chuck.

'Exactly, boy. Like a bloody wonderful dream… the type you don't wanna wake up from. Anyway, we got back to base, transferred the gold from the van and one of the guys then dumped the vehicle – I don't know where to this day. I warned everyone not to flash the cash for a while. We needed to stay quiet until the heat died down. Waste of breath, that was.'

'Why, Billy?' Chuck again.

'Some geezers just love to brag and rub the cozzers' faces in it,' said Billy. 'One even bought a big country house and invested in a pair of Doberman dogs, which he called Brinks and Mat, fackin' idiot. Trouble was, the coppers soon established there was an inside man on the job and worked out he was related to one of the crew. The inside man caved under police pressure and he, his brother-in-law and the bloke with the dogs all ended up eating porridge.'

'What did you do with the net closing in, Gramps?' asked Sly. 'The way you tell it, it sounds like you were the leader.'

'The other lads treated me that way sure,' said Billy, a hint of pride in his voice. 'Probably because I had my head screwed on and wasn't as thick as pig shit. I was planning to make sure I was around long enough to spend my share of the money. I kept my head down and as soon as I got my hands on the first instalment, I knew what I had to do … leave the country.'

WHEN his two grandchildren had retired to bed, pleasantly tipsy from Spanish lager, Billy the Kid Dolan hobbled along to a large wood-panelled room at the back of the house which he called his office. Opening a drawer in the sturdy oak desk at its centre, he pulled a mobile phone from a pile of similar devices, removed the SIM card and inserted a new one which he had taken from his pocket. Picking up an old leather-bound address book, he rifled through it until he came to the letter F. At the top of the page was written the word Factor with a number alongside it. It was an "in joke". Carefully putting the number into the phone, he pressed dial, then let it ring for a short while. Eventually, a familiar voice answered.

'Can't you sleep? Mozzies biting, so you think it's a good idea to get someone else out of bed for company. It's freezing over here you know.'

'Fuck off and listen,' said Billy the Kid. 'You don't dictate where and what time I call you. Remember who put you on that lofty perch... and I could bring you down just as quick.'

'All right… God, can't you take a soddin' joke? I'd say you clambered out of bed the wrong way, but I don't suppose you've been to bed. It's either Salsa night or you've been utilising those nice Spanish brothels, I shouldn't wonder.

Anyway, you know it's always been tit-for-tat. Without my help you would be dining at her majesty's pleasure tonight, not lording it out there. So what's up?'

'The Hackney thing,' said Billy. 'You said it would go away. It hasn't.'

'Fuck me! I can't do everything, you know. I was up to my eyes in Dando until recently. I thought that little nightclub fire would disappear off the radar or, at least, get pinned on the nail bomber… unfortunately, they caught him too soon. I don't give our forensic boys enough credit.'

'So what's the score with this incriminating video evidence I've been told about, eh, Max Factor?' said Billy. 'My acquaintances need to know they're safe… it wouldn't be convenient for your lot to march in and extradite them now. Brink'sMat looks like it's about to raise its ugly head again. Honestly, sometimes I wish…'

'What? That I'd never tipped you off about it? Where would you be now, eh?'

'Living a happy retirement in Chigwell, probably.'

'More like the Scrubs,' said the voice on the phone. 'Look, we're too old in the tooth for regrets. Both our lives could have been completely different if I hadn't shot your boy, y'know? You might not believe this, but it still gives me sleepless nights, and I'm sure my ex-girlfriend feels the same. I hear she still walks with a limp after what your boys did.'

'Don't give me no crocodile tears for some Essex tart you used to shag,' said Billy spitefully. 'If your wife knew, she'd thank me. I did you a favour and you know it. The top brass don't like scandal and if you'd kept her around, you wouldn't be sitting in that nice big office. Am I right, Assistant Commissioner?'

'Are you going senile?' The man on the other end of the line raised his voice in alarm. 'Never say anything that could give someone away, them's the rules. You never know who's listening. Some former colleagues of mine have been prostituting their surveillance skills to the highest bidder recently and every week some poor cunt or other sees their name splashed across that *News of the World* rag. What is it they call that bloke? The Fake Sheik? Cunt! Anyway, when you piss off to play 18 holes on your picturesque golf course just remember that for every scumbag you've helped me put away, I've repaid you in spades… which reminds me. What's happening with the other thing we discussed?'

'It's all a bit… delicate,' said Billy. 'Involves some nasty people. Colombians. We're talking Pablo Escobar-level shit.'

'I never know whether it's fairy tales with you,' said Assistant Commissioner Max 'Factor' Cooper. 'It's as I told you. The Spanish police would be very grateful for any help and for me personally a big international drug bust would push me right to the top of the ladder. Just to make myself entirely clear: do me this favour and I'll make sure the other thing goes away. Can't say fairer than that, can I? How is the golf, by the way?'

'Not bad,' said Billy the Kid. 'Funnily enough, I was thinkin' I might take the grandsons out on the course again in the morning.'

'Hope it pisses down,' said the policeman, chuckling.

28

'BET the food ain't cheap,' said Sly, casting his eyes around the decadent interior of *La Pescar de Noche,* a harbourside restaurant in the picture book town of Vilagracia de Arousa in northern Spain.

'Don't panic, they won't ask us to pay,' said Lucky, leaning over to tap glasses with him before taking a swig of lager. 'Galicia is a bit of a h… hidden jewel, so things might be a bit cheaper than you think.'

'You've been reading that bloody tourist book of yours, ain't you?'

Lucky smiled. 'Guilty as ch… charged. I'm glad the old man sent you with me for my first trip. I'm told this was one of Rafael's regular jobs. I'm sure I'll get used to it but ... you know, Colombian drug dealers seem a bit out of my league. Still, what's not to like about an all-expenses-paid mini break?'

They both looked over their shoulder as a waitress transported a sizzling plate of food to a table across the room.

Sly sat back, looking around at the crab nets, ship anchors and other fishing paraphernalia that decorated the walls. A large swordfish on a shield took centre stage on the stone wall to his right, its beady eye watching the two Englishmen. 'Granddad insists it ain't a holiday,' he said.

'We're here on business. I've been here before. Your predecessor brought us straight from Bilbao on the day our ship docked, but I'm glad the old man now trusts me enough to think I'm up to this kind of thing.'

'I remember watching you drive off. It took me almost t … two bloody days to get to Benidorm. I've never forgiven you.'

'My heart bleeds,' said Sly.

They chuckled, easy in each other's company, the banter between them a sign of the close friendship they had cemented since the Fuengirola shooting ambush.

'Why do you reckon the old man changed his tune and sent you? No offence but he has p… plenty of others capable of doing his dirty work. He doesn't need to send his grandson.'

Sly sat back, a grin tickling the corners of his mouth. 'La Rana asked for me personally, I reckon.'

'He did?'

'He's a she.'

'What?' Lucky sat back, a disbelieving look on his face. 'Oh… oh, I see. You charmer. So she said, what? "Please-ah, senor Billy, send that stud Sly to fuck-ah my b… brains out".'

'Shhhhh! Keep your voice down. Last time I said something similar I nearly lost my bollocks. She grabbed hold of 'em and threatened to wear them as earrings. By the look on her face, she wasn't joking…'

'Bloody hell! Is she hot?'

'Look, this lady ain't no cheap whore, neither is she the kind you find sat at home with her knitting, biding her time before dishing out the family meal. She's, umm, different.

A Colombian cartel boss, for fuck's sake… so be on your guard.'

'Wow, I believe you,' said Lucky, his hands held out defensively in front of him.

'You'll find out soon enough what she's like,' said Sly. 'From the instructions the old man gave us I reckon she'll be here any minute and…' He lowered his voice. 'Yes, she's sizzling!'

Sly looked around to make sure their conversation wasn't being followed by other diners. 'I'm glad granddad picked me, though,' he said. 'Chuck was desperate to make the trip. He doesn't trust me to tie my own shoelaces. Fortunately, the old man was having none of it – insisted my big brother had work to do for the Irish, which pissed him off even more.' He laughed.

'Seriously, though,' said Lucky. 'Aren't you a bit worried? She might decide to finish off what she started.' He nodded in the direction of his friend's groin area.

'To be honest, pal, I'm shitting myself,' said Sly. 'Excited, too. It's weird. You wait til you see her…' He lowered his voice to a whisper again. 'Sex… on… legs.'

At that moment they turned towards the entrance, recognising the faint thud of a car door closing. Immediately, the hubbub of conversation died as all eyes focussed on the restaurant doors. An impeccably dressed Maitre d' stood to attention, ready to welcome the new arrival. Outside, Sly saw a sleek black limousine parked at the kerbside. Two tough-looking men stood either side of the entrance and, as the Maitre d' pulled open the door, she stepped through.

Instantly, the breath was sucked from Sly's mouth, and his lungs tightened, as if squeezed in a vice. Dressed head to toe in a figure-hugging leopard print body suit, La Rana entered the room. Flanked by three bodyguards, one on each side and one behind her, she made her way to their table, expensive ankle boots gliding across the carpet. The two Englishmen stood up.

'Ahh, it seems you have learnt some manners since we last met, Sylvester Dolan,' she said. 'And you must be the one they call Lucky.' She held out her hand and Sly's friend took it.

'My real name is Luke... Luke Chalmers,' he said.

'Yes, I hope you live up to your *mote*, how you say, nickname though. Your predecessor did not have good fortune.'

Lucky nodded. Sly could tell the young south Londoner was nervous. It wouldn't be long before the stammer set in.

'Luke was very lucky for my grandfather,' he said, seeking to diffuse the tension. 'The scum who was responsible for trying to kill Billy would have succeeded if it hadn't been for this man.'

'I have heard the story,' said La Rana. 'It was fortunate you were there at exactly the right time… Sadly for Rafael, maybe a tiny bit late. A pity. I liked him.'

The table fell silent for a moment, thinking about her words. Eventually, she spoke again, her voice an even purr. 'Something like that must make you believe in fate, Mr Sylvester,' she said. 'I hope it will be kind to you on your visit.'

The woman seemed to be talking in riddles, but Sly let it pass.

'Now, we were never properly introduced. I imagine you know me by that idiotic nickname they seem to have given me. My real name is Estella Isabel Sanchez Montoya, but you can call me Stella,' she continued. 'Like that beer you English love so much, no?'

'People call me Sly, rather than Sylvester.'

'OK, Sly, well I have an, umm, proposition for you. Mr Chalmers can join my business partners at the bar to sort out the routine stuff. Ignacio!' One of the burly minders stepped forward. 'Escort Lucky here to the bar and give him our "special" Galician welcome, no? He can order anything he wants from the menu. He will be hungry, I'm sure. It's a long journey.'

The man nodded.

'I… I… think I should stay…'

'It's fine,' said Sly. 'You're not a million miles away. Do as the lady… umm, Stella… asks.'

'Bless him,' said La Rana. 'Do not worry about your friend, Mr Chalmers. I will not be removing his *cajones* today.'

Reluctantly, Lucky rose from his chair and was led to a bar area at the back of the restaurant.

'Now, if you would please stand, Sly, I wish to check you personally for weapons.' Before he knew it one of the other men grabbed him by the arms while La Rana sank down on her haunches in front of him, running her hands up and down his trousers. He could feel every digit of her slender fingers applying pressure, bringing goosebumps to the surface of his skin, his face flushing red in reaction to her touch. Daring to look down, he registered the 2-inch purple nail extensions and tried to think of a distraction to replace the salacious thoughts filling his head. The tactic was doomed to failure as soon as he felt the firm pressure of one of those nails running the length of his manhood, his body reacting despite his determination to keep it under control. It was over in seconds, but he knew he had lost a significant battle of wills.

'OK.' She climbed to her feet, the candle on the table reflecting in her dark brown eyes. He could read neither her feelings nor intentions. 'He is clean, Hugo. Go join your friends.' The second bodyguard released his arms, nodded and walked off in the direction of the bar.

'To business,' said La Rana. 'I am sure you are aware of what our product is, Sly, but to fully appreciate what we do here you need to see it for yourself. The life involves great risks and greater rewards. If we are to have a meaningful relationship in the future, I need to see you have the, ummm, stomach for this type of work.'

She took a seat and indicated he do the same. 'Let's eat,' she said. 'All this talk has made me hungry.'

29

A YOUNG tearaway materialised at the end of the table just as they were finishing their meal and Sly was surprised he hadn't been intercepted by La Rana's men. 'Well, this is an interesting party,' he said in English with the hint of an American accent. 'Am I invited?'

La Rana stood and air-kissed both of his cheeks. 'It is good to see you, Cerdito.'

'And you, Estella… This is the passenger?'

'It is.'

'Passenger?' Sly was confused.

'Ahh,' said La Rana, addressing her comment to the new arrival. 'I haven't told him yet, Cerdito. I didn't want to spoil the surprise.'

The boy chuckled. He looked to be around the age of Sly's brother Arnold, but where these days the younger Dolan had started taking a pride in his appearance, this kid's straggly hair and lived-in face gave him the appearance of a rock star or hippy. On the way into town, Sly had noted many young men and women sitting in groups on the pavement while others slept in doorways or wandered the streets aimlessly. The boy didn't seem far removed from the disaffected youth in these parts. Perhaps he was the Spanish equivalent of Tigger.

A slender hand grasped Sly by the knuckles, interrupting his train of thought. The gesture seemed strangely intimate, considering he and La Rana had known each other for such a short time. 'Sly, this is Cerdito,' she said. 'He has volunteered to take you on a boat trip, a guided tour of Galicia's beautiful rivers and estuaries. Do you know the coast here spans 930 of your English miles? Incredible, yes?'

Sly nodded. On the journey north, Lucky had explained that it was longer than the coasts of Majorca, Ibiza and Menorca put together. The conversation had stuck in Sly's mind because the name Ibiza revived memories of his 18th birthday celebrations when he, Chuck and a couple of mates had enjoyed a wild time on the party island.

'Galicia has wonderful wildlife and a rugged landscape,' La Rana continued, '...and, of course, it is famous for its wine. The climate and rich soil are perfect for growing the Albarino grape. The grapes for this bottle came from my own estate... Try some.' The liquid sparkled under the restaurant lights as she poured it into a wine glass and handed it over.

'Welcome to the Rias Biaxas,' said Cerdito, taking the spare seat at the table and pouring himself a glass. 'It means lower estuaries. There are four of them, including this one, Ria de Arousa. Our relationship with the sea is a close one.'

'Very close,' said La Rana, laughing. 'Cerdito's people are descended from cut-throat pirates, isn't that right, my friend? His ancestors lured ships in from the Atlantic until they ran aground, then boarded them and left the bodies of hundreds of mutilated sailors on the beach before stealing their cargo. It's where the name Costa del Morte came from.'

'If you say so, Estella.' The young man sat playing with his straggly, curling hair, the dandruff perched like sea foam on the crests of his bony shoulders. He wore a designer-label tracksuit and top-of-the-range trainers, but his wealth obviously didn't stretch to grooming products. The boy's nails were caked in dirt and a feint odour of sea and tobacco hung around him.

'Don't be shy, Cerdito,' said La Rana. 'You should be proud of your history. I'm sure Mr Dolan would love to hear how you came about your name... the story is most entertaining.'

The young man took a sip of his wine then leant in Sly's direction; his sharply angled elbows planted on the table.

'My father was a smoke lord,' he said, as if Sly was supposed to know what that meant. 'When the fascist Franco was booted out of power, the arseholes in Madrid left us to rot. Galicia was too far away for them to care about. The people here had no jobs, no money and no government help. All we had was ourselves and our cunning... of course, when I say *we* I mean my father and his friends. I wasn't even born then. To survive they smuggled things across the border from Portugal.'

Sly nodded to show he was paying attention. The kid continued.

'My father tells many funny stories about those days, though I know it was hard for him. One thing they used to bring across was scrap metal, and they did so by turning it into clothing. He would wear waistcoats made out of metal and leg warmers fashioned from tyre rubber. He and his friends must have looked like robots, moving around town in slow motion.'

Sly chuckled. 'Hell, I'd pay to see that!'

'As would I,' said Cerdito. 'On one occasion their bus broke down at the border. The driver could find nothing wrong. He was completely unaware his passengers were carrying 40 kilos worth of car parts, copper, tin and other goods on their bodies.' He took another sip of his wine and looked around the room.

'That was just the start though,' he continued. 'The next thing they moved onto was people. Portugal was at war in Angola and Mozambique, and many of their men wanted to avoid being called up to fight. My father's gang offered them a way out, bringing them into Spain in the belly of empty petrol tankers or in the boot of a car… for a good price, of course. After that, the idea of smuggling cigarettes seemed a ridiculously easy way to make money by comparison. The practice wasn't even illegal, though it cost the Spanish government a fortune in lost taxes. Running one of these cigarette smuggling gangs made you a smoke lord.'

'I'm guessing that led to bigger things,' said Sly.

'My father doesn't approve of drugs,' said Cerdito, leaning across the table with a serious look on his face. 'He felt he was earning enough money running a tobacco clan. He had gained plenty of influential friends – politicians, policemen and the like – and didn't want to spoil a good thing. He even worked with Celso Lorenzo Villa. You know?'

Sly shook his head. 'Never heard of him.'

'Then are you a football man? You must have heard of the team Celta Vigo.'

'Of course,' said Sly.

'Well, Lorenzo Villa was such a successful smuggler he became president of the club, pumping much of his spare cash into it. Because of this connection the team became known as "Marlboro Celta", after the brand of American cigarettes he smuggled. My father says there were always crates of smokes on the team bus from which the players could help themselves. It was hardly the encouragement they needed to perform at the highest level.'

'I guess not,' said Sly, smiling. 'Mind you, I suspect my team West Ham are on 40 a day, the way they're playing.'

Cerdito laughed politely. La Rana, meanwhile, was called away from the table by the big bodyguard, Ignacio. Sly watched nervously as the giant figure bent down to whisper in her ear at the far end of the bar. Cautious not to flag up his concerns to his new acquaintance he asked, 'Cerdito's not your real name then?'

'Oh no,' said the youth, laughing. 'I am Marcos and Cerdito is my nickname. It means, how you say, child pig?'

'Piglet?'

'Si. It is a joke, once again, concerning my father,' he said. 'You see, he was eventually drawn into the world of the white snow…'

'Cocaine.'

'Si. He saw how much money his friends were making and couldn't afford to be left behind. Pretty soon the cash rolled in and he had to, how you say, "wash" the profits?'

'Launder.'

Cerdito nodded. 'Well, to keep his wealth hidden from the authorities he invested in a pig farm. After one successful run the policia were nosing around and he was forced to hide his coke in the sty. Unfortunately, his prize pig wolfed down the entire batch. It must have been on one hell of a trip before it died. When I told this story, somehow I got stuck with the nickname, Little Pig.'

Suddenly there was a commotion at the entrance, a heavy-set woman bursting in, followed by two others. They wore peasant clothes and looked out of place in the grandiose surroundings. The Maitre d' tried to block their path, but the woman used all her strength to barge him out of the way, sending him crashing into a nearby table.

All eyes in the restaurant turned to watch the woman confront La Rana. The cartel boss simply took a step back, allowing Ignacio and Hugo to block the path of the onrushing interloper. 'Asesina! Asesina!' The old woman shouted and immediately the chant was taken up by her companions.

A string of words in a coarse Spanish dialect followed, and Sly looked at Cerdito for an explanation, but he simply shrugged. Before the situation could escalate, though, the doors burst open and four men in the uniform of the Guardia Civil rushed in, grabbing the old woman and her two sidekicks and ushering them towards the door. When they'd finally been removed from the premises, a hubbub of excited conversation filled the void.

'Time we left, too, I think,' said Cerdito.

'Hang on!' said Sly. 'What just happened? Who were they? She actually looked a bit frightened…'

'Who is frightened, Mr Dolan?'

Sly's heart almost stopped. He swivelled quickly, knocking a wine glass to the floor. It shattered, adding to the chaos. La Rana studied him, her anger simmering just below the surface. A silent tension descended on the restaurant. After what seemed an age, Sly saw a hint of amusement flicker across the face of the Cartel boss.

'Sorry, Stella, I didn't mean…'

'Fear is an interesting subject,' she said, the glint returning to her eye. 'It is easy to be brave with words, so now is the time to find out how you react to certain, umm, situations, Sylvester Dolan.'

Without further explanation, she turned and headed for the exit, hypnotising Sly with the sway of her hips.

30

'LUCKY!' he shouted. 'What the hell?' He watched as his friend disappeared along the harbour road, bookended by two of La Rana's men.

The woman herself appeared at his shoulder, the expensive scent giving her away even before she spoke. "Don't worry about your friend,' she said. 'We are simply taking Mr Chalmers to his hotel to continue our business. He will be in the lap of luxury, as you English say. He is indeed a lucky boy, like his name suggests, no? A little insurance, that's all.'

'Insurance for what?' he asked.

'Remember the boat trip we discussed? It's tonight. We didn't want you getting – what is it you English say? – the cold feet.' Her voice had an enigmatic quality laced with an aura of danger. It both petrified and excited him. He turned to face her. Cold, dark eyes bored into his and for a moment there was just the sound of the blustery wind howling through the streets and waves colliding with the harbour wall.

'You've got to be kidding?' His alarmed voice echoed around the quiet seafront, bouncing off the shutters of the closed shops. The police and protesting women had long gone, and Sly estimated it was close to midnight. 'We can't go out in a boat in this! It's blowing a gale and about to rain.'

He felt the first drops hit his face, big splotches announcing the oncoming storm. Studying her flawless ivory skin, prominent cheekbones, tapered eyebrows and full-bodied red lips, he battled to subdue his animal lust, sensing a night of hidden dangers and delights lay tantalisingly within reach. His train of thought was rudely interrupted, though, when his hands were jerked behind his back, handcuffs snapped in place, and a sack pulled roughly over his head.

'Hey!'

'Don't panic, English boy,' she murmured, her breath tickling his ear, her lips so close he could taste them. 'This is just a precaution because we don't want any outsiders getting wind of our, umm, secret places. Bend your head.'

'Look, I'm on your side,' he said. 'No need for fuckin' handcuffs!'

Instead of a reply, his body was propelled down and forwards, the smell of expensive leather invading his nostrils. His ears detected a low rumble as gentle vibrations rippled through his body and he pushed himself into a sitting position, realising he was in the back seat of a car.

'If all goes to plan, I will see you later,' said La Rana, her words accompanied by the gentle clunk of a door closing.

BEFORE he had time to consider his new predicament his body was propelled forward, the acceleration catching his breath, the sensation akin to riding a fairground attraction in a blindfold. Whatever this was about, he would find out soon enough. If only he'd visited the toilet before leaving the restaurant.

'Don't worry, English, I look after you.' Cerdito's voice came from somewhere in front of Sly as he sensed the vehicle twisting through a labyrinth of streets. Nausea rose in his throat and he clamped his mouth shut in an attempt to suppress the sensation. 'Sorry,' said Cerdito. 'I have to drive this way because we don't want to attract any, how you say, Tom peepers.'

'Peeping Toms.' Sly felt the sick sensation slowly receding. 'I would have thought driving at this speed would be a good way of attracting attention. Who are you hoping to avoid?'

'The coastguard, the police, Interpol and any other government agency interested in our business. We have to take precautions.'

'I'm no fan of the Old Bill myself,' said Sly. 'My brother and I had a little disagreement with them back in England. That's why I'm here.'

'So we are, how you say, birds of the same feather?'

'I guess.'

'In that case, let us speak openly. What do you think of Estella?'

Sly wasn't sure how to answer. It could be a trick question. For all he knew she could be sitting silently in the passenger seat, waiting for him to speak out of turn again.

'She can't hear us,' said Cerdito, reading his mind. 'Though I carry out work for her, I am not part of her network, more like what you call the sub-contractor... Look, let me say what we are both thinking. She is a very sexy lady, no?'

Sly weighed up the situation and decided to speak honestly. In the situation he was in, it couldn't hurt to nurture an ally. 'Yes,' he replied.

'Sexy, but very dangerous,' said Cerdito. 'Me, personally, I wouldn't have treated you in this way, you know, the blindfold and restraints, but she is very cautious. There are people who would like to lock her up and enemies that would see her dead, so I understand why she acts this way.'

A question had been nagging at Sly since the evening started. 'La Rana means frog, doesn't it? I heard this story about her rising in the cartels...'

'Who knows if it is true or not? It has served her well though. It prevents people taking liberties.'

'If she is such a force in Colombia, though, why is she here?'

'It is, how you say, a long and complicated story,' said Cerdito.

'We have time, don't we?'

At that moment Sly's companion slammed on the brakes, bringing the sports car to a skidding halt. 'We have arrived,' he said. 'Let's save the bedtime stories for when we are on the boat.'

'THAT'S some machine.'

The high-powered speedboat took pride of place in the vast converted barn. 'She is called *Marion*,' said Cerdito, proudly walking around the 35ft monster.

'Why *Marion*?'

'She is named after Marion Jones, the American sprinter. She is fastest in the world on land, no? This baby is the fastest on water around these parts.'

'I see.'

'Today you are very lucky, my friend, because you get to ride her.'

Sly felt a lump in his throat. He could hear water crashing against rocks nearby, the storm gathering momentum in this wild and windswept place. On arrival, Cerdito had whipped off Sly's blindfold to reveal he was sitting in a bright green Lotus Carlton parked on an exposed area of gravel at the side of a remote farm building. On each side of it, ominous cliffs rose into the black void while a high, chain-link fence topped with razor wire surrounded the compound.

'What—' Sly's question was shut down abruptly as Cerdito put his finger to his lips, staring intently in his direction. The unspoken message was that they were no longer alone. The Spanish smuggler crept over to the big wooden doors and peered out into the darkness, then relaxed and began to heave them aside.

'My team is here,' he announced.

Sly watched as a beaten-up Volkswagen camper van pulled onto the wasteland, its exterior painted in bright, psychedelic colours, like the Mystery Machine from his favourite childhood TV series *Scooby Doo*. The cartoon dog in the title spent each episode trying to get to the bottom of ghostly mysteries. With all the cloak-and-dagger precautions that had gone before, the vehicle seemed garish and out of place in its understated surroundings.

Joining Cerdito outside, he then watched as two men of roughly the same age emerged, dressed in heavy-duty waterproof smocks, oilskin trousers and rubber boots.

'Miguel, Javier... right on time!' Cerdito shouted to make his voice heard above the elements. He hugged each of them in turn.

Javier rattled off a few words in Spanish, looking to the skies.

'Ah, my cautious Javier, when did you ever know of a little drop of rain putting off the greatest speedboat skipper there ever was?' He turned to Sly. 'Javier, Miguel and I have known each other since we were babies. They worry about me, though. No need.'

'So you say,' said Sly. 'It's hardly a brief shower, though, is it? It's raining cats and dogs out here and seems to be getting heavier.'

'We Galicians are used to far worse,' said Cerdito. 'A small storm won't send us crying to our mamas. Now, we have work to do. These boys will help *Marion* into the water.'

SLY'S hair was plastered to his brow, the salty taste filling his mouth as a never-ending stream of water ran in torrents down his face. He ducked his head as another avalanche struck him full on, sending him rocking backwards, his fingers clinging to the slatted wooden seat for dear life. Even though he now wore waterproof clothing, it felt like every inch of him, inside and out, had been marinated in Atlantic seawater. In front of him, Cerdito stood perfectly balanced at the wheel, rocking from side to side with his feet planted firmly on deck in stubborn defiance of the onslaught. Rather than attempting to avoid the tumultuous waves, he seemed to be deliberately heading into them in a foolish demonstration of bravado.

'She's a beauty, no?' he shouted, the words barely discernible amid the squall and the roar of the engine. 'I have 1750 horsepower at my fingertips, six engines, and she can do 75 miles per hour. What's more she holds 20,000 litres of fuel and still has room for 10,000 kilos of *Farina*.'

'Farina?'

'Sorry, you English would say flour. What we really mean is blow or Charlie.'

'Cocaine.'

'*Exactamente.*'

The boat crested another gargantuan wave and Sly fell to the side, losing his grip for a second but quickly re-establishing it before his worst fears were realised. It was like being trapped under a constant waterfall while someone stood 3 feet away, directing a wind machine on overdrive straight into your face. His cheeks shook out of control, as if a giant had reached down and grabbed both sides of his face, pulling and poking them mercilessly.

Sly suspected this might be the kind of punishment you received when the Devil finally got his hands on you after a lifetime of misdemeanours. The noise was deafening; the ferocious thud of aluminium against water, the howling of the wind, the high-pitched roar of the engine bashing out an unrelenting rhythm on his eardrums. Below him, the bodywork grumbled and groaned, and he feared the whole thing was just one giant wave from splitting asunder, sending them to join the vast community of sunken ships lying on the seabed around these parts.

Then, just when he had given up hope of redemption, he saw a dim light in the distance, only for it to disappear as quickly as it came into view. A mirage, he thought, but no, there it was again, and it seemed to be getting nearer with each passing wave.

'*La Madre*!' shouted Cerdito, turning towards him, his excited eyes shining through a face bathed in shadow.

'What?'

'*La Madre* – the mother ship. Our destination. She has travelled all the way from Venezuela to be with us, and she has bought us many presents.'

'Thank God,' Sly mumbled, but Cerdito had turned back and was masterfully negotiating a path through the waves, the dark shape of a sea-going tanker gradually materialising through the mist.

31

SMALL packages rained down on them, Cerdito catching them expertly and transferring them into the hold. 'Each of these bales is worth around a million!' said the speedboat driver as he kept up a running commentary to his passenger.

'A million pounds?'

'Jesus, no.' He chuckled. 'I mean pesetas. I don't know the equivalent in your British money, but it is worth around 15,000 American dollars.'

'Still a lot of dosh,' said Sly as he moved forward to help, at last trusting his legs to keep him upright on the rocking boat, which was now moored to the side of the bigger vessel and shielded from the worst of the tempest.

'Yes. The percentage split is usually 70 to La Rana and 30 to us though she tends to favour us more when the weather is bad... which perhaps explains to you why I do this.'

'Not a bad pay day,' agreed Sly, thinking there were easier ways to make a living. He suspected Cerdito was a pure adrenaline junkie, getting his kicks from playing Russian roulette with Mother Nature. 'You were going to tell me about how Estella came to be here and how all this got started.'

'Ah yes.' Cerdito effortlessly continued transferring the packages as he spoke. 'Some time ago one of the Galician cigarette smugglers, a friend of my father's named Paredes, went to Panama with the intention of returning with clean money. While he was there, he met some Colombians living in exile. You know Escobar?'

'Pablo Escobar? Who doesn't! He's the most famous drug lord ever.'

'Si,' said Cerdito. 'Well, Escobar had the Minister for Justice killed in Colombia, and the cartels moved out of the country to avoid repercussions. Panama was a perfect place to regroup and carry on their business. They were looking for a way to expand into Europe and Paredes appeared to offer the solution. When he returned to Galicia, he brought with him a South American girlfriend.'

'Estella.'

'Si.'

Something was puzzling Sly. 'So what happened to Paredes?'

'Ahhh, he upset some of the other head honchos in the cartel. A shipment went wrong, and he was caught and sent to Carabanchel, the prison in Madrid. The cartel lost lots of money due to the failure of the mission and sent an assassin to shoot down Paredes on his release.'

'So he's dead?'

'No, but he lives now permanently in a wheelchair.'

A memory flashed through Sly's head. The day Rafael had driven them through the gates of La Rana's mansion a well-dressed man in a wheelchair had been among the welcoming party. At the time, they thought he was the cartel boss. 'I've seen him,' said Sly.

'Si, but he is no longer a full man, *comprende*?'

'I think so. His cock and balls don't function.'

'I think I would prefer to die.'

'Indeed.'

Above them, the constant stream of packages had been interrupted. One of the ship's crew shouted something from above, and Cerdito issued a short, sharp reply. 'Good,' he said. 'We can go home.'

'How much coke do we have here?' asked Sly, helping to drag a heavy tarpaulin over the illicit product.

'About 2,500 kilos if my calculations are right.' Sly whistled. 'A nice pay day, no?' said Cerdito.

'At least the weather is improving,' said Sly, looking to the skies. The rain was falling lightly now and the wind dying down. Above them, the clouds were starting to clear.

'A good thing and a bad thing,' said Cerdito. 'Good, because it shouldn't be such a bumpy ride, bad because it means the customs boys will be out on patrol.'

There was a rumble as the speedboat's engine burst into life again and they pulled away from the mother ship, setting course for home at a far more sedate pace. Despite the rapid improvement in the weather, Sly sat in the back of the boat shivering, icy tentacles reaching deep inside him and clawing at his internal organs. He had never felt so cold.

'Here, drink this,' said Cerdito on cue, handing him a hip flask. He could smell the strength of the liquor just by unscrewing the top but was prepared to try anything to ease his discomfort. Taking a long slug, he immediately felt a burning sensation as the liquid hit the back of his throat.

'Christ!'

'Is good, no?'

'Si,' he agreed, making use of his limited Spanish. It only seemed polite when he considered Cerdito's sharp grasp of English. 'What is it?'

'It is dark rum, like all the good pirates drink.' He laughed. 'Now, do you want to know the rest of La Rana's story?'

'Of course,' said Sly.

'Paredes married La Rana in a small ceremony in Vigo just before he was imprisoned, and they kept the wedding a secret. When he was shot, she wasn't so much devastated as angry. She took the cartel's actions as a personal slight, furious someone so callous could rob her of the chance to have children. Her being a woman, they underestimated her.'

'What could she do? They are pretty powerful.'

'Quite a lot, as it happens. As Paredes recovered, Estella returned to Panama where she still had a lot of allies. She used every weapon at her disposal to assemble a small army while keeping up the pretence of a broken woman reeling from the brutal attack on her husband. No one suspected she might be plotting against them until it was too late. The exact story of her revenge is shrouded in mystery, but when she returned to Spain, she was a leader in her own right. A few Galician clan bosses had their noses put out of joint at a woman muscling in on their business, but they soon learned that challenging her was foolhardy.'

'I can see why you wouldn't want to get on her wrong side,' said Sly. 'Who were the old women in the restaurant, though? They didn't look remotely intimidated.'

'Ahh,' said Cerdito. 'They are the Mothers Against Drugs. You have seen the junkies on the streets in town? It is a consequence of building your economy around smuggling and narcotics. The woman you saw shout at Estella is Maria Dolores. Her son died from a drug overdose. She kicked him out of the house after he stole from her, and he was found dead in a shop doorway 24 hours later. When you have nothing left to lose you are a dangerous opponent. Maria blames Estella, calling her 'Asesina' – "The Assassin". The Mothers accuse her of profiting from the corpses of dead children – 53 last year alone – and scenes like today are meant to awaken the authorities. Those women won't enter half the shops in the town because they are funded from the proceeds of drug money. Mind you, it works both ways. Vilagracia wouldn't have half the amenities it does without the smugglers.'

'Do the deaths not bother you, Cerdito?'

'Of course,' replied the speedboat skipper. 'Some of those street kids went to school with me. Javier, who helped us prepare the boat, had to watch his brother die. But you must make a living somehow and if I wasn't doing this someone else would. I have been around boats since the age of eight. It is my talent and I love it. You could even say it is my drug. Yes, perhaps one day it will kill me, too, but I refuse to scrabble around for a living doing shitty jobs others refuse to touch. I want the good life now because one wrong turn and I could be on the street myself.'

Sly could relate to Cerdito's sentiments. Plenty of kids from his school had ended up trapped in the straitjacket of drug addiction. He guessed they weren't a great deal different, both involved in lifelong battles for survival, and both determined to emerge on the winning side.

'Newspapers and TV have a lot of time for the Mothers,' said Cerdito. 'That is why Estella is so careful about how she acts around them. She isn't stupid. She knows unwanted attention is bad for business, so she lets them get on with it, while behind the scenes she wins favour with local businesses, politicians and certain police officials with her generosity.'

'She buys them off, you mean. Clever. Do these mothers follow her around all the time?' asked Sly. 'I mean, they seemed to know exactly where she was going to be tonight and at what time.'

'La Rana will be aware of this and will try to discover who tipped them off. Shit…'

'What's the matter?' asked Sly.

'We have company.'

A burst of acceleration deposited Sly back into his seat with incredible force, the wooden slats smashing into his back. Holding on for dear life, he was deafened by the roar of the engine, while spray hammered into him from every direction and he was soon drenched to saturation point again. Each time the boat rose to breast another wave he caught sight of a flickering light in the distance.

'Hold tight!' shouted Cerdito, his clenched fist waving in Sly's direction to emphasise his words. Suddenly, the boat swivelled in an arc and set off at breakneck speed towards a barrier of cliffs rising up in the distance. Within seconds the speedboat skipper had expertly manoeuvred his vessel between two rocky outcrops into a tributary, which had been invisible moments earlier. The pungent aroma of gasoline was so thick Sly could taste it, bile burning his throat. He leant forward and vomited onto the deck. Last night's seafood returned to the ocean as water sloshed about in the bottom of the boat.

Lifting his head enough to look back out to sea, Sly got his first glimpse of their pursuers, a high-speed schooner now turning into the same stretch of water, lights flashing. Looking to his right he realised with alarm that the waterway contained obstacles at first invisible to the naked eye. Cerdito remained totally unfazed though, zigzagging around partially sunken rocks with effortless ease. Though the customs boat appeared to be closing the gap, the smuggler seemed surprisingly relaxed, despite the vast amount of cocaine concealed under the tarpaulin which could net both of them a heavy prison sentence.

A crackling voice broke the early morning air and though Sly had no idea what it was saying, he guessed they were being ordered to pull over. Cerdito's response was to turn the boat sharply to the left into an even smaller tributary, rocks closing in on both sides. One small error now and Sly knew his life was over. He held his breath and shut his eyes, saying a silent prayer that this was a dream and that when he awoke, he would be in bed at the villa, Naomi's warm body curled up by his side. Instead, what he saw as he prized open his eyelids was a sheer rock face looming in front of them, so close that a collision seemed inevitable.

32

'FUCK ME!' he shouted, bracing himself for impact just as the vessel's nose rose out of the water and it performed the boating equivalent of a motorcycle wheelie. Petrified he might fall from the back and get churned up by the propellers, Sly wedged his foot under a piece of sturdy metal and gripped the struts of the bench with both hands, his eyes shut in silent prayer.

The impact didn't come.

Instead, he felt himself spinning, spinning, spinning like an abandoned sock in a supercharged tumble dryer. Squeezing open an eye with trepidation, his vision was obscured by water as the boat completed a 180-degree pirouette and crashed back down. As soon as it was horizontal, Cerdito gunned the engine again, and it roared back in the direction from which it had come, the faces of those on the now-stationary customs schooner frozen in shock as their target shot past at top speed. Sly found himself laughing maniacally as he saw *Marion's* swell drench law enforcement officers too hypnotised by the powerboat's daring escape to react and take cover.

'Let's go home,' said Cerdito and, despite the fact Sly was the only other person on board, he found himself enthusiastically applauding the skills of his young accomplice. Looking back, the customs boat was no longer visible.

MIGUEL and his small band of stevedores took just 30 minutes to unload the valuable cargo once Cerdito had guided the boat into a small, well-hidden inlet. Sly watched the military style operation with fascination as men formed a line and passed bales of cocaine hand to hand into the back of a waiting truck. Light was slowly breaking through the dark clouds above and though it had been a long night, Sly felt elated rather than weary, adrenaline still coursing through his veins.

Cerdito offered him a cigarette and though he'd been the one Dolan boy to resist the lure of tobacco until now, he took it eagerly and welcomed the smoke into his lungs, an immediate calming effect passing through him. Where before he had feared the health risks associated with the habit, at that moment he felt invincible. He had stared down death and come out the other side.

Their shared experience made Sly feel close to Cerdito now. He watched with admiration as the powerboat driver stubbed out his cigarette and walked off to supervise the finishing touches of the operation. When everything was in order, he banged three times on the metal shutter of the van with his palm and the vehicle rumbled into life, moving smoothly off up the hill in the gloom and fog.

'They drive without lights?' Sly said, as Cerdito returned.

'The drivers know every inch of these roads,' replied the Galician. 'The success of tonight's operation depends on them and they know they face heavy prison sentences if they are stopped and the van searched. My friend Javier is the best driver, but his father is very unwell so he took the night off and left it to one of the other men.'

'Dangerous business.'

'Yes, but most of the drivers have been doing it for years now and know every trick in the book. Miguel and Javier, they have been with me from the start.'

Their conversation was interrupted by the low growl of a car engine. 'Ahhh, it seems we have, how you say, the royal visit,' said Cerdito.

Sly watched a dazzling blue sports car wind its way down the mountain road and pull into the gravel area just above where they were standing. Moments later Estella Isabel Sanchez Montoya was heading down the path towards them. 'Good trip, boys?' she asked, removing a pair of black driving gloves and placing them with the Lady Dior handbag in her right hand.

'OK,' said Cerdito. 'There was a problem – customs – but nothing I couldn't handle.'

'And how about Sylvester here?'

'A natural.'

'I wouldn't say that,' said Sly, looking slightly embarrassed as he took in every inch of the woman in front of them. She wore a thick three-quarter length fur coat and black stiletto heels, which seemed totally inappropriate considering the rough terrain. Her expensive ensemble put his clothes in bleak perspective. The borrowed oilskins reeked of the sea from spending the best part of five hours being tossed about like chip shop leftovers in a refuse lorry.

'Well done, Mr Dolan,' she said. 'You have passed my little "test". Your efforts deserve a reward. It would please me, however, if you would remove that stinking fisherman's uniform.'

He thought for a moment she wanted him to strip in front of her, but she produced a sack from behind her back and threw it in his direction. 'Fresh clothes,' she said. 'I believe they are your size. I can't have you soiling the seats of the Porsche. Now, I suggest you find somewhere more private to put them on.'

Twenty minutes later he was strapped into the passenger seat of a 911 Carrera Turbo as La Rana expertly negotiated a maze of country roads. She barely dropped her speed below 50 but handled the sports car like a pro. Having been buffeted around on the high seas for hours he expected to be drained but actually felt alert and excited to be in this charismatic woman's presence.

'You've scrubbed up nicely, but it would be good to get a shower, no?'

He looked down at the borrowed jeans and sweatshirt and nodded. 'Yeah. Are we going to the hotel?'

'Sorry, no – a change of plan.'

The words sent a flutter through his nervous system. Hadn't he done everything she demanded? He had risked his life on that speedboat, not to mention his liberty, and now she was playing games with him. He locked eyes with her in the mirror, but she had the same enigmatic expression as ever, giving away no clues as to what would happen next. He had no choice but to sink back into his seat and stare out of the window, watching the Ria Arousa wind its way through the valley below.

Five minutes later they passed through the imposing gates of La Rana's mansion and pulled to a halt in front of the opulent building. Unhooking her seat belt, she then grabbed her handbag from the backrest and climbed out. 'Come on,' she said, looking back into the car where he sat, confused and uneasy. 'I need a drink and I suspect you would like one, too.'

Without waiting, she strode through the entrance, stopping briefly to whisper into the ear of one of the bodyguards. He responded by rushing across and opening the passenger door for Sly. He climbed out and the man waved his hand, instructing him to follow in the footsteps of his boss. Sly was starting to feel like a pet poodle being taken for walkies on the instruction of its owner. When he entered the house, he saw her halfway up the winding marble staircase and suddenly felt a crisis of confidence sweep through him. Was he supposed to follow? What was the etiquette in this situation?

Stopping halfway up, she looked over her left shoulder and inclined her head in his direction. She wanted him to follow. As the knot of tension twisted in his stomach he headed for the stairs and, once at the top, stared down from the circular balcony, realising just a wooden rail separated him from a 20ft drop. It would be easy to engineer a fatal accident here, plying an unsuspecting visitor with drink then pushing them and watching them tumble to their death. Perhaps he'd seen too many horror films in his youth, a scene from *The Omen* springing vividly to mind, the point where the devil child inflicts a similar punishment on his nanny. Refocussing his mind, a worm of apprehension wriggled through him. Where was his host?

Seeing a door to his right was slightly ajar, he approached with trepidation, noting his hand was visibly shaking as he raised his fist to knock.

'Come.'

The order came before he had made contact. Sly pushed the door open and a large room stretched out before him, its walls, curtains and furniture all a brilliant white. The impact was so unexpectedly dazzling he had to raise a hand to shield his eyes. Finally, when his vision adjusted, he took in an elegant chaise longue, a plush sofa and elaborate silk drapes. To his left, a couple of expensive looking paintings hung from the wall, and, to his right, he could see a huge four-poster bed through a set of partially open double doors. On a table along the far wall of the bedroom stood a large glass tank, and he wondered if the woman owned tropical fish.

When he noticed something pooled on the floor, his breath caught in his throat, the blood rushed to his head and his legs almost buckled beneath him. He thought for a moment he might be hallucinating and wondered if it was the after-effects of being in proximity to such a large haul of drugs. Slowly, he collected his thoughts and brought his racing mind under control. Then he looked again at the item blocking his route across the threshold. There was no mistake.

It was the fur coat.

Raising his eyes slowly he was instantly intoxicated by the sight of light bouncing off Estella Isabel Sanchez Montoya's smooth skin as, now dressed only in sheer black lingerie, she moved her body in time to an imaginary soundtrack.

33

SLY woke in a disorientated state, his vision hazy. It was as if he had been drugged. He recalled snorting coke from La Rana's smooth stomach but was pretty sure his state of mind wasn't the by-product of overindulging in recreational stimulants. He imagined this was how you might feel if your drink had been spiked with a date rape drug. Then again, if that was the case, he was pretty sure he wouldn't remember anything. On the contrary, he had a clear recollection of every salacious detail of his sexual encounter with Spain's most dangerous woman.

Rolling onto his stomach, he groaned from the aches and pains he'd accumulated during the previous night and wondered where she'd gone, this dark and deadly goddess. It was still almost impossible to believe the events had taken place. He'd enjoyed his fair share of sexual conquests during his relatively short life, but in this instance it was he who had been conquered, truly and utterly.

His mouth dry, he turned in search of a glass of water and leapt from the bed as he registered two beady eyes watching him intently. He'd thought he was alone, but evidently that wasn't the case. The other occupant of the room was peering at him through a nest of leaves in the glass tank by the bed. It measured barely 5cms, was coloured a dazzling yellow and, while it appeared harmless and friendly, Sly knew appearances could be deceptive. This had to be the golden poison frog Rafael had told them all about – one of the deadliest creatures on the planet.

'Ahhh, you've met Pablo.'

He moved quickly to cover his nakedness, feeling insecure and vulnerable as he realised La Rana was coolly appraising him from the end of the bed. 'He is beautiful, no? The greatest living treasure of my country. Somewhere in among all that greenery is Escobar as well. They are remarkable creatures… an inspiration. They taught me that whatever size you are, however you might appear to people, you are capable of delivering so much more. Do you know there is enough poison on Pablo's skin to kill two male African elephants? I think you English call it, "Punching more than your weight".'

Above your weight, thought Sly, but he said nothing, aware that correcting anything the cartel boss said was likely to be bad for his health. He watched as she stepped forward to make a closer inspection of her exotic pets. 'Now,' she said, tapping the glass. 'The maid is bringing coffee, the best Colombian variety, which should wake you up to the new day after the, umm, exertions of last night. Then you must dress. We have to conclude our business. I am sure you would like to get it out of the way as much as I do.'

'I thought Lucky—'

'Yes, well he will be there too, of course.'

As she turned to leave the room, Sly tried to commit every contour of her body to memory, pretty certain he would never get the opportunity to sleep with her again. She had virtually told him as much on inviting him to her bed the night before. Reliving that moment in his head, he felt an instant reaction in his groin region.

'You want me, yes?' she had said, matter of fact, as she stood with her back to him, the fur coat on the floor between them.

'Yes,' he had replied.

'Then I am yours, but only this one time.'

Slowly she had turned, permitting him to take in the magnificent sight – her body like a sculpture's work of art, partially hidden behind flimsy silk; curves and undulations visible through the fabric, hinting at the delights beneath.

Reaching out her hand, she had led him to the en suite shower room and instructed him to wash from head to toe and use the toiletries on offer, including an expensive brand of men's aftershave. He'd wondered briefly what she was doing with male grooming products in her personal washroom, then remembered the story he had been told about her husband. What if this was an elaborate game they played? Perhaps they had established a routine to spice up their relationship whereby she invited men to her bedroom, and he burst in with his bodyguards to drag La Rana's latest lover naked to a torture chamber down the hall.

This was the disturbing thought playing on his mind when he stepped out of the bathroom into her steely embrace, the woman's nails digging so deeply into his back that he felt rivulets of blood trickle between his shoulder blades. She bit him hard on the lip, her tongue darting in and out of his mouth.

'You know why you're here?' she had whispered, pulling away sharply then planting her hand between his legs, the slender fingers wrapping themselves around him while those long nails drew intricate patterns in tender places. Then, as if she had climbed inside his head at that moment and read his thoughts, she abruptly let go and pulled him into the bedroom.

'My husband cannot give me what I want,' she said. 'He was shot by our enemies, and now he does not function in the bedroom. This is why you are here.'

Looking directly into her eyes, Sly tried to read the woman's thoughts but was unable to see through the tinted windows to her soul. Confronted by his own reflection, he opted to remain silent.

'I sent you out on that boat to find out what sort of man you are,' she continued. 'From your previous visit it was obvious you wanted to bed me, but I only look for a certain type – the type of man who will walk blindly into the face of danger. You proved to me you have that level of courage. So what do you think?'

It was a strange question. He hadn't really thought anything past what he intended to do with this dangerous, beautiful woman.

'I don't understand,' he said. 'Are you offering me a job?'

She laughed, throwing her head back wildly, her long neck stretched out enticingly in front of him. 'A job, hmmm,' she said after subduing her mirth. 'What sort of job would you like, Mr Dolan? Drug runner? Personal driver? Assassin?'

When he failed to respond, she answered her own question. 'Far easier than any of those tasks, Mr Dolan. Your job is to put a baby inside me.'

WHEN the coffee arrived, he raised the cup to his lips, then promptly put it back down when he saw two sets of amphibian eyes focussed on him. How easy would it be for La Rana to introduce the tiniest trace of frog poison to his morning drink now she had what she wanted?

There was a knock at the door, and he went across to open it. Ignacio the bodyguard stood there, a pile of folded clothes in his arms. Without speaking, he handed them over and departed. The vest and shorts both had the names of well-known brands stamped on them and there was a pair of open-toed plastic sandals you could wear without socks. It took him a few moments to change before surveying himself in the shower room's full-length mirror. Everything fitted perfectly, as if she had been able to gauge his exact size from one night in his company. Returning to the glass tank, he paraded in front of the frogs. 'What do you reckon, boys?'

'It will do.'

Jesus, if the woman could sneak around this quietly, it was no wonder she had earned her deadly reputation.

'Thanks,' he said, turning to look at La Rana. 'For the clothes, I mean.'

She brushed his gratitude aside. 'Come! We will be late.'

'Lunch?'

'For some,' she said strangely.

She led him down the stairs, and two bodyguards joined them when they reached the ground floor. Turning towards the back of the building, they passed through a set of glass doors and out into a garden, the sun now shining where hours before the sky had been overcast and full of rain.

The garden was awash with colour, and he smelt a variety of different scents as they followed a path between the bushes. Eventually, it opened up into a large, rectangular paved area with a pond at its centre, the water teeming with algae. Underneath the surface he could see the faint outline of fish weaving gentle patterns through the reeds. Ahead of him, La Rana waved her hands around, issuing instructions to the guards, who walked away to do her bidding. 'Nice,' he said. 'Lunch on the terrace.'

'Yes,' she said. 'Take a seat. The others will be here shortly.'

Six or seven chairs were lined up along one side of a long table, shaded beneath a parasol. It was a strange layout not particularly conducive to conversation, but he thought nothing more of it as Ignacio guided him to his seat. Hearing a rustle from the pathway, he turned and was delighted to see a familiar face. Lucky marched in confidently, smiling a greeting and taking the seat next to him. He put a reassuring arm around his friend's shoulders. 'You OK?' asked Sly's partner-in-crime.

'Never better.'

'I thought you were going to join me at the hotel. I couldn't sleep. I kept looking out of the window expecting to see you arrive at any minute.'

'I didn't get a lot of sleep either.' Sly had a brief flashback, La Rana standing over him in stockings and heels, her foot pressed against his bare chest. Not all his bruises had come from the speedboat adventure. Before he could elaborate, there were more footsteps, and this time Cerdito joined the party. He looked haggard, his chin hidden beneath dark stubble and rivulets of red running through the corneas of his eyes.

'You OK, mate?' Sly asked as the speedboat driver sat down, his friend Miguel taking the seat next to him. They both looked confused and unwell, nodding silently at their fellow guests. It was a strange reaction, considering the experience Sly and Cerdito had shared the night before. Perhaps they were still shattered from the drug run or merely playing it cool.

Satisfied there would be no late arrivals, La Rana clicked her fingers and Sly expected servants to materialise with trays piled high with cold meats, cheeses and bakery products. Instead, from a pathway on the other side of the pond, a new party arrived. Two guards led the way, followed by another pair carrying a wooden cross between them, as if some obscure religious ceremony was about to take place.

The body attached to the cross was no statue. The figure was male but unrecognisable to Sly, the eyes hidden behind swollen and discoloured flesh, the mouth toothless and stained red with blood, the hair sporadically grouped in dark clumps, red blotches filling the gaps where sections had been torn out.

He knew the unfortunate soul was male because he had been stripped naked, rivulets of blood running indiscriminately down the body. The torso and legs were covered in dark marks and even from a distance away Sly could tell someone had been to work with lighted cigarettes. For a moment he held onto the hope that the poor unfortunate creature was dead, but this notion was quickly disabused when La Rana walked around the poolside and grabbed the prisoner by the face. A guttural cough emerged, more blood flowing over the lips, the head barely able to move of its own accord. 'You see what happens?' she said, looking at the crucified man but addressing her question to the horrified spectators. 'This is the result if you mess with me and put my operation and everyone who works with me in danger.'

She turned to face them. 'This man has been feeding information to the authorities. He confessed as much last night to my associates. Because of his lack of loyalty, you, Mr Dolan, and you, Mr Sotalongo, could be facing a long stretch in prison. As for me? Well, had he succeeded then all this,' she indicated the mansion and its grounds with her free hand, '...would be fatally compromised.'

She stopped talking long enough to let her words sink in. When she had looked each of them in the eye individually, she continued. 'You all need to know that this is what Estella does to traitors who endanger us and our freedoms.'

Sly was under no illusions. She was warning them they could expect similar treatment if ever they had the audacity to cross her. He looked towards the Spanish speedboat skipper, hoping to detect some kind of mutual acknowledgement that once again they were in the same boat. What Sly saw shocked him – this was no longer the devil-may-care character he'd shared an adventure with last night. Pain and hatred were etched in every crevasse of Cerdito's face and he noticed a solitary tear escape from the corner of one blue eye and travel down to settle on quivering lips. Next to Cerdito, his friend Miguel whispered one word that carried to Sly on the morning breeze.

'Javier.'

IT took Sly a moment to register where he had heard the name before. Then he twigged. Javier was the third member of the triumvirate, the school friends who had stuck together through thick and thin and set up a little drug smuggling operation off the Galician Coast. Javier, alongside Miguel, had helped prepare the speedboat *Marion* for Sly and Cerdito's daring ocean adventure. Cerdito spoke of him with warmth and admiration, an outstanding driver who could negotiate the winding roads of this remote region of northern Spain without headlights, even on the darkest night. Not last night, though. Last night Javier had missed the delivery, prioritising his sick father ahead of his lucrative business commitments. Or were more sinister forces at play?

Stripped of all looks, personality and dignity, the Javier Sly saw now was a mere husk of humanity. Only the occasional flicker of an eyelash or a bloody air bubble escaping the mouth gave testament to the fact he clung to life by his fingernails. La Rana was on her haunches in front of the prisoner, prompting an unbidden flashback in Sly's mind; the thin line between pleasure and pain.

Sunlight reflected off steel, and Sly saw a long knife nestling in the elegant fingers of the Colombian cartel boss. With one swift movement, she drew it from one side to the other, the impact on her victim hidden by her crouching body. Eventually she rose, moving to one side so that Sly and his fellow voyeurs could admire her handiwork. Sly reflexively moved a hand to his lap in response to the sight of blood dripping from the boy's manhood, then turned to see Lucky throw up in some bushes.

Bitch.

Had he really made love to this woman, fallen for her abundant charms and responded to her every demand? And how soon would she tire of using him as her toy and treat Sly with the same dispassionate disregard as her current plaything? He tried to look away from the macabre horror show, but morbid fascination compelled him to stick with it, reminding him of his childhood when he would watch scary scenes on TV through the gaps in his fingers.

La Rana walked towards them, pausing briefly to issue further instructions to her men. Cerdito stood, pain etched in every crag of his weather-beaten face. Sly could only pick up bits and pieces of Spanish, but was able to understand the gist of what the Galician was saying. 'Why?' he was demanding of the Cartel boss. 'Why you do this to my friend? He is a loyal *soldato*.'

'Si?' La Rana stared down her inquisitor. 'This is not what my informants at the Guardia tell me. This *puta* informs of our movements yesterday, bringing those women from hell to insult me at the restaurant and telling the policia of our operation out at sea, the one that nearly landed you and Mr Dolan in prison. This is your loyal *soldato* – your "friend".'

She spat the last word as if it left a horrible taste in her mouth.

'There is a mistake!' urged Cerdito. 'Let me talk to him.'

'Talking is finished. He has told my men all they need to know. This piece of shit must learn what the consequences are when you rat on your amigos. *Continuar*!'

With no regard to their victim's delicate state, two burly men in black tuxedos grabbed the cross while, through another gap in the foliage, two other dark suited foot soldiers emerged, carrying a wooden pontoon with a hole in its centre. Sly watched as they positioned it on the pond then lowered the cross onto it, their victim face down, the hole lining up perfectly with the young man's genitals. Then one of the guards carelessly kicked the pontoon from the bank and it floated slowly into the centre of the pond.

The next few seconds would live in Sly's mind forever. At first sporadic bubbles broke the surface, followed by a few splashes as a large number of dark shapes converged on the pontoon. As they disappeared underneath it, the silence was so pronounced that Sly could hear his heartbeat in his ears.

The shriek when it came pierced right through to his soul, forcing Sly to question whether human vocal cords were capable of such an ungodly sound. He watched the pontoon toss and twist on water now bubbling as if the pond was a saucepan abandoned on the highest heat setting. As the scream wore thin, he watched aghast as the body lifted momentarily, the head turning in their direction, a few anguished words escaping through the toothless mouth. Finally, giving up the fight, the victim slumped back down, resigned to his horrific fate.

Sly glanced over at Cerdito and mouthed the question, 'What did he say?'

The Spaniard wiped away the tears flowing freely down his cheeks. '*Matame ya*,' he mumbled. 'It means "Kill me now".'

34

'EXPLAIN to me, clever clogs, why trouble has come knocking at my door?'

Philippa Lee stood against the washing machine in the utility room, hands on her waist, giving her husband the cold stare. Geoff could only shrug.

'What am I supposed to do, Treacle, turn him away? Family ain't he?'

'Yeah, and he's caused you nothin' but grief,' said Philippa, pointing a finger aggressively in his direction. 'You know it, I know it. I don't want you throwing all this away, but I know the influence he has on you. Hell, you've told me enough times about how every time you got into a scrape it was down to him. This better not be an attempt to reunite the Glorious Lee brothers, I warn you.'

'What are you rabbiting on about, love? That was all a long time ago.'

Biting her lip, she grabbed the basket of washing, turned and headed out of the door. He felt the heat rush in to fill the void; another muggy day in paradise. Geoff Lee couldn't argue with a word his wife had said. Every poor decision he had made during his time growing up in London could be laid firmly at Arthur's door. It was only when his older brother was sent down that Geoff had wriggled out from under his wing and flown the family nest.

'Everythin' all right in there?'

Speak of the devil. Geoff left the utility room and walked through the open-plan kitchen to the spacious lounge. Arthur was sprawled out over the four-seat cream leather sofa, looking like a giant in a doll's house, his long legs stretched out in front of him, his head resting against a scatter cushion depicting a bull fight.

'There he is!' he said, a big grin spreading across his face. 'Let's have a proper look at yer, G, son. Bloody hell, I can tell from that fackin' belly life's been treating you well. You were all skin and bones back in the smoke.'

'Things change, don't they, Arthur? That was a long, long time ago. Business has been OK and the lifestyle here moves at a slower pace. Anyway, we couldn't have been poorer as kids, could we? We were hardly getting three square—'

'Too right. Not our mum's fault, though.'

Both men turned at the sound of footsteps padding down the wooden staircase outside. The door opened and Abby entered the room, dressed in frayed white shorts and a tie-dye purple and gold T-shirt.

'Well, well, well… if it ain't little Abigail,' said Arthur. 'Ain't so little now, are ya? Shit the bed, I remember when you was just a nipper. Let your uncle take a proper look at you. Wow! All grown up and everything.'

'Yeah, well, there are good reasons you haven't seen her,' said Geoff, unable to keep the edge from his voice. 'I'll be surprised if she remembers you at all… it's not like she's been inundated with birthday cards or Christmas presents from you to remind her of her loving "uncle".'

'Don't listen to him, girl,' said Arthur, his dark, impenetrable eyes locking on hers. 'I sent 'em, honest, love, but who knows what the Spanish postal service is like. Thieving bastards over here, I expect. Anyway, it's me who should be moaning. My brother seems to think he was born to a higher calling than the rest of his family. You'd think he'd have a better memory of how I helped him down the years, but not a phone call, a postcard, nothin'. Still, don't worry, babe, I can appreciate when I'm not wanted. This is just a flying visit… I'm out here to see my girl. A little bird tells me you've got yourself a young, fit lad… is that kosher?'

'Dad!'

'Sorry, sugar, I don't know how he heard about Chuck, honest. It wasn't from me. Perhaps your mother—' His words fizzled out as he realised he was about to dig a deeper hole for himself. Whoever had told him about her private life, Abby couldn't dispute her uncle's words. Chuck was certainly fit. They'd just spent a splendid week together, barely able to keep their hands off each other having been apart for four tortuous months. She'd been forced to go back to London after the Millennium celebrations due to work commitments but had returned to Spain over the Easter holidays and Chuck had travelled down to Marbella to be with her. They'd stayed in his grandfather's villa off the Golden Mile, and it had been bliss. No parents to tell them what to do or older relatives to order Chuck about. Now she couldn't wait to be with him again and was planning a surprise trip to Torrevieja in the next few days. She knew he had some work lined up with the Irishman, but would be happy to wait around for him while taking the opportunity to top up her tan.

'Londoner, ain't he?' said Arthur. 'Anyone I know?'

'I hope not.' She smiled, meaning every word but trying to disguise her response as a joke.

'Aww, don't be cruel to your uncle when I ain't seen you in ages.'

Something about his forensic gaze made her feel as if tiny bugs were travelling up and down her spine. Subconsciously, she folded her arms across her chest. 'Well, you're not my uncle are you? Not really. And I'm not sure there is such a thing as a step uncle. My love life's none of your business.'

'Abby!' Her stepfather's eyes flashed a warning. She didn't think he was cross with her, though, just trying to be diplomatic. Over the years, she had gained the impression Geoff Lee was a tiny bit frightened of his rarely seen older sibling. Now the bogeyman was in their front room, larger than life, getting comfortable on their expensive upholstery.

'Ahh, she's being protective,' said Arthur, addressing the comment to his brother but keeping his eyes on Abby. 'Out here because he's been a naughty boy, is it?'

'Enough, Arthur!' Philippa Lee entered the room, a lioness determined to protect her cub. 'My Abby doesn't need an interrogation from you. Hell, she don't know you from Adam. She ain't seen you for more than 10 years what with you being given bed and board courtesy of Her Majesty. Anyway, we should be equally inquisitive about your girl. How long has *she* been out here, yet we ain't seen hide nor hair of her? Is she on the run as well?'

'Don't be daft, she's a good girl. It's her job, in'it… keeps her busy 24-7. She ain't got time for visiting. I'll mention your invite when I see her, though, eh?'

'Do what you like,' said Philippa. 'Meanwhile, stop questioning my Abby as though she's in the dock.'

'Old habits die hard,' he said, laughing. 'Did I tell you I represented me'self in the Old Bailey? Jury was out for two days before they let me walk. Guess it was me innocent face what swayed it. Should have seen the look on those coppers' ugly mugs – wanted to kill me, they did.'

He chuckled, turning his profile towards them, a jagged four-inch scar meandering down his cheek.

Abby had heard her stepfather talk about the case on the odd occasion the alcohol and sun had combined to loosen his tongue. Arthur had been in a car chase, pursued by cops who suspected him of a robbery. When they caught up with him at traffic lights, he stabbed one of them in the neck with a screwdriver. The officer died from his wounds and Arthur had been stopped at Heathrow as he attempted to flee the country.

In court, he had claimed that when the plain clothed officer had approached him at a red light he believed he was about to be subjected to a road rage attack, the car having been following him since he left Orpington. He had the screwdriver in his hand for protection and in the ensuing scuffle the man had fallen on it. He had died at the scene, despite another policeman giving him CPR. By that time Arthur had panicked and driven away.

Arthur claimed self-defence in court and won his case. If the jury had seen his prior record beforehand, they might not have been so hasty in declaring him innocent. The man had a list of criminal convictions as long as his arm and had spent time in prisons up and down the country. Only recently he had been released from Wandsworth.

'I'm amazed they have let you out of the country,' said Geoff. 'Ain't there some sort of travel restriction placed on you because of your record?'

'Arthur Lee ain't here, though, is he? Bobby Stavanger is.'

'Who?'

'Bobby Stavanger.' Arthur let the smile creep across his face, addressing his answer to Abby rather than his brother. 'It's me new alias. Got a nice shiny passport and everything. Suits me, don't you think?'

'I pity the real Bobby Stavenger,' said Philippa.

'So do I,' said Arthur. 'Died when he was 2, poor dab. Buried in Nunhead Cemetery, he is. A pal of mine obtained a copy of his birth certificate and, well, Bob's your uncle, Fanny's your aunt…'

'Bloody fool,' said Geoff. 'You'll end up back inside again.'

'Oh, don't get so high and mighty, little brother. Let's not forget you wouldn't be here if I hadn't loaned you some of me ill-gotten gains.'

'Paid back with interest.'

'Yeah… but still,' said Arthur. 'This little palace would be just a dream if it hadn't been for me and that handout.'

'Handout? Ha! You were just laundering the fuckin' money,' said Abby's stepfather, finally unable to control his temper. 'Don't talk to me as if my head buttons up the back! That cash was dodgy, and you lent it to me so the cops wouldn't confiscate it when you got nicked. Granted, it was a gamble, but you knew where I was and could call in the favour any time. I paid you back in instalments over the years… all nice, clean cash from my legitimate business so no one could trace it back to your dodgy activities. Jeez! Do me a favour…'

'Geoff!' said Philippa, indicating Abby with a shake of the head. She didn't want their dirty laundry aired in front of her daughter.

'Sorry, your Lordship,' said Arthur, ignoring the intervention. 'Your shit don't stink like mine, I get it. It's all dosh, however you carve it up, G, and you would do well to remember that. Anyway, I ain't got time to sit around shooting the breeze. I've gotta make tracks. Hey, fancy a day out, Abigail? You and your cousin got on pretty well as kids.'

'I can't remember,' said Abby, being honest. 'Anyway, I've agreed to take Mum shopping.'

What Abby really meant was she couldn't spend another minute in the company of this uncouth man. You might not be able to choose your family, but you had even less leeway when it came to someone who was related to your mother's second husband.

35

MIGUEL OUTEIRO peered down at the crashing waves, then shone a small torch on his watch, the spray from the Atlantic Ocean depositing droplets on its face. It took him a while to focus, his hand shaking violently as his mind battled his body for control of his nerves.

A son of a Galician fisherman, Miguel had never felt so vulnerable and afraid, even though he'd been brought up with sea water in his veins. His nervousness was down to the fact that in the next few hours his whole life could change forever. Everything depended on the success or failure of the mission. Using his right hand to hold the left one still, he noted it was shortly after 1.35a.m. on Thursday, August 24, 2000.

Never before had Miguel been so directly involved in a mission. For years, his lifelong friend Cerdito had been urging him to step out of the shadows and take a more prominent role in operations. It would show their Colombian paymasters he deserved more respect and responsibility and, in turn, would provide the extra cash to feed his mother and three young siblings who'd been forced to provide for themselves after his fisherman father fell overboard in a storm four years ago.

When news of a large cocaine shipment from Venezuela had reached the ears of the Galician smugglers, their excitement had been palpable. The British gang organising the mission needed a local aboard the mother ship, someone with knowledge of territorial waters who could oversee the smooth transfer of 130 sacks of white powder to a speedboat off Spain's north-west coast. Cerdito, informed of the joint operation by La Rana personally, had recommended Miguel for the job, intending to keep his friend in favour after the terrible fate that had befallen Javier.

While Miguel had not objected at the time, the agonising twist in his gut and unstoppable case of the shakes told him now that accepting the job may have been a mistake. This was so much bigger than anything he'd done before.

More serious. More life affecting.

Until now, everything had gone to plan. Miguel had met up with his unlikely new *companeras* in the Port of Coruna. They were a gang of hardy British sailors resembling the character pictured on packets of those lozenges that burned the back of your throat. From northern Spain they had sailed south and east on a large fishing trawler called the *Atlantic King*, spending six days on the open seas before dropping anchor just off the coast of Anguilla, a British-owned territory in the Caribbean. On the morning of the seventh day, Miguel had spotted an elongated grey cigar shape moving towards them and feared it was a torpedo. When it surfaced, he had been astonished to see an ugly, custom-made submarine with odd tubes of metal protruding from the main body and a long black pipe trailing from the side.

'Meet the new top-of-the-range method of South American transport.' The words had been delivered in Spanish but with a heavily accented English voice. The speaker was Scally, the only crew member who could speak Miguel's native language thanks to a mother from Valencia. They had watched as an emaciated, stumbling creature was helped onto the boat from the narco sub.

'People travel in that?'

'Not many,' Scally replied.

On entering the vessel to organise the transfer of coke, Miguel had been overcome by the intense stench of urine, excrement and some decomposing matter he couldn't quite identify. Realising his discomfort, Scally tapped him on the shoulder and passed him an army issue gas mask before pointing further inside the vessel. As far as the eye could see, there were large woollen sacks tied off at the top. He couldn't imagine how much the cocaine would fetch on the street. It was only when they started transferring the product to the *Atlantic King* that he found the dead body of the submarine's second crewman lodged away in the corner by the satellite navigation system.

IT seemed ironic the pilot had died of dehydration and malnutrition while surrounded by water. On the journey back from the Caribbean, Miguel found it impossible to erase from his mind the horror of what he had witnessed. The dead narco was testament to what little value the drug gangs of South America placed on human life, something the young Galician had begun to realise when his close friend Javier had been fed to the piranhas in La Rana's pond. Scally's urging that he 'Let go of his demons' had fallen on deaf ears.

As the days progressed, the anxiety had gnawed at Miguel's insides, sowing seeds of doubt in his brain. Was he doing the right thing? Would this whole risky enterprise cost him his life? When the shout went up, he knew there was no turning back, the single word bouncing around his brain as it pierced through the turbulent squall.

'Boat!'

For a moment Miguel could just see the dark, inhospitable and menacing waves tossing and turning all the way to the horizon. Then he caught sight of a flickering, intermittent light and, focussing on one particular spot in the vast swathes of ocean, he identified a speedboat thrusting forward at speed.

Marion.

The vessel was closing in on *Atlantic King* rapidly, and Miguel felt his stomach perform somersaults every time his friend Cerdito crested a wave. This was the crunch moment, the climax of an operation that had been planned for months, and he knew his life depended on everything going smoothly.

AS Miguel sat in his cell awaiting the arrival of the operational commander, he watched the various actors in the play filter past him. First, he saw his fellow Galicians pulled and dragged down the narrow corridor. Many of them had played significant roles in his life, and the haunted looks on their faces hammered home the full extent of his betrayal. These weren't unscrupulous crooks, but ordinary people whose action had been carried out with the single aim of feeding and nurturing their families. With so few jobs around, they had resorted to helping unload the speedboats, driving the vans and doing the donkeywork required by the drug barons. None of them had made a fortune from the work, as Miguel knew only too well.

He felt another tug on his heartstrings as he saw his friend Marcos Sotalongo, aka Cerdito, being pushed along at the rear. If there was one person he wished he could have warned in advanced of the raid it was his friend, the brilliant young speedboat driver who risked life and limb every day out on the ocean. Miguel had been told in no uncertain terms, though, that tipping anyone off would not only jeopardise the success of the operation but put his own life, and those of his mother and sisters, at risk.

The man in charge had confessed that Javier had been sacrificed "for the greater good" of the operation when Colombian suspicions had become aroused. It was an unfortunate situation but had been completely necessary to protect the real mole, Miguel, from closer scrutiny. The young Galician had been assured the authorities would do their best for Cerdito, who would be offered an appetising deal to testify against the Colombians. Unfortunately, deep down in his soul, Miguel knew his friend would never take it. Not only did Marcos Sotalongo have a misguided sense of loyalty to the South American butchers, but he also loved the money and acclaim his life had brought him. In parts of this rugged land he was seen as a hero, a latter day El Cid, using his powers for good by pumping money into the local community and providing people with work.

Miguel felt no such obligation. Motivated by a desire to rescue his family from the stigma of narcotics, he'd entered into a pact with the authorities, offering his services in their battle to bring the Galician drug lords to justice. He felt enormous guilt because it was that decision which led to Javier being tortured then sentenced to an horrific death for "crimes" he hadn't committed. La Rana had been right about a mole, she had just identified the wrong person. After that Miguel was left with no option but to follow through with the plan and ensure his friend's death was not in vain.

His opportunity came along soon enough. Far from being a narco ship, *Atlantic King* was owned by HM Customs and Excise in the UK and undercover investigators had spent years infiltrating a British drug gang with affiliations to La Rana's Colombian operation. When it was discovered the two gangs planned to bring in a major consignment of drugs from South America, *Atlantic King* was put forward as the perfect vessel to meet their needs. What they didn't know was that its crew was made up entirely of UK customs officials. Miguel was the final piece of an elaborate puzzle.

Hearing more shuffling footsteps, Miguel looked through the bars of his cell again as the weather-worn *Atlantic King* sailors filed past, bound and shackled. It was all part of the deception, as the authorities had plans to continue using the boat and its crew for future operations and needed their capture to look legitimate. Miguel himself had been arrested when the lorry he was in began unloading cocaine at La Rana's mansion. As he was hauled away, armed officers rushed the building, seizing goods and arresting anyone they found on the premises.

The police had promised Miguel he would be provided with a fake identity and a new home courtesy of Spain's witness protection programme once the operation was wrapped up. His mother and sisters had been whisked away to their new life shortly after the raids, and he would join them as soon as the mission was complete. He'd worked out he could live comfortably on the reward money and still had hopes of nailing down a proper job in a new town far away. While his mother would miss her friends, he knew she had been coming under increasing pressure from the Mothers Against Drugs to disown her only son. The fact Miguel was shunning the life would more than compensate her for quitting her lifelong home.

Miguel's heart lifted. Now he could see the Colombians being dragged in, the familiar bodyguards Ignacio and Hugo protesting as they were led to the cells. Both of them had almost certainly played a role in Javier's torture and eventual death, and Miguel hoped the courts would dish out the sentences they deserved. He watched them disappear and waited for "Operation Snow White" to unveil its biggest prize.

As seconds turned into minutes and minutes turned into hours, though, Miguel's stomach began churning and his hands shaking. Eventually he uttered out loud the nagging question he had been turning over and over in his mind.

'Where the hell is La Rana?'

36

'YOU SHOULD wear a mask mate.' Lucky slammed his putter into the bag.

Sly's brow furrowed. 'What do you mean?'

'You're a bleedin' bandit,' said his friend. 'Taking my money through false pretences. You said you didn't play off a handicap.'

He waved the 500 pesetas note in Sly's direction.

'I don't,' said Sly, pocketing the fruits of victory. 'It's not like I play every week and belong to some exclusive club. Anyhow, when it comes to golf, your nickname couldn't be more inappropriate. How many times did you end up in a bunker?'

Lucky shrugged. 'They say it's a good way to spoil a country walk and they're right. Come on, let's go – the old man probably wants to head back to the ranch.'

'Where is he, anyway?' asked Sly. 'I thought he was gonna join us.'

'He's been on the big course with a mate who's flown in from the smoke,' said Lucky. 'Business, apparently. I'm only the hired help, so I didn't get an invite.'

'Don't be a mug all your life,' said Sly. 'He's got more time for you than the rest of us put together. Now come on, this cash is burning a hole in my pocket.'

Sly dodged the playful punch thrown in his direction then grabbed his friend around the head and ruffled his hair. When he eventually let go, Lucky shook himself like a dog caught in a shower before grabbing his golf bag and charging off in the direction of the buggy. When Sly was 10 feet away, Lucky turned the ignition key and put his foot down, the vehicle speeding off over the undulating terrain.

'Ha ha very funny, you prick!' shouted Sly, trudging after his golfing buddy.

WHEN they arrived in the main bar of the clubhouse, there was no sign of Billy the Kid Dolan or his guest. Sly asked the barman on duty if he had seen his grandfather and was told the old man was having lunch in one of the private hospitality rooms. 'My orders are "strictly no interruptions" but he's set up a tab behind the bar for you gentlemen,' said the barman. 'He'll join you when he's ready.'

'Doesn't want his grandson showing him up in front of his important mates,' said Sly to Lucky.

'Don't let it bother you, mate,' said Lucky. 'You're not missing out on anything, I'm sure. What are you having?'

'A bottle of that Spanish lager,' said Sly, waving his hand in the direction of a large fridge behind the bar. 'But first, I need a wazz.' He walked away, pushing through the double doors leading to the toilets. The feeling his grandfather didn't trust him with any of the important stuff still weighed on his mind. Hadn't he risked life and limb on that mission to Galicia a few months ago? He'd expected at least some Brownie points, but it was Lucky who'd received all the pats on the back. When they'd returned from the north, his friend spent hours locked away with the old man in his private study, discussing the trip. Sly had a nagging feeling there was some hidden agenda he knew nothing about.

Standing at the urinal moments later, he tried to figure out which one of his grandfather's many associates would deserve such VIP treatment. Billy seldom confided in him about his UK connections other than during his Brink'sMat revelation and on that occasion, he'd been careful not to name names. Perhaps one of the original gang had arrived to touch base with him after all this time or claim a share of the robbery proceeds.

Hearing a noise behind him, he glanced over his shoulder to see a large man emerge from one of the cubicles and wash his hands at the sink. His thick dark hair was tinged with grey and he wore a sharp black suit. It wasn't *déjà vu* exactly, but Sly had a nagging feeling he'd seen the bloke somewhere before. If anything, he looked out of place in these surroundings, but despite searching his brain for answers, Sly came up blank. Moments later, the man was gone.

On his trip back to the bar, Sly snatched another quick glance into the hospitality room – and froze. His grandfather was now standing, his arm draped around his guest. It was the tall stranger, and the two of them looked like they were sharing a joke. They were obviously as thick as thieves.

'CAN'T believe you got here so quick,' said Billy the Kid Dolan to his guest.

'Wonders of modern travel,' said Assistant Police Commissioner Maxwell Cooper. 'When you get to my position, everyone drops everything to get you where you want to be.'

'So you said you were playing golf in Spain with a wanted criminal and they all said, "Yes, sir. No, sir. Three bags full, sir". Surprised you didn't order a blow job from one of those sexy young WPCs while you were at it.'

'Come on, I only use my superpowers for good,' said the policeman, laughing. 'Of course I didn't mention I was coming to give you a thrashing at golf. I'm here about "Snow White".'

'Oh, going into the fairytale business, are we? It'll suit you, judging from some of the bloody porkies you've told in the past.'

'Now, now,' said the AC. 'I told you about Snow White. It's a little project we put together with the Spanish, French and Germans, designed to smash up the networks bringing cocaine into mainland Europe from South America. But, of course, you know all about that.'

'Ahh, how lovely,' said Billy. 'The combined brains of Europe all working together and you on hand to take the credit. Just don't forget who gave you the intel, son.'

'And I've kept my end of the bargain,' said AC Cooper. 'I'm flying back for the big press conference tomorrow. Remember to tune in.'

'Don't watch TV,' said Billy. 'Every time I turn it on I see your ugly mug.'

'Perhaps you should make an exception. I wouldn't want you to miss out.'

Billy scowled. His relationship with his special guest had never been straightforward. There had been plenty of ups and downs, and he still felt uneasy about climbing into bed with the enemy. Years ago, as a newly trained firearms officer with Special Branch, Max had accidentally shot and killed Billy's youngest son. He'd been about to take the ultimate revenge when the policeman traded his life for vital inside information about a warehouse which stored large quantities of cash and valuables near Heathrow. The Brink'sMat tip-off had healed their relationship, and from that moment it had gone from strength to strength.

'Are they anywhere nearer catching her?' asked Billy.

'Who?'

'Don't be thick. That Colombian cunt. You said the plan was foolproof and "Snow White" went like clockwork. Not the way I hear it.' Billy's voice had climbed an octave, his reddening face the result of high blood pressure. He prodded AC Cooper hard in the chest.

'Hey!' said the Assistant Commissioner, grabbing Billy's hand and forcing it away. 'The Spanish authorities say they're closing in. It seems someone might have tipped her off, no doubt some bent Spanish cop in her pay, and she's flown the coop. I wouldn't worry, she'll head straight back to South America. There's nothing left for her here, and if she sticks around, she'll just end up behind bars. Her charge sheet reads like an A-Z of criminal offences and if she goes down, they'll throw away the key.'

'You don't know Estella,' said Billy. 'She can get to anyone. Do you know—'

'The poison frog story? Jeez everyone does. It's a gangland fairytale.'

'You think? You wouldn't be so sure if you looked in her eyes.'

'Yeah, well, maybe she can get away with that sort of shit in South America. The authorities are all corrupt. This is Europe, though. Those tactics don't work over here.'

His damning verdict on police corruption was volunteered without a trace of irony in his voice.

37

'EXCUSE ME, love, can you find somewhere else to dust for a minute?' Chuck realised how condescending he sounded, talking to the 'help' in the same way his grandfather did. He was still suspicious of Naomi, though, and didn't want her knowing his personal business. Thankfully, she nodded and left the room without any sign her nose had been put out of joint.

He pulled the sliding doors shut behind her and searched for the remote, eventually finding it down the side of the big sofa. *Why couldn't Sly put things back where he found them?* Pressing the "on" button, the first thing he came across on the tv was a soap opera about a hospital, the popular American show having been dubbed into Spanish. He had to laugh at how out of sync the nurse's mouth was as a string of words bombarded his ears.

Clicking through the channels, he paused when he saw a well-known BBC anchor woman wrapping up the midday news.

'*...Now over to sport, where there is news of England's first Test series victory over the West Indies since 1969.*'

'Lummy days,' said Chuck, sitting back. He was pretty sure his brother Arnie hadn't rung to inform him about a sporting event he didn't give two shits about. A man appeared on the screen and rattled through the sports news. As well as the cricket, there was a report on Arsenal's come back from 2-0 down to draw 2-2 at Chelsea and an interview with rower Steve Redgrave about his bid to notch a fifth Olympic Gold medal at the Sydney Games later in the month. Finally, the camera panned back to the newsreader.

'*Those main headlines again*,' she said. '*After almost 18 months, a police investigation into the cause of the London nightclub explosion which resulted in six deaths and 25 serious injuries has finally announced its conclusions…*'

A face appeared on the screen and Chuck recognised the man immediately. It was the bodyguard he had chained to the desk before the grenade exploded. *Shit*! He gripped the arms of the sofa.

'*Morgan Wynstanley, an illegal immigrant from Jamaica, has been deemed responsible for the explosion that ripped through the Ottoman Club in the London Borough of Hackney. He died instantly in the explosion and in an interview with the BBC earlier this morning, Assistant Metropolitan Police Commissioner Max Cooper revealed it had been established beyond reasonable doubt that Wynstanley had planned the attack alone in what is now believed to be the first suicide bombing in this country. Police have uncovered worrying evidence that the bomber, a new convert to Islam, had links with the Middle East terror group al-Qaeda and had been planning the attack from the moment he entered the country illegally six months earlier. We will have further revelations in a* Panorama *special investigation later this evening, but this is what Assistant Commissioner Cooper had to say…*'

'Hold up, who's that geezer?'

Chuck swivelled to see Sly standing in the doorway, looking dishevelled. He'd been out on the town with his mate Lucky the previous night having spent a few hours at the golf course in the afternoon. Chuck guessed they had spent time in the 19th hole then carried on the party in Torrevieja.

'He's the copper who investigated the Hackney job,' said Chuck excitedly. 'Looks like we're in the clear, bro. Fucking hell, Sly, we can go home! Hang on, I've got to tell Arnie… he's on the blower.'

The older Dolan boy hurdled the sofa and walked towards the glass doors, only for a hand to shoot out and hold him in place.

'He's a copper?' Sly looked like he'd seen a ghost, the effect no doubt magnified by the excess alcohol sloshing around his system.

'What of it?'

'That pig was at the golf club yesterday, having a cosy private lunch with our Granddad.'

'Don't be daft.' Chuck didn't have time for his brother's nonsense.

'I'm serious,' said Sly.

'Nah. You were pissed. Look, that TV interview is taking place in London. How…?'

'Look, I was standing as close to him as I am to you now,' said Sly. 'We'd only just come off the course and I hadn't touched a drop. He was in the bogs and I later saw him with Granddad's arm draped all over him, like they were best mates. It was in one of the hospitality rooms. They didn't know I saw them and Billy never introduced us.'

Chuck held his brother's gaze and realised he was telling the truth. 'Wow!'

'Yes wow, right?' said Sly. 'It looks like our granddad's a fuckin' grass.'

'Don't jump to conclusions.' Chuck's mind was ticking over, testing alternative scenarios. 'It's probably the other way around. Someone's been helping Billy avoid arrest all these years, don't you think? The bloke could just be a bent copper on Billy's payroll.'

'Maybe.'

Chuck could tell his brother wasn't convinced. 'Let's discuss it later,' said the older Dolan boy. 'I've gotta get back to Arnie. The good news, my son, is that copper says they've completed their investigation into the Hackney fire and we're in the clear.'

He pushed past Sly into the hall to pick up the receiver. 'Still there, Arnie?'

'You've seen it?'

'This is kosher, right? It's not a windup. What about that CCTV? The fingerprints?'

'Shhhhh!' said Arnie, reminding Chuck they were talking on granddad's home phone. 'Come on, don't look a gift horse in the mouth. They're closing the fuckin' book,' said Arnie. 'Do I have to spell it out for ya? You boys are coming home!'

For a moment, Chuck needed to compose himself. He pushed the receiver into his chest as a plethora of emotions swept through his insides. He couldn't wait to let his mum know. He'd missed her, his sister Anjelica and youngest brother Bruce, not to mention his mates down the pub and his old haunts. He wasn't generally this emotional, but at that moment he was torn between laughing and crying.

Despite his overwhelming delight and relief that the chase was over, there was also a nagging feeling he was going to miss certain things about Spain: his grandfather and, more importantly, the way he and Abby had been able to conduct their relationship away from prying eyes. Even though they only saw each other on her occasional trips out, their relationship had been able to grow and flourish without the constant hassles and pressures of London life. Still, every time she returned to England, he had to admit he missed her terribly. Now there would be nothing to hold their relationship back.

SLY flicked through the channels on the TV. He needed to find out more, fearing it might be a clever ruse designed to lure them into a trap. He'd seen his grandfather cosying up to one of the Met's top coppers. Could Billy the Kid have pulled the strings to get him and his brother off the hook? Or had he sold them out in return for a free pass over the Brink'sMat business? Sly knew money could buy an awful lot of things, but he wasn't sure even his grandfather's riches would be enough to tilt a multiple-murder investigation firmly in the wrong direction.

'Hey, you.'

He turned to see Naomi enter the room dressed in her working uniform. She always made him feel horny, raging hangover or not. The short black skirt perfectly showcased her tanned, shapely legs, while the lacy gold top afforded him an eyeful of cleavage. More than the uniform, though, he guessed it was the upstairs-downstairs scenario which really turned him on. From the first moment he set eyes on her, he'd this vision of her attending to his every desire. When he'd followed up on his interest, he had not been disappointed. She was a dirty little minx.

He thought about her sinking to her knees in front of him now, pulling down his zip and taking him in her mouth, and was about to suggest as much when he was distracted by something on the screen. He nodded to her and turned his attention to the Spanish news channel now showing. Though he couldn't understand a word of what was being said, he was pretty sure he knew what was going on. Law enforcement agents were displaying a large collection of neatly wrapped packages, an officer cutting one open to reveal white powder. The packages looked exactly the same as the ones he and Cerdito had unloaded from the mother ship out on the Atlantic during his trip north – solid bricks of cocaine. Before he was able to properly process the image, the scene switched to a group of men being frogmarched along a dock to the waiting vehicles of the Guardia Civil.

Finally, a news reporter spoke Spanish into the camera, a collection of small boats bobbing around on the swell behind her. When the camera spun around for a shot of the harbourside, a steak and seafood restaurant was instantly recognisable to him. He and Lucky had sat in that same restaurant talking to a powerful Colombian cartel boss and a fearless young speedboat driver. Suddenly, all thoughts of sexual gratification were washed from his mind.

Now he thought he knew exactly what had happened, and it sent chills down the length of his body.

'You fucker, Billy,' he said under his breath.

38

SLY found his grandfather in the pub. The Rolling Stones were blasting out 'You Can't Always Get What You Want'.

'Ah come in, boy, have a drink,' said Billy the Kid, shouting to make himself heard. 'You look like you could do with a hair of the dog. You and Lucky painted the town red, eh? He didn't look too good this morning either, so I gave him the day off. I've not much on today, anyway.'

Billy was looking far better than Sly had seen him for a long while, younger somehow, as if he had been given a new lease of life.

'You fuckin' used me, Granddad,' he said.

'What's that? Speak up, son. You're muttering.'

Sly took a few steps further into the room, summoning up the courage for a confrontation. Billy might not be a threatening physical presence any longer, but he still possessed an intimidating aura.

'La Rana,' he said. 'The Galicia trip. That's what I'm talking about. You made me go through all that so you could get what you wanted. You pimped me out, Granddad.'

'Not sure what you mean, son.' His grandfather was sitting at the bar, a glass of single malt in his hand and the bottle beside him. He waved his hand in the direction of an empty stool. 'Sit down. The way I heard it you had a whale of a time up there. Still, you've obviously got a bee in yer bonnet. Let's sort this out mano y mano, as they say in these parts. Have a drink.'

Sly wasn't sure his grandfather knew the real meaning of the Spanish phrase. It referred to hand-to-hand combat, not man to man as he suspected the old man thought. Against his better judgement, he wandered over. He was furious and wanted to maintain that anger, to feed it, but it was so easy to get sucked in by his grandfather's persuasive manner. The old man was a master at winning an argument and Sly reminded himself that everything he was about to be told was probably a tissue of lies.

'It had to be done, son,' said Billy, 'for your benefit – you and your big brother. If it wasn't for me, they'd be extraditing you now. You'd be given a life sentence in one of her majesty's fine institutions... just like that waster of a father of yours. Way I hear it, they're jam-packed with body-building bum boys who would just love some tasty fresh meat like you. I guess you could run, but that would be your whole life, right there. I should know. This way, you can carry on living life the way you want. You should be grateful to me.'

'You don't deny it then?' said Sly. 'For Christ's sakes, Granddad, you've put a massive target on my back!'

'Look, it's unfortunate La Rana got away,' said Billy. 'But the way I see it you're safe as houses. The Colombian cunt is a business woman first and foremost. I've got a lot of her money tied up in certain places and she knows she will never see it again if she upset me. Scoring points comes way down her agenda. Anyway, what would you have done if I'd told you what was going on?'

'I would have refused to go,' said Sly.

'Refused a request from La Rana?' Granddad Billy smiled. 'Don't piss up my back and tell me it's fuckin' raining. It was written all over your face, son. You fancied your chances. You should think of me as one of them dating agencies that are all the rage these days. You know the ones? You give them your details, likes and dislikes, what you ate for brekky etc, and they match you with your ideal partner. We could call it Rumpy-Pumpy.com, eh?'

'You think it's funny?' Sly raised his voice.

'Oi!' His grandfather growled, the old man's demeanour changing in a second, the laughing comedian gone. 'You never heard the phrase, "Don't cheek your elders?" You can't come down here shouting the odds like I'm one of your fuckin' siblings.'

'But La Rana, she'll…'

'Either spend the rest of her life in prison or go back to South America where she belongs. Don't worry about La Rana. The fact we can't trust her is the exact reason why I did it… that and to enable you boys to go home.'

'What did you do anyway, Granddad? I saw you with that pig from the Met. Are you a fuckin' grass? Chuck won't be happy to hear that, let alone the rest of the family and the members of your crew.'

Billy sighed. 'You don't get it, do you, boy? I've heard you can be a bit slow on the uptake. Sometimes you have to make compromises to keep the world spinning. I scratch your back, you scratch mine. You, of course, wouldn't know about that because you've been spoon fed all your fuckin' life. Don't think I didn't hear about that mess you got in with them prostitutes down in Torrevieja. The way you've been acting, I've started to think Chuck and my dearly departed brother-in-law should have left those scumbags to finish the job. Seems to me you ain't got the balls these days.'

'I'm trying to protect them,' said Sly, answering fire with fire. 'I'll lose them soon enough if La Rana thinks I double-crossed her. Have you seen what she does to people she believes have ratted on her? No? Well, I have. It involves some hungry fish with sharp teeth, a plank of wood with a hole in it and—'

'All right, all right, don't get your knickers in a twist,' said the old man, cutting him off in full flow. 'You seem to be forgetting I'm a big fish in these parts myself, and anyone who tries to mess with my family knows what's coming to them. See them guards outside?'

Sly knew who the old man meant. Security had been beefed up with three or four new men patrolling the grounds at any one time.

'Those geezers are either ex-police or ex-military,' Billy explained. 'All recommended by my mate Max, the bloke you saw at the golf club. He and I have a mutual understanding. It's fair to say I wouldn't have all this if he hadn't tipped me off about Brink'sMat years ago. In return, I've thrown him the odd scrap designed to make him look good to his superiors.'

'La Rana ain't a scrap,' said Sly. 'Your latest titbit could come back to bite us all in the you-know-whats.'

'Man up, son,' said Billy. 'As long as you don't do anything stupid, you'll be fine. Pretty soon you'll be back in England, and all this will be forgotten. I can't see the Colombian cartels wandering around Barking just to find your sorry ass. La Rana will need to keep her head below the parapet now Interpol is on her tail.'

'Interpol?'

'You really are a fuckin' novice, ain't ya?' said Billy. 'It's like an international police force that hunts down major criminals. La Rana has been one of their top targets for some time. They hadn't been able to touch her, and the slag was getting too big for her fuckin' boots, threatening our arrangement with her greed. To be honest with you, I wonder whether she was responsible for Rafael's murder. You told me yourself she used the word puta when talking about the mole in her operation. Maybe that bullet I got came from her.'

He looked wistfully at the ceiling for a few seconds before taking another large gulp of his whisky and swirling the glass around. 'When she suggested I send you – my grandson – along with Lucky, I was fuming and became even more determined to take her down a peg or two,' he continued.

'So why did you send me? What was my part in this operation?' Sly was confused. 'I don't remember hearing anything useful that would have helped you fit her up.'

'You just had to play along, that's all,' said Billy. 'Look, let me tell you a story. Hopefully it will help you understand. There was this illusionist in the East End once who I used to go to see with my first wife. Could make you think black was white, that one. Amazing. Anyhow, I got talking to him after a show and asked him his secret. He said it was all about misdirection, getting people to watch one thing when the main part of the trick was happenin' somewhere else. Do you see?'

Sly's expression was blank.

'For pity's sake, boy,' said the old man, raising his voice again. 'You were the misdirection. While La Rana was concentrating on everything you were doing, Lucky was looking after the important stuff.'

'Really?' Sly's mouth dropped open. 'The way I saw it, all he did was have a slap-up meal at their expense and a complimentary night in a hotel. Meanwhile, I was risking my life out on the fuckin' Atlantic in a powerboat during a raging storm. Not content with that, I then got dragged back to La Rana's place where she used me as a… anyway, remind me to congratulate Lucky on all his "hard" work, won't you?'

'I didn't know about the boat,' said Billy. 'Sorry about that. I might have changed my plans if I had. Teamwork is the key, though, and you'll see the benefits of it if this Boxer Boys caper ever takes off.'

Sly faded out the old man's words as he tried to analyse every moment from his trip north. He could remember telling Lucky certain things about his encounters with Cerdito and La Rana on the journey home, but they were both tired and shocked from seeing the horrendous punishment meted out to Javier. As a consequence, much of the trip was conducted in silence.

'Let's have a celebratory drink,' said Granddad Billy in an effort to lift the sombre mood. 'After all, you boys are going home, and it might be our last opportunity to enjoy each other's company. We should get Chuck in here too.'

'Did Chuck know?' asked Sly. 'I mean, about the real reason for that trip north?'

'Give it a rest, boy,' said Billy, the sneer returning to his voice. 'You gonna be a mug all your life? I hope not. What is it the spooks say? Need to know, that's it. There was no need to tell him. Shit, imagine what would have happened if your big brother found out? He would have gone off half-cocked in his typical, hot-headed way. This was a delicate operation, and I didn't need him blundering in and ruining it all. Every day I see more of his father in him.'

'What you mean is Chuck would have been wise to you. He would have insisted I didn't get on that boat and would never have let me go alone to La Rana's mansion.'

'Exactly,' said Billy. 'Now you're getting it.'

'Bloody hell, Granddad,' said Sly. 'You really are a piece of work.'

Billy smiled, then winked. 'Thanks, son.' He poured himself another drink, blissfully ignorant to the fact that Sly didn't mean it as a compliment.

39

'WHAT'S WRONG, babe?' Naomi raised her head from where it had come to rest on Sly's belly then brushed her fringe from her eyes so she could look at him.

'Sorry, I'm not in the mood.'

'Excuse me?' Her face contorted in disappointment; her voice laced with annoyance. 'What am I doing wrong, your lordship? I thought you couldn't get enough of it.'

'Oh, cut the master-servant crap, eh? It's not been a great day.'

'Soooo…rry,' she said. 'Don't you want me to act as your personal slave? That's the way you treat me… The hired help, expected to jump at your every beck and call. I guess it was inevitable you'd grow tired of me. Found another fuck buddy, have you?'

'No, look, it's not that… I… well, just not today, OK?'

Sly could feel his temper rising and took a deep breath to quell his anger. It would be wrong to take it out on her. He couldn't understand what was happening to his body. He had never failed to rise to the occasion in the past, however pissed he was and whatever shit was going on in his private life. Christ, he hoped this wasn't a sign he was getting old.

Sensing his mood, Naomi pulled her shirt down over her breasts and manoeuvred her way up the bed, cupping his face with her hand and turning it towards hers. 'Don't worry, it happens,' she said. 'What's bothering you, babe? Tell Auntie Nay Nay all about it.' She brushed her hand across her body. 'I know I got all this, but I do have a brain as well.'

It made him smile.

'I'm not sure I can,' he said.

'Bad as that, eh?' She smiled, too. 'Has the old man sworn you to secrecy?'

'Fuck him,' he snapped. 'It's his fault.'

'Oh?'

'Too bloody right. He doesn't give a shit about anyone, particularly not me. The "family man" has been talking crap all this time. Hell, look at how he treats Alisha, eh? And she's his wife. She doesn't deserve it.'

'What do you mean?'

'Well, it was in order to protect him that her brother-in-law Rafael was killed yet he shows barely a hint of remorse. What sort of man is that?'

His brown eyes locked on hers, burning with intensity. The strength of feeling was overwhelming, stronger than anything he'd felt about any issue before. He was starting to realise he might actually hate the old man.

'Go on,' she said. 'Get it out of your system.'

'Look at the way he treats his own fuckin' grand kids,' said Sly.

'Well, I don't want to sound like I'm taking his side,' she interrupted, 'but he seems to have given you free run of the place… and it's not like you have to beg him for money, is it?'

'No, I have to shovel horse shit for it and other things besides!' he stormed. 'You don't understand, do you? I'm muckin' out the fuckin' stables while golden boy Luke gets to drive him around. Why didn't he give me that job? I can drive a fuckin' car.'

'Maybe he feels that after the shooting it's too dangerous for his own relations to be doing that sort of job. Perhaps he's just protecting you.'

'Ha! You see! I should have expected you to side with him,' said Sly. 'He's your boss. Can't you see, that's exactly what he wants people to believe? He's brainwashed you into thinking he's this caring old bloke who will do everything to protect his own. Well, what you don't know is he put my life in the hands of the most dangerous criminal in Spain. I was sent out on a speedboat to do a cocaine run which could have seen me locked up for life or, even worse, killed ... and Billy the bloody Kid knew all about it. It was a deliberate tactic so that he could find out certain things, and once he had what he wanted he double crossed this Colombian crime boss and handed over the information to some copper friend of his. Now there's been a major drug bust, and it's all down to my grandfather, the bloody police grass. Not only that, but the criminal he double crossed has escaped and who will she think betrayed her?' He raised his eyebrows to invite a reply.

'Oh, I see.'

'Yep,' he said. 'Dopey bollocks, that's who. She warned me what she was capable of, even gave Lucky and me a demonstration, feeding some local kid's privates to her pet piranhas.'

'I'm sure you are safe here, though, babe.'

'Oh, you think that bunch of old PC plods and squaddies are up to the job? I ain't so sure. That's what annoys me... if he wants proper protection, he should ask us. Look at

Chuck. Hard as nails, sharp and loyal as the day is long, yet what's Granddad got him doing? Working for some Irish nutcases who would slit our throats as easy as look at us! Still, we won't have to put up with it for long.'

'Eh? What do you mean?'

'We're going home… He's packing us off back to Britain. It can't come soon enough as far as I'm concerned.' He stopped abruptly, looking down at her. 'What's wrong?'

She turned her face away. 'Nothing.'

Despite the warmth in the air, he sensed the atmosphere had turned decidedly chilly. It took him a moment to catch on. 'Oh, for fuck's sake. Really?'

He heard the sniffle. 'Doesn't matter,' she muttered.

He felt for her wrist and pulled her towards him, her head turning as he wrapped a protective arm around her. He kissed her below the eye, tasting the salt. 'I just didn't realise…'

'Well, you wouldn't,' she said. 'How could you? Maybe you have a bit of your grandfather's cruel streak in you.'

'What? Hell no! That's not fair. I ain't anything like him. It's just I thought… well, that you felt the same about all this, that you were happy the way things were.'

'And I was, but now you're going and I… it's difficult to think we won't have this.' She looked around the room. 'It means something, you know, perhaps more than I realised. God knows, there ain't much else in my life other than breaking my back working for the old man. It was great when Alisha was about, but I hardly see her now. To be honest, these days you're the only person I talk to properly. I have feelings for you, Sly.'

'I like you, too… even though I have had a bit of trouble showing it today.' He nodded downwards, then smiled, feeling her warm breath disturb the tiny hairs on his neck.

She ran her hand down his chest then on through the thick expanse of hairs below his belly until fingers encircled him, her grip delicate yet firm.'Ah, you're back,' she said. 'How would you like your leaving present early?'

Turning her back to him again, she pressed herself against him.

'Shit. Really?'

'Won't tell if you don't,' she said. 'Can't guarantee I won't cry, though.'

'Nor me.'

He shuffled around until they were spooned on the bed, then manoeuvred into a position from where he could enter her. Then, enfolding her in his arms he placed his hands on her breasts, rolling the firm, chunky nipples between his fingers.

'Oh no, master,' she said. 'You shouldn't.'

'Oh yes, I should!' he said, driving forward with his hips and moving his hand to stifle the yelp that burst from her lips.

There was a quiet knock at the door.

'WHAT the fuck?' Sly mouthed.

'Who is it?' Naomi whispered back.

'Have I got X-ray eyes? I know as much as you do!'

'Sylvester…, darling?' A quiet voice laced with a Spanish lilt. Alisha.

'Shhhh!' Sly put his fingers to his lips, urging his lover to stay quiet, the anticipation of what they were about to do fading rapidly. Naomi twisted her head and spoke softly into his ear, her breath tickling his skin. 'She calls you darling?'

'Sylvester, are you awake? I need you. It's about the horses. I am worried.'

'Shit.' He rolled away from his lover and planted his feet on the floor, reaching down for his jeans. 'Is… is that you, Alisha?' he said, feigning a bewildered, disorientated reaction. 'I was asleep. Just give me a minute, eh, I'll come and find you. Wait in the lounge. Whatever it is, we'll sort it out. OK?'

'Hurry please, darling.'

He held his breath, hearing the soft patter of her feet against the polished wood flooring.

'Really?' Naomi sounded hurt. 'You're just going to leave me like this?'

Sly cursed himself for his insensitivity. It was the second time he'd upset her in a matter of minutes. He hesitated briefly before standing and pulling on his sweatshirt. 'I'm sorry,' he said. 'I can't very well ignore her.'

'You're supposed to be riding me, not the fuckin' horses,' she hissed. 'I thought you wanted me. Now I know the truth.'

'Don't be like that,' he said. 'There will be other…' He stopped, realising what he was about to say.

'You're going home, Sly, in case you'd forgotten.'

'You can visit,' he said. 'On your holidays, and I can come out here again. You must go home to your family sometimes?'

'Sure,' she muttered to his retreating back. 'My family are a bundle of laughs… jailbird father, drug addict mum.' She was talking to herself. He'd disappeared out of the door.

Rolling over, she looked at the clock. 4.25a.m. Why the fuck would Alisha be talking about her horses at this time of night? She wondered whether Sly might be sharing his affections with the lady of the house, his own grandfather's wife. She was young and sexy enough but, no. Despite his phenomenal sex drive and narcissistic tendencies, she couldn't envisage him stooping that low.

She reached for her clothes.

Talking of families… perhaps it was a signal she should get in touch with hers.

40

ALISHA was standing by the panoramic patio windows peering into the misty half-light of dawn when Sly entered the lounge.

'Everything OK?' he said.

'I could hear them,' she replied. 'They sounded distressed.'

'Who?'

'My babies,' said Alisha. 'The horses! Who did you think I meant?'

He shook his head. Of course she meant the horses. 'Maybe they were disturbed by one of the new guards,' he said. 'Have you spoken to anyone?'

'They are your grandfather's men.'

'Well, maybe he could have a word.'

'I'm not asking,' she replied. 'We don't speak.'

'Yes, but…'

'I'm sorry. I know he is your grandfather but I cannot bring myself… look, will you help?'

It took him less than a second to make up his mind. This woman had been kind to him, treating him as if he was one of her own. Not just that, but with her guidance he'd become attached to the magnificent animals and would be distraught if anything happened to them.

'Let me go and check,' he said.

'I'll come too.' She turned and marched towards the hallway.

'I'm not sure that's a good idea. What if…?'

She stopped and looked over her shoulder, pinning him with her large, dark eyes. 'They are my horses.'

'I know it's just… it might not be safe.'

'If my children are distressed, I should be there to calm them down.'

Sly wondered if he should call Chuck or Lucky for backup.

Fuck it. It was odds on they'd just been spooked by a wild animal. Anyway, was he man or mouse? His grandfather had suggested the latter. Damn the old bastard. OK, Billy, it's time to man up. 'Promise you'll do as I say,' he told Alisha. 'If there's danger you run back to the house and raise the alarm. I'd be pretty surprised if anyone could get past Granddad's security. Those guys are armed to the teeth. We had better get going. There's just one more thing I need.'

Alisha nodded.

He disappeared downstairs and returned, dragging the German Shepherd behind him. 'Come on, Major,' he said. The dog barked, saliva dripping from its jaws.

'I don't know,' Alisha said. 'He makes the horses nervous.'

'Look, this is no ordinary situation,' said Sly. 'Do you have a gun? I'm not sure where Granddad keeps his weapons.'

She moved over to a tall, slim oak cupboard against the lounge wall, fiddled around behind it before drawing out a key on some string. Detaching it from a hook, she then twisted it in the cupboard lock and opened it, removing a shotgun. He held his hand out, expecting her to pass it to him.

'Can you shoot?' she asked.

Her dark eyes were like lie detectors, and he knew he wouldn't fool her. He shook his head.

'I can,' she said. 'I lived on a farm and was brought up with guns. In my younger days, I was on the Spanish junior shooting team. By the time you have deafened yourself, missed the target and dislocated your shoulder from the recoil I could have dealt with the intruder.'

The words stung his male ego, but she moved across to massage the side of his face with a cool hand. 'You look after the dog,' she said. 'Maybe in the future I can give you lessons on how to use one of these. Now, shall we go?'

He grabbed a quilted jacket from a peg by the front door to shield him from the damp of the early morning. 'Ready?' he asked. She nodded but didn't speak, her body radiating apprehension.

He unlocked the door and strode out into the chill morning air, the dog pulling hard as it raced out in front. Behind him, he heard the gentle click of the front door shutting. All around them it was quiet and Sly was beginning to suspect the Spanish woman had dreamt about the horses, then woken up and imagined their alarm was real.

Major seemed to know exactly where he was heading, though, ploughing forward and tugging at the chain so hard that Sly found he was running to keep up. 'Hold on, dog,' he said. The animal turned, tongue hanging out, eyes fixed on him. 'Sit,' he ordered, but it just gave him a quizzical look. Leaning forward, he loosened the chain and let the dog run free, jogging on behind.

MAJOR'S howl – desperate and unearthly – was the first warning that something was terribly wrong. For a moment they stood still, looking at each other, their eyes betraying a fear neither was able to translate into words. Then Alisha was tearing past him, running in the direction of the barn, the rifle held against her right side.

'Wait!' he shouted, but she didn't break stride. Sly shook his head and gave chase, gaining on her as they neared the collection of outbuildings. The dog was in the doorway to the barn turning circles, its painful lament cutting through the mist. As he approached, he could hear no sound coming from inside when he might have expected nervous whinnying in response to Major's presence.

'Oh no, no, no,' Alisha exclaimed as Sly caught up with her, registering the abject terror on her face. Her complexion, usually a sun-kissed shade of light oak, was bleached white with shock in the pale light. He grabbed her by the arms, feeling the ripples of anxiety pass through her body, her eyes wide and questioning, the gun rattling as it shook against her leg.

'Please, Alisha… let me!'

'You are wasting time. Every second might be…' She tore herself from his grip and opened the door to the stables before racing to the nearest stall. He watched on helplessly as she sank to her knees, the dog's howls mimicking the despair she felt. Gingerly, Sly followed, looking left and right to ensure he wasn't jumped by an intruder lurking in the shadows. When he was convinced they were alone, he walked across to where she had collapsed, her face resting against the beautiful white head of her prized stallion. Caja de Oro was lying flat against the hay as if it was a pillow, but he clearly wasn't sleeping. His eyes were wide and unblinking, mirrors that reflected Sly's alarmed features back at him. The body was stretched out across the stable floor, the legs at an awkward angle, suggesting the animal had no time to prepare itself before collapsing. He put his arm out tentatively to touch the stallion's flank and though he could detect heat, the torso was still as the morning air. There was no rise and fall to indicate a heartbeat within its mighty breast.

Sly Dolan felt tears trickle down his face, coming to rest at the corner of his mouth, the taste of salt bitter and sharp. Then he put his arms out and embraced the shell of the woman beside him. They sat silently together for what seemed like hours, consumed by their grief. He thought he should at least rush back to the house and call a vet, but he knew it would be pointless. The horse was dead and there was nothing anyone could do to revive it.

After a while, Alisha shook him off and clambered to her feet. Setting off to check the other stalls, she slowly shook her head as she passed each one. Following her, he began ticking off the catalogue of destruction. There were two more animals sprawled across the barn floor, their eyes wide open, no hint of life remaining in their bodies. The only one of Alisha's horses left was Rocco, who was still in Marbella after the Christmas visit, and if this was an act of revenge against Billy there was no guarantee he was safe.

'Your grandfather,' she hissed under her breath. 'He did this.'

'Alisha, I don't think…'

'No, he did, as if he had taken a gun to their heads and shot them himself. That old man dances with the Devil, and it's the rest of us who pay the price.'

41

WHEN Sly returned to the house after waiting for the veterinary pathologist to arrive, Naomi was helping Alisha load suitcases into the boot of the car. He could understand the woman's desire to get away. The death of her prized horses was the final thrust of the knife in a relationship so wounded it seemed impossible to heal.

She gave him a knowing look and wiped her eyes, then raised her hand tentatively in a gesture of goodbye. She mouthed the words 'Thank you' before climbing behind the steering wheel, turning the key and revving the engine as it grumbled into life. Then she was off, sweeping past him up the driveway towards the gates of a home which, little by little, had become a prison for her.

His thoughts were interrupted by a shout from behind, and he turned to see his grandfather staring after the car, his mouth open in shock. Billy the Kid had to be the only person on the estate taken aback by the turn of events, considering how long he and Alisha had been living separate lives. It was about nine months since the horrible afternoon her brother-in-law Rafael had been gunned down in the car park of a supermarket on the outskirts of Marbella, and slowly but surely the fallout had ripped their relationship asunder.

'Where… where is she going?' Billy's question was directed at anyone and no one. 'Alisha!', he shouted as the car disappeared through the gates, leaving a cloud of dust in its slipstream.

I might as well get this over with, thought Sly, approaching the old man as his brother Chuck and friend Lucky appeared at the front of the house. Eventually they converged on the old man and Chuck, assuming the responsibility thrust upon him by age, was first to speak.

'What's happened?'

'Alisha,' mumbled Billy who, in his moment of despair, looked like a tired, ordinary, confused old man. 'She… she's gone. She packed her things and just drove away. She's left me.'

Sly couldn't hold back. 'For fuck's sake!' he exploded. 'How can you be surprised?'

Chuck put a hand on his arm and flashed him a warning look, but he shrugged off his older brother, twisting the words like a corkscrew, designed to pierce the old man's tough exterior. 'Her brother-in-law was murdered and now her horses are dead, too.'

Billy the Kid stared back at him. It was as if he couldn't understand one word his grandson had spoken. Then, slowly gathering his wits about him, his lips began to move. 'Horses?' he said.

'Yeah, you know, those beautiful four-legged beasts that once galloped around these fields without a care in the world. Not that you paid them much attention. That wonderful Andalusian Caja de Oro is dead, the one which Alisha taught me to ride. The one you bought her as a wedding present. I bloody loved that horse but once again, you've found a way to ruin it all.'

'What are you talking about?' Chuck stepped into the void between them, breaking the eye contact between his brother and grandfather. 'What's happened to the horses?'

'All dead,' said Sly, 'Poisoned I reckon. Flat out in their stalls, no signs of life. I tell you, Chuck, it's an horrific sight.'

Chuck looked into his brother's eyes, detecting a mixture of unhappiness and loathing just below the surface. There was something else, too, the unmistakable hint of fear.

'You know who did this,' said Chuck, a statement of fact rather than a question.

'Yes,' said Sly, 'and so does he.' He tossed his head in the direction of the old man.

'Billy?' Chuck transferred his gaze to his grandfather, who was fiddling with a loose piece of thread hanging from his jacket.

'Hmmm?'

'Sly says you know who killed the horses.'

The old man shrugged, the action in complete contrast to the message his eyes portrayed.

'Don't fall for his bullshit,' said Sly. 'He knows… It's all part of the silly bloody games he likes to play.'

'Bollocks… You little—'

'Come on then,' said Sly, beckoning the old man into a confrontation, reasoning that the only way he would be able to justify laying out a pensioner would be if Billy threw the first punch.

'Wait!' Chuck pushed his brother back and grabbed his grandfather by the arms, forcing him to look in his direction. 'What does he mean? Why does he think you're responsible?'

'He's convinced himself it's the Colombian bitch,' said Billy. 'We had a bit of a, ummm, dispute.'

Sly let out a sarcastic laugh. 'Dispute?' he said. 'Is that what you call it? Fuckin' hell, Chuck. The *truth* is our wonderful grandfather is a fuckin' police informant, just like I told you, and his dirty work is all over the news. The whole of La Rana's coke operation was shut down and everyone arrested except for the woman herself, who miraculously escaped. It was the result of a joint operation between Interpol, the Spanish police, and the old bill back in England, one of whom is our granddad's best mate. Weren't you surprised that one minute we were Britain's most wanted and the next we were free to go home? And who did Granddad use as bait in the little trap he set for La Rana? Muggins here.'

'You!' said Billy, rediscovering some of his old fire. 'Why would I ask you to help out, eh, Sylvester? For goodness' sake, everyone knows you're a walking disaster. Thank God Lucky was around to do the real work.'

'Hang on, I didn't know…' said Lucky, speaking for the first time.

'Don't give Sly a hard time, Billy,' said Chuck. 'He's just upset.'

'Yeah, well, you're as bad as each other. You've upset my business partner again. He's heard you went behind his back to release one of the "prisoners" he was intent on using as an example to others of what happens when they cross him. You think no one knows about that? Boy, Senor Tel is fuming.'

Chuck wanted to respond, but before he was able to his grandfather turned his back on them and marched into the house. Lucky looked to see if he would be summoned, but the old man kept his head down and continued walking.

Sly turned to Lucky. 'You knew?'

'No, I swear,' said the south Londoner. 'He asked me to k… k… keep notes about the trip and to report back everything that happened, that was all. I had no idea what he was planning.'

'If I ever find out you're lying, you and me are gonna fall out big time,' said Sly, poking his finger into the other man's chest. 'I risked my neck and my freedom on that fuckin' boat, and it turns out I was just a stupid decoy.'

'Wh… what was I supposed to say?' asked Lucky. 'He's my boss. I was told not to mention anything to you, though, in case you let something slip with La Rana that got you into trouble.'

'Hang on… you mean when I was in bed with her,' said Sly. 'He planned for me to sleep with her?'

'Well, n… not exactly. I suppose he suspected that given your track record…'

'Bloody hell!' Chuck grabbed Sly around the waist and hauled him away just before he could unleash the punch.

'Arguing will get us nowhere,' said the oldest Dolan boy. 'We're on the same side. We have to figure out what's going on. Sly, you obviously think this is La Rana's doing.'

'I'm not s… sure,' said Lucky. 'Your grandfather insists she's back in South America.'

'Like she hasn't got anyone else to do her bidding,' said Sly. 'Hey, maybe it's you? For all we know her mob offered you a tidy little sum to switch sides? It's strange that someone could approach the horses, feed them poison and walk away without setting alarm bells off with the guards.'

'You think I'd do that… after all your grandfather has d … done for me?'

'This is getting us nowhere,' said Chuck, cutting in again. 'Sly, why do you think this is La Rana's doing?'

'Oh, come on, Chuck,' said Sly. 'You were there when Rafael told us about the frogs and how La Rana uses poison to dispose of her enemies. It's her method and I've seen the bloody creatures myself. She kept them in a tank at her mansion. I bet those horses died in minutes, in absolute agony, and there can't be many poisons that work so quickly and effectively. I've been reading up on her little "pets" since I got back. When they're agitated, threatened or in pain, they produce this chemical. A tiny amount of it applied to other animals, birds or humans brings on instant paralysis followed by a heart attack. There is no known cure. It seems a pretty open and shut case to me. Perhaps we should search our friend Mr Chalmers' room to see if we can find any suspicious substances lying around?'

'Oh c… c… come on, S… Sly.'

'Yeah, I noticed the stammer was back,' said Sly. 'It always comes out when you're nervous doesn't it, Lucky old son?'

'Leave him,' said Chuck. 'He's bound to be nervous, having all these allegations thrown at him. The best thing we can do at this time is wait for the vet's report.'

'Take his side, why don't you?' said Sly. It was his turn to storm off in the direction of the house.

WATCHING from a distance, Naomi had mixed feelings. The family was destabilising, each member consumed by suspicion and doubt. The old man was becoming increasingly isolated, Rafael was dead, his wife gone, and now his grandchildren were turning against him. All he had left was Lucky and a couple of easily malleable guards in his camp, which was exactly how she wanted it. Of course she'd known all along that Lucky wasn't the person Billy deemed him to be.

Her only real regret was that she could see Sylvester was hurting and, despite her better judgement, she really did have strong feelings for him.

42

ABBY was on the coach from Marbella to Torrevieja, looking forward to surprising Chuck with her visit. The journey would take around 10 hours, with numerous stops along the way, but she wasn't bothered. She had plenty to read and music to listen to and was actually relishing the chance to be on her own. The journey would give her time to work out what she wanted to say. There was so much to plan, and she couldn't wait to see him. It was the first chance for them to be together since Chuck had told her his exile in the sun was reaching an end.

It seemed crazy to think they'd been together ever since that bizarre night in Hackney, which led to his banishment. That was well over a year ago, yet in all the time since they'd spent little more than a month in each other's company. It had to be a good sign they felt ready to commit to each other even though they got together so infrequently.

She was pretty sure Chuck was being true to his word when he said he hadn't been led astray by the scantily clad women who flocked to the Costas during the summer months. She believed she was a good judge of character and personality but could never know for sure he wasn't pulling the wool over her eyes. Plenty of her friends would be willing to warn her she shouldn't trust a man so implicitly, women who loved to convey horror stories starring their own husbands or boyfriends. Why should she be unique in the relationship stakes? Yet ever since their first encounter as lustful teenagers, she felt she'd spotted something in him – an inherent sense of fair play and honesty – which other boys his age lacked.

Hearing her tummy rumble, she realised she hadn't eaten since breakfast. That was almost five hours ago, so she put down her magazine on the seat beside her and reached for the sandwiches her mother had lovingly slipped into her bag. Lifting out a small plastic container, she then opened it, casting her eyes across the various foil-wrapped packages, an orange, a chocolate bar and a white envelope. It made her laugh. Her mother always surprised her with little treats. It was one of the things that made their relationship so special.

Her mum had scrawled an affectionate "Ab Fab" across it, a pet nickname, and embellished it with a big heart and a couple of kisses. Perplexed, she ran her finger under the flap and opened it, pulling out a letter and letting two Polaroid photographs fall into her lap.

Hi dear, I just thought you might be bored, and this would cheer you up. After Uncle Arthur's visit the other day, you asked me about his daughter. Of course, she isn't your real cousin. In fact, you aren't related in any way which is fortunate, really, because it means you have none of that crook's twisted blood! Ha ha. But I'm waffling, and you probably have better things to do. I found these photos of you and Arthur's girl from back in the day, so thought you'd like to see them. Lots of love, Mum.

She looked down at the square prints in her lap, a smile playing across her lips. Good old Mum. Turning the pictures over, she then pulled one closer to study it in more detail. They'd been taken in one of those bus station photo booths, two young girls staring back at the camera making funny faces. They were 11 or 12 years old, and she felt a pang of longing suddenly for those carefree days when she had her whole life ahead of her. At the time the picture was taken she was wearing her hair relatively short, a blonde nest sitting atop her thin freckled face, her eyes dancing with amusement as she stuck her tongue out for the camera. The girl next to her wore a black bob framing a round face, her goofy look exacerbated by the fact she was leaning with her head to the side with a finger in her ear.

Abby laughed as the memories came flooding back. A day out in London window shopping with her new 'friend' while their parents met up in Soho for a meal. Though they had only met a couple of times, they seemed to get on like a house on fire and Abby wondered what had happened to the girl she used to call "Cuz". It was more than 10 years ago since they last saw each other yet… that mole, just below the right side of the girl's mouth. It was awfully familiar and, thinking about it, she had seen one exactly like it recently.

Where? She wracked her brains, examining different settings and scenarios, thinking of people she had encountered at work, on nights out and on the bustling streets of Marbella. At first, she drew a blank, the answer frustratingly out of reach, before it came to her with blinding clarity, the impact causing her head to spin. She dropped the photo like a red-hot ember and considered the implications. How could it be?

'SORRY, Chuck, there's no sign of him.'

'Bloody hell! He needs to hear this.'

Lucky looked nervous, flicking his eyes to each corner of the room. There was also a trace of a stutter in his voice, and Chuck knew he was hiding something.

'What is it? Spit it out, mate.'

'It… w… well… it's just that Sly…'

'Take it slow. I know my brother's name. What's he done now?'

Lucky sat down in one of the living room chairs, clenching his hands together in front of him. He was wrestling with his conscience and finally made a decision.

'He's gone out on the razz, Chuck,' said Lucky. 'He said he wanted one f… final fling before you guys went home. He knew the bloke was coming to tell us what had happened to the horses but said he already knew what the results would be and wasn't prepared to listen to anything I had to say any m… more.'

'He's convinced they were poisoned by La Rana,' said Chuck. 'Same old tune. Still, if it turns out to be true, surely that's a really good reason for him to stick closer to home. If she can kill such beautiful animals out of a desire for revenge, then it could be one of us next. A pissed-up Sly wandering the streets of Torrevieja would be an easy target. Fuck! I'm gonna have to go after him.'

Their conversation was interrupted by a buzz on the intercom. Lucky pressed the button and listened to the visitor announce himself. 'Please come in, senor,' he said. 'We're straight down the hall and through the double doors. Meet us in the lounge.'

Turning to Chuck, he said, 'Any idea where your grandfather is?'

'I'll get him,' said Chuck. 'I'm sure he's as keen for answers as we are. After all, if this was an act of wilful destruction, I suspect he will want to get his hands on whoever cost him his marriage.'

'SPANISH FLY… Have you heard of it?'

'It's a song ain't it?' said Billy the Kid. 'Or is that the Spanish flea? Done by that Herb Alpert geezer?'

Chuck and Lucky looked at one another, both thinking the old man had totally lost his marbles. Then all three of them blankly stared back at the veterinary pathologist. He was a small man with rimless spectacles and dark hair combed over a rapidly advancing bald patch.

'You don't mean frog, do you?' asked Chuck. '...One that comes from South America and produces a strong poison?'

'No, not frog, senor. Why you say that?'

'Oh, no particular reason. It was something I read, that's all… its poison seems to have a deadly effect on animals.'

'No, I can assure you I have checked everything,' said the vet. 'It was really quite simple for me, as I have seen cases like this before. When you mention frogs, it reminds me of a story from back in the 1800s. A French military doctor was asked to examine a group of soldiers complaining of terrible weakness, stomach upsets, dry mouths and… well, how you say, the permanent erection…'

He looked down.

'Bloody hell, man, we know what an erection is,' said Billy.

'Granddad!' Chuck shot Billy a warning look. 'Carry on, doc.'

'Well, after some examination he realised the soldiers had all eaten frogs' legs for tea…'

'That's what I said isn't it... frogs?'

'Let me finish, senor, please,' said the vet. 'The reason their legs contained poison was that the frogs had ingested the Spanish fly.'

'It sounds like that bloody nursery rhyme,' said Lucky. 'There was an old lady that swallowed a fly. Perhaps she'll die.'

Chuck ignored him. 'This fly, what does it do then?' he asked. 'Does it just buzz around, the horse somehow swallows it and what?'

'No, no, it's not actually a fly,' said the vet. 'It is a species known as the Blister beetle, a bug that can secrete a highly potent poison called Cantharidin. It is designed to protect it from, well, anything that fancies it as a meal. Your horses have eaten this poison in large quantities, and it has resulted in their sad deaths.'

'But how... our feed is top-of-the-range stuff,' said Billy the Kid. 'We order it from the best suppliers. Why would they need to eat bugs when they're so well fed? Fuckin' hell I should sue...'

'They probably haven't contracted it from the horse feed you buy in,' said the vet. 'Some species of this beetle feed on Alfalfa and, even if the bugs die in the hay, the toxin remains in their bodies. Horses are highly susceptible to it and if they happen to eat any of the alfalfa, it causes them to bleed internally and drop dead. It can happen in no time at all. Strangely, cows and sheep don't seem nearly as badly affected.'

'The far field,' said Chuck, thinking about what the doctor has said. 'There's plenty of hay up there. It's possible the horses grazed on it before...'

'Fuck,' said Billy. 'So, it's not...'

He fell silent, aware of the stranger in the room.

'I am so sorry for your loss,' said the veterinary pathologist. 'If you are going to destroy the grass you must take precautions, wear strong gloves for protection, you only have to digest a bit of it, maybe put your fingers in your mouth after touching it and it can make you severely ill. If a beetle gets on your skin, it can bring out severe yellow blisters.'

'Hence why they call them blister beetles?' said Lucky.

'I don't know,' said the vet.

Granddad Billy shook his head, trying to work out a conundrum, the hint of amusement showing on his face despite the horrendous revelations. 'So,' he said. 'The erections… what's all that about?'

'Ah,' said the vet. 'Some stupid men believe Spanish Fly is an aphrodisiac, that it works in the same way as… how you say… the little blue pill.'

'Viagra,' said Billy.

'Si. Some of the worst sorts of men have been known to lace women's drinks with it or have taken it themselves because they assume it will make them more, how you say, virile.'

The men swapped looks, each wondering whether it might actually work.

'Seriously, you don't want to try it,' said the vet, reading their expressions. 'The truth is that the effect it gives is not really an erection. The beetle inflames the urinary tract and, though it looks like you have, what you say, a rod of iron, it is actually just a severe inflammation. Let me tell you, it has not only killed horses. It is every bit as powerful as cyanide, and there is no antidote. It strips away the lining of your stomach and you bleed internally. The truth is, senors, those horses would have suffered an agonising death.'

'So you don't think this, um, poison… was put deliberately into the horses' feed.'

'No, senor, who would do such a thing?'

Plenty of people with a bone to pick with Billy the Kid, thought Chuck.

'Maybe to be on the safe side you should have the feed tested,' said the vet. 'But I have seen and heard enough about the blister beetles to suspect this was purely an unfortunate accident.'

43

SLY sat at the counter of the Irish bar, Mulligan's, and took a big pull on his third pint of Spanish lager. He needed something stronger. If the Colombian bitch and her people were coming for him, he wanted to be fully anaesthetised. His mind was a teeming mass of conflicting emotions, and he wondered whether he might be in the middle of a breakdown. He kept thinking of the night he'd spent with the cartel boss, how she had managed to instil in him a toxic mixture of lust and fear. Automatically his hand reached for his back, where the bruises had faded but he could still feel them, unsure whether it was his mind playing tricks or she had caused permanent damage to him by walking across his flesh in her stilettos while wearing only a black basque. It was at that moment he had realised her aphrodisiacs were power and control. He shivered just at the moment a hand came down on his shoulder. The pint glass wobbled in his hand, beer splashing across the bar.

'Fuck!'

'Shit, sorry.'

A familiar voice. He turned to face her.

'Didn't mean to scare you, hun. You're jumpy today, ain't you?'

'I didn't think you'd come.'

'You don't know me very well then.' Naomi bent down and kissed him on the cheek, then turned to track down the barman. 'Excuse me, senor, por favour?'

He came across, wiped the beer from the counter, and looked at her eagerly. 'What can I get you?'

'Vodka and lemonade.' She looked at Sly. 'You need a refill?'

'This beer isn't doing the trick. Get us a shot… maybe a double? I need something to numb the senses.'

'I know just the thing.' She looked at the barman. 'Two double sambucas, please.' Turning back to Sly, she said, 'I guess this is your leaving do, then? Not a great turnout. Where are your mates?'

'I don't have any.' As he said it, he realised the sentence was soaked in self-pity.

'Oh, come on… where's the happy-go-lucky joker I know and love?'

'He's an idiot,' said Sly. 'You're better off without him.'

'I don't think so.' She paused for a moment. 'This is about the horses, isn't it? Look, what happened, it wasn't your fault. It was just one of those things… probably someone taking revenge on your grandfather for some despicable act or other. You now know the kind of man he is… the things he's done over the years.'

He was hearing her words, but they weren't really registering. After what she'd said about her feelings, guilt weighed heavily on him in the same way he considered he was to blame for the fate of Alisha's beautiful horses. He pushed the beer away, more of it slopping on the counter. Grabbing her by the upper arms, he pinned her in place, registering the hurt look on her face. He felt he had no choice. He had to make her understand. If she saw him for what he really was, a millstone around her neck rather than a caring lover, perhaps…

'What are you doing?' said Naomi. 'You're hurting me!'

'You know nothing!' he said, spitting out the words, flecks of saliva landing on her face. She turned away to lessen the impact of his verbal assault, the tears starting to flow. 'I made a pact with the devil, and it's come back to punish me… punish us. Poor Alisha, if she knew what I'd done she would never forgive me. Just as you shouldn't. I … I slept with the boss of a drug cartel, and all this is happening because she thinks I…'

The effort of the revelation drained him, and his grip on her arms loosened. For a moment she looked him in the eye, and he noted the blobs of mascara smudged on her cheek. Then she slowly turned and walked out of the bar, the door swinging shut behind her. He stared at it for a long time, hoping she might return, lock him in an embrace and tell him he was forgiven, and that she loved him, despite his many sins.

The door stayed closed.

'Where is the lady?' He turned to the see the barman standing there. 'I bring the drinks.'

'Leave them there,' said Sly, handing over a large note. 'And keep them coming until that runs out. The lady had another appointment, but I'll help her with these.' He lifted one of the glasses, tilted his head back and downed the drink in one, before reaching across for the other. He wondered how many it would take to make the pain stop and turn his head into a big ball of nothing.

IT WAS dark outside, and he had totally lost track of time. Though he tried to make sense of the clock at the far end of the bar, the task proved beyond him. Finishing the remains of another pint, his fuzzy mind prodded him, advising he couldn't leave it any longer. Slipping from the bar stool, he lurched on unstable legs before crashing to the ground in slow motion. 'Stupid pisshead,' someone muttered, adding that the person in question should be 'thrown out for his own good'.

Climbing to his feet, Sly collided with another customer – an old guy in a flat cap – and mumbled 'bog'. The man looked at him oddly, then pointed to his left. With no time to waste, Sly pushed his way past another couple of drinkers before throwing himself at the door.

Where were the urinals? He swivelled around, feeling disorientated, only to be disturbed by a scream. Spinning, his eyes focussed on a figure with shoulder-length blonde hair stepping out from a cubicle.

Shit, he was in the Ladies'!

He muttered an incoherent apology and stumbled out. To his right were steps disappearing down into the depths of the ageing building. He experienced a lightbulb moment, his memory alerting him to the fact the gents were on the lower level. Clinging on to the wide wooden banister in order to remain upright, a feeling of nausea swept over him, the alcohol pushing him over the edge from numb to decidedly ill.

Stumbling down the steps, he barged through the door marked SENOR then tripped and fell head-long into a stall, his head cracking against the porcelain cistern. He put his hand up to inspect the damage and pulled it away covered in blood. The sight caused his stomach to emit a strange gurgling sound and he quickly locked the door before throwing up, some of the putrid bile splattering his favourite blue T-shirt.

'Yer man's very keen to get it done tonight.' The words came from the other side of the cubicle door, and for a moment he thought the Irish voice was addressing him. There was a silence as he pondered how to reply, followed by the sound of liquid hitting stainless steel.

'Aye. He's not happy with that London fella now, is he?' The other man spoke in a similar dialect. The two men were addressing each other. It had nothing to do with him, and they appeared to be unaware of his presence. He listened.

'Tel's worked with yer man ever since he arrived here from Belfast, y'know?' said the first man. 'They bought the golf course together, then moved on to timeshares. Made a lot of money, they did, and no mistake. But Tel thinks the old man's taking him for an eejat. There's even a whisper he's in the pay of the peelers. Some big wig bastard from London was seen up at the course the other day. Our Sammy recognised him from the TV.'

'Billy the Kid's a fuckin' rat?' The other man sounded genuinely shocked. 'His rep is that of a top villain. They say he got away with a huge pile of gold from some warehouse caper back in the day.'

'Brink'sMat?'

'Aye.'

'Happen they're right,' said the first man. 'It's a mite strange he never got himself locked up like the others, though, is it not? Some of them boys are still inside and others were only recently released. Never had his collar felt for anything, so they say.'

'Odd.'

Sly was now listening intently to the conversation, the use of his grandfather's name sobering him up instantly.

He had to get back to the villa and warn his family of this imminent threat.

Slap!

Damn. The sound of Sly's wallet hitting the floor echoed off the tiles. It had fallen from his trouser pocket as he overbalanced in an effort to hear what was being said.

'Shhhh!' said the first Irishman.

'What?'

'Did ye not hear that?'

'I heard nowt, but there's a godawful pong in this place, like puke. Uuuurgh, it makes me feel like boking mesel', so it does. Let's go, eh?'

'I don't know,' said the other man. 'Maybes we should check it out.'

Silence engulfed the room, Sly holding his breath as he brought his feet onto the seat so they couldn't see his legs under the door. He listened intently for movement, hoping they'd leave, but there was just deathly silence. Then, just as he was thinking about sneaking a look, a pair of large black brogues appeared in the space beneath the cubicle door. Sly had the sense the two men were communicating with hand gestures. The gentle tap of knuckles on wood made his heart thump against his chest.

'Ye awright in there, sonny?' asked the man with the harsh Ulster brogue. 'Can we help you out there maybes? By the smell of ye, ye could do with some assistance.'

Sly was willing them to go away, but knew he was trapped. The only way out was through them and the amount of alcohol in his blood stream was bound to prove a hindrance. He had to do something: His grandfather, Chuck and Lucky might be in danger.

Tap, tap, tap.

'Come on, Sonny Jim, we know you're in there. You fuckin' stink pal. Either you come out or we'll have to act all Big Bad Wolf and blow this here door down.'

Sly felt the bile rising in his throat. Not now. One retch would give the game away.

'Could have fallen asleep in his own vom,' said the second man, speaking for the first time in a while.

'That's what I'm worried about,' said the other. 'Can't have the wee tosser dropping dead on the premises. Too many questions.'

The feet disappeared from view and Sly's hopes rose again before the door disintegrated in an explosion of flying wooden shards.

'YOU know who this is, don't ye, ye pair of spoons?' Senor Tel looked out from beneath thick, caterpillar eyebrows. He was holding Sly's wallet in his hands. The gang boss had appeared on the scene just as they were about to jettison Sly through the tradesman's entrance into the alleyway out back. Sly had seen the glimmer of recognition on Senor Tel's face as he told them to bring the drunk into his office.

'We thought he was just some pished looper,' said the guy in the brogues.

'And that's why you don't get the good jobs, y'see?' said the Ulster gang leader. 'This here mess of an individual may be poleaxed but it don't mean he's some ordinary wee tourist out on the razz. This here is one of the Dolan boys, you divvies, grandson of Billy the Kid, no less.'

The two men looked at each other, their expressions betraying their alarm.

'Aww, no,' said Senor Tel. 'Don't tell me… Yer fuckin' didn't, did ye? Hell! How many fuckin' times have I told ye to keep yer mouths shut. Who discusses business in the crapper? Eejits! You two have been jabbering away without a care, ain't ya?'

'N… no, boss,' said the second gang member, who was short and stocky, with red hair and freckles. 'He couldn't have heard anything anyway… he was two sheets to the wind. I'm sure he was just sleeping it off.'

'And yer willing to bet yer life on that statement?' Sly watched the two men attempt to stare each other down. There was only going to be one winner. Sly sensed his situation was growing worse by the minute, and began to consider how he might fight or argue his way to freedom. 'Yous two are an absolute liability and no mistake, y'know that?'

'I saved you from my brother at the golf club, Senor Tel,' Sly blurted out.

'Oh, here we go,' said the Ulster gang boss. 'It speaks. Not sure what language, but let's listen.'

'Don't you remember?' Sly tried to elucidate more clearly. 'If it wasn't for me, you'd still be buried in that bunker.'

'So you did,' said Tel, 'which means it's an almighty shame what I have to do now. I'm sorry, son, but it's just business, you see?' He turned to the two men, who were awaiting their instructions. 'Go fetch Sammy. Tell him to bring his tool kit.'

44

NAOMI gave Lucky both barrels the moment he walked through the door. She could tell she'd taken him by surprise. Their relationship might have been one of mutual convenience, but they'd been getting on well over the last few months. He'd agreed to meet her at her favourite pizza haunt in Torrevieja after she'd phoned to say she'd found Sly propped up against the bar in Mulligan's. Though she was seething, she'd managed to keep her powder dry until they were face to face.

'You knew, you bastard!' she said. 'You knew he'd slept with that South American bitch. You went on that trip with him.' Her eyes shone brightly, the flame from the candle on the table reflecting back at him. It was clear he didn't know how to respond. She'd confided in him about her relationship with the younger Dolan brother, but probably hadn't made it clear how serious she was about him.

'L... look,' he said. 'S... sit down and we'll t... t... talk.'

She threw her bag over the back of a chair and flopped into the seat like a petulant child. 'OK,' she said, 'I'm all ears.'

Lucky was trying to remain calm under fire, speaking slowly and no doubt hoping to cut out the stammer, which always made him sound guilty. He explained painstakingly that he didn't really know what had happened, as he and Sly had become separated on the trip to Galicia. After further prompting, he revealed he had assumed Naomi's relationship with Sly was an open one. 'You must know what he… he's like,' said Lucky. 'He told me "What goes on tour, stays on tour" and if he found out I'd blabbed my life wouldn't be worth l… living.'

'Oh? Think it's going to be worth living now, do you?'

At that moment, a waiter arrived to take their order. Naomi asked for a large red wine to go with her slice of margherita and salad, then sat back, her eyes daring him to keep talking so she could unleash another volley of abuse. When the meal arrived, they ate in silence, Naomi mulling over what the last few days meant for her. She desperately wanted to get away from the villa now that Alisha had left, and was considering her next move. Even if she stayed, she had a nagging suspicion it would be only a matter of time before the old man dispensed with her services. He was cutting back, and with the marriage now over in everything but name she guessed he would find her surplus to requirements. A shame. She'd served Billy the Kid well for six years. She'd worked herself into the ground, but still felt the advantages of life in the Spanish sun outweighed the drawbacks.

With Billy's wife being so much younger than him, Naomi had developed a close relationship with her, sharing their thoughts on current trends, music and fashion. Even though it had been just a few days since Alisha's departure, she missed the woman greatly and was hanging on to the slim hope she would get a call to join Mrs Dolan in Marbella. The woman had retreated to the couple's second home on the Golden Mile so she could be near her one remaining horse, Rocco, but Naomi suspected she wouldn't stay long. Once the marriage was annulled, she could buy somewhere of her own. Then, when all the turmoil died down, she would hopefully need a maid and send for Naomi.

'Are you staying in town?' asked Lucky in an attempt to broker an uneasy truce.

'There's a small hotel on the seafront,' she said, lightening up a bit. 'I've booked for a couple of nights. I can't face going back and, anyway, I'm expecting a visitor.'

'Oh?' This came as news to Lucky but she wasn't going to answer his unasked question. He would find out soon enough. Then he would have real cause to worry.

LUCKY manoeuvred the car into a side street, heading for the promenade.

'Shit,' he said, spotting the commotion outside the darkened Irish bar. 'Some poor bloke looks the worse for wear.' He knew having visited Mulligan's on numerous occasions that closing time was an hour ago, it being a week night with the summer season almost over.

He watched three burly blokes fighting to get a bedraggled figure into the back of a stationary car.

'Fuck!' said Naomi.

'What?' asked Lucky.

'That's Sly, between those two boneheads,' said Naomi.

'Shit!' He moved his foot towards the brake.

'Drive on.'

'What? Look, I know y… your angry with him but we can't just l…. leave him.'

'And what are you going to do?' she glared at him. 'You're up for taking on those head cases, are you? Maybe they're going to give him a lift home. Thought of that? Chuck works with them, don't he? They could be just doing him a favour.'

'Th… they don't look like the type of people who do favours. Fuckin' hell, I thought you c…cared for the bloke.'

'I do… did… look, drive past then take a left and park up. I need to think.'

He didn't look convinced, but did as he was told. 'Now what?'

'I'll wander down and check what they're doing,' said Naomi. 'They don't know me and they won't suspect a woman. If they are Senor Tel's men, they would have seen you hanging around with Billy plenty of times.'

'True, but I could…'

'You got a gun?'

He shook his head.

'Then, with the greatest respect, you can do fuck all. Hell, they would probably see it as a bonus. Two for the price of one.'

'You agree then,' he said. 'You think Sly's a prisoner.'

She nodded. 'That's the way it looks. You go and ring the villa, sharpish. Chuck needs to hear about this. He knows these blokes, works with them. If anyone can get Sly out of the shit, it's his brother.'

'OK.' He nodded. 'Be careful, though.'

CHUCK had just spoken to his mum and was itching to get the show on the road. He had a suitcase on the floor and was throwing in things he didn't think he would need for the last few days at Granddad Billy's. He wondered what the old man would do without them. At least he had Lucky.

Hearing the phone ring in the hallway, he waited for Naomi to answer then remembered she was on a couple of days off. Billy the Kid said her presence reminded him too much of Alisha and was contemplating firing her, but Lucky had persuaded him otherwise. 'She's almost like family, Mr Dolan,' he had protested. 'You'd only have to find someone else to do the job, and it won't be easy to come across someone so trustworthy.' While Chuck couldn't disagree, he did wonder if the boy's protest was further evidence there was something going on between the two of them.

Reluctantly, he left the bulging case on the floor and stepped out into the corridor. The caller was persistent and his grandfather nowhere to be seen. It was pretty late, and he was probably indulging in his daily routine of drowning his sorrows in the pub. Picking up the phone, he recognised the voice immediately. Lucky sounded breathless and was stuttering, and Chuck sensed something was wrong. 'What is it? I thought you were off dancing the night away in one of those tourist discos.'

'W… w… we've got a problem, Ch… Chuck,' said Lucky.

'Fuck, you OK?'

'I'm fine,' said Lucky. 'It's S… Sly.'

'Shit, what's he been up to now? Bloody women again?'

'More s… serious, I think. I've just seen him b…b… bundled into a car by some of Senor Tel's boys. Your mate Sammy was with them. Sly didn't look good. Honest to God. He had a c… cut on his head and his clothes were a m… mess.'

'You think they've given him a battering? I'll fucking kill that Sammy... you got the car?'

'I... uh yeah but... I'm not sure what I can do on m... my own. I could grab him but...'

'No. I'll sort it. You need to keep an eye on them, though ... see where they go. You OK with that?'

'Sure.' The voice sounded uneasy. 'It's l... late though, they may s... stop to find out who's f... following them.'

'Take extra care then,' said Chuck. 'You're Sly's mate, ain't you? We have to do this right, Lucky, or he'll be floating among the flamingos tomorrow morning. Sammy's a creature of habit, so I'm pretty sure I know where he'll be going. I just need you to confirm it for me. I'll do the rest.'

'You'll need b... back-up, Chuck.'

'Of course,' he said. 'I'm not stupid. A couple of granddad's men can come with me. We'll have to leave the old man alone for a bit, which isn't ideal, so once you find out what I need to know you'd better get back here sharpish. OK?'

'OK, Chuck,' said Lucky.

45

THE walkie-talkie buzzed, and Chuck picked it up, pressing the button as his grandfather had instructed. Holding it in front of him, he spoke into the microphone.

'Yeah.' He released the button and listened. His grandfather's voice boomed into the stillness of early morning.

'It's meant to be "Yeah, over", not just "Yeah", OK? Over.'

Chuck thought his grandfather had seen too many movies, but didn't waste time questioning the order. 'We're five miles from the lake. Over.'

'Lucky just rang. You're right. That Irish bastard's nothing if not predictable. Over.'

Chuck felt an uncomfortable sensation in the pit of his stomach. The fact the Shankill Whisperer followed routines made him fearful for his younger brother. Chuck had rescued Sylvester from many scrapes in the past, but this was trouble at a whole new level. Sammy McMahon was a stone-cold killer and Chuck felt ill when he thought of the sickening condition in which the paramilitary's victims ended up. A vision of Sly being given the horrific six-pack treatment formed in his mind.

'Can't you do something, Billy?' asked Chuck. 'Thought you and Tel were thick as thieves. Over.'

His grandfather fell silent, and Chuck wondered if the connection had been lost. Mobile phones were all the rage these days, yet the old man insisted on using antiquated military equipment for communication.

Just as the oldest Dolan boy was about to put the walkie-talkie down, it crackled to life again. 'Sorry, son, I tried to call Tel, but he ain't picking up,' his grandfather said. 'This is my fault. I'll never forgive myself if anything happens to Sylvester. Those Irish… you can't trust them. Bastard's got a bee in his bonnet over a couple of timeshare deals. He thinks I'm holding out on him. I've told him the Spanish cops have launched an investigation and moving money now would be foolish, but he won't listen. Maybe he intends to use Sly as a bargaining chip to get what he wants, but negotiation isn't his way. I had a feeling he's been planning something, and maybe this is it. Over.'

'OK, Billy. Well, Lucky's on his way back to keep an eye on you… just in case. I need to focus on Sly. Over.'

'Ahh, buzzer just went. That'll be the boy now. Over and out.'

'Be careful, Billy, you don't know…'

Too late, his grandfather had gone.

Chuck glanced to his side at the driver, a thick-set man with a dark beanie perched on his shaven head. A former squaddie called Scottie, he'd seen action in Desert Storm when UK and United States forces fought in the Gulf War. The third member of the group, a former officer of the now-defunct Special Patrol Group called Dazzler, was sitting in the back seat massaging a pistol. The ex-cop had worked for the mobile unit of the Metropolitan Police during the early 80s when they were renowned for their questionable tactics in handling riots in Brixton, Southall and Tottenham. Chuck didn't imagine either man had qualms about using excessive force, which was no bad thing when Chuck considered who they were up against.

He touched Scottie on the arm and pointed ahead. 'Turn off the road here and park up. We can do the rest on foot. We need to stay invisible for as long as possible, right? My fuckin' brother's life's at stake.'

'Got it, boss,' said Scottie. 'Clear as crystal.'

'Daz.'

'Yes, chief.'

'Get out those wire cutters.'

'NAOMI?'

The line was silent for a couple of seconds.

'She just nipped out, son.' There was a harsh chuckle. 'This is her dad.'

Lucky froze. It was the first time he had heard the voice in months, and it so disturbed him he nearly sent the car skidding off the road into a ditch. What the fuck? Chills travelled through his bloodstream.

'H… how…?'

'You're stuttering, son. Get a grip.'

Lucky was too shell-shocked to reply.

'Guess you're wondering what's going on here, me answering Naomi's phone, right?' the voice continued. 'Let's just say I thought it would be nice to check in on her. Anyway, never mind all that, let's get down to business. You've had an easy ride so far, considering you fucked me over good and proper. I was hoping you might have wormed your way into his confidence enough for him to tell you where I might find my gold, but you've learned the square root of fuck all. I'm disappointed in you, Lucky. After all that pleading and those promises. It's time to be a bit more proactive.'

Lucky took a deep breath, trying to muster some courage. The voice was still talking, the underlying menace causing a sick feeling in the pit of his stomach. 'I hear those two boys are otherwise occupied, which gives you the opportunity to put the squeeze on the old bastard. Go to Naomi's room. There are things in her bottom drawer that can help you. Not the kind of things most young girls keep in their bottom drawer, I'll grant you.' The harsh chuckle attacked Lucky's eardrum like a power drill. He felt a headache coming on.

'There's a pistol she's been saving for a special occasion and some knock-out drops… you'll know what to do with them, but I'll send a text to explain, anyway. They ain't for the old man, you need him conscious. If you want to bump him off later, I've no problem with that. Hell, feel free to drown the fucker in his own pool – that would be ironic.'

The cackle came again, and Lucky had visions of Billy the Kid Dolan bobbing face down in the water, his grandsons attempting to fish out the body. 'That old cunt ain't played fair with me over nothing, after all the years I've known him and the favours I done him,' said the voice. 'He promised a number of times he would see me right but zilch, nada, nowt. Now he can pay the full price – I need to know where he has stashed it all. The gold, the cash, traveller's cheques, jewellery, whatever. You owe me, son, so get that information and we'll call it quits. Fuck me over, though, and you're a dead man walking. I've found you once and I can find you again, so don't even think about doing a runner.'

When the phone went dead Luke Chalmers stared at it for a good 20 seconds before dropping it on the passenger seat as if it was a hot potato. The shock of hearing from Arthur Lee did that to a person.

'WHAT a lovely surprise!' Billy the Kid's voice crackled through the intercom. 'I was expecting someone else. No one told me I'd be getting a royal visit, ha ha. They've left me on me Jack Jones. Come in, come in.'

The grounds of the Dolan villa loomed dark and silent as Abby's taxi drove through the gates. Usually the driveway was illuminated, the lighting particularly bright around the security hut. On this particular night it was bathed in shadow and the only reason she could make out anything was because of the full moon blinking through the trees. *Perhaps there's been a power cut*, she thought. Or maybe Grandpa Dolan was becoming more frugal in his old age. Chuck had told her things had changed dramatically since Alisha walked out.

The taxi pulled up in front of the house, and she stepped out. Leaning through the driver's window she told him, '*Uno momento. Por favor esperame*?' He nodded. Yes, he was prepared to wait.

She needn't have worried. In seconds the turning circle on the driveway was illuminated in glaring white light and the next moment he was standing at the door. Chuck's grandfather, Billy the Kid Dolan. She had always thought it a funny nickname, more suited to a native of the Wild West than a London pensioner, and it seemed even more out-of-place now.

She hadn't seen him in months, and it was frightening how much he'd aged. Where before he tended to stand ramrod straight, he was now bent down over a stick, the silver flecks in his hair having multiplied to the point where it was the most prominent colour on display. The brightness of the porch light highlighted the deep worry lines on his forehead, cheeks and under his eyes, vast areas of his face bathed in shadow. He walked forward to greet her.

'It's fine, Billy. I can handle it,' she said, holding out her palm to instruct him to stay where he was. Moving around to the back of the taxi, she took her favourite Louis Vuitton suitcase from the driver, lifted the handle and rolled it on wheels towards the house. Billy leant forward to kiss her on the cheek.

'Nice to see you again, girl,' he said.

She hated people who called her girl, finding it patronising, but in his case, she would make allowances. The old man had been brought up in a completely different era.

'Nice to see you too, Billy,' she said. 'What have you been up to? It was all a bit eerie out there… I thought someone would be on the gate.'

'Waste of money,' he said. 'I don't need all those people no more. They were draining me bank account and, anyway, I've had to send some to Marbella to look after Alisha. Life's changed so much since you were last here and I don't see the point in frittering away all my ill-gotten gains. At some stage I'll have to leave something to my, umm, family. Having the two boys here, my grandchildren, got me thinking. If you two have long-term plans, for instance…'

'Don't be silly, Billy,' she said. 'Plenty of time for all that.'

'Silly Billy, ha ha, I like that girl. You're very kind, but what have I got left to live for? With Alisha gone…' He stopped abruptly. 'Anyway, where are my manners, keeping you on the doorstep? It's late. Do you need cash for the taxi?'

'No, it's fine. I've got it.'

She walked back and paid the cabbie who then turned the car around and headed back down the drive. When she returned, Billy ushered her into the house. 'Look, girl, you've had a long journey and I ain't sure when our Chuck will be back… he's just out on a little job at the moment. Come and rest your pegs. In fact, join me for a nightcap. I don't usually permit girls to enter the sanctuary of my pub, but I reckon I should make an exception, you being Chuck's girl n' all.'

What she really needed was her bed after such a taxing journey, but she didn't want to appear rude, as the old man was letting her stay in his house. More than that, he seemed a bit down and from their earlier conversation she guessed he was experiencing a moment of introspection after Alisha left. Maybe some company would lift his mood.

'Just the one then,' she said. 'I could do with a drink after all that travelling. Where's, umm, Naomi isn't it?'

'Night off,' he said. 'No matter, just leave your suitcase in the hallway. Chuck will take it up when he gets back. You should consider yourself a very privileged young lady. You'll be the first woman ever to set foot in my private boozer.'

46

THE THREE men moved at speed around the periphery of the lake, pushing through clusters of hogweed and tamarisk, huge white pyramids of salt rising up on the horizon. Chuck guessed that somewhere in that direction, the Shankill Whisperer would be dragging Sly towards a tortuous fate. Chuck had insisted his men dress predominantly in white. Camouflage might be an advantage when pushing through the local flora, but he reasoned it would offer little protection when they were travelling across the vast expanse of salt flats.

CRRAACK!

They hit the deck in unison as a flamboyance of flamingos rose from the surrounding marshlands to saturate the moonlit skies above.

'Shit!' said Chuck.

'Just birds,' said Scottie, his tone reassuring.

'Yeah, but what a fuckin' racket. Something disturbed them.'

Chuck levered himself to his feet again slowly, looking left and right before continuing the trek around the vast expanse of water. 'We've a bit of a way to go. I hope…' He cut off the negative thought.

'Not much we can do about it, skip,' said Dazzler, reading his mind. 'Scottie's trained to take out a target from here in the daylight, but it would be pretty tricky right now. We'll just have to trust to luck and forge on.'

SLY had no reason to recognise the terrain. The last time he'd been anywhere near the place he was lying comatose in the back of a van. He knew the story off by heart though, Chuck having taken him through it step by step. When it came to Sammy "Shankill Whisperer" McMahon, he hadn't skimped on the detail. Anyone capable of subjecting a fellow human being to the sort of treatment he liked to dish out had no moral compass, hardly a comforting thought when you were his latest prisoner.

A thump in the back encouraged him to hobble faster, his arms tied behind him and his progress hampered by the removal of his shoes and socks, which had been discarded alongside his stinking clothes. All that protected his dignity now was his underwear, while blood had seeped down from the wound on his head to his shoulders and chest. He could smell his own stink and was in desperate need of a bath, but the thought of submerging himself in water rapidly dispersed when he saw the vast lagoon reflecting the bright full moon. Would his body ever be found if he ended up dying here? He could just imagine his family searching for answers in the days that followed, while the police drew a blank in their efforts to solve the mystery. He shivered, but not from the cold.

No one spoke as the grim route march continued. One of the guys he had encountered in the toilets led the way, followed by Sammy and Sly with the bloke in the brogues bringing up the rear. Why hadn't he been nicer to Naomi?

Why had he told her about his brief encounter with Estella? His brain was full of irrational thoughts at the moment, the confession largely due to the alcohol sloshing around his system. He should have had a couple of drinks with her, kept his mouth shut then taken her to her hotel and banged her brains out. He was in this situation purely because of self-pity, a trait which seemed destined to cost him his life.

The Northern Ireland gang boss Senor Tel had rightly come to the conclusion that Sly had overheard the two men discussing a raid on his granddad's villa. Nothing he said or did at this stage could persuade them to let him walk away. He felt his bladder release – control of his bodily functions seeming irrelevant in his current predicament – and was so disgusted by his own ineptitude that tears filled his eyes. He made a vow that if he somehow got out of this situation, he would set about changing his impetuous ways.

'HERE, boss,' said Scottie. 'Just behind this bloody great mountain.'

Yes, thought Chuck. Thank fuck Sammy McMahon was such a predictable psychopath.

'What's the plan, chief?' asked Dazzler.

'When the time comes, you two take out the smaller guys and leave the big fucker to me,' said Chuck.

'Personal, chief?' said Dazzler.

You don't know the half of it, thought Chuck, but he didn't answer. Instead, he said, 'Let's split up. Work your way around to the other side of the mountain and when the time comes draw the attention away from me. Then I'll rescue my brother.'

'What's the signal?' asked Scottie.

'Hand me a flare.' Chuck pointed to Dazzler's backpack. 'I know it's blatant, but it's more instant than the walkie-talkie, and we know it will work. Also, it should cause a useful distraction, if just for a few seconds. When it goes up, you're straight in. No delay.'

'Shoot to kill?'

'I don't want a full-scale war, but these fuckers started it. Whatever it takes to get my brother out of there.'

'You ever thought of joining the forces?' asked Scottie. 'You'd do OK. Think like a commander.'

For a moment, Chuck's mind flashed back to his uncle Clive, the contrasting memories of him before he set off for the Falklands and after he came back, the way war had changed him.

'Not for me,' said Chuck. 'Now come on, there ain't much time.'

The two men headed off around the back of the huge white obstacle standing between them and the target.

'YE SHOULD finish him off now, Sammy,' said the man in the brogues, his strong Ulster accent bouncing off the mountain. 'Tel won't want any dramas. He just needs the kiddie out of the way.'

Sammy was wrapping ropes around Sly and tying him to a wooden pole. Peering through watery eyes, Sly saw the lake in front of him and wished he could break away and drown himself. Anything was preferable to being at the mercy of this muscle-bound madman.

'I want his brother to know he suffered,' said the Shankill Whisperer, speaking for the first time since they'd arrived at the lake. 'The arrogant shite needs to be taught his place in the world. Maybe's I'll mail him some body parts just so's he's aware what went on here.'

The two foot soldiers knew better than to argue with the Whisperer. They stood back now, looking nervously around as Sammy secured the restraints, pulling them tighter than necessary in order to make Sly wince. Any effect the alcohol might have had in numbing his senses had worn off long ago. If only he could shut down his thoughts and stop agonising over the different ways this barbarian might choose to inflict pain on him.

'Pass the mallet, Jimmy boy. Think I'll do a job on the wee man's ankles.' The red-haired man delved into his rucksack and pulled out the hefty wooden tool. Sammy reached over with one massive hand and snatched it away. He stroked it tenderly, as if it was about to go on display in a museum and needed a final polish. Then he put it between his knees, spat on his hands, rubbed them together and lifted it again, nodding as he got a true sense of its weight.

'You and me need some private time, boy,' said Sammy. 'Forget these eejits, the lake, the salt… I need ye to concentrate on me and me alone. It's a shame, so it is, that you're related to that sad loser Chuck. If you hadn't been, I could have spared you a lot of pain, but that bastard thinks his shit don't stink and I want to show him it does.'

He shot a look at the man in the brogues. 'You bring that video camera, Micky?' His accomplice gave a slight nod. 'Then get it out, why don't ye, so's we can send this kid's nearest and dearest a nice home movie?'

Turning back to Sly, he said, 'It's interesting, don't you think? You look remarkably like yer man Chuck, which makes life a lot easier for me. It will feel like I'm going to work on his sorry ass... D'you see what I'm telling yous? Chuck was supposed to do what I told him but instead he decided to deliver some wee scrote to the hospital, which earned me a bit of grief from the boss when the kid's face turned up in the paper with his dad demanding action from the peelers. So if you need someone to blame for this it's him.'

Sly noticed the red-haired gang member looked slightly queasy, though he knew neither of the Whisperer's accomplices would have the balls to talk him out of his plan of action.

'You say something, pal?' The Whisperer walked forward until he was standing so close that Sly could smell the man's rancid, fetid breath.

'Chuck's more of a man than you'll ever be,' muttered Sly, finally mustering some defiance. A bit of the Dolan gene filtering through. What was it his dad used to tell his mum?

Might as well be hung for a sheep as a lamb.

Sly decided that if he had to go down, he would go down fighting – verbally, if not physically. He lifted his head and looked his captor in the eye. 'Chuck will rip your head off and piss in the bastard hole.'

'Wha...? You little...'

Sammy's eyes widened, and he took a step back, lifting the heavy mallet up high and over his left shoulder...

Shhhhhft!

A bright red trail shot into the night sky and Sly watched in wonder as it exploded over their heads. For a moment, he thought it was the start of one of those religious festivals the Spanish loved so much. Then he heard a ptt, ptt sound and saw the red-haired man – the one called Jimmy – crash face first to the floor. The one called Mickey then broke into a run, hands over his head, his brogues crunching on salt as he sought cover.

Sammy lowered the mallet, turned in the direction from which he perceived the shooting to have come, and saw two men emerge from behind the salt mountain. What he didn't see was the charging figure arriving from the other direction. Chuck wrapped his arms around the waist of the giant Ulsterman and Sly watched in awe as the two figures disappeared into the lake under an explosion of water.

47

ABBY sat in the corner by the snooker table and looked around the pub. It was amazing. It didn't matter that some of the materials used to construct it were undoubtedly fake. The overall impression was of a cosy, rustic bar in the heart of England. There was the famous snooker table she had heard all about, two fruit machines, a set of ornate tables and one of those old retro jukeboxes. *If you had to treat yourself to one indulgence from dear old Blighty why not a traditional pub?*

She watched Billy pour the drinks then walk across and place a large glass containing an orange liquid in front of her. 'Looks interesting,' she said, lifting it to the light so the ice cubes clinked together. 'What is it?'

'A little pick-me-up,' he said, taking a pull on the large whisky he had poured himself. 'It contains champagne, orange juice, cognac and syrup. Hope you like it. Alisha swears by it.'

She feared talk about his missing wife would lower the mood, so jumped in quickly to take his mind off things. 'Wow, you have a jukebox. Anything good on it?'

'That depends,' he said. 'What do you like?'

'I don't know… something uplifting.'

'You like the Rolling Stones?'

'My dad did... he used to listen to it on his Walkman when...' She stopped suddenly.

'OK?'

'Yeah, sorry... it's just I don't talk about him much. He died when I was young. When you spoke about music, I guess it just awoke a memory.'

'Sometimes I think music is the only thing I have to hold on to from the past,' said Billy, walking across to the jukebox. He pushed a couple of buttons and Abby watched, mesmerised, as the round disc moved up and around on the end of a metal arm before being placed in position. There was a crackling sound as needle connected with vinyl, then the melodic tones of a keyboard, joined by female soprano voices. For a moment she thought he must have got it wrong, the music having little in common with rock-and-roll, the singers repeating a high-pitched mantra. 'You can't always get what you want.'

'Are you sure...?'

'Shhhh...' he said, holding his fingers to his lips, his eyes focussed not on her but something in the far distance. At that moment, the singing stopped and the chords of an acoustic guitar broke in. A brass instrument joined the ensemble, playing a haunting refrain, before it faded away and the rough, nasal tones of Mick Jagger echoed around the room, introducing them to a girl at a reception holding a glass of wine.

'It's true,' said Billy, breaking the spell.

'What's that?' she asked.

'I've found to my cost you can't always get what you want.'

Abby hoped he wasn't going to bring down the mood. She was feeling better now, nicely relaxed and excited to see Chuck.

'You have to reflect on the good things,' she said, hearing her mother's voice coming out of her mouth.

'Oh, I do… I do,' he said, knocking back the whisky. 'That's why I love my single malt, for instance. I may sound morbid at the moment, but when I think about my life, I've been luckier than most. I have wonderful grandchildren, two nice houses, no money worries… I ain't wanted for much, really.'

God, she thought, *he sounds like he's about to make a deathbed confession*. She hoped he wasn't mistaking her for a female priest, here to give him absolution.

'Of course, there were times it could have gone very wrong,' said the old man, warming to his theme. 'I had my fair share of luck, back in the day when I used to cross the pavement.'

'Sorry?'

'Oh, it's a term we used for doing some of the naughty stuff, you know, bank heists, security van raids, that sort of thing.' Leaning across the table towards her, he placed his hand on top of hers and looked her in the eye. 'You know I ain't always walked on the right side of the law, don't ya girl? I'm sure Chuck would have told you…'

'Not really, no,' she said, slipping her hand from beneath his and hoping he didn't take offence. His actions made her feel uncomfortable. She didn't know the man, and although he seemed like a harmless enough old soul, she felt he had a tendency to act a bit too familiar.

'Chuck's a good boy,' said Billy. 'Always has been. When he used to come and visit me with his father, he always gave me a present, like a drawing or something he'd done at school. He'd learnt respect, even at that early age.'

'Your grandson's a gentleman,' she said. 'You should be proud.'

'I am… I am,' he said. 'And I've done my best to keep him out of trouble while he's been here. I wouldn't want him taking after me.' Leaving the words hanging between them he stood and declared, 'More music… and another drink I think.'

'Oh, maybe I should…'

'Nonsense, nonsense!' He raised his voice. 'Not going to deny an old man a bit of company, are you?'

She felt uneasy but didn't want to cause a scene. He was Chuck's grandfather, after all, and if push came to shove, she just had to mention her boyfriend's name and he would surely back off.

'Will Chuck be long?' she asked.

Billy looked at the clock on the wall, and she thought she detected a hint of concern in his expression. 'I'm sure he'll be back any moment,' he said, slurring his words slightly. It was at that moment she realised these were far from his first drinks of the day. 'He went off to find that crazy brother of his. You know Sly? Black sheep that one. Lucky he's got Chuck around to keep an eye on him. He's always been like a dad to that kid, particularly with Mo, my eldest, being absent for much of their childhood. He'll make a good dad himself one day…' He winked, and she felt a shiver pass through her. Maybe she was just feeling paranoid, but it was like he was making a play for her. To distract herself, she stood and looked at the books on the shelf.

'Do you read a lot?' she asked, intent on changing the subject.

'My wife did,' he said. 'Viola, I mean. Sadly, she died a few years after we came out here. Loved her books… reminded her of home she said.'

'I can understand that. What about magazines? There's one here...'

She pulled it from the shelf. There was a picture of a stack of gold bars on the front, a person's hands on the table holding a framed picture of the outside of a warehouse. It was the colour supplement from one of that Sunday's British newspapers. 'Where did all the gold go?' the headline asked.

'Yeah, well...' He came across and handed her a fresh drink, taking the magazine from her as he did so. 'Wouldn't they like to know?' He winked.

'Do you?' she said, wanting to keep him focussed on other things rather than her.

'I could tell you, but I'd have to kill you,' he said, liquid splashing over the rim of his glass as he broke into a laugh, followed swiftly by a coughing fit. She thought perhaps she should rub his back, but the thought of touching him made her queasy. Instead, she sat there, slightly embarrassed, until he eventually brought the attack under control.

He sat down with the magazine in front of him and for the first time she noticed the jacket hanging over a chair, a handgun visible in the inside pocket. Harmless little old men didn't carry guns, she thought. 'Fuck it!' he said. 'I'm gonna tell you a story.'

'I don't know, Billy.' She took a long drink from her glass. 'It's really quite late and I've nearly finished my—'

'Don't!' he said, and she thought he was ordering her to stay. 'Don't you want to know? I bet you do! I'm gonna tell you about the biggest bullion raid of the century.' He tapped the magazine. 'This gang of herberts got away with 28million fuckin' pounds worth of gold and cash and, guess what?'

She shook her head, feeling nervous about the direction in which the story was heading.

'I was one of them, and some might say I was the leader. After all, it was all my fackin' idea.'

The crazy smile on his face transformed him instantly from harmless old man to dangerous master criminal.

48

LUCKY'S head was all over the place, his mind a bundle of conflicting emotions. As he drove at speed back towards the Dolan villa, he knew his entire future depended on what transpired over the next few hours. It was a real catch-22.

During the nine months Luke Chalmers had lived and worked alongside the Dolans he had established a special bond with them, Sly in particular. Although the old man could be a cantankerous git, even Billy the Kid wasn't too bad, treating Lucky like one of his own grandchildren – and the pay was good too. The problem was that the only reason he was there in the first place was because a former prison acquaintance of his had presented him with a fait accompli. That man was Arthur Lee and refusing to do his bidding would have consequences far too grim to countenance.

On several occasions he'd considered confessing all to Sly. Yet whoever had come up with the adage about honesty being the best policy hadn't worked inside London's criminal fraternity. In that world, quite the opposite was true. Tell it like it is, and you were likely to end up taking a midnight dip in the Thames with concrete blocks as armbands.

When Luke had met Sylvester Dolan on the ferry to Bilbao, he was convinced he was escaping those who had lured him into the life. After the Hole in the Wall plan bit the dust, leading to high-profile arrests south of the river, the inevitable witchhunt ensued, and he knew it wouldn't be long before the failure was laid at his door. He was the new kid on the block and for that reason alone certain big cheeses in the syndicate were likely to suspect him of being the informant.

His escape route had been provided by his friend Rob, who'd invited him to rep for a popular British holiday firm in Spain. Money, girls and fun were on tap, and it seemed the ideal getaway. At first, everything had been wonderful. Luke had enjoyed the work, meeting the 18-30s crowd off their flights from various outposts in the UK, taking them to their hotels, organising party nights and sorting out their little problems. Not only that, but there was one huge perk in that he was able to take his pick of the sex crazy young women who threw themselves at him after a few overly generous cocktails. Luke had never had much success with the ladies and getting locked up at an early age had put a large dent in his social calendar. To find himself Mr Popular boosted his self-esteem and for a while even his stammer faded.

Unfortunately, the past has a nasty habit of catching up with you. One fateful night before Christmas Arthur Lee walked into a popular Costa Blanca drinking establishment where Luke was entertaining, and everything changed. Arthur was a real big hitter in the Hole in the Wall Gang and as soon as Luke saw him, he knew his running days were over. The story he'd told Sly about his mate being dragged aboard a boat was based on truth, but differed in one crucial aspect. It was Lucky who had been forced aboard that yacht, wrapped in chains and heading for a watery grave.

How had Arthur found him? Through his own stupidity. He'd posed for a publicity shot with two bikini-clad girls; unaware it would appear on the cover of a holiday brochure for Luke's company. One of Arthur's cronies had spotted it in a travel agent's window in London while booking a week away in Tenerife. He had relayed the information to his boss and as a consequence, Luke found himself stuttering and stammering for his life out on the Mediterranean, in the vain hope something he said might resonate with the ruthless gang boss. When he let slip the name Dolan – the boy he'd met on the ferry – little did he realise he'd found the one trump card capable of saving his ass.

'Shit. Here we go,' he said to himself as the ornate gates of Billy the Kid's villa loomed large in front of him. He pulled up, got out, and approached the security pad. It was eerily quiet, which added to his unease, and he questioned whether he would have the strength to stand up to Billy the Kid when the time came.

Inputting the code, the gates then swung inward. Lucky was banking on Billy following the same predictable pattern of recent weeks. With any luck, the old man would have passed out on the counter of his bar. When his phone beeped to break the silence, Lucky almost jumped out of his skin. It was the text message he'd been promised.

WATER plugged his nose, salt stung his eyes, and he began to choke. Fighting the unpleasant sensations, Chuck put his full concentration into maintaining his grip on the bundle of fury he had dragged into the water with him. A stray elbow administered a bruising blow to his cheek, but he refused to let go of the thrashing, writhing figure. Chuck imagined this was how it might feel to wrestle an alligator determined to sink its monstrous teeth into your flesh.

Of course, his opponent was not a creature from the swamp, but an entirely different animal: 18-stone of furious, steroid-enhanced Irish gangster. Chuck knew, though, that if he lost his concentration for barely a second the consequences could be fatal.

As a decent amateur boxer, Chuck liked to let his fists do the talking, preferring a straightforward punch-up to a no-holds-barred grip-and-grapple wrestling contest. Feet slipping and sliding on the uneven terrain, he struggled to anchor himself to the bed of the lake. Eventually, by digging his toes in, he achieved a solid base and launched himself upwards, breaking the surface and gulping in air.

The Irishman rose with him, an expression of pure hatred on his face as his head careered forward on a trajectory programmed to collide with Chuck's nose. Calling on all his ring skills, Chuck weaved to his left a fraction of a second before impact, feeling the rush of air brush his cheek. With nothing to halt his momentum, the big man staggered and lost his balance, and Chuck released his grip immediately. Directing all his anger, effort and hatred into his right fist, Chuck let fly, the shock waves of the punch rippling up his arms as he made brutal contact with the giant's ribs and pushed through to a target a few feet beyond. The blow was so perfectly timed and accurately delivered that the recipient's bones buckled then snapped beneath the skin, collapsing inwards on organs they were designed to protect.

Chuck heard an agonised grunt from his opponent, saw the man's mouth open to draw desperately needed oxygen into his lungs and watched as his face dissolved in agony as pain flooded his chest cavity. The result was a high-pitched shriek, so unearthly and uncharacteristic that it was hard to believe it could have come from the paramilitary killing machine in front of him. Punctured lung? Yes or no, Chuck knew the big man wouldn't be distracted for long.

In a surreal moment he saw his father's stern face in his mind's eye, recanting the lesson from his childhood, the voice of Big Mo suddenly and unexpectedly resonating around his brain.

'When you have a fish dangling, you don't let 'em off the hook.'

He knew now was the time to seize the advantage having detected a chink in his opponent's armour. Yet a moment's hesitation almost cost him dear. Chuck saw the splash of water first but was powerless to prevent the well-directed foot making contact with his knee. Fortunately, the resistance of the water deadened the impact and though Chuck staggered, the kick didn't seriously impair his movement in the way it would have done on land. He let his body roll with the blow, falling back into the water and maintaining eye contact with his assailant. The Irishman flung himself forward, groping fingers clawing for Chuck's eyes as he believed his opponent to be on the retreat.

It was all part of the deception. Chuck was still in control of his senses, like a champion boxer caught momentarily on the ropes. Going into defensive mode was all part of the strategy and in reality, his mind was still two moves ahead of his slow-witted and badly injured rival. Twisting his body, he felt the nails scratch down the side of his face, missing the intended target. The Shankill Whisperer slumped forward with the effort, his head disappearing below the surface of the lake.

It was all Chuck needed. He wrapped one arm around the man's neck, then grabbed hold of his own wrist with his other hand. His opponent tried to scramble to his feet, to lift his head free from the water, but his splashing and wriggling were uncoordinated and desperate. Learning from his previous mistake, Chuck wrapped his body around the Irishman's lower torso, preventing the man from using his legs. Increasing the pressure on the windpipe, Chuck knew the man's lungs would be screaming under the strain. Eventually, Sammy opened his mouth, but instead of a gulp of air he took in a mouthful of water, sucking it in so greedily that he spluttered and coughed, allowing more liquid to fill the void.

Chuck maintained his grip, building pressure on the throat until gradually the body beneath the water began to go limp. He held on for what seemed like minutes, long after resistance had stopped, wary his rival might be faking the seriousness of his plight. Finally, he saw the bubbles drift to the surface from the man's open mouth and turned the head so that he could study the lifeless mask. At that moment, he knew it was all over.

'Fuckin' cunt!' he growled through gritted teeth. All the hatred and anger and frustration he'd been harbouring for months came out in one angry cry. With a last, unnecessary effort, he punched the corpse in the mouth before letting his hands drop to his sides and bowing his head, muscles aching from the intense effort invested in the battle.

Pushing the body away, he then lifted his eyes and watched as the giant form rolled over twice before settling just below the now calm surface of the lake, the eyes staring sightlessly at the full moon above.

49

'WHAT the hell happened, Sly?'

Chuck stood with one arm around his brother, the ex-copper Dazzler holding him up at the other side. The younger Dolan boy could hardly stand, and Chuck wasn't sure whether that was because his brother had been maltreated or simply because he had been on a serious bender.

'I was in the bogs… at Mulligan's. These blokes came in … I overheard them… they were… talking about an attack … granddad… they heard me… kicked door down.'

'Wait… What attack? When?' said Chuck.

Sly lifted his head. One eye was blackened and his nose badly swollen. Chuck imagined Sammy hadn't been able to resist having his bit of fun on the journey to the lake. Looking at Chuck through his one good eye, Sly shook his head slightly as he gathered his thoughts and tried to dispel the fog clouding his brain.

'I… I dunno. Tel knows about that copper… the one from the Met. Obviously, someone spotted him… at the golf club and word got back. Now he suspects Granddad of being a grass.'

Chuck looked around for the other security man. On cue, Scottie appeared from a patch of vegetation to his left. 'Any luck?'

'He gave me a run for his money, but I got the fucker.'

'…And?'

'He won't be telling tales.'

Chuck had hoped they could limit the number of casualties, but with the new information he had been given, taking prisoners would have just slowed them down. Time was of the essence, though he would be slightly surprised if Senor Tel launched an attack without his destroyer-in-chief Sammy McMahon.

'We need to get back to the villa,' he said. 'Sly thinks the old man's in danger.'

'Is Granddad Billy on his own?' asked Sly.

'Lucky should be with him by now,' said Chuck. 'He saw you being bundled into that car and told us what had happened, so you owe him big time. I guess I was wrong not to trust him. Even so, he can't fight off an organised raiding party on his own. The best he can do is hide Granddad away and wait for the cavalry.'

'Us,' said Sly. 'Some cavalry…' He laughed.

Good, thought Chuck. After all that's happened, his brother had retained his sense of humour. 'We'll be OK. These two guys' – he indicated Scottie and Dazzler – 'they've proved over the last couple of hours they can handle themselves, and their weapons. Me, I reckon I can go another ten rounds. Finishing off that bastard has made me feel pretty good. Now, come on. We don't want to be late for the party.'

'Chuck,' said Sly, looking up at him.

'What's the problem?'

'Thanks. You've always been there for me, I appreciate it. I vowed I would do more to look after myself, stay out of trouble, but…'

'Don't be a wimp,' said Chuck. 'I'm your big brother. That's what I'm supposed to do. If you weren't getting yourself in a fix all the time, life would be boring. Now come on, before we find ourselves in bigger trouble.'

Soon they were on the move again, and Chuck stared out of the front window as the Land Rover ate up the winding country road in front of them. His mind was a million miles away. When he had told his younger brother that the outcome of his showdown with the Shankill Whisperer had made him feel good, it was a lie. Although he had hated the Ulster thug with all his heart, it was still the first time he'd taken a man's life. Yes, the guy was a psycho, but even so, Chuck was beginning to realise that once you stepped over that line from fighter to killer there was no going back. Of course, there had been the unfortunate incident with the grenade in the nightclub, but that had been an accident, pure and simple. He hadn't pulled the pin, and he hadn't looked the victim in the eye as his life drained away. The whole Hackney incident was regrettable, but this was different. It had taken all his strength, in terms of both physicality and mentality, to apply pressure to a human being's neck and hold on until his life ebbed away. While he felt a certain amount of relief when it was done, he knew the wounds to his mind would take some time to heal… if they ever did.

He could imagine the disappointed look on his mother's face if she ever discovered her eldest boy had committed the ultimate sin. Even more worrying was the fact he would need to conceal his secret forever from his beloved Abby. She was so sweet, bubbly, natural and honest, he had no idea how she might react to the news her boyfriend had committed murder. They'd vowed not to lie to each other, but in this case he had to make an exception.

'Chuck.' Sly's voice interrupted his moment of self-reflection.

'What?'

He swivelled to see the sorry figure in the corner of the back seat. Sly was wrapped in a camouflage jacket two sizes too big for him. They'd scrubbed him down as best they could with water from a container they had in the back of the vehicle, removing some of the blood, puke and piss that caked his body, but he looked shattered. The sight of him reminded Chuck exactly why he'd done what he had done.

'I'm frightened,' his younger brother confessed.

'We'll be OK... You're safe now.'

'It's not just the Irish though, is it?' said the younger Dolan boy. 'That Colombian bitch is still around somewhere and after what happened to the horses...'

'Ahhhh,' said Chuck. Without warning, he burst into laughter.

'You think La Rana's some kind of joke?'

'No,' he said, bringing his giggles under control. 'I just forgot. You haven't heard, have you?'

'What are you on about?' Sly had an uneasy expression on his face.

'The horses had nothing to do with La Rana. It was an accident... at least, no one deliberately poisoned them.'

'But the frogs...'

'Just our imagination getting the better of us. Apparently, the deaths were caused by a bug.'

'What?'

Chuck told him the story about the veterinary pathologist's visit and his explanation about the Spanish fly in the wild alfalfa. 'So basically, you got drunk, threw up, got captured, and almost lost your life over something that didn't happen,' he said, the smile creeping back across his face. 'Perhaps next time you should wait for the post-mortem.'

THEY reached the gates to the villa. Chuck opened the door, but Scottie shot out an arm to prevent him leaving the vehicle.

'Let Dazzler get it, boss. He can change the codes... the fewer people that know what it is, the better.'

Chuck watched the ex-squaddie walk over to the intercom, pull down a panel and press digits into the keypad beneath. The gates opened, and he climbed back in next to Sly.

'Something's wrong,' said Sly.

'How do you mean?'

'Just a feeling.'

'You're confused,' said Chuck. 'I'm not surprised after what you've been through. There are no guards because they're in here with us. The gate's intact and...'

'I can't explain. We just need to be careful.'

'Fair enough,' said Chuck as the vehicle moved through the gates and onto the driveway leading to the house. 'Stop,' he ordered, putting a hand on Scottie's shoulder.

'What's up, boss?'

'Let's go on foot,' said Chuck. 'If what Sly says is true, we need to check the grounds to make sure no one got here before us. If so, they'll be expecting us to drive up. It could be a trap.'

Scottie pulled onto the verge.

'You and Dazzler take the right side and go in through the front entrance. Sly and I will take the back.'

'You sure that's a good idea?' Dazzler interrupted, directing a subtle nod in Sly's direction. Chuck followed his gaze and saw Sly's head jerking about in panic as if at any moment armed men would charge from the cover of the trees and subject the vehicle to a hail of bullets.

'It's fine,' said Chuck. 'He's my brother, and I want him with me. He's stronger than he looks.'

'If you say so, boss.' Dazzler climbed out and went to the rear of the vehicle, opening the back doors and lifting out a couple of automatic weapons. He threw one to Scottie, who performed a couple of quick movements to make sure everything was as it should be.

'You want one?' asked the ex-soldier, looking in Chuck's direction.

'No, mate, not really… I wouldn't have a clue how to use the bloody thing.'

50

'IT ALL began when I heard about this warehouse out at Heathrow through one of me trusted contacts, see,' said Billy. Abby noted how his voice had morphed from companionable old man to feral low life. It was becoming obvious that Billy Dolan had reinvented himself to fit in with his elevated position in modern society. The real Billy the Kid hadn't been too far below the surface, waiting for an invitation to emerge. Now it was happening, it was a rapid and unpleasant metamorphosis.

'Obviously I needed help, so I put the word out and these fackin' geezers south of the river got in touch. Lo-and-behold, one of them had a brother-in-law who worked there on security, guarding cash and jewellery before it was flown out of the country.'

Billy was getting into the story now, showing off to a young woman he believed was falling under his spell. The real truth was that Abby was keeping one eye on the doorway, hoping Chuck would arrive at any moment to rescue her. She'd spent enough time in the company of Billy the Kid and didn't want to hear any more. It did make her wonder, though, how a bright young woman like Alisha had been lured into the web of such a boorish man and how the marriage had lasted so long.

'Anyway,' said Billy. 'We did a bit of a recce of the place and came up with a date, a Saturday morning in November while it was still dark. We would pounce during the shift changeover. We had to time it right though, see, but with an inside man, things went as easy as blinking. Drink up!'

Without waiting for her permission, he strode over to the bar, poured another cocktail then grabbed the whisky bottle for himself. Weaving back across, he plonked everything on the table, ignoring her protests. She sipped at her first drink, hoping her boyfriend would turn up before she could touch the new one.

'I reckon we need something a bit livelier,' said Billy, returning to the jukebox. A percussion rhythm started to revolve around her. The stereo effect amplified as a pair of congas joined in, the beat chugging along at the steady rhythm of a train. In the background a high-pitched solitary scream emerged, enhanced by an echo effect. A piano came in next, its haunting melody building up the effect before Jagger's voice purred, introducing himself as "a man of wealth and taste".

It occurred to her that this was Billy's view of himself, though she saw an entirely different human being in front of her.

'Excuse me, are you listenin'?' he said, interrupting her thoughts. 'I don't tell this story to everyone, y'know? Not even the wife or me right-hand man. You're fackin' privileged, young lady, that's what you are. Over the last 20 or so years, the only people I have trusted with this secret are me grandkids, but as you and Chuck are so close, I thought, what the hell, you should hear it too.'

Not really, she thought. *I'm not impressed by gangster stories. They just remind me of the pain inflicted on other people.*

She didn't say any of that though, settling for an apology. 'Sorry, I got distracted by the music.'

'Ahhh, I'll let you off,' he said, nodding. 'Great fackin' track this... Sympathy for the fackin' Devil. That was the way they thought of me, wasn't it?'

'You've lost me,' said Abby. 'Who did?'

'Everyone,' he said. 'I was the Commander, the leader of the gang, and the other members were as scared of me as the cunts who were hired to protect the place. I was the devil with a few tricks up me sleeve, see? Ways to get what I wanted. We needed to be straight in, straight out: Blam, blam. The best way to do that was to scare 'em shitless.'

'Scare who?'

'Security, girl, security... do I have to say everything twice? These guards obviously thought they was hard geezers, but once they met me, they pissed themselves like little kids.'

'Really?'

He suddenly had her attention, and she wasn't sure why. There was something tapping away in the recesses of her mind, a long-ago recollection.

'Hell, I ain't proud of it now, but, well, you do what you can, don't ya?' he said. 'I mean, to get what you want. You have to make them think you're off your bloody head and will do anything. They need to be shittin' themselves, so scared they'll do exactly what you want just to escape relatively unharmed.'

'Commander,' she said it out loud.

'Yep, that was me,' he said. 'They called me that because I planned everything like a military operation, and in a military operation you have to make sacrifices to achieve victory. It's all about the bigger picture.'

'Picture,' she said, her mind far away, an alarm bell ringing faintly in the distance. Perhaps it was warning her not to pursue the matter farther and to end the conversation here and now.

CHUCK and Sly were moving slowly through the grounds in a wide arc, passing the villa on the right-hand side. All seemed quiet. No obvious signs anyone had entered the grounds that shouldn't have been there. Chuck led the way, with Sly following, his head moving jerkily back and forth.

'You OK?' asked Chuck, even though he knew the answer.

'Shhhhh!' said Sly. 'What the fuck's that?'

'I don't hear… oh, hang on,' said Chuck.

'It's the alarm.'

'Shit. It sounds like it's coming from the back of the house. We'd better get a move on.'

They began to move quicker, neither prepared to put their worst fears into words. Chuck could now see the far end of the pool and the pathway leading up to the stables, but nothing seemed out of place.

'Fuckin' hell!' Sly hissed from behind him. 'Mate, I can't keep up with you.'

Chuck stopped and turned to see his brother staggering towards him in the oversized coat and scruffy pair of jogging bottoms. 'Look, I know you aren't in any fit shape, but I'm not sure we have time to waste. Let's get this done… think about this, we could be on our way home tomorrow.'

Sly had his hands on his knees. When he looked up, Chuck could tell his brother was in pain. 'Yeah, I can't wait to get back,' he said. 'Who wouldn't want to trade sun, sea and sangria for rain, concrete and pissy lager in Barking? You've always had good taste, Chuck.'

The two young men chuckled, the light-hearted banter between them easing the tension. Even at times of maximum stress, Sly was able to inject a comedy note into proceedings.

Chuck hooked his arm over his brother's shoulder, taking his weight before setting off towards the house again. They'd only gone about 50 yards before he stopped again.

'What's that?'

The younger Dolan brother stared in the direction Chuck was pointing. Lying on the paving stones by the side of the pool nearest the patio doors was a familiar shape. 'Fuck, it's Major,' said Sly. Before Chuck could stop him, the younger man was limping rapidly down the grassy incline towards the prostrate form. Cursing under his breath, Chuck set off after his brother at a measured jog, carefully monitoring his surroundings. It looked like the perfect trap, and his brother was running straight into it. He could only hope he'd read the signals wrong.

Sly reached the point where the ground flattened out and slowed down, carefully looking in the direction of the house before coming to a halt beside the dark shape on the patio. Chuck waited for a second, carefully scanning all around before weaving his way down to join his brother.

'Is he dead?'

Sly had his hand on the dog's flank.

'No, still breathing,' said Sly. 'It's very shallow, though. Shit, do you think he's been poisoned?'

Their eyes locked on each other, registering each other's fear, their stark features illuminated by the dawn light creeping slowly over the horizon.

'La Rana,' whispered Sly.

51

'IS THAT an alarm, Billy?'

'Never mind that,' said the old man. 'It's always playing up. Lucky can sort it wherever the fuck he is. He was due back by now. Some bloody bodyguard, eh?'

Thank God, Abby thought. If Lucky was on his way, she wouldn't be alone in the house with this man much longer. Hopefully, Billy's right-hand man would seek him out at some stage to make sure everything was all right. Then she could make her escape. Only…

Something inside of her was demanding to know the rest of the story.

'You were telling me about them calling you Commander,' she said against her better judgement, her eyes flicking again to the gun in the inside pocket of his jacket. Bloody hell! It was so close she could make a grab for it and shoot him if things got out of hand. Let's see who acted like a frightened child then.

He shut his eyes and took another swig of the whisky, obviously trying to sort out the thoughts scatter-gunning around his head. He's really drunk, thought Abby.

'Sometimes, see… shumtimes you get someone who wants to play the fackin' hero, and ya got ta kick that in the head straight away,' he said. 'F'instance, there was this bloke, supervisor-type, who we'd been told had the codes to the fackin' vault. Now, without that code, we were stuffed and the whole operation would go tits up. Loading the van was gonna take long enough without some cunt acting like James fackin' Bond.'

The tiny seed taking root inside Abby's memory was starting to grow. It was as if she had seen the movie before and knew what happened next.

'Hero?' she said. 'Who?'

'Shit, girl, it was 27 fackin' years ago.' He grabbed the bottle, filled his glass, and knocked back the lot in one gulp. She imagined him digging deep into his memory, travelling back down the years, transporting himself to an airport warehouse on a winter's morning in 1983.

'I just wondered…'

'Of course, I remember!' he said. 'I'm only pulling your fackin' leg, girl. Shit, I remember every moment of that fackin' day. Not very often you take part in the biggest crime in British history, is it?'

'No,' she agreed, leaning across the table towards him, her eyes homing in on his and imploring him to continue. Without warning, his hand shot out and enclosed hers again, gripping it so tightly she almost cried out in pain and shock. His eyes were blazing with excitement, the thrill of recalling his greatest 'hit'. On the jukebox the music had changed, heavy organ giving way to thunderous guitar chords, a singer blasting out lyrics about 'fighting in the streets' and 'shotguns singing songs'.

'I can still see him in his uniform,' he said. 'He thought he was pretty fackin' smart until we poured petrol over him, and I threatened to light him up. Jeez, I just rattled that matchbox and he came up with the code pretty swiftly, the cunt. Remember watching him tap it in and can still recite it now. Well, you would, wouldn't ya? Those numbers changed me entire fackin' life. One. Two. Oh. Five.'

Oh fuck. The fog in her brain was clearing, the truth solidifying in front of her.

'He had this name tag on... Flynn. Don't remember his first name but his mates called him...'

'Errol,' she said.

'Yeah, that's right!' He suddenly sat back, releasing her hand and roaring with laughter. 'Fackin' Errol like the fackin' film star... you know who I mean? I'm surprised you got that, girl. I didn't think you would have heard of Errol Flynn. He was a swashbuckling Hollywood hero from the old days, long before your time... Hey, what are you doing?'

His chuckles began to subside when he saw his own gun pointed in his direction, Abby's hands shaking as she held it out in front of her.

EVERYTHING had so far gone to plan for Lucky. He'd sneaked into the house, liberated a piece of nice juicy steak from the fridge and inserted the knockout drops. It was no coincidence the prime cut was where he found it. Billy loved his steak, and Naomi had only bought some the previous morning. He wondered if she had done so on the instruction of her boss or her father.

During the months he'd been living with the family, he had grown fond of Major, taking the dog for daily walks around the grounds. He considered the German Shepherd to be both obedient and intelligent but knew that if someone had threatened Billy, he would have seen a different side to 'man's best friend'. Major was a former police dog trained to work with the tactical firearms support unit. At the first sign of a threat to his master, he'd been coached to take down the aggressor without mercy. Arthur Lee had insisted Lucky couldn't take any chances with the dog. He feared it might interrupt Lucky's progress in finding out the whereabouts of the missing gold, particularly as a confrontation with Billy was inevitable.

Having slipped in through the back entrance, Lucky had found Major patrolling the corridor outside his master's study. The dog licked its lips when he saw the treat in Lucky's hand and went along obediently, sitting to attention by the poolside when Lucky produced the prime cut from behind his back. He felt traitorous deceiving the dog that way, but at least when Major recovered, he would be none the worse for his ordeal.

It didn't take long for the drugs to work and soon the dog was out for the count, giving Lucky the all-clear to go about his business. He touched the gun in his pocket nervously and entered the house, expecting to find the old man passed out in the pub. It was as he made his way down the corridor towards the staircase leading to Billy's favourite haunt that the alarm went off and he realised he hadn't shut the patio door properly.

Damn! What did he do now? He couldn't go back. He had to act quickly. Then Lucky saw the suitcase and heard raised voices filtering up from below.

'HOLD ON, babe, what the bloody hell are you doing with that?' said Billy. 'You gotta be careful. That thing's loaded, it ain't no toy. You could do yourself a nasty injury. Hell, you could do me an injury. You're just getting excited by all this talk of…'

'My dad.'

'What?'

'Errol.'

'What about him?'

'His real name was Peter. He was my father.'

Billy spluttered and gave a nervous laugh, suddenly unsure of his ground. 'Nah, don't be daft, girl,' he said. 'You're just having a joke with me, ain't ya? You told us at dinner your dad's called Geoff and he sells motors. I also remember you told us your name. Can't remember what it was, but it wasn't Flynn, that's for sure. Good one!'

'I changed my name when Mum remarried.'

'Oh, come on,' he said. 'Even if that's the case, it don't mean that loser was even related to ya. There are loads of Flynn's around them parts, you only have to look in the soddin' phone book, and I bet most of them are nicknamed Errol... specially men of that age.'

He was talking too much now, and the words were flowing over her like a tsunami, the tears of fury forming in her eyes and blurring her vision. She had to shut him up and before she realised what she was doing, she smashed the pistol butt down on his hand.

'Aaargh! Fack! You crazy little bitch.' He grabbed his hand to his chest and looked at her, his eyes black and thunderous, confusion and pain contorting the lines on his forehead. 'What did you do that for? Jeez, you got a fackin' screw loose. Does our Chuck know he's going out with a fackin' mental case?'

Strangely, having done the deed she now suddenly felt calm, like she'd stepped out of her body and was watching the scene from a distance, like a theatregoer at a play. The other version of her, the one with the gun, was speaking with a cool, measured voice. 'When I first heard the name Commander, it rang a bell, and I couldn't think why. Then when you said those numbers – One, two, Oh, Five – it all became clear. They should be read twelve 05. They represent the 12th of May. My birthday. Peter Flynn was my father, and you killed him.'

Looking at her from beneath his bushy, mean eyebrows, the hand cocooned under his armpit, he still looked unsure. 'Nah,' he said. 'That ain't right. I never killed anyone on that job. In fact, I never killed anyone on any job. It went just like I said, straight in and out, no messin'.'

'Oh, he didn't die that day,' she said. 'It was a slow, agonising death that went on for more than two years. I was just a young girl the day you took my dad from me. What you did lived with him right up until the moment he could bear it no more and took his own life in a nursing home. After what you did with the petrol and the matches, he was forever petrified of fire and would freak out if anyone spilt liquid. I saw one of his carers spill some water once and he just lost it. He was shouting what I thought was "Come and hurt" and they had to sedate him. It wasn't that though, was it? It was Commander. You might not have been with him at the moment he died but you were there, inside his head, infecting his brain like a slow-dripping poison, right up until he took his last breath.'

'Hang on… you can't blame me if he went doollaly,' said Billy, mustering up the bravado to fight back. 'He must have been weak to start with, possessed some bloody character flaw that stopped him dealing with things. It was his job to handle stuff like that.'

'You poured petrol over him!' she spat the words into his face. 'He thought he was going to die, that he would never again see his wife and child. I was only seven, for Christ's sake, and I can't remember the friendly, loving, guitar-playing Dad I was told about, because you stole him away from me. What…?'

She suddenly became aware of a subtle shift in the atmosphere, as if the man she held at gunpoint no longer had her full attention. She swivelled to see Lucky standing in the doorway, mouth open and a perplexed expression on his face. He was holding a pistol, too. *Was it a bring a gun party and she'd missed the memo?*

'For fuck's sake, Lucky, do something you daft sod,' urged Billy. 'Shoot the bitch!'

'Ab… Ab… Abby, isn't it?' said the new arrival. 'Why don't y… you hand it to me, eh? I'm sure you don't want to sh… shoot anyone.'

Didn't she? She wasn't so convinced. Or maybe she was. Deep down she was unable to imagine taking the life of any human being, even the Devil incarnate, sitting opposite her.

'Look,' he said. 'I… I'm in the same b… boat as you. I… I'm here to collect a debt for someone Billy owes big time. G… give me the gun and I'll m… make sure he doesn't go anywhere. OK?'

She didn't know how to respond.

Billy, however, looked perplexed. 'What d'ya fackin' mean, Lucky? You work for me! Are you telling me someone made you a fackin' better offer, son? Talk ta me, you st…st… stuttering little shit.'

Lucky ignored the mocking imitation, directing his words at Abby. 'Give the gun here, eh? I d… doubt you have ever handled one. W… when I have what I want I'll c… come and consult you about what we do next. If you shoot him it will be the end of you and Chuck, won't it? Think about it.'

'What you said.' Abby looked confused. 'Does this have anything to do with Naomi and Arthur Lee?'

'Eh? H… How do you know that?'

'Arthur's my uncle.'

Billy interrupted, his furious voice echoing around the bar. 'Ahhhh, now I get it. You two are in league. That's your second name, aint't it? Lee? I should have put two and two together and sussed you out, you crazy bitch.' He turned his attention to Lucky. 'And you've been sent here by that numbskull because he thinks I've got some gold stashed away. Why the fack would you want to work for him, son? Bloke would kill ya as soon as look at ya. All he did was smelt down a bit of gold for me back in the day and now he thinks I owe him. Jeez, he owes me! Bloody hell, I took his daughter on as a favour, and this is how he repays me?'

'You know?' Suddenly Abby was confused. Seeing the picture of Naomi Lee her mum had sent her had rung an alarm bell in her head and she'd been able to put two and two together. It explained the strange look Naomi had given her in the corridor all those months ago on her first visit to the villa. It was one of recognition. The mole Abby had spotted in the picture had been the thing that persuaded her that the maid and Arthur's daughter were one and the same. After discovering the link all she could think of was that this was something Chuck needed to know, not realising Billy was fully aware of Naomi's background.

'Course I knew,' said Billy. 'Arthur told me his girl was struggling to find work in the UK, so I took her on. I thought as she spoke a bit of the lingo, she would be a big help to Alisha. The little bitch must have been spying on me for years.' He turned his attention back to the young man in the doorway. 'Look, Lucky son, this ain't gone too far yet. Help me out here and I'll double yer wages. You'll be my number one man, and we can deal with Arthur Lee together. I ain't getting any younger so I need a partner to take over when I…'

'Shhhh… shut up,' said Lucky. 'I've heard enough of your c… crap. If what Abby said about her dad is true I d … don't want anything to do with you.' He turned to Abby. 'My dad was a security guard, too. I know how I would have felt if the same thing had happened to him. Now, w… why not let me sort this, eh? Hand me the gun and go and w … wait in Chuck's room. I'll come and find you when I've worked out what to do.'

Mired in confusion, she hesitated for a moment before dropping the weapon to her side and slowly climbing from the chair.

'Aaaargh!' Pain cascaded down through her body as her wrist was encased in Billy the Kid's steely grip. He might have been drunk but he was still alert enough to fight back. Shocked and afraid, the stubborn side of her still wasn't prepared to surrender the advantage to the creature that had destroyed her family. Gritting her teeth, she then pulled the prone figure across the table and, though he was strong for an old man, she had the advantage of sobriety. Just when she thought she'd regained possession of the gun, the table collapsed and sent the two figures – the old man and the young woman – sprawling on the floor amid broken glass and spilt alcohol. For a minute she wasn't sure where the gun was, then…

BLAMMM!

As she looked down, she watched in detached wonder as a red puddle of blood began spreading on the floor. Then his heavy weight collapsed across her, sending them both sliding in the direction of the jukebox.

52

'WAIT.' Chuck pushed himself to his feet, looking around. He made his way, at a crouch, to the far end of the pool, studying something on the floor. Quickly, he returned to Sly.

'No,' he said. 'Not La Rana, or, at least, I don't think so. That dog would be dead by now if this was her doing. Remember how quickly we were told that poison acts? Major wouldn't have lasted 10 seconds. I think he's been drugged. There's a piece of steak up there half eaten, and it seems to be studded with small capsules. Some kind of knockout drop is my guess.'

'Who then?' asked Sly. 'The Irish?'

'I dunno,' said Chuck. 'Bit subtle for Senor Tel and his thugs. I've been around those bastards for a long time. I know how they work. They'd shoot the fuckin' dog and have done with it.'

'What are you thinking, then? Doesn't leave many candidates, unless Billy's got enemies we don't know about. Remember him telling us about the curse of the Brink'sMat gold?'

'Whoever is responsible is someone Major trusts,' said Chuck. 'It's pretty exposed here, there's nowhere to hide. It's not as if you could just chuck a bit of meat over a hedge, is it? And he's a cantankerous beast. Remember how he reacted when we first arrived here, and how he acts when strangers are about?'

'Sure,' said Sly. 'That narrows it down. Who then?'

'There are a couple of people that spring to mind. Naomi?'

'Shit, come on!' said Sly. 'Why the hell would she do this? She's worked for Granddad for years, and well, she often walks Major. She loves dogs.'

'Easy for her to get close then,' said Chuck. 'I know you've got a soft spot for her, but the only other people that spring to mind are granddad, Lucky and Alisha.'

'…And the guys we came here with.'

'…Who haven't been out of my sight. They didn't have time to coordinate all this.'

'Some of the blokes he laid off?' suggested Sly. 'They would have an axe to grind.'

Chuck made a decision. 'There's something I have to tell you.'

'Go on?'

'Purely by chance, I saw Lucky and Naomi having a quiet little meal together in a small village restaurant near here.'

'What? You think they're shagging? Why didn't you tell me?'

'Come on, Sly, that's why. I didn't want you to overreact. Honestly, it means nothing on its own. They both work here and it's hardly a surprise they decided to have a meal together on their day off, particularly when you were in Marbella. They speak the same language, and they're both working far from home. What's happened now, though, has got me wondering.' The two men fell silent, thinking about the implications.

Eventually, Chuck said, 'There's only one thing for it. We have to check the house.'

Leading the way, Chuck peered through the patio doors into the summer room at the back of the villa. He couldn't see anyone. One of the glass partitions was partially open though, which was the reason the alarm was still chirping. Chuck slipped through, Sly following in his footsteps. Sly approached the alarm box on the wall, but Chuck shook his head, fearing that any changes would alert the intruders to their presence.

The two men crept into the corridor, pushing themselves hard against the wall, knowing they were now fully exposed if anyone came from the other direction. Chuck's eyes darted one way and another, then settled on an object in the middle of the hallway, an oblong box on wheels. For a moment he thought it might be some kind of explosive device, primed for detonation by someone waiting in the shadows. It looked familiar, though, and as he got closer, he recognised the well-known logo and designer initials on a brown background, unlike any military device he had ever seen. LV. Louis Vuitton.

Abby's case.

Pushing aside precautions, he broke into a run, Sly giving chase. 'Chuck, Chuck, what the fuck?'

He glanced back. 'Abby… she's here.'

'Well, you won't be much good to her if you're dead, will ya?'

His brother had a point. He pulled up abruptly and dived back against the wall. Standing still and breathing heavily for what seemed an age, the brothers listened for any noises that might betray the intruders' whereabouts. There was nothing but the constant chirp of the alarm.

Slowly he started up again, feeling the tension creep into his body like ice, his breathing jerky. What had he got her into? Abby, his Abby, was here, paying him a surprise visit, only to walk straight into a gangland war. He was distraught and pledged to cause serious damage to anyone who laid a finger on her.

The suitcase was inches away from him, standing to attention in the middle of the empty hall, an object so out of keeping with the scenario they found themselves in that it was as if someone was playing a schoolboy prank on him. Maybe they were watching now, laughing at his indecisiveness, his fear, his total inability to know how to react to what amounted to an unfathomable conundrum. Thankfully, Sly wasn't so burdened by the latest development.

'Downstairs,' he hissed. 'Granddad's pub. Perhaps he, Lucky and Abby have locked themselves in and are waiting for the cavalry. When you think about it, as a panic room it makes sense. Billy designed it to keep unwanted visitors away, including his Mrs.'

'You're right,' said Chuck. 'Let's go.'

Leaving the suitcase in the hall, he tracked across to the stairs and descended slowly, gripping the handrail with clammy fingers. Sly followed in a crab-like manner, walking sideways while looking up the stairs in case someone tried to trap them in the stairwell.

'I thought the boys would be here by now,' whispered Chuck.

'Maybe they met some resistance,' said Sly. 'Hey, you hear that?'

The sound of voices filtered up the staircase. Neither brother could hear what was being said, but it sounded like some sort of negotiation was taking place. Chuck leaned forward, sneaking a look around the bend in the stairs. The door was open, and the lights were on, the sound of The Who's 'Won't Get Fooled Again' blaring out.

'We might be too late,' said Sly.

BLAAAAM.

Shit! The two men ducked instinctively as the sound echoed around the walls. Chuck looked at Sly and saw his own fear reflected back at him through his brother's eyes. The younger Dolan mouthed, 'Gun!'

Timidly, they both began to push themselves back into a standing position.

BLAAAAM.

53

CHUCK took the last few steps in a hurry and pushed himself up against the wall outside Billy the Kid's pub. Sly leapt forward and made for the other side, the two Boxer Boys bookending the entrance.

Chuck pointed at his eye, and Sly nodded. Yes, he could see something. He was in a better position to get a look inside the bar. From Chuck's vantage point, all he could see was the snooker table and the fruit machines. There was a red streak spreading across the floor and disappearing behind the door frame.

'Fuck!'

Sly tore past him into the room.

'Sly! What the…?'

'There's a body,' said Sly. 'So much blood, it's…'

Throwing caution to the wind, Chuck stormed through the gap and ran across the room, falling to his knees and sliding the rest of the way on the blood and debris coating the floor. The slumped form was lying against the bar, green eyes locked on him, long blond hair splayed out like a model's in a glamour photo shoot.

'No,' whispered Chuck, the word catching in his throat. 'No, no, no, no, no.' He leant over, looking for signs of life, hoping he would detect the faint breath of hope on his cheek.

Nothing.

'Abby! Abby! Come on, baby.' His pleas were getting louder now, the tears pooling in his eyes. 'Shit, babe. It'll be OK. We'll get you to a hospital, find the best doctors… Talk to me, babe, please. Abby, come on… don't leave me. Open your eyes, babe. I love you… we can…'

'She's dead, son.' Both men turned to see Billy the Kid slumped beside the door, his T-shirt soaked in blood, the head of another casualty cradled in his hands. Lifeless eyes looked back at them; the mouth half open as if a switch had been flipped mid-sentence.

'Lucky too?' muttered Sly. 'What the hell…?'

Suddenly, the two security guards burst into the room, guns at the ready. They quickly moved in opposite directions, scanning every corner for intruders.

'Clear,' shouted Dazzler.

'Clear,' echoed Scottie.

Walking over to the old man, Dazzler asked, 'You hurt, sir?'

Billy shook his head. 'I… I… no. I don't think so. No.'

'You're covered in blood. We'd better get you checked over. Has anyone called an ambulance?'

'No!' he shouted. 'I'm fine. No ambulance.'

'I was thinking about…'

'It's too late for them,' said Billy hurriedly. 'They're gone. Dead. Bring an ambulance here and you bring the police. We have to talk this through first.'

'The people who did this could still be on the grounds,' said Scottie. 'The gunshot was only a minute or so ago. I can't see how…'

'No need.' Billy indicated the prone body lying across him. 'It was him.'

'What?' Sly interrupted. 'That ain't right. Lucky wouldn't…'

'I always said you were too trusting, son,' said the old man. 'Lucky wasn't who you thought he was.'

'What the hell are you talking about?'

'Don't worry, he duped me, too,' said Billy. 'Good and proper. All the time he's been here, your pal has been trying to track down that bloody gold. He worked for one of my old "acquaintances". Apparently, the untrustworthy bastard turned against me. I told you about the Brink'sMat curse, remember? It's taken another victim.'

'Two,' Chuck whispered, his voice light as he clutched his girlfriend's body to his chest and kissed her forehead. 'How the fuck could you let this happen, Billy? You should have been looking after her…'

'That's what I was trying to do, son,' said Billy. 'I couldn't have expected Lucky, of all people, to burst in here like fuckin' Al Capone and shoot the place up. Me and your girl were getting on famously, having a drink and a good natter until… well, he burst in and tried to shoot me. Somehow poor Abby got in the way, and the next thing she was on the floor. I wanted to help straight away, but I had to act quickly and catch him off guard. He was shocked at what he'd done and was just staring at her. I took advantage and jumped him. It was him or me, honestly, boy. I managed to wrestle the gun away and shoot him. I had no choice.'

'Really?' said Chuck, the tears reflecting on his cheeks from the glare of the bar lights. 'There's somethin' not right about all this.'

'You're upset, son,' said Billy. 'Bound to be. You lost your girl, and it's a bloody tragedy, a horrible accident. I know …'

'Shut the fuck up!' Chuck pushed himself to his feet and fixed the old man with a glare, one finger thrust out in front of him. 'Bloody hell, everything you touch turns to shit, doesn't it? You're like the grim fuckin' reaper. First Rafa, then the horses, now these two. You destroy anything that means anything to anyone.'

He felt hands grab his forearms and turn him around. Shaking himself free, he did what he always did when he felt threatened, pulling back his fist with the intention of punching his assailant. Then he saw his younger brother standing in front of him with a defiant look on his face.

'Go on then, punch me if it'll make you feel better,' said Sly. 'God knows I ain't been battered enough tonight. Look, losing your temper won't solve anything, Chuck. It sounds like Granddad says… a terrible accident. I know you loved her, mate, but nothing can bring her back now and from what I'm hearing, Granddad did all he could. Can't you see? He's only an old man. He was lucky to escape with his fuckin' life.'

Chuck felt himself being pulled into his brother's embrace. Putting his head on the familiar shoulder, he wept uncontrollably. Behind his back, he heard his grandfather barking out instructions. 'Scottie, we need to act quickly. Bring the van around front and wait for me.'

Chuck broke away. 'Why do you need the van? You're leaving? After what's happened? Surely…'

'Chuck, I'll discuss it with you in a minute, OK? We need clear heads. If any of us stay here, we're gonna be asked a hell of a lot of questions we can't answer. I'm happy to face the Bill but I'll do it on my own terms once we get our stories straight. After the thing that was recently hanging over your heads, it's better you two make yourself scarce, too.'

Chuck shook his head in disbelief, turning back in the direction of the slumped body at the bar. He bent down and began to lift Abby into his arms, holding her close as a parent might cradle a sleeping child. He could still smell her intoxicating perfume mixed with a strong metallic odour.

'Put her down, son,' said Billy, softening his voice to suit the situation. 'I'm so sorry.'

He gave his grandfather a withering look. 'What? You get her killed and then you…'

'Think about it,' said Billy. 'She was your girl, your fingerprints are all over the body, along with hair particles and God knows what else, and the first thing her parents will say was that she was on her way to see you. Whatever conclusions the police will draw about this business, the forensics don't lie. You'll already be their chief suspect because they'll look at those with a close relationship to the victim first. They'll be thinking of a lovers' tiff and when they get their test results, it will back them up. Believe me, you wouldn't want to go to jail for murder, son, especially over here. I've heard bad things… they'll throw away the key.'

'I don't care.'

'You say that now, Chuck, but in time…'

Chuck stood frozen for a second, the body heavy in his arms. Then he gently returned Abby to the floor, and Sly rested a calming hand on his shoulder.

'Granddad's right, Chuck.'

'No,' said Chuck. 'No, he fuckin' isn't. He knows what happened. If he just told the police the full…'

'No!'

The guttural growl shocked Chuck, and he guessed that by the expression on his brother's face, Sly was stunned, too.

'Scottie, Dazzler… I'll call for you when I need you. I need to talk to my grandsons. OK?'

The two men didn't need a second invitation, leaving the room without glancing back at the scene of carnage spread out behind them.

54

SO MUCH deceit. So many lies. Chuck was finding it hard to extricate the truth from the avalanche of bullshit. As he sat on the plane at Alicante airport while the pilot waited for the all-clear to fly them back to London, his mind tossed around everything his grandfather had told them about the previous night's craziness. Abby's death had still not sunk in properly. It was as if he had been injected with some powerful anaesthetic and was living in a dream state, unable to separate myth from reality. On occasion he even found himself planning the next step in their relationship before hastily having to reset his chaotic thoughts to factor in reality. If this was karma for Sammy, it really was a bitch.

He wished now that he had listened to the alarm bells ringing in his brain long before things got out of hand. He'd always harboured suspicions about Lucky and had been annoyed by the way his brother had formed such a close relationship with a relative stranger. Seeing Lucky in that restaurant with Naomi should have been enough to rubber-stamp his initial impression, but for some reason he'd given the bastard the benefit of the doubt. He'd told himself his feelings were all rooted in paranoia and, to a certain extent, jealousy. Before Lucky came along it had been him and Sly against the world, and Chuck felt the south Londoner's appearance had driven a wedge through that bond. Not only that, but Lucky had been given the job Chuck felt should have been rightfully his – right-hand man to his grandfather. For putting aside his natural cynicism, he'd ended up paying the ultimate price.

After finding his lover's blood-soaked body, Chuck had every intention of carrying Abby up the stairs to his room and laying her on the bed. He felt she deserved that level of respect, rather than being left bloodied and broken on the floor of the pub, another thing to be swept up and removed with the broken glass and spilt drinks after closing time. Eventually, though, his grandfather had talked him out of it with the full support of his brother. They insisted that the 'crime scene' – as they were now calling it – should be left exactly as they found it. Now, nine hours later, Chuck was regretting he hadn't been more vehement in his protests. 'Fuck!' he shouted, making Sly jump and earning confused looks from the other passengers on the aircraft. 'I'm so sorry, Abby,' he muttered. 'It's my fault. I should never… I should have…'

He could feel the anger rising within him again, ready to explode. He hadn't felt emotions like this since his father was arrested for armed robbery when he was a kid. 'Fuck, fuck, fuck!' he repeated, quieter now, his eyes filling with water. He focussed on the suitcase he'd stored in the compartment opposite, remembering how just 24-hours earlier he had been packing it, anticipating the future and the chance to take his relationship with Abby a step further.

Why had she turned up at the villa? It was another mystery. She hadn't told him of her visit and if he had known…

What? Would it have changed anything? Would he have abandoned his brother to that psycho Sammy? Of course not. He might have tried to change Abby's mind, though, things having been so fraught around the villa since the incident with the horses and Billy's split from Alisha. Abby was strong willed, though. She would have insisted on travelling, anyway. In which case, everything would have panned out in exactly the same way it did.

Chuck cursed again, but this time under his breath. Not for the first time, he was thinking about Abby in the present tense. His head was banging. He knew at some stage he would have to get in touch with Philippa Lee to talk about the death of her daughter. It was a frightening thought. Physical threats didn't scare Chuck but when it came to openly discussing his feelings and showing empathy to others, he was petrified and wasn't sure he'd be able to follow through on the course of action suggested by Billy and Sly. He needed to get the lies straight in his own head before imparting them to someone else.

The story went like this: Sly and Chuck had gone out for one last night in Torrevieja in order to say farewell to Spain in time-honoured fashion. They'd taken their suitcases with them and left them at the home of some English ex-pats they knew in town and they'd then all gone out together to one of the nightclubs, without having to worry about getting back to the villa. At the same time, their grandfather had decided to return to Marbella to make one last effort to patch up his failing marriage and had stopped off on the way south to sort out some timeshare business. This little detail meant that Alisha wouldn't be able to contradict his story when the police called to interview her about the dead bodies found in Torrevieja. In truth, Billy had left for

Marbella first thing in the morning, accompanied by his security men. The gruesome scene had been left untouched for Naomi and the poor cleaners to discover.

The plan worked because it enabled Sly and Chuck to claim complete ignorance about Abby's surprise visit to the villa, having gone straight from town to catch their flight. It even meant that Philippa Lee could back up part of the story, because Abby would have told her the visit was intended as a surprise. Of course, the fact that few people even knew the Dolan brothers were in Spain made it highly unlikely the police would pay them a visit once they were back in Barking unless, of course, it was suggested by Abby's family.

The plane's engines rose in pitch and Chuck looked out of the window as it began taxiing down the runway, shielding his eyes from the brightness of a scorching day, the terminal buildings in the background bleached of colour by the dazzling sun.

Another bloody day in paradise.

As the aircraft gathered momentum and began to rise into the air, he shut his eyes in an effort to quell the jackhammers bouncing off his skull. He tried to clear his mind, but thoughts kept indiscriminately popping into his head. Why, for instance, had Lucky immediately tried to shoot Billy when his main purpose was to find the elusive gold? Surely, he wasn't going to get the answers he needed by killing the only person who possessed them?

Then there was Abby's presence. Once Lucky had discovered her there, his original plan would have been thrown into chaos. Logically, in those circumstances, he could have been expected to postpone his mission for another day.

There would have been plenty of opportunities to seek out the gold when Chuck and Sly were back in London.

Chuck's thoughts were interrupted by the crackle of a speaker.

'Ladies and gentlemen, good evening. Welcome on board flight no. 4401e from Alicante to London Heathrow. This is Captain Matthew Honeyman speaking, and I'd like to give you some information about today's flight—'

He tuned out and closed his eyes again, his thoughts coming at him in waves. The only thing that tended to confirm the old man's story in Chuck's mind was the stutter. It marked Lucky down as the nervous type, and he had rarely seemed confident in Chuck's presence. Maybe, therefore, he got jittery and pulled the trigger by mistake. A tragic accident. Then again, if he knew he was inclined to nerves surely he would have applied the safety catch? Chuck knew nothing about guns but was pretty sure there were built-in fail-safes to prevent them going off accidentally. Indeed, would Lucky not have kept the gun hidden in his pocket once he became aware of Abby's presence?

There were many, many questions that needed answering, yet the way they'd removed the gun from Lucky's pocket to dispose of it meant when the police arrived they would quickly draw the conclusion that it was a break-in gone wrong – the two bodies those of a young couple rudely interrupted as they enjoyed a drink, some music and each other's company.

So many lies, so much deceit.

BILLY the Kid Dolan sat on the plush mulberry leather sofa in the lounge at his villa outside Marbella and dabbed at his head with a plastic bag of ice cubes. A large bump was beginning to form at his temple, which he had told Alisha was due to having cracked his head on the car window when they had struck a large pothole on the journey down. Billy had made a big thing of criticising the Spanish authorities in the past over their failure to maintain the highways adequately, so this was nothing new to his long-suffering wife. In truth, however, it had happened during his scuffle with Abby when he had wrestled her for the gun, using all his strength to turn it in her direction before exerting pressure on her trigger finger. In effect, the stupid bitch had shot herself.

Bloody hell, what a night it had been. He was still trying to get his head around it. How could he have known that Chuck's girlfriend was the daughter of that security guard he'd doused with petrol almost 20 years ago? And what chances her mother would have remarried into the Lee family, who had been notorious back in the day for holding a monopoly on the north London crime scene?

Added to that there was Lucky, who had pulled the wool over his eyes well and truly. He'd trusted him implicitly from the moment the kid saved his life. Now he suspected Rafael's shooting had been a set-up, the rescue an elaborate ploy designed by that prick Arthur Lee to get the boy inside Billy the Kid's inner circle.

Well, choosing Luke Chalmers to do his dirty work was an enormous sign of disrespect. The boy might have been good at acting the part, but when it came to the crunch, he failed to follow through. Too squeamish.

Billy could still remember Lucky's shocked face as Abby rolled over, her dead green eyes fixed to the ceiling. The moment's hesitation was all the old man needed to pull the gun from the girl's lifeless fingers and fire two bullets into Lucky, who slid down the wall in increments. Pushing Abby from him, Billy had rushed over to the dying man. Nestling his head in his hands, he asked him gently, 'Where do I find Arthur, son?' Lucky's last act was to spit out a mouthful of blood before Chuck and Sly burst on the scene.

Christ, if Alisha knew the truth about Rafael's death, there would be no going back. As it was, she still hadn't forgiven him, but he suspected it would be only a matter of time. The news that the horses had not, after all, been poisoned by one of his enemies but had in fact been struck down from eating bugs in their own feed had helped in that respect. Rather than blame him it meant she now had to take a closer look at herself and ask whether she was responsible for not removing the infected Alfalfa from the top field. In not doing so, had she killed her own horses? He had put a comforting arm around her shoulder when the tears came, telling her she shouldn't chastise herself over a mistake anyone might make, the subtext being that she had made the error.

Redemption was halfway there.

He had to tread carefully now, though. Senor Tel would be out for revenge after his No.1 boy Sammy McMahon was removed from the picture, that cunt Arthur Lee was still around somewhere nursing his groundless grudges and as for La Rana, well, who knew where and when that Colombian head case would raise her beautiful head again. At least he felt on top of things for the first time in ages. Whereas before he was unsure where the threats were coming from, now he had a clear picture of who constituted his enemies. It was time for some pre-emptive strikes. If there was one positive to take from the last few days, it was that the entire incident had replenished his lust for life. He had repelled an attack and survived to fight another day. At that moment, he really did feel on top of the world.

A leader of men.

A Commander.

Now, he only had to play his cards right and he would find himself sharing the marital bed again. He was actually feeling quite horny.

55

'DAD?'

'That you, Naomi? Thank fuck! I was worried about yer girl.'

She looked out of her hotel window, fearing that at any moment Billy's men would pull up outside and she would have to make a rapid escape.

'I haven't heard from him,' said Naomi. 'I think we have to assume it's not worked out for Lucky. Nothing on the local news either.'

'The little shite,' said Arthur Lee. 'He better not be having it on his toes with that money or betraying me. If he is, I'll string him up and cut off his tiny scrote… I knew I shouldn't send a boy to do a man's job.'

'He seemed onside last night, Dad. I'm worried.'

'Don't be,' said the north London gang boss. 'Things go ahead as planned. Meet me in Barcelona and we'll get out of here. You've done well, babe… you'll work for me from now on. I'm sure I can find something more suited to your abilities than washing that old bastard's undies. You ain't no skivvy, you're better than that.'

She thought about his proposition. There was no future in the job with Billy anyway, now that her dad had laid his cards on the table. All her worrying over continuing to work for the Dolans had been rendered irrelevant. A shame, too, because she really had liked Sly and the developments over the last day meant any hope she had of a future with him was completely shattered.

She patted her stomach. A pity. She would have to think seriously about an abortion.

ON the other side of the world, another woman was paying special attention to the bump in her belly as a man dressed in white hospital scrubs passed a device over it. Estella Isabel Sanchez Montoya directed her gaze at the small monitor by the side of the bed and stared with fascination at the broad bean-shaped outline as it floated in carefree abandon against a colourless background.

'You want to know?' said the doctor.

'Of course, I want to know.'

'Well, Senora, I am delighted to tell you that you are going to be blessed with a son.'

For a moment she was silent, thinking over all the possibilities life held in store for the child in her womb. She was glad it was a boy. Though she was living proof that a woman could defy the odds and rise to the top of an extremely cutthroat profession, she didn't want her offspring to have to overcome similar prejudices on his way to the summit. Life was tough enough as it was.

Look at her current plight, for instance. She should have been enjoying her pregnancy in the exquisite grounds of her beautiful home in Galicia, but instead she was holed up as a guest of her brother in a miniscule retreat bordering the Amazon rainforest in Bolivia. Numerous law enforcement agencies throughout the world were still searching for the notorious drugs cartel leader known as La Rana but, as always, these things were inclined to die down pretty soon, given time. As soon as her baby was born, she would be back on her feet again, and then she had plans… big plans.

She looked down at the small bump in her midriff and stroked it gently. ‘Hello, little one,’ she said. ‘I am your mother, and I cannot wait for the moment when we meet each other face to face. You are going to be a great man one day, a leader of men. I will teach you how to be a good leader, a brave leader, because I know you have that bravery gene inside you. Now, I am sure you would like to know about your father. Well, to be quite honest, I don’t know where he is at this moment in time. Never fear though, for when the time is right, we will track him down and pay him a visit. I bet you would like that, wouldn’t you, chico?’

EPILOGUE

PHILIPPA Flynn Lee bent and placed the flowers in the small receptacle which sat in front of the unassuming headstone in the quiet surrounds of the East Finchley Cemetery. Although the grounds were close to the busy A406, better known as the North Circular Road, the only sound reaching her ears was that of birds chirping respectfully in the trees.

'I've brought someone to meet you,' she said to the stone, which was carved with the words 'Peter "Errol" Flynn'.

She held out her hand and Chuck stepped from the shadows of the surrounding trees and into the light of a grey January morning. 'Pete, babe, this is Chuck. He was our Abby's bloke until she was sadly taken from us. He was the love of her life, and I am sure you would have got on famously with him if you'd met him. He is very thoughtful and took great care of our daughter before the unthinkable happened to steal her from us. We've just been to visit her now and I'm so glad you're together here in a way that you couldn't be when you were alive.'

Chuck bowed his head and composed his thoughts. Eventually he spoke.

'Hello, Mr Flynn,' he said, feeling slightly self-conscious about speaking to a patch of earth and a carved lump of stone. He was doing it for Philippa, though, glad she'd invited him to visit the graves with her. 'It's lovely to meet you. I want you to know that I'm sorry… I know something horrible happened to you that meant you were never the same person, but Philippa has explained to me what a wonderful father you were before things went so badly wrong for you. It's only fair I tell you that Abby never forgot about you. She spoke about you often and missed you greatly, just as I miss her now.'

Chuck looked up, noting that though the day had started crisply, the skies were beginning to darken. Wiping a tear from his eye, he thought about everything he had lost. He was so grateful to Philippa and Geoff Lee for not holding a grudge against him even though they could have done so easily. The truth was that the incident took place at his grandfather's house and the sole reason she was there was to pay Chuck a surprise visit.

He still felt guilty for being forced to lie about how she met her end, but was able to see now why Sly and his grandfather had insisted it was for the best. If Abby's parents had known of the major contribution Geoff Lee's brother Arthur had played in the tragic death of their daughter, the pain and self-recriminations would have run deeper, the period of mourning far more painful, the list of victims much longer.

'Right, I think we're done,' said Philippa, rousing him from his private thoughts. Clutching his hand, she rose onto the tips of her toes and kissed him on the cheek. 'Thank you for coming with me,' she said. 'I think we'll spare him the gory details. That's just about perfect. Now, let's go. I'm hungry and you promised me lunch, Chuck Dolan.'

At the mention of his surname an angry growl of thunder erupted around them and the first drops of rain, heavy as gasoline, landed on his shoulders.

THE END

About the Author

NICK RIPPINGTON is the award-winning author of gritty UK gangland and psychological thrillers. His debut novel ***Crossing The Whitewash*** received an honourable mention in the 2016 Writers' Digest self-published eBook awards with judges describing it as 'Evocative, unique, unfailingly precise and often humorous'. The other Boxer Boys novels ***Spark Out*** and ***Dying Seconds*** also received great acclaim while ***Rabette Run***, a standalone psychological thriller, was popular with book bloggers. ***Bare Lies*** is the fourth novel in the Boxer Boys series. You can track him on facebook at facebook.com/buckrippers or on twitter @nickripp. He also has a website: www.theripperfile.com

Printed in Great Britain
by Amazon

42703411R00239